WHO WOULD HURT
HER CHILDREN?

Who wanted to hurt Allison, a bright, beautiful
fourteen-year-old? Who wanted to hurt eight-year-
old Jake, a nerd at school but a real computer whiz?
Who in the nice safe suburban neighborhood of
Garden Place was tightening the screws of terror
around the newly arrived single mom and her kids?
Young, attractive Hollie Ganz was more than a
woman struggling for personal survival. She was
caught in the clutches of a brilliant, psychopathic
master of fear . . . a mother fiercely fighting to
protect her children. And with every new savage
act of violence, with every fresh refusal of anyone
to believe or help her, she was losing . . .

A
SHADOW
ON THE
STAIR

A
SHADOW
ON THE
STAIR

GLORIA MURPHY

A SIGNET BOOK

SIGNET
Published by the Penguin Group
Penguin Books USA Inc., 375 Hudson Street,
New York, New York 10014, U.S.A.
Penguin Books Ltd, 27 Wrights Lane,
London W8 5TZ, England
Penguin Books Australia Ltd, Ringwood,
Victoria, Australia
Penguin Books Canada Ltd, 10 Alcorn Avenue,
Toronto, Ontario, Canada M4V 3B2
Penguin Books (N.Z.) Ltd, 182–190 Wairau Road,
Auckland 10, New Zealand

Penguin Books Ltd, Registered Offices:
Harmondsworth, Middlesex, England

First published by Signet, an imprint of Dutton Signet,
a division of Penguin Books USA Inc.

First Printing, October, 1993
10 9 8 7 6 5 4 3 2 1

In memory of

**Muriel Elizabeth Wilks Murphy
and Joseph S. Murphy, Sr.**

ACKNOWLEDGMENTS

Thanks to Laurie and Bill Gitelman, my editor Audrey LaFehr, and to Alice Martell's mother, Grace Fried . . . for their feedback, enthusiasm, and expertise.

Prologue

Bugs made Hollie squeamish. But after being at the house a week, she finally clipped back her dark blond hair, put on old jeans and an oversized T-shirt, and got busy on the cellar. Sweeping trash, making order, finding storage for those dozens of miscellaneous-marked boxes she'd brought from the other house, most of which were filled with useless items that ought to have been tossed. Breaking ties was never easy—not with things, not with relationships.

In the copper piping above she spotted a spider-web, and as she raised the broom to it, she winced. Though the bruise in her upper right arm was a week old and barely noticeable, she could still feel it. With a sweep at the spiderweb, the sticky threads fell to the concrete along with a daddy longlegs that made Hollie's heart beat faster until she had squashed it soundly beneath her sneaker.

The stairwell coming from the kitchen above ended mid-cellar. Along the left back corner were the gas burner and hot-water heater; she had used the empty adjacent wall to stack most of the cardboard boxes. Straight on from the stairs, next to the fuse box, were the washer and dryer—the hookups were there when she moved in—and the upright freezer. Off to the right were three stairs leading up to a green bulkhead that opened to the backyard.

The single thing she liked about the cellar was the small room off to the left—the finished room.

"Where did you hear about it?" Kathy Morrison, the young realtor with the ivory skin and a bright red braid, had seemed particularly curious to know when Hollie stopped at Sampson's Realty to inquire about the house a couple of months ago.

"Actually, it was my boss who told me," Hollie said. "I think someone had mentioned it to him. He knew I was looking in this area, of course, and in a low price range. Since the house was on the market so long . . . Well, he thought the owner might be eager."

Kathy went to a file drawer, picked out a listing, and brought it back to her desk. She handed it to her. "It needs a lot of work, outside as well as in; that's why it's still on the market. To be frank, we haven't bothered to advertise for a while."

Hollie studied the photograph of the exterior, trying to picture the potential beneath the chipping paint and overall shabbiness. The yard, too, had gone to hell. Certainly it bespoke bad business on the part of the owners—why hadn't they simply hired contractors to do the cosmetic repairs, then upped the asking price?

"But it's still for sale?" she asked finally.

"Oh yes, of course. But as I mentioned, it needs work. And with you being alone . . ."

"What you mean is, if I were a man."

"Oh dear, did it sound like I meant that?" Kathy winced, as though Hollie might begin a sermon on sexism.

Was she beginning to sound like one of those overly defensive women, the insecure kind who seem always on the lookout for a fight? Gingerly, she backed out of that one. "I'm sensitive these days, is all. Just ignore me."

"Don't say another word. You mentioned you're in the process of a divorce." Kathy lifted a three-ring binder labeled MULTIPLE LISTINGS onto her desk and began to leaf through it for similarly low-priced properties. "My parents went through one years back. And as much as they insisted it was for the best, I always wondered, who for? One little mistake—as they say—and I watched two perfectly sweet, sane people turn violent and insecure and vindictive."

Not a pretty picture, and if Kathy could have come up with more descriptives, she might have. But instead Hollie, eager to get the conversation safely back to the house, put in quickly, "Now, with respect to that handyman special—my main concern is location. I have two children who'll be on their own every day after school. So most important is a safe neighborhood."

Kathy, who didn't seem overly excited at her continued interest, shut the listing book finally and shrugged. "Oh, well, it is that. In fact, I was around that neighborhood a lot as a kid. It's quiet, the houses are substantial, set back on double-sized, well-maintained lots. Actually this particular house is sort of an oddball, if you'll forgive me for saying so. It's quite a bit smaller than the others, and set on a much smaller lot of land.''

Poor guy on the block, Hollie thought, then shrugged it off. Not a major problem.

Kathy smiled, but brought out yet another objection.

''You did mention kids. I'm afraid this neighborhood doesn't have many, if any at all. Mostly it's middle-aged or retired people whose kids are grown and gone.''

Her buyer-beware tactic—if that's what it was—was definitely working, albeit doing a job on Hollie's patience. ''Are you trying to sell this or keep it for yourself?'' she asked.

''Excuse me?''

''Or maybe you're using reverse psychology.''

''You mean, the house?'' It seemed Hollie's direct return was also effective: Kathy's white cheeks had begun to turn pink. ''No, no, that's not it at all.''

''Good, then show it to me. Please.''

Number 8 Garden Place was your basic ranch: pale yellow, five rooms, one bath, a driveway but no garage. The pluses were central air, lovely brass ceiling light-fixtures in every room, and, of course, the finished room in the cellar with the wall of bookshelves. Two crayon pictures lying on one shelf and a half-dozen forgotten thumbtacks in a wall, one with a wad of blue crêpe paper sticking from beneath it.

''She used to baby-sit,'' Kathy explained.

Hollie had thought as soon as she saw it, what a nice office it would make. She had that marvelous old mahogany desk her folks had given her when they retired—she'd never been able to find the right spot for it. Maybe she could pick up a secondhand word processor. By occasionally taking work home, she ought to be able to keep overtime to an absolute minimum. As it was, she was leaving the children to fend for themselves more than she cared to.

The inside of the house, too, needed cleaning and painting. According to Kathy, the previous tenant, Nina Richards, had moved to Colorado more than two years earlier, leaving the house during one of the worst marketing slumps in years. And though Hollie didn't relish the thought of needing to do all that dirty work to get the house livable, it was something she was capable of doing.

Less than a week later she had an engineer come to check the plumbing and heating and structure. Most of the problems were minor: a broken banister on the back stairs that led outdoors, two missing doorknobs, three loose floor tiles in the kitchen—some of which she could do herself, others she would deal with in time. The most serious problem, one which in fact almost dissuaded her from buying at all, was the roof. Something she couldn't do herself, and though it didn't need instant re-shingling, it wasn't likely to hold out beyond the coming winter.

But Hollie had apparently come along at just the right moment. . . . Though the owner wouldn't budge earlier, she was able to negotiate the price far lower than even *her* expectations. In fact, according to her best friend Elaine Byers, who ran a one-person realty business back in Bloomfield, Hollie got the property for a steal.

Now, after filling and tying two twenty-gallon bags with trash inherited from the former people, Hollie cleaned and polished the paneling of the soon-to-be office. Then, with a pailful of disinfectant and water, she scrubbed the red tile floor. She hadn't noticed the low built-in compartment on one of the bottom walls until she was standing right in front of it. The door was slightly ajar. Perhaps a viable place to store office supplies. She leaned the string mop against the wall, then dropped to her knees and opened the door wider.

First a foul odor made her withdraw, then she spotted the dead kitten in the corner. She pulled a piece of broken broomstick from the trash bag and, using it to wedge beneath the gray-and-white kitten, began to pull. The bloodied paws slid out first, then the head. Suddenly she dropped the stick, and gasped, her hands stopping short of her mouth: the kitten's eyes were dangling by threads. . . . Like the animal had simply scratched them out.

CHAPTER
One

Allison wasn't a complainer, so keeping Dylan's harassing from her mother for nearly two weeks wasn't really unlike her. Indeed, if Hollie hadn't detected tension in her daughter's voice on the telephone that afternoon and dug for the source of it when she arrived home, she still might not have known. Rubbing her feet, Hollie now sat in the kitchen after putting groceries away, listening to the details: apparently Dylan Bradley, a senior at Union High School, had been making a pest of himself since Allison's first day, and though she was trying her best to ignore him, it was becoming increasingly difficult.

Allison, who had cut fresh vegetables for a salad earlier, took a carrot stick from the bowl and, leaning against the counter, bit down. ''Kind of long hair, unshaven, and rude,'' she said in her initial description of the boy. ''He wears tight jeans, a gold earring in his left ear, and leaves his three top shirt buttons open. That's to advertise his chest hair, I guess. And I hate how he looks at me.''

''How's that?''

Allison swallowed the last of the carrot, then folding her arms across her chest and looking toward the ceiling, color flowed through her cheeks. "You know . . . like he sees under my clothes."

"Overdeveloped hormones, underdeveloped brains," Hollie's mother used to say of all males below the age of twenty-one. Not that Hollie ever agreed much with her mother. Her fourteen-year-old daughter was bright and responsible, usually showing such remarkable good sense, Hollie sometimes wondered where she came from. She hated the idea that along with all the other confusion and change in her life now, this kind of thing had to be added.

"Has he asked you out?" she asked.

Allison faced her mother: a strong, straight nose that tilted slightly up at the end and wide-set eyes, the blueness of them stunning. "That's how it started. I said no."

"By your description of him, you made a wise choice."

Allison went to the refrigerator, removed a six-ounce can of apple juice, then pulling off the tab, dropped it into the pail under the sink. She tipped the can to her mouth, swallowing, then stared out the window over the sink. "I just wish he'd back off. The more I say no, the more he bothers me."

"What exactly does he do?" Hollie asked, wishing her daughter would turn to face her.

The slim shoulders rose, then fell. "I don't know . . . anything to embarrass me."

"Like what?"

A noisy sigh that meant Allison was annoyed at

her mother's continuing to push. But she nonetheless came out with an example. "Well for instance, today. As I was about to leave the cafeteria, he was standing there, chewing gum—every time I see him he's chewing gum. Anyway, he wasn't just standing, he was blocking my way out. He had one hand against the wall and was leaning in toward me, smiling and swaying his hips in a gross way. You know how I mean."

"I get the picture," Hollie said.

"All his friends were standing around watching, enjoying the sideshow. He's popular. At least there always seems to be kids hanging over him."

Though Allison had started dating last spring and older boys had shown interest in her long, leggy blond looks, she chose to be with boys nearer her age, boys she'd grown up with. Of course they were no longer living in the same old, familiar neighborhood. Which didn't make Hollie any too comfortable with the situation herself.

"He hasn't tried anything . . . I mean, like try to put his hands on you, has he?"

Allison finally turned around and faced her. She folded her arms at her chest. "He would never . . . I know he wouldn't," Allison said, her sureness wavering.

Silence; then: "If he really makes you nervous, I suppose I could call the school."

"And talk to who? You might as well announce it over the PA system."

Hollie knew that idea would be rejected, and was inclined to agree with her daughter. Certainly it would be better if Allison could defuse the tension herself. Trying to fit into a new school environment was tough enough without unwanted attention drawn by a parent running interference. Besides, Hollie had seen those Dylan types before: a small mind, a big mouth, and an even bigger sense of self-importance. But otherwise harmless.

"The best thing to do is what you're doing—ignore him," Hollie said, her palm coming down on the tabletop. "The less reaction he gets, the less fun it'll be. And likely he'll latch on to a new and better activity."

With lips pressed, Allison nodded. Hollie glanced at the clock on the wall oven, surprised to see it was six-thirty. She stood up and from one of the lower cabinets, dragged out a deep pot. She filled it three-quarters with water, lit a back burner, and set it down. "Any calls?"

"Yeah, Daddy."

"Oh?" She didn't mind Jeremy calling—after all, he had every right to talk to the kids whenever he wanted to. But more often than not he would call at night, speak briefly to the children, then ask for Hollie. If she wasn't home, he'd leave a message to call—SOS. But it was rarely important, and it was getting annoying.

"He just wanted to move up the time Friday night," Allison said, tuning perfectly to her mother's reaction. "He'll be coming for Jake and me at six."

"Fine. By the way, where *is* Jake?"

"Playing with his computer, where else?"

Hollie smiled—her eight-year-old had become fascinated by computers when he was only five, and since Jeremy had surprised him with his very own PC last year, his fascination had only grown. His computer was strictly a "don't touch" item—much like his hamster, Popeye. Jake had nearly taken the head off the moving man who had dared attempt to carry those items in.

"When's supper?" Allison said.

"Give it about twenty minutes."

"Need help?"

Hollie shook her head, then reached out, smoothing a flyaway strand of her daughter's hair, a half a dozen shades lighter than her own, and following the strand to where it was cut blunt at her shoulders.

"I really like this haircut."

"You don't think it's too short?"

"Uh-uh, not at all . . . it shows off that pretty face. Oh, by the way, thanks." She gestured toward the salad; Allison nodded, then headed off to her room. It was odd—sometimes looking at her daughter was like looking at an old snapshot of herself, except Allison had been lucky enough to escape her mother's teenage gawkiness.

Hollie had been painfully tall for her age, skinny, and what she perceived back then as plain. Always the girl without the dance partner. To compensate for such inequities, she sometimes did weird, reckless things. Her parents were Polish immigrants— simple, hardworking, decent people. And knowing little about kids and nearing their forties when she was born, they were unprepared to deal with such a difficult model.

When she was twelve she cracked open her red

ceramic piggy bank the day before Thanksgiving and with the assets boarded a bus to Manhattan to see the Macy's Thanksgiving Day parade. She got ejected from the Girl Scouts for marketing their cookies three days before the official sale starting date, resulting in her being first to sell two hundred boxes of cookies, winning first prize—a purple mountain bike—then to her disenchantment, having to return it.

She was responsible—or so her folks had told her regularly—for Daddy's painful recurring stomach ulcer and Mom's migraines and hair loss.

Her impulsiveness continued throughout high school, ending with her running off and marrying Jeremy Ganz in her sophomore year at the University of Connecticut. Confident, handsome, and passionate—the first person to have made her feel special.

Allison was clearly nothing like her mother . . . or for that matter, like Jeremy. Hollie pushed away thoughts of her estranged husband as Allison popped back into the kitchen, grabbing her current issue of *Seventeen* off the countertop and asking, "Why'd you wear that red-and-white-striped pinafore to work?"

"It's a dress, not a pinafore." Hollie looked down, reassessing her clothing. "Why . . . is it so bad?"

"It has ruffles, Mom."

"So?"

Her expression seemed to hem and haw.

"You started it, you might as well finish," Hollie said.

"It's too young for you. It makes you look silly."

Though Hollie'd been the one to push it, Allison's words jarred her: a tie in the back, and only a few insignificant ruffles at the neckline. Besides, at what point had she and young and silly begun to butt heads?

While the pasta was cooking, Hollie wandered to the picture window in the living room. She got down on her knees with her elbows resting on the sill and looked out. Just getting to be dark . . . but there was no shortage of streetlights on Garden Place. She counted ten. A black Buick backed out from the driveway of the large stone colonial up the street. Though she couldn't make out the driver, it was likely the young man. She had passed him before, and though he hadn't stopped over to introduce himself, he had waved. Clearly friendly.

It was mid-September, but the weather was more like August. Though they had been living in the neighborhood two weeks, everything still seemed new and strange. She really hadn't had much choice but to move, and Union had seemed the right spot. It was almost an hour from their old neighborhood in Bloomfield, but only ten minutes from Stern-Adler, the mid-sized pharmaceutical company where less than three months earlier she'd been hired as an assistant public relations director. Her first full-time job since earning her bachelor's degree five years earlier.

Besides it being convenient to work, because of its outlying location—abutting nearly twenty miles of state forest—it was more reasonably priced than communities closer to the Hartford business district. It was a place where the twenty-five thousand dollars her parents had given her would make a reasonable down payment on a home for her and the children. Her parents were now in their mid-seventies, retired from their dry cleaning business, healthy, and alert and living in Palm Beach. The letter accompanying their generous check criticized her one last time for picking a gambler for a husband.

She craned her neck to look to the top of the street: beginning at Ashmore, it made a winding path that ultimately semicircled back to Ashmore. It was short and wide and distinguished, with only twelve houses in all, each distinct from the others and all but hers, impressive. Lovely old sycamores and maples lined the street, and a small buffer of wooded land ran along the backyards on both sides, providing a sense of isolation from the houses on the adjacent streets.

So unlike the old Bloomfield neighborhood with lookalike contemporaries, a single sapling in every left front yard, flagstone paths, back decks, barbecues, swing sets, swimming pools, and noisy kids riding bicycles and big wheels around the cul-de-sac. Noise . . . yes, that's what was missing—Garden Place didn't have any noise.

She turned her head, and as she did, in the window across the street, she thought she saw a figure dart away. She stood up, grabbed the curtain cord, yanked it, and the white nubbly cotton-lined draperies sailed together. Though the watcher had caught her off-guard, surely it was innocent enough. After all, hadn't she been looking out the window too?

* * *

Dinner was almost over when Hollie noticed the thin red scratch on Jake's forehead. She reached over before he could stop her and pushed his hair aside. He had thick straight brown hair like Jeremy, and intelligent brown eyes that were usually hidden behind glasses that dwarfed his impish smiling face.

"What's happened here?"

"Nothing." He reached out, tore a chunk of Italian bread from the loaf, and buttered every corner.

"Definitely something."

"I don't think Popeye likes it here much," he said, neatly changing the subject to his hamster.

"Why, what makes you say that?"

"He's acting real weird—one minute he's angry, he won't even look at me when I talk to him, then the next minute he's banging up against the cage trying to get my attention."

"He'll get used to the change," Hollie said. Then, placing a hand on her son's arm: "I still didn't get an answer to my question."

A sigh; then he said, "I was running home, is all. I tripped over a branch on the sidewalk. No big deal."

"What were you running from?"

"A kid," he said, with a kid's practiced nonchalance. He diligently rolled pasta onto his fork, took a mouthful, a third of it falling back onto his plate.

At least one bully in every class, and the new kid always at the top of the hit list. When she was Jake's age, despite her angry protests, her folks had bought into a bigger house in a better area. And to make the transition worse, Mom stuck her nose into every neighborhood battle that followed. Not that it's easy for a parent to sit by and see his kid get picked on, but sometimes it's the best thing to do.

"Someone picking on the new kid, is that it?"

"I guess. . . ."

"What's his name?"

Silence.

"Jake, I'm not going to rat to his mother. . . . I would never do that—at least not without your okay. So come on, talk to me."

"Gary Anderson. He's in my class. He's big; I bet he weighs eighty pounds."

A twenty-pound edge. "Really? Where does he live?"

Jake's glasses slid, and with two fingers he pressed them upward. "Across from the school. There wouldn't have been any trouble if it wasn't for his stink-face older brother."

"Why, what did he do?"

Jake's no-big-deal attitude was waning—she could see the hurting in his eyes. "He's a high school kid, so he's out earlier than us. Well, anyway, the big brother and his friend were waiting for Gary after school. They were heading across the street to the pharmacy, so Gary tagged along . . . and they ended up in back of me. Gary's brother, Ray, started saying things to get him going at me."

"What kind of things?"

He shrugged. "Like I was a four-eyed egghead, and that I thought I was too good for the kids around here. He said my nose was out of joint and maybe Gary ought to straighten it."

"So Gary hit you?"

"Uh-uh; he tried, but I booked it. He couldn't catch me."

Jake's dad had been the runt in his class until he was sixteen, at which time—as his story goes—he amazed all who knew him by sprouting to six-foot-one. And by the looks of it, his son might follow suit: being smaller than most of the boys his age, Jake hadn't a chance in a match of strength. But he was a fast runner, usually managing to elude any would-be opponents.

"How did the older brother know you were new in town?" Hollie asked.

Jake shrugged. "I guess Gary told him."

"I don't get it. Why would a kid that age want to start a fight between fourth-graders?"

"Oh, I've seen it happen before," Allison said. "Some of the high school boys are such babies." She was about to go on when there was a knock at the front door.

Hollie got up and went through the living room to the door. Aside from Elaine, who had come by unexpectedly the other day to bring an old computer and printer she'd found in her attic, the Ganzes had yet to have visitors. She pulled the door open: he was bald, except for a sparse patch of auburn that sat on his large head like an old bird's nest. His wire-rimmed glasses, clearly too small for his face, held thick lenses that magnified his pale eyes, now staring. . . .

"Roger Spear," he said finally, turning and with his hand gesturing to the wood-shingled, flat-topped two-story almost directly across the street. "We're neighbors."

The house where she'd seen someone scoot from the window. She opened the door wider and smiled. "Hi, glad to meet you, I'm Hollie Ganz. Come in."

"Oh, no. I wouldn't want to both—"

"No bother . . . really."

Again he hesitated.

"Please," she said, wondering if she wasn't sounding a little too desperate. If the man didn't want to come in, then fine—no need to push. But as it was, she didn't need to push further: as though suddenly working up courage, he stepped inside. He had a medium build, muscles that had gone flabby. And although his look and manner projected a certain fatigue, judging by his fairly tight skin she figured him to be no more than fifty-five. She accompanied him to the sofa to sit, then took the chair across. "I'm so glad you came by, Mr. Spear."

"People call me Roger."

"Roger," she said smiling, and wishing he'd stop staring at her. "You're our very first visitor, at least from the neighborhood. So if I sounded eager or excited, it's only because I am."

No smile, no laugh. He apparently took her seriously, which now made her feel foolish. She began to get up. "How about some tea? It'll just take—"

"No," he said. "Thank you, but no."

She sat back. "Do you live alone?"

"I live with my sister. Margaret."

"How nice." She waited for more, but when she realized there was no more, she said, "Well, I have two children. Allison's fourteen, and Jake's—" She spotted Jake peeking from the kitchen and seized the opportunity for assistance. "Jake, come on in here and meet our neighbor. Allison, you too."

"Oh my, I hope I didn't interrupt dinner," Roger said.

"No, not at all. We had just finished." The children walked in and Hollie introduced them. Roger nodded, Allison smiled and said hi, and Jake said, "I know you—you're the one who's always staring at us from your window."

"Jake!" Hollie said.

"Well, he does. Even Allison—"

"Come on, squirt, the dishes," Allison said, quickly cupping a hand over his mouth from behind. "And it's your turn!" She crossed her arms around his neck and over his chest and playfully began to drag him backward.

"But you said last night . . ."

"Forget last night, I must have been delirious. Come on!" she insisted. And he went, laughing and grumbling as she dragged him away.

Hollie turned back to Roger, wondering if she should laugh or apologize—she did neither. Which forced Roger to take the lead. "My reason for coming here," he said finally, "was to tell you about trash pickup. Once a month the town takes the larger items. Old appliances, whatever. The first Monday."

"Oh. Well, isn't that good to know. I think everything is out and gone though. Last week I finally got to the cellar—pounds of dust and trash and spiderwebs and water bugs—all of my worst nightmares." She remembered the kitten, then pushed it from her mind. "But now that you mention the pickup, I ought to check the shed."

"If there's anything I can help you carry . . ."

"Thank you, but I doubt there's much, certainly nothing too heavy that one of the kids and I can't handle. As I said, I'm pretty well settled. Not that I don't appreciate the offer."

He began to stand, and she couldn't say she was sorry—though she had tried, the conversation had been awkward at best. "I understand it's not easy for a woman alone," he said, as he headed for the door.

She beat him there, opening it. "Yes, true, but we're doing fine. It's a lovely neighborhood. I do hope to get to meet your sister, Margaret, one day soon."

"We don't get out much. Either of us."

"Oh?"

"Margaret's getting on in years—sciatica, that kind of thing. And too much ultraviolet doesn't agree with my fair skin."

She looked at his skin: definitely sallow.

"So I mainly get my exercise in the night hours. Not that you should ever hesitate to call if you need help."

"Well, it's nice to know. But—"

"No buts, Hollie," he began to scold in his mild voice. "I'm one of those early retirees, so I have nothing better to do with my time." He stepped outside, then turned back. "The other one didn't meet a happy end, you know."

"Excuse me?"

"The other one . . . Nina Richards, the one who lived here before. She was alone, high-spirited like yourself. But look what happened to her—she got herself killed."

CHAPTER
Two

It was only eight-fifteen when he left, so Hollie didn't hesitate to make the call. And though Kathy Morrison wasn't in her office, an associate was—one that was familiar with 8 Garden Place.

"I assure you, Mrs. Ganz, the former tenant did not die in that house. In fact, there's no knowledge of any death, let alone a murder. Though there was some kind of suspicion floating around at the time, the police found no basis for it. According to what we know, the lady moved to Colorado." She chuckled. "Why, who's been filling you with grisly stories?"

"No matter. Actually, the person didn't say it happened in the house, so I guess that part was my imagining. It's just that I recalled Kathy not being so enthusiastic about my interest in the house. So I thought maybe there was something—"

"Hold on, wait, time out." The woman was already chuckling as she went on. "The reason it might have seemed that way is, before you came along, Kathy had a few good bites on that house.

But always for one reason or another, the deals bottomed out. So it got to be a standing joke around here; don't waste your time showing that property because it's jinxed. Not serious stuff, just typical broker talk.''

At this point Hollie felt more than a little foolish, and while she might have inquired how that kitten had gotten trapped in her cellar, she didn't bother. She had decided the answer to that one the same day she found it, and it still made perfect sense: the house had been vacant for more than two years, certainly time enough for kids to climb through a window, let the kitty in with them, and play out some sick prank.

The *Tonight* show had just ended when the phone rang, and Hollie quickly scooped up the receiver so it wouldn't wake the children.

''Ah hah, caught you, still up,'' the voice said. ''What's the matter, can't sleep?''

A sigh. ''Okay, what do you want, Jeremy?''

''I want to be in bed with you, spread my palms across that gorgeous ass, and squeeze—''

''Good night.''

''Wait, don't cut me off!''

Come on, Jeremy, get with it. You're on your own now, just like me. So don't expect me to walk you through it when I'm having a hard enough time walking through it myself. ''It's late,'' she said finally. ''I thought something was wrong.''

''And if I had called earlier?'' He paused; then: ''Look, forget that, there's nothing as pathetic as a man who snivels. Hey, princess, I've got great news.''

Though her aspirations had never been so lofty as Jeremy's, she used to love to watch his gray eyes fire up when he went on about grand ideas. But the enthusiasm and high-on-life she heard in his voice now seemed flat—a hoax.

''Well, aren't you going to ask?''

Silence; then: ''Okay, what?''

''I've got me a job. At Travelers, selling. Only a small draw to start, but not to worry, I have no intention of staying at that level. Just wait'll I show my stuff.''

''That's great. I'm happy for you.'' And she was, too. But how long would it be before the interest waned, before he decided it wasn't moving fast enough?

''It'll mean I'll be able to send you money . . . you know, as in child support.''

''Then I'm happy for me, too.''

She didn't know if it was intentional or not, but she noticed the skepticism in her voice, too. In any event, the ''happy'' hoax was quickly ended. ''You never forgive, do you? You're still holding that fight over my head. I only meant to stop you, to keep you there long enough to listen, that's it. It was an accident, Hollie, a fucking accident. How many times do you want me to—''

It had taken a moment to recover from the unexpected tirade before she put the phone down and turned off the bedside lamp. Just as her head sank into the pillow, the phone rang again. She picked it up, this time furious.

"Dammit, Jeremy, get off my back!"

Silence.

"Jeremy?"

More silence.

"If it's you, this isn't funny." Still no reply. Finally she put down the receiver. With his call coming right before, her first thought naturally had been Jeremy. But then when no one answered . . . Would he try to scare her?

Hollie was putting out corn muffins, cereal, and juice the next morning when Allison brought it up.

"Who called so late, Mom?"

"Any bananas?" Jake asked.

Hollie picked a banana out of a wooden bowl on the counter and tossed it to him; then, to Allison: "May I ask what *you* were doing up at that hour?"

"I couldn't sleep, so I wrote a letter."

"Who to?"

"Grandma and Grandpa."

Strangely enough, Allison and Hollie's folks got along famously, and though they'd never come out and said so, Allison was clearly the kind of daughter they'd had in mind for themselves. Hollie smiled; funny how things worked out, wasn't it? *Sorry, Mom and Dad, once again foiled by your own daughter.*

Again: "So who was it?"

Hollie looked at her. "Oh, that. Your father."

"Don't tell me he wanted to change times again?"

"No, no, he's still coming for you at six; at least he didn't say otherwise."

"Then what did he want?"

Hollie poured herself coffee, then picked out a muffin. "He's found a job."

"Really," Jake said. "Where?"

"Travelers Insurance Company."

"Does this mean you'll forgive him for losing all our money?" Jake asked.

"It's not a matter of forgiving him."

"Then what?"

"I thought I explained this already. Your father and I—for many reasons that have nothing to do with you kids—have decided to go our separate ways. Better to end it now rather than hang on to something already gone . . . and begin to hate one another."

"Daddy could never hate you."

"Emotions between a man and woman are very fragile."

"But what if he changes?"

Like her, Jake was avoiding the word *gamble*, but in truth, the problems were no longer limited to gambling. It had to do with trust and confidence and respect and all kinds of other things marriages ought to have. . . .

"It doesn't matter, Jake, it's too late to go back. And you've got to understand, your father has only himself to answer to now. He doesn't need my forgiveness."

"Yeah, but I bet he'd like it."

She decided to give up. "Want more milk?" she asked.

"Uh-uh." He looked at the clock, stood up. "I'll be late if I don't hurry." He took his green book bag off the counter, opened the refrigerator, then lifted his bagged lunch and tossed it inside. Then he began looking around.

"I saw what looked like a math book sticking from underneath the sofa," Hollie said.

Jake rushed to the living room and Allison asked, "Who was the other call from?"

"A wrong number. Well, not exactly a wrong number . . . more like a crank call. One of those silent ones."

Allison drank her juice, stood up and put the glass in the sink, then headed toward the bathroom. At the doorway, she stopped for a moment and turned.

"This may sound silly, but . . . well, you don't think it was Dylan, do you?"

"No. He may be a nuisance, but I really think it's unlikely he'd go that far."

Jake, carrying his math book in from the living room, ducked under Allison's arm.

"Why would *he* call here anyhow?" he asked.

"You ask that like you know him," Hollie said.

"Not really."

"What does that mean? Who is he?"

"Well, that big kid with Gary's brother yesterday . . . his name was Dylan."

Between second and third period, Toby Cramer, a skinny, freckle-faced girl who was a whiz in Biology, and who had been friendly to Allison since her first day of class, verified that Ray Anderson was Dylan's best friend.

"Dylan's got lots of followers though," she said.

"I don't see why, he's such a jerk."

"Yeah, but he *is* hot."

"Sounds shallow."

"I agree, but we're in the minority. He usually gets his way with girls, at least with the scatterbrains he normally chases. I know of a girl who came within inches of being date-raped by Dylan. And with his disgusting reputation for dumping on girls, I wouldn't be surprised to learn there were others."

Allison's eyes widened. "Really? What about the one girl, what happened to her?"

"Joyce. She moved last year to the west coast. Well, she invited Dylan over to her house when her folks were out. They started kissing and stuff . . . you know. Well, it began to get out of hand and she wanted to stop, but he wouldn't. She screamed, kicked him and everything. According to her, he ripped her jeans right up the seam."

"How awful!"

"Yeah . . . luckily her brother came home in time. He was in college and not expected back till the next day."

"I hope he wiped the floor with him."

"Well, he tried. Stanley's not as good a fighter as Dylan though. Anyhow, as it turned out, Dylan gave him a black eye and nearly busted his jaw. The next day he told his friends a pack of lies about what he and Joyce did together."

Allison shook her head. "Is Ray like that, too?"

"I suppose, but I never heard any stories about him. I'm surprised you haven't seen Dylan with Ray. They're usually together."

"Whenever I see Dylan I do my best to head in the opposite direction."

"It must be hard, with you two living so close."

Allison slowed to a stop, her face moving in closer to Toby's. "What do you mean, 'so close'?"

"You do live on Garden Place, don't you?"

"Yes. But what—"

"You know the concrete house with the green roof? It's big and—"

"Yeah, yeah," Allison said, as though she were pulling the words out faster.

"Well, that's where he lives."

"You're lying."

"Why would I lie? Besides, I can't believe you didn't know." Toby now looked at her suspiciously. "Wait a minute. Are you putting me on, maybe just looking to get the scoop on him? Am I going to see you next week in the corridors walking arm-in-arm with Dylan and kissing up to his snotty friends?"

Allison's mouth dropped. "Gee, thanks a lot. In other words, you think I'm a liar."

Toby sighed, then put her hand on Allison's arm. "I'm sorry. The fact is, you turned down Dylan. I've never heard of another girl doing that. It took guts."

"Guts? Why?"

"I don't know. Well, look what happened to Joyce and her brother."

When Jake was fifteen minutes late getting home, Allison went out, headed toward the elementary school. She met him two blocks from the house.

"Where're you going?" he asked, clearly not thrilled to see her there.

"No place." She turned, stuffed her hands in her denim jacket pockets, and started walking with him. "You're late. Where were you?"

"I stayed after, signed up for a computer club."

She nodded. "What day's it going to be?"

"I don't know yet. Mr. Woodbury, this real excellent guy who's going to teach it, said they'd announce it in a few days." He glanced around—no one was nearby—then said to his sister, "And don't come snooping around like this again."

She started to explain, but that was silly—he knew exactly why she was there. She wondered why boys had to act so macho. Was it a learned behavior, or scripted somewhere in their genetic makeup? She'd have to ask her biology teacher about that.

It was four o'clock when the phone rang, and she picked it up.

"How's it going, babe?" the voice asked.

She knew immediately it was him—in fact, she felt her heart drop about a mile. "Dylan?"

"See that, recognized my voice right off. I like chicks who pick up fast. Some guys need their blondes dumb and submissive, but I'm not one of those."

"Gee, how secure of you," she said, hoping he was smart enough to recognize the put-down.

"See that—you do have a sense of humor after all."

She didn't want any of his compliments on her sense of humor. "I have to go," she said finally.

"No, not yet, not before you hear me out. I want to get to know you . . . and I want you to get to know me. It's that simple. Why're you so afraid of me?"

"I'm not."

"Sure you are, I can tell by the way your voice

gets jumpy and breathless when you talk to me. Unless, of course, I'm misreading the signals here. Maybe it means you want me.''

Her mouth opened, but nothing came out. She twiddled with the phone cord, winding it around her finger so tight it hurt . . . then immediately undid it.

''Come on, babe, tell Dylan. Do I excite you?''

Finally finding her voice, she said, ''No, you make me sick. And don't call me 'babe.' ''

''Okay, I'll stop. See how easy that was? Now, be honest here, what is it about me that bothers you?''

She took a deep breath, then in a voice that didn't sound anywhere as strong as she had planned on it sounding, said, ''For starters, you think your God's gift.''

He laughed, the same smart-aleck laugh as in the cafeteria yesterday. ''Hold it, wait a minute,'' he said, catching his breath. ''You mean to say, I'm not?''

''I know you're the one who phoned last night.''

''Oh, yeah. What'd I say?''

''And I know it was you who put Gary Anderson up to going after my brother.''

''Did your brother say I held a gun to little Gary's head?''

''Grow up, Dylan, and leave me alone!'' This time her voice came out big—he would have no trouble at all recognizing her anger.

''Wait!''

''What?''

''If I promise to stop bugging you for a week,

babe . . . then will you do me? Because if that's the case—''

Allison hung up while he was still talking. She was glad he wasn't there to see her blush. She went into the living room, pulled aside the draperies at the picture window, and looked up the street. She could see his house: unpainted concrete . . . an oak tree in the front yard, one thick branch reaching within inches of a second-floor window. She wondered if that was the window to his bedroom.

''Why didn't you call me at work?'' Hollie said as they did the dinner dishes that night and Allison relayed the gist of her conversations with Toby and Dylan.

''Why, what could you have done?''

She sighed. ''Okay. But if he phones again, hang up. I know it's tempting to go off on him, but give a creep attention and he'll misconstrue it as encouragement.''

''How do you know so much? I thought you never had much to do with guys.''

''I didn't; at least, not until college. Then I was sort of bombarded.''

''And Daddy came to the rescue?''

She considered the idea for a moment; then: ''I suppose in some respects, he did.''

Allison nodded, then started to her bedroom. ''Think I'll give Chelsea a call.''

''You already used your one call this week,'' Hollie said. ''Besides, you'll have plenty of time to talk this weekend.''

Hollie hated to put restrictions on calls to Bloomfield, but with the long-distance rates, she hadn't much choice. As is, relying on her salary, which was all there was to rely on, they would barely squeeze by. Soon both kids would have friends in town, and though they wouldn't forget their old friends, the need for so much contact would fade.

She picked up the newspaper from the coffee table, then put it down. With Jake already busy at his computer and Allison likely in her room for the night, it was a perfect time to go downstairs and familiarize herself with the IBM clone Elaine had given her.

In fact, she could even begin one of the articles her boss had asked her to do for the company newsletter. The deadline wasn't until next Tuesday, but with all the other work piling on her desk, it wouldn't hurt to get a head start. She went to the kitchen, opened the door to the cellar, then started down. Still feeling uneasy, but determined not to think about the damned kitten.

Allison had no intention of talking to Dylan again. She went off to her bedroom and fell across her bed, studying her room: Mom had let her do the decorating herself—all white and hot pink, touched off by two furry black rugs. On one large white wall she had painted a cheerleader holding a bullhorn: from the bullhorn came half a dozen sayings she liked, each expertly scripted with colored magic marker. The other three walls were covered with banners and pictures, all reminding her of good times and best friends and Bloomfield.

Her homework done, she had nothing to do. She

rolled over, picked a pen from her desk, and began to doodle on her three-ring binder. She was good at caricatures—capturing the face's focal point, then expanding on it. In Bloomfield she'd had the most intense book covers in school. But so far here, her covers were much like her life: empty and boring.

Saturday was Chelsea's visit—they had gotten permission almost a week ago, and though the visit was now only two days away, it still seemed an endless wait. Bad enough that Allison could barely see her friends, but what made it more unbearable was that she could no longer simply pick up the phone and call them. When she'd first learned they'd be moving, she did her best to hide her feelings from Mom. She was going through enough misery with Daddy already, and then needing to sell the house and all. . . . Well, no need for her to make it worse. But right now Allison was the miserable one, so what about *her*?

She hated Union, she hated the new school, and she hated this neighborhood, with weird Roger and his sister from across the street always looking out their front window. She missed Daddy, too, though she never knew what to say to him these days when she did see him. And Dylan, he hadn't really touched her, and she couldn't imagine him trying. Besides, she had no intention of getting close enough to give him the opportunity. But he was right about one thing: unlike any of the boys she'd grown up with, he made her nervous.

Finally she reached out, picked the telephone off her desk, and brought it beside her on the bed. Mom had always paid the household bills, and Allison had never known her to go through each individual phone charge. So what made Allison think she would now? She couldn't believe she was actually doing this. She was usually such a wimp, even her friends would attest to it. But pushing all reservations aside, she began to press in Chelsea's number.

CHAPTER
Three

"My boss asked me to dinner," Hollie told Elaine the next day from work.

"The one who sweats a lot?"

"Right."

"So what did you say?"

"Elaine, come on," she said, looking out the window. "You know I would never go out with my boss."

Hollie had a six-by-ten enclosed cubicle on the third floor at Stern-Adler, directly across from Harvey Boynton's office. Taking up part of one wall was a large window overlooking the chimney stack from the laboratory building below. Three secretaries and four technical writers shared an office two doors away, and the space between had a Xerox machine and a long blond wood table used to lay out copy for promotional and instructional leaflets, booklets, and newsletters.

"Really? Suppose he was Robert Redford—and single?"

"Okay, I'll clarify. I would never go out with Harvey Boynton."

"Fine, so what did you say?"

"I thanked him, told him no."

"And?"

"And nothing. He accepted it gracefully."

Hollie used twenty minutes of her lunch hour to tell Elaine about her first days in Union. She had been her closest friend ever since the day Hollie had moved to Bloomfield. Hollie remembered that first day well: left alone with the job of lugging, unpacking, cleaning, hanging curtains, shopping for groceries, all the while trying to keep her patience with an overtired and over-stimulated four-year-old, Hollie had run to answer the doorbell.

"I would have brought a casserole," the darkly tanned woman with the large mouth, perfect teeth, and sensational smile said as she stood on the doorstep with toddler in tow. "But I can't cook, at least not well. So I offer you something even better than food: time, free of child. One day baby-sitting, take your pick which day . . . just give me eight hours' notice." And Hollie tested her by taking her up on her offer the next day.

"Just what you don't need, more aggravation," Elaine said now, after hearing about Dylan Bradley.

"I would personally like to staple his ears back, but at this point Allison wants to handle it, and I'm sure she's right about it. Maybe I'm an optimist, but I'd like to believe this turkey is about to turn his attention elsewhere."

"Actually, he sounds like the short-attention-span kind."

"A good point."

"Have you spoken to Jeremy?"

"About Dylan?"

"No, anything."

Hollie began to tidy up her desk—she hated to work in chaos, though with the premium on space, she more often than not found herself immersed in it. "Oh," she said, sliding a few papers into a vertical file. "It's just I'd rather Jeremy not know about it. I don't need him flying off the handle or finding excuses to get over-involved in my life. He's got more than enough to do fixing his own mess. But he's called, if that's what you mean."

"Mike told me about the job."

"Right, and now he'll be able to help out financially. But I'll believe that when I see it. Meanwhile, he's coming for the kids tonight, taking them to dinner and bowling. It would be nice if the new paycheck would afford him a larger apartment, large enough to have the kids overnight occasionally."

"Looking to pawn them off already?"

Hollie smiled at her friend's teasing. "You know better. It's just that I know they'd like it, especially Jake. And of course Allison is dying to be able to spend time with her friends. As is, I need to limit her long-distance calls. Lucky me, I get to make mine from work."

"Send her here a weekend. You know me, the one who still can't cook but buys the best takeouts. Besides, you know Allison's welcome here anytime."

Hollie put the last paper in place, then swiveled

her chair toward the window. "Thanks, Elaine, I'll keep it in mind. This weekend, Chelsea Grant is coming over. God, I miss you. What was it I told you I liked about this neighborhood?"

"As I recall, you bragged about nearly everything. Hollie, I just had a marvelous idea. Mike's going to be in Cleveland on business this weekend. What about you and me meeting in Hartford Saturday night? We can do a long, leisurely dinner."

The capital where Hollie had grown up was only a forty-five-minute drive from Union, mostly highway. But with this pesky kid right in the neighborhood and Allison having an overnight guest, well, she didn't know if she ought to. . . .

"Yoo-hoo, I don't hear a response."

"I was just thinking about the kids."

"First off, I'm sure the kids will be delighted to have you out of their faces. My experience says, load up the refrigerator, then make yourself scarce. And if you're thinking of that boy, stop it. While he's certainly annoying, Allison is bright and responsible—she's not about to open the door to him. More important, you don't want her thinking you don't trust her to handle things."

It was the last point that registered strongly with Hollie. "Okay, convinced."

She put down the phone, staring at the smokestack. *Damn you, Jeremy, why did you have to screw up?*

Allison was on the way home from school, about to walk the last block on Ashmore, when a car pulled to the curb.

"Want a ride?"

Allison looked into the blue Torino with the black fur dice hanging from the rearview mirror. Dylan's shaggy hair was pushed away from his face, showing a strong jawline. Bristly brows ran an uneven ridge over cool green eyes. She swallowed hard, shook her head, and backed up. In the passenger seat was some boy with a toothpick sticking from the side of his mouth. Probably Ray.

"Come on, babe, we're neighbors," Dylan said, as he reached over the seat to open the rear door. But she shook her head and started to walk. He followed along in his car.

"I'd rather walk," she said.

"No problem, we'll keep you company." He took out a pack of Juicy Fruit from his pocket, popped a stick into his mouth, then stretched out his arm with the pack. "Want some?" he asked.

"No thanks," she said, becoming aware of her green denim miniskirt, wondering if it was too short and wishing she had worn jeans instead.

"Don't you ever loosen up?"

"Don't you ever stop being a pest?" she said, looking straight ahead.

He threw the gear into park, began to open his door . . . and she started to run. Suddenly he shifted gears and the car shot forward, caught up to her. She slowed, it slowed . . . she quickened her step, it accelerated. A game of follow the leader, except she hadn't agreed to play.

"Going somewhere, babe?" he asked.

She didn't answer or plead with him to stop. She

knew it would be useless. Finally she turned into Garden Place, saw her house up ahead, and started across the street toward it. Dylan brought the Torino to a stop in front of her. She moved forward, but as she moved, the car moved too, closing off her path to cross the street.

She looked at him, then rushed toward the rear end of the car. But as she did the car backed up, again blocking her access to cross over. The routine was repeated half a dozen more times while Dylan and the other kid laughed at her futile attempts, her face reddening with growing frustration and anger.

Then, as if things weren't awful enough, she began to cry: a couple of silent tears that escaped down her cheeks without her even knowing they were coming. And though she quickly wiped them away, Dylan and his pal had noticed.

"What have we here," Dylan mocked, "a damsel in distress?" Then in a pretense of tenderness, "Come on, babe, I won't hurt you. Come here and let me dry those tears."

She couldn't talk. If she did, more tears would come. She needed help—the old lady or Roger . . . maybe one of them. She turned quickly to the Spears' window just in time to see a figure draw away.

Suddenly there was a hand on her shoulder and she jumped. "It's okay," he said. Not too tall, but big, likely in his early twenties. He had a square look to him—wide jaw, blunt features, and brown hair cropped about an inch and a half from his scalp. He looked into the Torino at Dylan.

"Get lost," he said.

"Who's going to make me, Wood Face?"

The stranger walked to the front of the car, laid his hand on the polished hood, and rubbed it with his palm. "Nice polish job here," he said. "What do you use on it?"

Dylan's face was half out the window, annoyance showing all over his features. "Spit," he said.

The stranger folded his arms at his chest and nodded, his mouth drawing forward. "Is that right?" he said. "Ever see that wax commercial on TV? They wax the car hood, pour lighter fluid on it, toss a lit match to it and *voilà*—fire. Then they extinguish the blaze, wash away the residue, and presto—not a mark to be found. You know what they say about me: always a sucker for an experiment."

For the first time, Dylan didn't look so sure.

"I'll give you to ten."

Dylan mumbled something to Ray beside him, then put on a face-saving smile. "Hey, no problem, see you people later." Then his finger pointed at Allison. "That means you, babe."

While the stranger escorted her across the street and up the walk, she kept her eyes on the ground. She was so embarrassed she couldn't even face him to thank him.

"Don't let him see how upset you are, it'll only make his day. You don't want to do that, do you? Besides, you see at least a few of those nitwits in every high school, right?"

She nodded, and they walked silently up to her door.

"Your mother home?"

She shook her head.

"When does she get home?"

"Usually about five."

He took the house key from her hand, fit it in the lock, then turned it and pushed open the door. "Look, I'm not going to have to worry about you, am I? I mean, you won't go sticking your face on the waffle-iron, something distasteful like that?"

He was trying to make her smile, and it was working. Finally she looked up at him, and when she did, she found his smile comforting. "I'm okay," she said. "Thanks."

"Not a problem." He started to go, then stopped. "Listen, my name is Woody. If he hassles you again, just come rap on my door." He pointed across the street. "I'm that big stone colonial over there. What's your name?"

"Allison."

Suddenly a series of beeps sounded. Woody pulled a beeper partway from his jeans pocket, and with the tip of a thick, nail-bitten finger moved the switch to off.

"Good to meet you, Allison." Then, gesturing to his pocket, he frowned. "Duty calls."

Needing to stop at the cleaners and the bank, her mother didn't get home until nearly six that night, just when her father showed, so Allison didn't have a chance to tell her what had happened with Dylan before she and Jake and Jeremy left. By that time none of it seemed so awful, and maybe that's why she didn't think it was a big deal when she talked about it with Daddy at dinner.

Or maybe it was just something to say to cover the awkward silences that seemed to come up with the three of them alone. But whatever the reason, as soon as she told him and saw his eyebrows rise, she knew it was a mistake. When they got home at eleven-thirty that night, the first thing he did was walk up to Mom and say, "What the hell is going on with Allison?"

Hollie, taken by surprise, took a quick step back, then looked at Allison. "What happened?"

"I was going to tell you—" she began.

"She nearly got assaulted this afternoon," Jeremy said, grossly overstating what she'd told him. "And from what I can make out, you're aware this kid's been on her since day one."

"Dylan?" Hollie asked.

Allison moved closer to her father, trying to calm him. "But it wasn't that bad, Daddy."

Jeremy turned, his face softening as he reached his arm around her shoulder. "Hey, come on, baby," he said, "don't be upset. Let the folks handle this one. The last thing you need to do is defend this loser. What the kid needs is to be taught a good lesson."

"Tell me," Hollie said to Allison.

Allison took a deep breath, angry and embarrassed and feeling like a two-year-old, with both of them talking about her and fussing over her like this.

"He didn't touch me, anything like that. He followed me with his car, then wouldn't let me cross the street to get home. Some guy called Woody—one of the neighbors—came over and got rid of him. That was it."

Mom sent her and Jake to their rooms, but Jake made a fuss, refusing to go. Daddy though—as always—knew how to calm him down: nearly six-foot-one and well-built, he went over and lifted Jake off the floor. "Hey, buddy," he said, swinging a laughing Jake through the air as easily as if he were a sack of onions, "you mind your mom. Do you hear?"

When his father had set him down, Jake hugged him like he would never let him go, but he did finally and went off to his room. Allison had already rushed off, glad to escape the argument likely to follow. She only wished she hadn't been the one who'd started it. She fell onto her bed, going over the story as she had just retold it to her mother. Almost exactly as it had happened, except for the fear and humiliation . . .

Was Dylan just a clown with a big mouth? And was she making it worse by being such a baby?

"Okay, Jeremy, thanks for bringing it to my attention," Hollie said once the kids were out of earshot. "I'll take it from here."

"Can you?"

"What does that mean?"

"Just that we're talking about some schmuck kid who likes to play big-man-on-campus games. It sounds like something I ought to be handling, not you."

He always had the habit of moving in closer as he spoke, as though to strengthen his point, but now she found it intimidating. She moved away until the sofa was a barrier between them. "It's funny, Jeremy, but I don't remember you wanting to handle kid problems before.''

''We're not talking about one ten-year-old giving another a bloody nose.''

''Stop it! Don't treat me like a Stepford wife waiting to receive instruction. I'm the one who took care of the house and kids and everything that goes with them—not you! Now let me repeat, I'm aware of the problem, and I'll handle it.''

Jeremy pushed once again—his voice slow and deliberate and infuriating. ''Don't you see? The boy wouldn't be doing this if he didn't think he could get away with it.''

''Do you think I'm simply going to stand by and watch him harass Allison?''

''Oh, isn't that what you're doing?''

''No, it's not. His behavior didn't seem that serious—at least not so that I needed to interfere. Allison wanted to handle it herself and I agreed. We were hoping it would go away on its own—what often happens with these things.''

''Okay, you've waited . . . and it hasn't. Now what? Are you going to pummel the little son of a bitch . . . or am I?''

The statement didn't even deserve a response— she stood there glaring at him.

Knowing he'd gone too far, he tried to backtrack. ''Look, all I'm trying to say is—''

She went to the door, opened it. ''Suppose you refrain from saying anything more. Good night, Jeremy.''

''Hollie, I'm not trying to work against you. I'm just offering my help. I love you, I love the kids. . . .''

You're my whole fucking life. It's not fair to shut me out!''

Knowing Allison would still be upset, after checking door locks and turning out lights Hollie stopped at her room. She was lying on the quilt with only a dim light on, and when the door opened she sat up. ''This doesn't mean you're going to call . . .'' she began.

Hollie went and sat on the edge of her daughter's bed, then took her face between her hands and kissed her forehead. ''Stop worrying, okay? First off, I wouldn't do anything without first discussing it with you. But I want you to promise that you'll tell me if this escalates.''

''I would have, Mom, honest. It's just that when I was out with Daddy . . .''

''It's okay, honey, you don't have to explain.'' She drew down the bed covers, and Allison climbed beneath them while Hollie tucked her in for the first time in years.

Years. Where in the world had they gone? She went off to her room, now thinking about Jeremy. The trouble had actually started way back with Jeremy's gambling: once-a-week poker with the boys had turned into twice a week, then he'd added a ''friendly'' game on weekend afternoons at the local Am. Vet. hall that looked far too serious to be friendly. The lottery tickets she'd found torn and ditched in the car ashtray or in his pants pockets . . . the endless bets on sporting events. And the rub-away game tickets—instant gratification. Now how could he resist that?

Actually gambling was only a byproduct: Jeremy pretty much knew what he wanted, but he had little patience with the process of getting it. In his senior year of college, raring to join a business venture, he'd come close to dropping out. And he would have, if the venture hadn't fallen through first. Hollie admired his hunger and eagerness—too young and foolish herself to conceive of the pitfalls.

"You watch me—right to the top, traveling first-class. And how's this for crazy luck," he'd say, magically scooping a cardboard stub from behind one of her ears, "you've got the seat right next to mine. Anything you want, princess, just name it. What's that, a big black mink babushka with emerald studs?" Jeremy Ganz meant fun and adventure, and though he had dozens of coeds vying for his attention, he gave it to her. Now how could *she* resist that?

She couldn't—that is, until Jeremy got his degree and began the search for the "right" job. She was five months pregnant with Allison when Jeremy finally agreed to accept a lesser job so they could quit freeloading off his cousin Larry in New Britain: he moved them into a claustrophobic two-room apartment over a delicatessen. The only roach she had ever seen until then was in some picture book in the library when she was in fifth grade. Reality sank in swiftly.

Having quit college, her parents offered to pay her tuition if she would return. Accepting the offer, Hollie began evening classes at the University of Hartford when Allison was four months old; just about the time Jeremy skipped two consecutive days of work to visit the racetrack in Rhode Island. When his boss at Merrill Lynch cut him down in front of coworkers for his absence, Jeremy lost his temper, swung at him, and was terminated immediately.

Jeremy had already begun the shift to serious gambling, always just one number or card short of the big prize. It took a few more such episodes, and too many arguments between them to count, before she dared admit that the marriage was crumbling. Nearing the end of her patience, she threatened to take Allison and move back to her folks' home, a situation she wasn't at all sure she could live with. Though with a baby to care for, night classes, and no certainty of financial help from Jeremy, what other choice did she have?

But it worked: just as she was about to cart the last suitcase through the door, he pledged to quit gambling. Within four months he had opened an insurance agency in a two-room storefront. Jeremy gave to the new business the same passion he infused into everything he did, and in less than two years they were able to put a down payment on a lovely seven-room split-entry house in Bloomfield, a thriving young community outside Hartford. Jake was born a couple of years later. It was a wonderful time—the very best of their marriage—and it lasted nearly ten years.

Gone . . . along with a sixteen-thousand-dollar savings account, three thousand dollars in stocks, two fifteen-hundred-dollar bonds that belonged to the kids, and seventy-five thousand dollars still owing to bookmakers. What a coincidence—just about the amount of equity she and Jeremy had in the house.

"No, I won't sell the house," she had said.

"I could be roughed up more. Or worse."

They sold the house.

Nearly a year, and she hadn't even guessed. Now it was so easy to see in retrospect: she had noticed the distractions, the increasing evening appointments, the frantic activity—all of which he had blamed on business falling off, the recession. But she should have known—though Jeremy had a volatile temper, he had never raised a hand to her. The night he told her about his gambling debts, shattering whatever might have been of their marriage was the same night he slapped her in the face.

Now, she touched the still tender bruise on her arm—the one he'd given her the day she left.

Hollie sighed deeply as she picked up the newspaper and laid back on the sofa. She had been relaxing for less than five minutes when the phone rang.

She jumped, then lifted the receiver. "Hello . . ." She waited; then again: "Hello."

Silence.

She hung up, thinking about the call the night before. Both times it had come late, both times the caller had hung on a while, to give the person answering the full effect of the discomfort. Was it possible that this kid Dylan would go to such lengths over a wounded ego? She stood up, went to her window, pushed aside the flowered cotton drapes, and looked up the street. Except for a single light on a front post, his house and yard were dark. Suddenly her thoughts doubled back to Jeremy.

A chill curled at the nape of her neck, making her jump. She yanked the draperies closed, then looked toward the hallway door. She'd heard or seen nothing outdoors to warrant such uneasiness. It was just a feeling that someone was watching. . . .

CHAPTER
Four

Jake asked as they passed a sign along the state forest, "What's public conversation land, Mom?"

"Look again . . . conservation. And it's exactly what it says: land the state owns and cares for. It can't be sold to an individual, and it can't be built upon."

His head leaned over from the backseat. "You mean, to save the environment?"

She nodded. "And provide a home for wildlife."

"Are there bears in there?"

"I knew he would ask that," Allison said, rolling her eyes.

"Is there?" Jake asked.

"I suppose, black bears."

"Can we go see?"

"Talk to me about it in the spring," she said; then, glancing over: "You wearing your watch?"

He held high his right wrist, showing his psychedelic green plastic Swatch.

"Good. When we get to Bloomfield, you'll have until noon to do the rounds of your friends, then meet me back at the cul-de-sac.'' Then to Allison: ''You and Chelsea as well. On the way home, we'll stop for groceries.''

Meanwhile, Hollie did her visiting. She stopped in at three former neighbors, and by the time she met the kids at noon, she had overdosed on caffeine. In the entire time there she hadn't snuck a peek at what was once her house, nor had she asked about the people who had bought it and were now part of the community.

Once back in Union, she stopped at the Fieldstone Shopping Plaza for the week's groceries, doubling up on snack food. Jake stayed with her, and Allison and Chelsea went off to browse through the specialty stores. They didn't reach home until after two, and it was nearly four before Hollie had put away the groceries, made lunch for the kids, and headed out to do some yard work.

She wondered if the regular garbage pickup would take leaves and cut-off branches. As she turned, she noticed a person scuttle from the Spears' window. Roger? Well, she would put out the yard stuff. If it didn't belong, he would surely point out her error.

She was hoping the hedge clippers were in the shed along with a rake, but no such luck. She lifted the bulkhead to the cellar and went downstairs. Now that the cellar was semi-orderly, she had little trouble finding both the clippers and rake next to the water heater in the back. Before heading outside, she paused at her office: last night, while the kids were with Jeremy, she had finished the newsletter article, save some editing which hopefully she'd get to by tomorrow.

But now, glancing at the desk, she didn't see the article. She walked closer, sure she'd left the printed copy right on top. Everything was neat, nothing to move around and look under. Finally lowering the garden tools to the floor, she ran partway upstairs and called out, "Have either of you kids been in my office?"

A silence, then two "no's" came back—one from the kitchen, the other from Allison's room.

"Have you seen an article—two sheets of paper?"

Again, negatives. Jake appeared at the top of the steps, eating a peanut butter and jelly sandwich.

"What was the name of it?" he asked.

" '*Stern-Adler pushes for Orphan Drugs.*' Why, do you think you've seen it?"

He took a big bite of his sandwich, then shook his head. "Uh-uh; just wondered."

She went back down. Could she have put it someplace else, and not remembered? She went to the computer, booted it up, then went into the newly constructed Stern-Adler file. A sigh as the article came up. What had she expected, *that* to be missing too? Finally she turned on the printer and ran another hard copy. This time she would put it in the top. . . .

As soon as she opened the top drawer, she saw the article—two pages neatly clipped together, lying on top of a yellow-lined pad. She went out again to do gardening, but found herself unable to dismiss the silly episode—no matter how hard she tried to remember putting the copy in her desk drawer, she couldn't.

Still feeling uneasy about going off and leaving the children, Hollie thought about canceling her dinner plans, but when she suggested it to the girls, they wouldn't hear of it. Chelsea, a dark-haired, animated pixie who was always quick to voice her opinions, said, ''We don't need a baby-sitter, Mrs. Ganz.''

Hollie looked at Allison, who nodded agreement. ''Okay, but promise you'll keep the doors locked. I'll leave telephone numbers; if anything happens, you call.''

Hollie—wearing a white short-sleeved blouse, black-and-white-checked cotton blazer, and black skirt—left the house at six-thirty. And by eight she and Elaine were eagerly digging into platters of fried rice, chicken and shrimp with vegetables, and egg rolls. The spacious booths of the dimly lit restaurant were separated by bamboo and wicker, and the walls were covered with a green silk print.

''I hate Chinese,'' Hollie said. ''There's something so addictive about it.''

Elaine slapped the hand that was reaching for more. ''No more eating, no more complaining.''

''Get out of my face,'' Hollie said, laughing as she took another shrimp. ''You know I only said that to ease my conscience.'' A few moments later: ''Maybe I ought to call the kids.''

''They know where you are. By the way, Mike spoke to Jeremy today. He ran into him at the post office.''

"Oh?"

"You've heard of Gamblers' Anonymous?"

"Know it? During our marriage, I had a drawer filled to the brim with their literature."

"Well, he's going. There's a chapter in New Britain, it meets every night of the week. Not that I suppose he goes that often, but still I—"

"Stop," Hollie said finally. "Look, that's good. Really, I'm happy he's doing something about his gambling. Not that I believe it's his only problem." She hadn't been able to tell anyone about the few abusive incidents . . . even her best friend. It was odd, intellectually it fell flat; she didn't feel responsible, but she did feel ashamed. In any event, what would be the point in telling anyone now that she was out?

"What other problems?"

Hollie shook her head, hoping she hadn't already said too much. "Just that sometimes he behaves like a child, is all. He has a habit of leading with his emotions, not his head."

Elaine poured duck sauce on her plate. "Sounds like a lot of men I know."

Hollie shrugged, wanting to get off the subject. "In any event, it's no longer my concern."

"He's still your husband."

"Merely a technicality, my dear. The divorce will be final by summer." Hollie lifted her napkin from her lap, wiped her hands, then opened her purse to take out change for the telephone. She picked out a loose key from her change purse and tossed it across the table to Elaine. "Here, before I forget."

"What's this for?"

"A spare house key. You're supposed to give one to your nearest and dearest."

"I thought it was nearest neighbor, not friend."

Hollie shrugged. "I figure either will qualify." She stood up, holding some change. "I'm going to check in with the kids. When I come back we'll talk fashion, politics, work, even my severely failing memory, take your pick. But please, not Jeremy."

"What'd Mom want?" Jake asked as soon as Allison had hung up.

"Nothing, go back to your own business," Allison said as she applied glue to Chelsea's chewed-down fingernail, then carefully pressed the fake already-shaped nail over it. "You know, all this wouldn't be necessary if you'd just let your nails grow."

"I've tried, but I can't. Most of the time, I don't even know I'm biting them. Would you believe I gnaw on them in my sleep? Gracie says there's some vile-tasting stuff you can paint on. That way when you go to bite your nails you—"

Allison bared her teeth. "I get the point. It sounds awful."

"Well, it's that or this." Then, to Jake still standing there, listening, a piece of hair sticking up in a cowlick: "Get lost, squirt."

"I'm bored. I feel like talking to someone."

"Go talk to your hamster."

"He doesn't want to play," Jake said sullenly, then went to the window, pushed aside the curtains, and looked out. "Hey, there's Roger taking a walk."

"Who's he?" Chelsea asked.

"You don't want to know," Allison said. "A very weird guy who happens to be our neighbor."

Now was Jake's chance to make his contribution. "He watches us from his window," he said excitedly. "And he comes out only in the nighttime. Just like a vampire."

This time Allison glared at him. "Come on, Jake. *Go.*"

He let go of the curtain, pushed up his sliding glasses, then headed for the door. "I'm hungry."

"There's Doritos in the kitchen . . . top shelf. Pour some in bowls—one for us. Cokes, too."

Both girls were wearing their rattiest Madonna T-shirts, so big and stretched they made perfect nightshirts. Once Jake had left, Chelsea said, "Only out at night?"

Allison shook her head, waved her hand. "I think he's allergic to the sun."

"Oh," she said, satisfied. "Okay, tell me more about Dylan."

"There's nothing more to tell—he's a jerk."

"But cute."

Silence.

"Allison, you *said* he was cute."

"Okay, so he is," she conceded, trying to keep Chelsea's hand steady. "At least everyone seems to think that."

Chelsea's dark eyes narrowed, trying to search Allison's eyes, but Allison kept her concentration on what she was doing. "Are you sure you don't like him?"

Allison bounced up off the chair, dropping an emery board onto the floor. "Of course I'm sure, what a dumb question."

"Take it easy. Just asking."

Jake came in with the snacks, and the subject was forgotten.

It wasn't until ten o'clock, as both girls were sitting on Allison's bed, their legs crossed, talking, music turned up loud, that Jake burst in. Photographs were lying in a pile between them. "You're supposed to knock," Allison snapped.

"Sorry. You hear the noise?"

Allison reached over, turned down her tape deck, and listened. She shook her head, looked at Chelsea, who also shook her head. She got up, went to the window, looked out front and into the driveway: no cars, no one.

"I heard it, I know I heard it," Jake said, jumping around the room for more emphasis.

"Where was it coming from?"

"The front, the back . . . all over."

The girls followed him through the other rooms, coming last to the kitchen and the back door.

"Wait! Listen," Jake said. There was a tap against the door, then a bounce onto the porch.

"It sounds like an acorn dropped," Chelsea said, rushing to the door and opening it. She stepped outside into the cool air, barefoot, stooped down. She picked an acorn off the landing and held it up for Allison to see.

Allison looked at it, then into the darkness. She opened the screen door.

"Chelsea, get back in here."

"Just a second, there's another one. . . ." And it was then that a dozen kids carrying white paper bags and six-packs appeared, seemingly out of nowhere. They pushed their way by Chelsea, then by Allison. Dylan was the last one inside.

"Hi there, babe," he said, stopping in front of her.

She stared at him, still not quite believing what was happening. And there she and Chelsea were, standing like idiots wearing next to nothing. "Get out of here right now!" she shouted. "And take your friends with you!"

One boy with razor-cut hair backed up, giving Allison the once-over. "Not bad. Hey, Dylan, remember that blondie used to live here, the baby-sitter?"

He nodded his head, smiled. "Like I would forget."

"Holy shit, remember how she would dress, those halter tops, short-shorts, and how she'd sun herself in that bikini? What ever happened to her?"

"I heard she took a hike one day . . . vanished. No one's seen her since." He looked at Allison and shook his head in mock concern. "What sometimes happens to pretty blondies."

What was he trying to do, threaten her? "I don't know what you're talking about, and I don't care," she said, her arms crossed over her chest. "I just want you out of here, Dylan."

"I say, let's party!" a girl shouted. Someone pushed the big round coffee table to the side of the room, then put on it cardboard containers of chicken and fries and beer.

"Get some ice," someone said. "Find a bucket or something."

Suddenly everyone was making themselves at home—tossing off shoes and jackets, lying back on furniture, lighting up cigarettes, looking through drawers and cabinets, scooping out ice cubes from the freezer compartment. Music, talk, laughter.

The police, 911 . . . Allison picked up the telephone, but her fingers were so shaky that when Dylan rushed her, he was easily able to snatch the receiver from her hands. He returned the receiver to the cradle, then to further infuriate her he dropped his hand onto Jake's shoulder and said, "Hey, kid, come on in here and join the party."

Allison slapped Dylan's hand away and yanked Jake toward her. "Don't touch him," she said, stooping down to his level. She whispered in Jake's ear, then pushed him in back of herself.

Dylan raised his palms in a showy pretense of innocence.

"Hey, don't go getting violent on me. I'm just a friendly guy trying to do a good deed. I figure it's Saturday night, new girl in town, why not throw her a welcome-to-town party? But I don't know . . . what is it with you little freshman girls from Bloomfield?" He looked at Chelsea. "Are you one of those cold fishies, too?"

"Her mother's going to kill you," Chelsea said.

"Yeah?" Dylan brought a can of Budweiser to his lips, took a deep swallow, then said with an arrogant smile, "I've seen her mother—not bad for a lady her age. She didn't look all that mean and tough to me, but hey, what do I know?"

* * *

Dylan didn't see him go out the door, and the other kids couldn't have cared less. Once Jake was outside, he raced to the front yard. *Woody, across the street in the stone colonial,* his sister had told him. When he came up to the front door, he slowed: only one dim light on downstairs, all dark upstairs.

He couldn't find the bell, so he used the brass knocker. Less than thirty seconds later he heard footsteps coming toward the door, then the door opening.

"Mr. Woodbury, is that you?"

When Hollie walked in the house less than two hours later, feeling remarkably happy and rested, Chelsea was just emerging from the bathroom and Allison was on her hands and knees in the living room, scrubbing a section of carpet.

"Okay, gals, what spilled?" she asked as she set her purse on the coffee table. Then, without waiting for the answer, "Allison, where's your brother?"

Silence.

"Allison?"

"He and Woody are in his room," Chelsea said.

"He and *Woody*?" Hollie had started toward the bedroom when Jake came out, the young man from across the street behind him.

"Hi, Mom," Jake said.

Hollie looked at Allison, still scrubbing. "Will you please stop with that carpet!"

Allison looked at her as though she were in a semi-daze.

"What's going on here?"

"Maybe I should . . ." said Woody, coming forward.

"No, I'd rather *she*."

At her tone of voice, Woody drew back.

"Don't be mad at him," Jake said. "He didn't do anything."

"Jake, please!" Hollie wanted answers here, and from her daughter. Why wasn't she getting them? She went over to her, stooped down, laid a hand on her shoulder.

"One of them dropped a piece of fried chicken," Allison said finally. "And then someone stepped right in it and left it. Can you believe the nerve of those pigs?"

"Who're we talking about?"

Chelsea stepped forward. "Dylan. And his pushy friends; there were about ten of them, maybe more. They wanted a place to party, so they decided they'd do it here. Not caring of course that they weren't invited or wanted. They brought food and beer."

"How did they get in?" Silence; then louder: "Allison?"

"We heard a noise on the back porch—an acorn hitting the floor boards."

"It's my fault, Mrs. Ganz," Chelsea cut in. "I'm the one who opened the door. We had no idea they were there until they shoved inside."

"I went to call," Allison said. "But he . . . Dylan pulled the receiver out of my hands. So I sent Jake over to get Woody."

"Woody's my computer club teacher," Jake added.

Hollie sighed, nodded, then turned to the young

man with the light brown eyes standing there, waiting. "I didn't mean to be rude, Woody, it's just that . . ."

Again he came forward, this time putting out his hand—thick, blunt fingers with short, clean nails. She took his hand—it was cool to the touch. "I understand," he said. "What's this fellow doing in your house is what's going through your head, right? It's okay, really it is. Hollie's the name, right?"

He had a nice voice—deep and calming. "It looks like I owe you twice, Woody," she said. "Allison told me how you helped her yesterday."

He shrugged it away. "Not a big deal."

"Oh, it is to us." Then she turned to Allison, still holding the wet rag. "Why don't you go on to bed, honey? We can talk about this more tomorrow."

"But I want—"

Hollie put her arms around Allison, lifting her to her feet. "You did a fine job. Really."

As Allison rested her head against her mother's shoulder, tears that she had been holding back let go. With her hands fisted, she pushed them aside. "I was so angry, Mommy, and I didn't know what to do. They took over our house as if they owned it. I wanted to get back at him, but I felt so helpless."

It took almost fifteen minutes before the children quieted down, though Hollie suspected the girls would be whispering to each other until all hours. She asked Woody if he wouldn't mind waiting, and apparently he didn't because when she got back to the living room he was sitting in the easy chair, elbows on the rests. Looking at him, she suddenly felt weary. She removed her blazer and tossed it onto the sofa.

"Thanks for staying," she said. "Woody, can I get you something, maybe a cold drink?"

He shook his head, and as he did his attention went to the faded bruise on her upper arm. But seeing her discomfort, he quickly averted his eyes. "No, I'm fine," he said. "How about you?"

She laughed, a thin laugh, then sank onto the sofa across from him. "I'm afraid I don't feel so fine. I'm so infuriated with this boy—the nerve of him. He's made it so my kids aren't safe left alone in their own home. I hate to think what would have happened if you hadn't come over."

He looked down at the carpet for a moment, then at her. "Look, the truth be told, I didn't do much. As soon as the gang saw me come up the front walk, they made a beeline out the back. Leaving an incredibly messy trail behind, though. Allison and her girlfriend were troupers cleaning up. Still, it was obvious that they were pretty uptight even after the place was cleared out. So I decided to stay till you got in. Again, I didn't mean it to be a problem."

"Please, don't apologize," she said.

"Okay, quit, finished." He smiled and threw up his hands, and she thought how sure of himself he seemed for such a young man. "How did this Chinese water torture begin?" he asked.

Hollie shrugged. "It seems Dylan wanted to date Allison, and she turned him down. And ever since it's been a constant stream of harassment."

"He's a pain-in-the-neck kid."

Her energy picked up, piqued by his remark. "Then you know him?"

"Well, he grew up in the neighborhood and so did I," he said. "I'm a few years older, of course."

"How few?"

"Four, five years. I figure him for seventeen, I'm twenty-two."

"Really? You seem older."

A smile in his voice, he lifted a finger of mock warning. "You say that now, but wait till you get to know me."

She studied him—he's nice, she thought. And though he might not be considered good-looking, there was something quite appealing about his plain, intelligent face. "You live with your parents?"

"My mother. She's house-bound—rheumatoid arthritis."

Hollie's smile faded. "I had a great aunt who suffered with it. It's a real stinker."

"Well, Mom's deteriorated a lot since my father died—that was about six years ago. The disease put an end to her career, and her career and Dad were pretty much what her life was about."

"I'm sure that isn't all—" she began.

"Ever hear of Eleanor Egan Woods?"

"The pianist?"

His eyes sparkled with pride. "The same," he said. "Woods is her stage name."

Eleanor Egan Woods wasn't known nationally, but she was certainly what one would refer to as a local celebrity, having appeared in most of the concert halls in the East.

"Yes, of course," Hollie said. "She was marvelous, and so lovely. I saw her perform in the Bush-nell Auditorium in Hartford years ago. Maybe I can stop by one day, tell her how much I enjoyed her music.''

''I have no problem with it, but I'm afraid she'd never agree. She doesn't go out these days, and doesn't receive visitors. I have a hard enough time getting her to let in a cleaning woman twice a month.''

''Oh, I see,'' she said, though not sure she did.

The sparkle was now gone from his eyes—pain had replaced it. ''Maybe it's ego,'' he said. ''There is some deformity, especially in her hands. Or maybe it's just an aging woman angry at the world because her talent and beauty have gone. I'm not sure which, I just go along with what she wants.''

At Hollie's request, Woody told her more about Dylan. As far as he knew, there was no juvenile po-lice record—not that such an oversight couldn't eas-ily be rectified, Hollie thought bemusedly. But he definitely had been a major pain growing up.

Woody's description of Dylan was soon halted by a beep from his front jeans pocket. He pulled the electronic beeper out, checked the number, then asked to use the telephone to call home. He let it ring a while, but apparently his mother wasn't an-swering. He left soon after.

Hollie watched him sprint across the street. Elea-nor Woods, her neighbor. How heartbreaking to have one's talent stamped out by a crippling dis-ease. Then her thought quickly returned to what had occurred in her own living room that night.

Though she would discuss it with Allison tomorrow at breakfast, she had already decided it was time to confront Dylan's parents. As she went to bed, she went over in her mind what she would say to them. No parent wants to be told his kid is nasty or ill-behaved. Isn't that essentially an accusation of bad parenting? So here she was, new neighbor on the block, about to do exactly that. But still, don't responsible parents want to know what their child is up to, particularly when that child is causing others grief?

CHAPTER
Five

All night Hollie was plagued with nightmares about her and the children: giant, malevolent eyes were all around them, watching and studying their every move, even while they slept. . . . So when she awoke finally at five the next morning in a sweat, she ached to race across the street and vent her outrage and anger on the Bradleys. But if she had any hope of enlisting their cooperation, she needed to be civil. And part of that civility, she guessed, required that she not bang on their door before ten on a Sunday morning.

So it was exactly at ten that, wearing a light jacket and jeans, she walked up the street. Three cars were in the wide circular driveway. The small woman who came to the door had a pursed mouth and round green eyes that registered instant disapproval.

"I'm Hollie Ganz," she said, pointing at the ranch. "The new neighbor."

The woman nodded, looked across to the little ranch as though she needed to confirm its existence, then brought her gaze back to rest on Hollie. She reluctantly opened the door wider.

"Yes, do come in. I'm Pauline Bradley."

She wore a paisley silk dress with low-heeled pumps, and the hand lying on her chest fingered a single strand of cultured pearls. "We go to eleven o'clock mass," she said.

"I'd like to talk to you about Dylan."

"Oh? Let me get my husband." She led her guest into a living room that was close to the size of Hollie's entire house, and while Hollie slipped off her jacket and took a seat on the sofa, Pauline hurried upstairs. In a few minutes she was back. "Charlie will be right with us," she said. "He just stepped out of the shower."

"I'm sorry if the timing is bad," Hollie said, immediately annoyed at herself for apologizing.

"What church do you go to, Mrs. Ganz?"

"Hollie . . . And I don't."

A woman carrying a cane peeked in. "Mother," Pauline said, "this is our new neighbor, Hollie Ganz. You've seen the little girl and her brother walking to school."

So she *was* aware of their existence. Hollie greeted her, and the old lady, whose name was not mentioned, looked her over carefully, nodded, then addressed Pauline. "We're not going to be late to church again, are we, dear?"

A smiling man with a brisk walk, a badly matched hairpiece, and a booming voice came in, drawing their attention. He held out a manicured hand while he eyed Hollie and nodded his head appreciatively.

"Charlie Bradley, Hollie, glad to meet you. The wife failed to mention you look so good."

It didn't take a sage to see where Dylan picked up his attitudes. Charlie's body language was that of an aggressive salesman—maybe used cars. He continued to leer at Hollie while he gestured to Pauline. "Go tell Ma to give us five minutes."

Pauline started to get up.

"No, please," Hollie said. "I'd like you to hear this, too."

"Charlie is really the one. . . ."

"Relax, Hollie," he said, reaching over and resting a soft white hand on her bare arm.

"Take your hands off," she said, feeling crowded by his sudden familiarity.

"Hey, I didn't mean anything!"

"My goodness, what's wrong with you?" Pauline said.

"What's wrong is your son," she said, wishing she hadn't started on such a negative note. But she had, so she went on. "Since my daughter started school, he's been bothering her. And what I need is for both of you to listen."

"Well, we *are* listening," Charlie said, his words slow and hostile.

"Allison is only fourteen years old, she's a freshman," Hollie began. "Dylan asked her out and she turned him down. But he simply refuses to take no for an answer."

Charlie's eyes reexamined Hollie's legs, the slight scoop of her cotton shirt, then her face. "So he's persistent and has good taste—that is, if the little girl takes after Mommy."

Did he actually think he was scoring points with her? "Please listen," she said, realizing that this was going to be harder than she'd thought. "He telephones my home late at night . . . then hangs up."

"What makes you think it's Dylan?"

"It adds up; there's no one else it would be."

"Oh?"

Even to her, the assertion seemed weak—she never should have mentioned it. So instead of pursuing it, she went on to other complaints. "He caught up with Allison on the way home from school Friday—he purposely maneuvered his car in such a way that she couldn't cross the street to get home. And last night he and his friends broke into my house while I was out."

"Broke in?" Pauline said.

"I'll handle this, dear," Charlie said patting his wife's hand, then directing his attention to Hollie. "Are you saying he came into an empty house?"

"My children were home."

"He smashed a window, forced a door lock?"

"One of the children opened the door. They heard noises outside."

"I see. Which child are we talking about?"

"Chelsea," she said, her annoyance mounting, but sticking with him as he fired off questions. "A friend of my daughter's. She was staying the night."

"Then there was already a party going on."

"Not a party, simply a friend staying the night."

"It sounds to me like two little girls looking to have fun." He rested his arm along the top of the sofa, his hand falling within inches of her shoulder. And when she pulled back to gain more space, she saw his eyes mocking her. "It's not a crime, you know, Hollie—girls these days like to have fun, too. It's a liberated age we live in."

"Dylan was not invited into the house."

"I see. Did he rough anyone up? I mean, to get inside?"

Hopeless, impossible. Why was she going on with this? "Mr. Bradley, your son not only invited himself and his friends into my house, but when ordered out, he refused to leave. They made a total mess of the place and scared my kids. He and his entourage only left when they saw a neighbor come up the front walk."

"Really? Which neighbor?"

"Woody."

"Leon Woodbury." Charlie Bradley shook his head, smiled. "Woody the White Knight."

Hollie stood up and put on her jacket. "Look, this is really simple—what I want is for your son to stop, Mr. Bradley. I don't want him approaching my daughter or son. I don't want to be nervous every time I leave my children alone. When I bought the house, I was told this was a safe neighborhood."

"It is; at least it *was,*" Charlie said, as though he were defending something sacred. "And I don't believe my boy is doing what you say he is—at least not in the mean-spirited way you suggest. What I think is the problem here is an overactive imagination. I'm just not sure whose imagination we're talking about, though—your daughter's or yours. Perhaps both."

She stared at him, stunned. "Why would you say that? You don't even know me!"

"Not ten minutes ago, you distorted an innocent gesture of friendliness," he said. "A simple touch on the arm you made to appear obscene. And though I'm aware that a woman without a man is more at risk in this day and age . . ."

She wouldn't listen to any more from this insufferable bully. She headed for the door, so angry and frustrated she wanted to scream. Instead, she turned back—Pauline was right at her heels, but Hollie looked past her to Charlie, still on the sofa, and said in her most civil voice, "If Dylan bothers us again, I'll go to the police."

He shrugged, smiled. "You do what you think is right."

"Charlie is a lawyer," Pauline said.

Great. Not a used car salesman, a lawyer.

As Hollie opened the front door, Pauline put her arm out, stopping her; then in a small, pinched voice: "I know you . . . and your type. You're one of those women who comes on to men, then when they respond, you accuse them of being dirty."

For the next twenty minutes Hollie concentrated on the trees lining the sides of her house, clipping and examining them, then clipping some more. Suddenly, she became aware of someone standing in back of her. She jumped, the hedge shears nearly flying from her hands.

"Roger," she said, recovering her composure. "I didn't hear you coming."

Roger Spear was wearing a tan trench coat and a stiff wide-brimmed hat that she imagined was to protect him from the sun, all of which was now behind clouds. He smiled; then, holding out his hand to take the shears, he said in his quiet, formal manner, "May I, Hollie?"

She looked at the shears, at him, then relinquished them. He went to the trees and turned. "Now, these are called White Pine, a very nice buffer between yards, affording you good privacy. But," he said, sticking the shear points in to demonstrate, "it's important you cut these lower dead branches if you want them to stay full and lush."

He proceeded to cut them. Hollie glanced across at his large yard—neat and trimmed, not a piece of paper or stray leaf. "Do you do your own landscaping?"

"Yes, indeed. But of course, the night's my outdoor time. Most yard work I do after dusk. So don't be surprised to look out and see me crawling around in the darkness, weeding." When she didn't respond, he turned and peered at her in that same disturbing way he had the other night. "Have you ever seen me out there, Hollie?"

She shook her head. Why would he ask such an odd question anyway? What possible difference could it make if she'd seen him? "Maybe you shouldn't be out in the sunlight now," she said, wishing he'd take the hint and leave.

"No, you're probably right," he said. "And I thank you for your concern. But seeing you so flustered and upset when you came back from the Bradleys' house, I thought today maybe I ought to make an exception."

Actually the physical activity had been working to calm her. But now, standing there listening to him admit to watching her since she'd come back from the Bradleys' made her insides sizzle. "Margaret thought I ought not to interfere," he said as an afterthought. "But now and then we have to follow our instincts."

Okay, so how should she respond? He was polite and soft-spoken, and from what she could see, he was trying to be helpful. But the man gave her the creeps. Hollie ended up saying nothing about his window-watching, and he continued to prune the dead branches.

"Charlie Bradley is not a man of high moral fiber," Roger mused, so quietly she couldn't be sure if it was meant for her or not. He went on. "Married men who chase women are the worst kind of sinners of all. But Charlie will find that out someday. Oh, yes, indeed . . . his time will surely come."

After lunch they drove Chelsea home, and it was on the way back in the car that Hollie told Allison about her unsuccessful attempt to reason with the Bradleys.

Allison, sitting in the front passenger seat, turned to her. "They think I'm lying?"

"They don't really," Hollie said. "It's just a defense mechanism some people use to close out what they'd rather not hear. In this case, the Bradleys choose not to hear that their son is a delinquent."

"What're we going to do now?"

"Well, I've been thinking about that. What do you say to me talking to Dylan?"

"Oh, no!" she cried. "Why would you—"

"Wait, hear me out, honey." Hollie paused, glancing left at the thruway, then merging into the traffic. "First off, I'd need to find out if he's willing to talk to me. If he is, we could arrange to meet somewhere, a neutral territory, so to speak."

Allison sat back, leaning her head against the headrest as her mouth sank. "To say what?"

"Hopefully to appeal to his sense of honor. He's older than you—only a few years, but at your ages, it's a major difference. And he's definitely more experienced." Hollie had been thinking about approaching Dylan since Roger's ramblings that morning. Maybe it was hearing about Charlie Bradley's flagrant infidelities, or meeting the Bradleys face-to-face earlier. In either case, she could only imagine that communication between son and parents was, at best, minimal. So maybe before going to the police she ought to try to reason with him herself.

"It'll never work," Allison said, shaking her head from side to side. "Besides, he'll probably run straight to his friends and tell them. And I'll end up the joke of the entire school."

"We have no choice, Allison. Certainly we can't allow him to restrict your freedom or trash our house like he did last night."

"Suppose he won't listen? Suppose this gets worse?"

"Then I'll go to the police. There are laws against harassment. And if talking doesn't work, then okay . . . at least he can't say he wasn't sufficiently warned."

* * *

After the Sunday supper dishes were done and the kids were in their rooms—Allison on the telephone and Jake playing with his hamster—Hollie was about to go downstairs to finish the Orphan Drug article when the doorbell rang. She opened the door to find Jeremy standing there. Smiling and confident and acting too much at home, he stepped inside. He was wearing a crisp striped shirt, blade creases in his slim-fitting slacks. One hand played a coat hook, his sport jacket hung elegantly behind his right shoulder. Like he had come out of a magazine ad, except for those deep circles underlining his eyes.

She stepped back. "What're you doing here?"

"What's a matter, no visitors welcome on Sunday?"

"I clearly recall asking you to phone before dropping by."

He shrugged, tossed his jacket over the chair. "So I forgot—shoot me. Come on, Hollie, relax a little. Don't you think you're being overly inflexible here?" Before she could object, he raised his hand. "Besides, I want to apologize."

"There's no need."

"No, no, I disagree. I pissed you off the other night trying to dictate how to deal with that kid. I had no business insinuating you couldn't handle him yourself."

She looked at Jeremy, thinking about the phone call that had come after he'd left. . . . It would be so much simpler if she could be direct, simply ask him if he'd done it. But she knew him well enough to know that if he had, he'd never admit to it. Then again if he hadn't, she'd be opening a slew of inroads, giving him more reason to think she needed his protection. "I realize you were concerned, too, so let's forget it ever happened. Okay?"

He headed toward the easy chair—she stepped over before he sat. "Please, Jeremy, not now."

"When?"

"I don't know. Please don't pull this."

He threw up his hands. "Jesus Christ, what the hell am I pulling? I come over to visit with my family, and you act like I'm committing a crime."

She got between him and the chair. "I mean it, I want you to lea—"

She was cut off by Jake's voice calling his father, then Jake rushing into Jeremy's arms. "Hey, Mom, why didn't you say it was Daddy at the door?" And before she could answer—assuming she could come up with one that would be acceptable to Jake—he was saying, "Stay for a little while, okay? Want to see the house, Daddy? You never once saw the whole house."

He took Jeremy by the hand and went from one bedroom to another: Jake's, Allison's, then hers. After what seemed to be a long time in Hollie's bedroom, he took him to the cellar.

From upstairs, she could hear them tossing a rubber ball on the concrete, roughhousing, then talking and laughing, at times louder, at other times so softly she could barely hear. It was a good thirty minutes before they returned upstairs—Jake flushed and excited and grinning, his world temporarily put right.

Jeremy handed Hollie a small photograph—a woman's picture, but someone had used a black marker to thicken the eyebrows, add a beard, a mustache, and glasses, then mark out a couple of front teeth. "What's this?" she asked.

"I found it taped inside the door of the fuse box."

She looked away from the picture, to him. "What were you doing in the fuse box?"

Jeremy shrugged. "Just checking it out to make sure your system is good—nothing mysterious." He nudged her arm, "Take a look at the woman."

Hollie again examined the picture. "Yeah, so?"

"She doesn't look familiar?"

"No. Why, should she?"

Jeremy and Jake looked at each other and laughed.

"What?" Hollie said.

Jeremy shrugged, shook his head. "Naw, forget it."

Finally Hollie said to Jake, "Tell me."

Jake nudged his sinking glasses upward, stifled a giggle. "Well, when Daddy and I first saw the picture, we thought it was you."

She looked at Jake, Jeremy, and again at the picture. Then, her voice making it clear what she thought of the comparison, she said, "Gee, thanks a lot."

"But look closely, Hollie, there's a definite—" Jeremy began, but she stepped on his shoe.

"I'm warning you guys, not one more word!" And biting down laughter, she tossed the photograph onto the kitchen counter.

A nice moment that Jeremy quickly tried to turn to his advantage: he put his arm around Hollie's waist, drawing her toward him. Stunned, she yanked away, feeling like a schoolgirl, embarrassed to have been so naive not to have expected it. Right in front of Jake, too—just another something to confuse a little boy already confused. By the time she'd managed to get Jeremy to the front door, he was already looking to pick a fight, and among other things was insisting to know what she had done with respect to Dylan.

"It's taken care of," she lied, closing the door on him. Jake went to his room and Hollie, a headache coming on but determined to finish her newsletter article, headed for the aspirin. She took the bottle from the kitchen cabinet, then looked down again at the photograph on the counter, wondering what it had been doing in the fuse box. Who was it? She was sure it hadn't been there when they moved in. And then lifting it and examining the defaced features more closely, she saw it, too: a definite resemblance.

Once settled at the computer, she found it hard to work. Jeremy, Dylan, the peculiar picture, and a multitude of creaking walls and groaning pipes kept distracting her concentration. But it wasn't until she again experienced that feeling of being watched, that her production stopped cold. The muscles in her arms and shoulders began to tighten, her hands became clammy.

She looked up and around the room—nothing. She swung her chair toward the short, narrow window to the side: the red curtains were parted, but exposed only darkness. Still she went to the window, raised both her arms, and yanked the curtains closed. Finally she returned to the desk and shut down the computer.

CHAPTER
Six

When Hollie called Dylan the next afternoon, it took no time for him to agree to a meeting. Though it had been easy—easier than anticipated, so she should have been encouraged—she couldn't help but wonder about his eagerness.

"There's a bar out on Fairlawn Avenue," he said, a smirk in his voice.

"Not a bar, Dylan. What about a coffee shop?"

"I could pick you up," he said.

"Look, let's not complicate this, okay? I'll meet you right after work. You just tell me where there's a diner or coffee shop convenient to both of us."

He named one not far from the high school. So what did that mean, there'd be a bunch of his pals looking on? "Look, if you plan to make this into a comedy routine for your friends' benefit, we might as well forget it. I'd like this to be a serious talk, hopefully between two adults. And I'd appreciate it if you'd keep this meeting between us."

It was five-thirty when Hollie walked into the Hillside Diner. Dylan, wearing jeans and a brown leather jacket, was already sitting at a booth—she picked him right out by Allison's description. About to take a stick of gum from a pack, when he saw her, he returned the pack to his pocket. Maybe she *wasn't* doing the right thing. She looked around: mostly adults, except for a young couple a few booths away from him—none of whom seemed to be paying attention to her or Dylan. She headed for his booth and sat down.

"Mrs. Ganz, if you're going to accuse me of—"

"Call me Hollie, please. And I'm not here to ask you a lot of questions or go into details. You know what's going on as well as I do. I'm just here to ask you to please stop: it's been making Allison's and my life hell. I don't know if you've ever had the experience of moving to a new town, having to make new friends. . . . Well, it's not easy to do—particularly when you're just beginning high school."

He looked at her as though he were drawing a blank. "I only want to be friends."

She studied him a moment, his piss-ass expression as he flaunted his obvious lie. "What you want is to date Allison—and she refuses," Hollie clarified. "So what's the big deal? Surely a boy with your good looks has no trouble finding dates." For a moment—maybe it was simply the way he was tilting his head—he reminded her of his father. She winced, determined not to let it distract her from what she was saying. "Besides, Allison is too young and unsophisticated for you, as I'm sure you're aware."

A noncommittal shrug, but she could see that she'd struck home on that one.

"Want something to eat?" he said.

"Just coffee, please."

He hailed a waitress, ordered two coffees, then she went on. "You know, I spoke to your parents."

"They told me."

"Oh?"

"Yeah. Dad said if I was doing anything wrong, I should cool it. Of course, I told him I wasn't. And Mom warned me to watch my step around you." He tilted his head, his eyes speculating. "She says women like you get unsuspecting guys like me in trouble. Sounds like you two didn't hit it off so good."

No, Pauline Bradley was hardly a fan. Hollie was suddenly conscious of the red short-skirted suit she was wearing, and could only imagine Pauline's disapproval. "I'm afraid not," she said.

"Well, I can relate there—she's not easy. She drives my father nuts with all her talk about religion and evil and sin. She talk to you about going to Hell?"

Hollie shook her head, thinking for the first time that maybe Dylan's homelife wasn't so great.

"Give her time, she will."

He laughed, and though the idea of any further association with Mrs. Bradley was not a laughing matter, Hollie smiled for the sake of what might become friendly relations between her and Dylan. "Well, what do you say, Dylan?" she said, eager to move the subject away from his parents. "Can we come to some kind of understanding?"

"What kind you have in mind?"

"Leave Allison alone."

He smiled, shrugged. "But I haven't done anything."

She raised her hands. "Look, let's suppose for a moment. If you *were* doing something, would you stop?"

"Sure . . . that is, if you were willing to cooperate."

Now it was she who drew a blank—a legitimate one. Maybe he wanted her to run some kind of interference with his parents.

His green eyes began to wander from her face to her chest, then back. "What's the ante, Hollie?"

He was leering. . . .

"In this game you're calling, you want something from me," Dylan said. "Fine. So what are you offering in return? One side makes a concession, the other side makes a concession, that's how these things work."

He *was* his father . . . she should have suspected it. But now she felt like a damned fool, and like Charlie Bradley, the son was pleased with himself and laughing at her. "A 'contractual agreement,' I think my dad calls it," Dylan went on. "I bet you thought you were playing games with a dummy."

She lifted her purse, got up.

"Hey, where're you going? I listened to you. What about hearing what I want?"

"You're a pig, Dylan," she said, starting to go; then turning: "Just so you know: if you bother my kids again, I'm going to the police."

For a while it seemed as though the talk had done some good. Except for a couple of late-night calls the following week—assuming, of course, that they were Dylan's calls—he stayed pretty much out of Allison's face.

On the other hand, Allison wasn't so quick to concede him credit: only she knew the maneuvers she went through to avoid running into him in school. And even though it was only a temporary solution—actually no solution at all—it was all she could manage.

So when a boy with braces on his teeth piled into her after school, spilling her books and notebook on the sidewalk coming from the annex, her first thought was that he must be one of Dylan's followers and her luck had run out. And even though the boy was full of sincere-sounding apologies, she was not about to hear any of it.

She pushed his hands away from her notebook, then grabbed it up herself.

He picked up two other books, handed them to her. "Did I hurt you?"

His remorse is just for effect, she thought.

"If I did, I'm sorry. Really." He stooped down where she couldn't help but look at him, then carefully enunciated, "Can you understand what I'm saying?"

She smiled. He had hair the color of sand, and gold flecks in his brown eyes. And studying him carefully, he *did* look way too clean-cut to be a friend of Dylan's.

"I'm not deaf," she said.

"You're just *that* mad at me?"

"Not really."

"I don't remember you from last year. You a freshman?"

"Uh-huh."

"Jones . . . Highland?"

"Neither. Bloomfield. I just moved here." She wondered if her voice had revealed the pride she felt when she said Bloomfield . . . versus either of the Union Junior Highs. But if it had, he let it pass. "My name's Barry Connors," he said. "A remorseful sophomore. Really, I didn't mean to plow into you like that."

"Allison Ganz, and I know you didn't mean it." Her hand went to her hair, fingers scooping, raising, trying to give her hair lift.

"Then why were you so angry?"

She shrugged, looked up, then back. "I thought you were someone else."

"Someone you don't like?"

"Right."

"I'm glad it's not me."

Though it meant he'd have to run all the way to his part-time job to make it by three-fifteen, he walked and talked with Allison another twenty minutes before he jotted down her phone number and took off. Barry Connors was a runner, took two foreign languages, was a reporter for the school newspaper, and was someday going to be a foreign correspondent, but right now he worked after school as a stock boy in Kings, the supermarket in the Fieldstone Plaza.

So by the time she ran into Jake at the corner of Ashmore and Garden Place, Allison was feeling a whole lot better about things. Maybe her mother was right about Dylan giving up.

"I didn't plan to meet you," she said to Jake before he had a chance to accuse her. "If you want I'll walk ahead of you, pretend I don't even know who you are."

"It's okay, no one's around."

She looked up the street. No one was *ever* around, and if they were, it was only to get in and out of a car. She wondered if she screamed at the top of her lungs, would any of the neighbors even stick their heads out the door to see what was wrong, or would they only turn their televisions louder to drown out the noise? She looked at Dylan's house—his car wasn't in the driveway.

"Meet any new kids?" she asked Jake.

"One . . . a kid who plays chess."

"Great, maybe he can beat you."

"Probably not."

Jake sort of prances like one of those show ponies when his head goes too big, Allison thought, a little like the way Daddy does. Men can sometimes be unbelievably full of themselves. She gave him a playful wallop on the arm. "You may not be as good as you think."

"I beat *you*."

"That's not saying much," she said, heading across the street. "Of course at Scrabble . . . now that's different, that's where I destroy you. Where's the boy live?"

"What boy?"

"The one who plays chess."

They walked to the front door, and she took the house key from her purse.

"Oh, Ricky, he lives on Tremont Avenue. I could ride my bike over someday . . . or go straight from school."

"Yeah, you probably could. But ask Mom first." She put the key in the lock, then pushed the door open as Jake rushed in, headed toward the hall closet.

"Where're you going?"

"There's a box of cupcakes . . ."

"Mom's saving those for lunches," she said, knowing this was likely to turn into a big deal. She really had no desire to waste her time playing the bad guy.

"Just *one* is all. . . ."

"I wouldn't if I were you, you might end up dead meat." She figured now was about the time when he'd begin to turn hostile, and judging by his next statement she was right.

"Yeah, well, you'll be dead meat for going out and leaving on the TV in your room."

"I didn't," she said, dropping the keys back in her purse and paying little attention to his attempt to get back at her. Usually the most effective way to deal with him.

"Yeah, you did, I can hear it from here."

This time she could see that he wasn't bluffing. She listened, then sprinted to her bedroom and looked around, stunned. The television was on, the dresser and desk drawers were wide open, clothes spilling out, the closet had been ransacked, the bottle of Obsession her friends had given her at her going-away party was spilled on her glass vanity.

The call came at four o'clock through her direct line. And when Hollie recognized the tension in Allison's voice, she knew another level had been reached.

"What happened, Allison?"

She took a deep, shaky breath. "Someone was in here."

"In the house?"

"When I got home—Jake and I walked in together, actually. I knew something was wrong as soon as I heard the television on in my bedroom. I never turn it on before school."

Hollie sat forward at her desk, her stockinged feet automatically in search of her shoes. "And?"

Allison took another deep breath. "Mom, someone went through my things . . . my clothes, my personal stuff. My drawers were open, everything was a mess. The perfume my friends bought me was all over my vanity." With that last bit of information, her voice cracked.

Damn, I'll get him for this. "Allison?"

Silence. Harvey Boynton wouldn't be thrilled at her leaving work early—he was a real stickler for time. But she hadn't any choice. Though before she bothered to deal with that issue, she called the Union police.

Sergeant Gus Paterson was slim and had a wide snub nose and smooth upper lip and jaw, giving him a boyish look at odds with his receding hairline.

When Hollie arrived at the house he had already gone over the premises and questioned the kids, so he led her directly to the window in Allison's room.

"Look at this," he said, demonstrating the ease with which someone from outside could lift it and the screen. "What you need here are screen locks as well as—"

But her eyes had gone to the desk and dresser and closet . . . clothes and other items strewn on the floor, over the bed: the pictures and banners and artwork Allison had labored over, ripped right off the walls.

"Mrs. Ganz," he said, seeing he'd lost her attention. "If you'll look here, I'll explain."

"Sergeant, what I'm interested in at the moment, is this." With a tilt of her chin, she gestured to the chaos, a wisp of fear settling in as she wondered if she and Allison had underestimated Dylan. If he was capable of this, then what else might he be capable of?

"According to your girl, there's nothing missing. Of course, I'd like you to doublecheck that. Anything missing needs to be reported." His voice was so flat and unemotional, it was hard for her to believe they were seeing the same things.

"But what if there isn't anything?" she asked.

"Then consider yourself lucky. And if I were you, I'd get the windows fitted with good locks."

Still, she proceeded to state and ask the obvious, what any foolish citizen might think or expect. "Someone broke into my house, Sergeant Paterson. Regardless of theft, isn't that a crime in itself?"

"Sure it is—you see someone do it?"

"No, but we know who it was. Didn't my daughter explain all this to you?"

He stood legs apart, hands tucked at his belt, face lifted—apparently her concerns were trying his patience. He sighed deeply, then said, "Sure. But it's like I said to her, we don't arrest people on maybes. We need proof. So unless we find something here that ties this boy to the break-in, or you or your kids or a neighbor actually saw something . . ."

Certainly his lack of concern was trying *her* patience. "What about fingerprints?"

"This isn't television, Mrs. Ganz. We don't even attempt to get prints on a petty crime like this."

"Why not?"

"For one, they're difficult to get, at least clean ones you can use. And assuming we could get some, what would we do with them? Surely you don't think this boy you suspect is a felon with his prints on record?"

She stretched her arm out, clenched one hand around a bedpost, then tried to keep her voice calm. "No, but you can get his prints, then compare them."

"I'm afraid it's not all that easy. There's such a thing as a constitution."

"You can skip the sarcasm," she said.

He lifted his hands and shrugged. "Look, Mrs. Ganz, I didn't mean to get your feathers ruffled. I just figured you for a lady who wanted to hear the facts straight out. Now it works like this: we can't simply knock on doors to ask for fingerprints, at least not unless we have solid proof indicating a person is involved in a serious crime. And we sure in heck don't have any of that here, do we?''

"It sounds like a real Catch 22."

He nodded his head like she had finally said something right.

"Sometimes it's just that," he said, then paused. "Your girl told me how you're new in town. . . ." He waited, but when Hollie didn't respond, he went on, "So who's to say it wasn't one of the moving men who broke in? A perfect opportunity to case the place, find the easiest access. That happens quite a lot, you know."

She tried to picture such a scenario, but she was having difficulty with it. "Are you saying the moving man would go to that trouble, trash only my daughter's room, then not take anything?"

"I grant you, that's not the usual. Neither would it be usual if it was the kid broke in. In this neighborhood, I'm sure he doesn't want for anything."

"But this boy's motive isn't stealing, it's harassment."

"Trust me, Mrs. Ganz," he said, "catching this intruder is a long shot . . . and surely not worth the trouble."

Her eyes did a retake of the room, the impact of the destruction registering yet again. "Doesn't it count that someone invaded our space . . . that someone would commit such a malicious act?"

Though he was yet to provide her with satisfaction or even hope of any, he now shook his head sympathetically. "Of course it does," he said. "I'm not insensitive to the violation. I have a wife and three kids. In fact, unlike you, she would have freaked out about now. But what I'm saying is, use this warning wisely, stop tempting fate. Get your house tight and secure so you won't find yourself in this same position again."

She stared at him, annoyed that he seemed to be turning the blame back on her.

"What about the telephone calls?" she asked finally.

"Just like I told your daughter: your best bet is to hang up. If it *is* this boy like you think, trust me, he's going to get tired of talking to an empty line."

"And the harassment of my daughter?"

"Typical kid stuff from what your girl says . . . didn't put his hands on her or anything. Sounds to me, what this boy needs is a good swift kick in the butt. And much as I'd like to help out there, they don't let us do that."

Really now, Einstein. . . . Then what're you doing here at all?

At the door he stopped, and as an afterthought he added, "Of course, you can always file a complaint."

It wasn't until eleven o'clock, when Allison was nearly finished cleaning her closet, that she stepped on it. She moved her bare foot, looked down. When she recognized what it was, her jaw dropped. She bent, picked up the pack of Juicy Fruit gum: the paper was ragged and torn—only two sticks left.

CHAPTER
Seven

According to his Criminal Law professor, who had
claimed she wasn't coming on to him, Frank Lorenzo had undisciplined good looks: a square chin,
a high-bridged, slightly crooked nose, unruly
patches of brows over brooding eyes. And coarse,
dark curly hair that most men past thirty would pay
bucks for. As it was he had just passed forty, and
the hair-of-plenty was holding out.

Frank had come a long way to where he was:
seven years as a Union cop before entering law
school. Once he passed the Connecticut Bar, though,
it was those handy cop connections that got him the
State's Attorney appointment in Union, where two
days a week he prosecuted penny-ante crime in the
court annexing the forty-person police department.

And though the money wasn't great, it was
enough to enable him to maintain a private practice
a block from the courthouse. But now that his practice was rolling—affording him a nice car, apartment, membership in a snooty health club, and a lot
of fancy clothes that seldom looked right or felt

right—and he could have put those hours to better use, he was reluctant to give up the job.

Not that he conned himself into believing that what he was doing had any real impact. He dealt with the speeders, disturbers, and disorderlies, breakers and enterers, drinkers, and druggies. Some got a slap and sent on their way; others got jail or community service or put into a rehab program where available. Yet no matter the method, the same faces seemed to turn up with frustrating regularity.

No, he thought, more likely what he'd miss would be the early-morning kibitzing with the guys on the force who—despite the career move—he still felt a part of. Aside from a feisty sister-in-law and adored sixteen-year-old niece in Boston, whom Frank tried to keep an eye on by occasional visits and weekly phone calls, there was no other family. So in a way, he supposed, the cops were substitutes.

This morning, it was eight o'clock when Frank entered the station through the courthouse door, took doubles on coffee—one for the chief—and the woman walked in.

She was tall and carried herself like she knew who she was. Her blond hair didn't quite reach her shoulders, but she pushed it from her face as though it were a nuisance. Good facial structure and magnificent eyes: big and blue, and able to reel him in from at least a twenty-foot distance. She leaned her elbows onto the high desk where Sergeant Lewis sat, and said in a voice that immediately betrayed her anxiety, "Who do I talk to about filing a complaint?"

Sergeant Lewis took a form from his drawer. Then, holding pen to paper, he asked, "Name?"

She took out a little brown paper bag from her jacket pocket and held it in her hands. "Look, maybe this would be easier if you read over Gus Paterson's notes."

Slowly, his gaze shifted back to her. "You've been here about this before?"

"Last night Sergeant Paterson answered my call. Though his analysis of the situation was discouraging, and he was hardly what I would consider aggressive, I suppose I might as well see him." She nodded toward the bag. "Besides, I now have evidence that I'm hoping will make him see things differently."

"It seems you're a lady with a lot of complaints."

"I didn't mean—" she began, but stopped.

"Look, it's too early in the morning to spar. I'm going to try this again, ma'am . . . your name?"

The complaint was filled out and sent to Paterson's desk. While Frank sat in the chief's glass cubicle, drinking coffee and bullshitting, he watched. Later, after she left and Paterson had gone to the conference room for the usual morning briefing, he went over to the sergeant's desk, picked up the notes and signed complaint, and read them.

Then he looked in the little brown paper bag, the case number already indicated on it in heavy black marker pen. A wrapper and two sticks of chewing gum?

Harvey Boynton summoned Hollie into his adjacent office; from the position of his desk, he had a perfect view of Hollie's desk and of Hollie. Of when she came and went, and whatever she did in between.

"You asked to leave early yesterday, and I didn't give you a hard time, did I?"

She shook her head. Why was he doing this?

"I consider myself a fair man. . . ." He pointed his finger toward the clock on his office wall.

"Look," he said, and she looked. "Can you see it says nine-fifteen?"

"Yes, and—"

He folded his chubby hands on his desk. "Which means you are forty-five minutes late."

Yesterday, she had told him briefly what was going on in her home, and that only because of necessity. Now she faced him, not wanting to open up more of her personal life than was necessary, yet feeling pressed to do so. She said, "I had to file a complaint at the police station."

"Then they haven't caught the offender?"

"No. I know who— Well, it's a long story."

He studied her a moment, then shook his head. "Look, forget I even said anything. I know you're having a tough enough time without me getting on you. Tell you what, why don't you fill me in on all this over dinner?"

Another dinner invitation, but this one came with a pretense. She shook her head.

"No thank you, I can't," she said. Then, when he didn't respond, she added, "It's important, particularly now, that I be at home with the children." It was true, of course, but damn it, why did she even feel the need to say it?

* * *

On the way home from work that afternoon, Hollie stopped at the humane society. The animal was tan and black with a white left eye patch—still a puppy, but not for long. At least, that's what the fellow at the pound assured her. "By summer, he'll be half your size," he said, gesturing to the little German shepherd he was holding to his chest. He had just removed him from his cage.

"It doesn't bite, does it?" She reached out, then quickly drew her hand back.

"Shepherds are fiercely loyal. If you mean, once he's grown will he protect his territory or his master from danger, the answer is yes. And you would have it no different."

Hollie had never had a pet herself. Her parents had been convinced that animals were dirty, surefire transmitters of disease. And though she had always been quick to put down their theories, maybe that's why she never felt particularly at ease around animals. She had, of course, agreed to let Jake own a hamster. But then again, there was a cage standing between it and her.

"Why is he here? I mean, why would someone give up a healthy puppy?"

"He's a mongrel—a cross between shepherd and collie, not worth the money of a thoroughbred. The litter was big, more than the people could handle." He shrugged. "They tried to place all the pups in good homes, but ran out of takers."

Leash, collar, bed, chow, bones, vitamins, food dish, and teething toy—all of them she found in the hardware store in Fieldstone Plaza. Hollie also picked up twelve new window locks and twelve hooks and eyes to put on the screens. The hooks and eyes would be easy enough, but the locks might present some problem.

The pup peed all over the car's backseat on the way home. Apparently, as tense as she was.

"A dog?" Jake shouted.

"That's what they said it was. Be a nice guy and get the bags from the car," Hollie said.

Jake ran out and Allison came over and petted the puppy.

"He's so cute. Oh, look, he's shaking . . . he's scared." She lifted him onto her shoulder, petted him, then said to her mother, "Okay, why all of a sudden a dog?"

"What do you mean, why?" Hollie said, heading into the kitchen.

Allison followed along. "You always said you wouldn't let a dog in the hou—" She stopped, and putting the pieces together, said in a somber voice, "You spoke to the police and they won't do anything. Is that what this is about?"

Jake came in with the bags, dropped them on the kitchen table, then took the animal from Allison's arms. He put his face down to the puppy's face and looked him square in the eyes. "Come on. Want to meet a hamster named Popeye?" he said, heading toward the door. "Maybe you can get him to play again."

"The puppy is here to protect us?" Allison asked.

"I filed a complaint."

"What does that mean?"

"It means Sergeant Paterson will talk to Dylan."
Hollie filled the dog's dish with water, then set it on
the floor next to the cellar door.

"And?"

She faced Allison, took a deep breath. "And . . .
he's hoping that'll work. We don't have proof it was
Dylan . . . or witnesses, at least to anything signifi-
cant."

"What about the gum I found in my closet? Isn't
that proof enough?"

"According to the sergeant, it's not proof. It might
have been anyone's gum. It might even have been
put there purposely to make it look like it was his."

"But why would anyone—"

"I agree, it makes no sense. And though anything's possible, it's quite unlikely." She gathered
up the puppy food and vitamins and put them away
in the cabinet beneath the sink. "He will question
Dylan about it, of course."

Allison threw up her hands at the absurdity of it.
"Oh, that's just swell. Dylan will lie."

"I imagine he will. Then it ultimately comes down
to your word against his. It would have been better
had someone seen him enter the house."

"Even better if they got him on video," Allison
said, sighing. "So that's it?"

"Unless something more serious happens . . ."

"Like what?"

"I don't know, Allison. And please stop badger-
ing me."

Hollie had asked herself all the same questions,
and was just as frustrated. What exactly had to hap-

pen before the police could do more—would one of the children need to be hurt? Sergeant Paterson had worked on her for fifteen minutes that morning. And though Hollie couldn't stomach the man, he'd made his point well: she could speculate all she liked, but without proof, she had no case.

It was seven o'clock that same night when Sergeant Paterson, holding a copy of the signed statement against Dylan, rang the bell at the concrete house on Garden Place. Charlie Bradley opened the door; his necktie was off, his shirtsleeves were rolled, his belt undone, and his pants loose. In his hand he cupped a short glass.

"Hey there, Gus, come on in," Charlie said, opening the door wider. "What brings you around?"

Paterson stepped inside, shifted his feet uncomfortably: Charlie had done a few favors for him, one of them being pulled strings at Immigration for his cousin to come here on a visa from Ireland. He had always found him to be a regular guy. Not like some lawyers who looked down their noses at cops, treated them like scum.

"I've had some complaints issued against your boy, Charlie. Nothing that's gone beyond the warning stage, of course. But I'll tell you, the lady's mad as hell. She's from up the street—Hollie Ganz." He handed over a copy of the statement and waited while Charlie read it.

"I pegged her as trouble the minute I laid eyes on her," Charlie said, sliding his hand beneath his front waistband to scratch. He led Paterson into the den where there was an enormous wet bar, then gestured to his own drink. "Can I offer you something?"

"Thanks, but not while on duty. What's the story, Charlie, you have some kind of run-in with this lady?"

"Well, she was here all right . . . all upset because my boy wants to go out with her girl. Can you beat that? Now she's gone and gotten the police involved. I tell you, the trouble these days of mass divorce is there's a shitload of single mothers running around not knowing how to handle their kids. So they figure, get the police to do it for them. If you want my opinion, I think this one has a screw loose."

"Yeah, why's that?"

"Listen, if the wife wasn't sitting here at the time, I wouldn't even mention this because you'd figure I got to be lying. But if you don't believe me, confirm my story with Pauline."

Though Charlie wasn't beyond delivering a good con—in fact, it's what made him such a good lawyer—he'd always been up front with Gus. "Go ahead."

"Hollie Ganz came here, all frantic and distressed. We're neighbors, so naturally I tried to be friendly, do whatever I could to calm her. I went to touch her arm—totally innocent. Like this." Charlie put his hand on Paterson's lower arm. "As God is my witness, Gus, that's it. Well, she nearly went through the roof. You would have thought maybe I rubbed my prick up against her." He chuckled. "No mistake, not that she doesn't look good enough that a guy might have those thoughts. But no thanks, loonies I'll pass on.''

Charlie's reputation as a ladies man was not to be sneezed at, and now, with him approaching his mid-fifties, he still seemed to know how to handle the ladies. A reason why Paterson could buy that Hollie Ganz had misinterpreted Charlie's attempt at friendship: the last thing he needed was to steal a feel, and from a neighbor no less. ''Listen, Charlie, either way, I've got to talk to Dylan. He home?''

He got up, put a friendly hand on Paterson's shoulder. ''Sure, no problem. He's upstairs, doing homework.''

Five minutes later, Dylan was sitting with the two men.

''Dylan, I hear you're a real chewing gum addict.''

A slow smile, then he said, ''What've you been reading, copy for the Union High School yearbook?''

''Then it's true?''

''Cut the crap,'' Charlie said, turning to Paterson. ''He likes to race his car, wear designer jeans, and eat junk food, too. Him and the rest of the fucking kids in the nation. Now, are you alleging some kind of crime here? Because if you are, I sure as hell want to know what it is before he opens his mouth again.''

No need for any legal rigmarole, Paterson thought as he cleared his throat. He shook his head. ''Forget it, Charlie, just some sticks of chewing gum found at one of the scenes. I needn't tell you—strictly circumstantial.'' He addressed Dylan again. ''Your dad tells me you want to go out with this girl." He looked down at his notes. "Allison Ganz."

"Yeah, sure, so what?" Dylan said. "Since when has that been against the law."

"It's not, but if you're harassing her, that is. So I want you to stop whatever the hell you're doing."

"Okay, but what'd she say I'm doing?"

Paterson handed the statement to him and waited while he read it.

"This is a bunch of crap," Dylan said finally.

"Yeah? You sure?"

"Hey, I said I wanted to go out with her, not take the lead on her shit list."

Paterson smiled, rolled the statement, then tapped him playfully on his head.

"You've got a point there. Listen, do me a favor, stay away from this chick, will you? Ask your dad, he'll tell you, none of them are worth this kind of trouble. Besides, look at you: a good-looking stud like you can have his pick."

Barry Connors called Allison that night as soon as he'd finished his homework, and though they'd just met the day before, he was easy to talk to. Before she knew it, Allison found herself telling him how she wanted to study commercial art in college.

"I knew you were artistic," he said.

"Yeah, how?" She looked around her room, feeling kind of bad as she did: though she had cleaned up the mess after the break-in, she hadn't bothered to put back the artistic touches.

"I saw your book covers."

"Oh," she said, shyly. "And here I was thinking maybe you were psychic."

"I would have known without that tip-off, though. Something about you . . . you're different."

Silence.

"You're smiling, right?"

"I'm not saying."

More silence; then: "Allison, who'd you think I was yesterday afternoon?"

"What do you mean?"

"You know, when I knocked into you."

"Oh, that. You know Dylan Bradley?"

"Sure, I know who he is."

"Well, he's been sort of bothering me."

"How?"

"I don't want to talk about it, okay?"

It wasn't really okay, she could tell by the sound of Barry's voice, but he backed off. By the time they ended the conversation fifteen minutes later, he'd asked her out. But because of his work schedule this week, Friday was his only night available.

"Sorry, it's the night I see my dad," she said.

"Your folks divorced?"

"Yeah . . . just."

"Mine too, but it happened so long ago, I can't even remember them together."

She thought about what Barry had said, wishing for a moment that she couldn't remember her parents together either. But then all the good stuff would disappear, too. Did she really want *that*?

Hollie had installed the screen hooks with no difficulty, but after an hour of trying to figure out the window locks, she went to the yellow pages and looked up a locksmith. She found a local guy who worked from his house, and though he couldn't come out immediately, he promised to be there the next day at four. It was after eight o'clock when she went downstairs, intending to finish the article. She went first to her top desk drawer to get the hard copy: the yellow-lined pad was there, but again no article! She rushed upstairs, frantic—either she was going nuts, or someone was moving it!

Allison, who had just hung up her telephone, looked up, startled when Hollie burst in. "What's wrong, what happened?"

Without answering, Hollie asked, "Have you been in my office?"

"No. Why would I be in your office?"

"I didn't ask if you had a motive. Just give me a straight answer."

"Okay, fine—no. Is that good enough?"

"I don't like your attitude!"

"Well, I don't like yours either! You come bursting in here, then talk to me like I'm sneaking around your office. I didn't notice you asking Jake the question."

"Only because I haven't gotten to him." Suddenly noticing that Allison was close to tears, she dislodged the anger from her voice. "What's wrong?"

Allison shook her head. "Nothing really, at least nothing new." She gestured toward the telephone, then said, "I was just talking to Toby. She told me there's gossip going on about me in school." Hollie waited for Allison to go on. "Dylan and another boy made a hundred-dollar bet over me. Dylan bet that he'd 'do me' before the year was out."

Hollie stooped down, put her hands on Allison's shoulders. "That's just macho garbage, honey. And that's all it is. You can't let that kind of talk intimidate you."

Allison nodded, and Jake, who had apparently come in in the midst of all the emotion, stood there with his legs spread and his hands on his hips. "I'm here now, Mom. What do you want to ask me?"

Hollie, her agitation somewhat diffused, stood up, looked at him. "Were you in my office?" she asked.

"When?"

"At any time in the last few days."

He thought about it carefully, then shook his head. "Uh-uh. Why?"

"I can't find the hard copy of my Orphan Drug article."

"Isn't that the one you lost last Saturday?" Allison asked.

"In a way," she said, not really wanting to go into it. "I found it, though, and put it away in my top desk drawer. Now today it's missing again. I just can't imagine misplacing the same item twice."

Allison's eyes grew larger. "Then what you're saying is, you don't think you did. Someone could have come in the house again. Do you think it was Dylan?"

"Wait, stop, we don't know that. And we can't just make that assumption." She said it, but did she really believe it? If not Dylan playing some sick game with them, then who?

"Is the article still in your computer?" Jake asked, taking her mind back to the original problem. And she grasped at it because she had no desire to deal with the rest. She headed downstairs, booted up the computer: the article was there.

Her suspicion again went to Dylan. Except that he didn't know about her article or for that matter, her office downstairs. But he could have been walking around the house, hit upon her office accidentally, moved things just for kicks. . . . Her heart skipped: hadn't Jeremy been in the basement Sunday night? But Jake was there with him the entire time. There was no way Jeremy could have gone into her office, opened her drawer, taken out the article. Not without Jake seeing. And why would he? She remembered what the broker had said about the house—jinxed.

Now she began going through each drawer, dumping the contents on the carpet, then putting them back. She ended with the top drawer: the yellow-lined pad fell to the carpet first, and there it was beneath it: the lousy article! She sank to the floor, tears pressing against her eyelids. She hadn't even looked under the pad, she had been that sure. My God, what was happening to her? Hollie took a long, deep cleansing breath, trying to get rid of the turmoil in her head.

A mistake: she had placed it under the note pad, not over it. And no wonder her mind was in such turmoil, with all the stress in her life: trying to cope with single parenthood, emotionally and financially; leaving her friends; moving to a new home, a new city. Jeremy coming around . . . Allison's room being trashed . . . Dylan. That pig—right now she wanted to wrap her fingers around his throat.

By this time the next day, every window in the house would have double locks. Including the one in her office that no one but a child could squeeze through.

CHAPTER
Eight

There was a knock at the door just as they were finishing dinner the next evening, and Jake ran for it. When he returned to the kitchen, Woody was following him. He wore jeans and a sweatshirt. "Did I interrupt dinner?" he said, looking ill at ease when he saw the dishes still on the table. The puppy ran up to him and began to growl.

Jake picked up the puppy he'd named Chester, and scratched his neck. "We got him yesterday from the dog pound. Isn't he neat?"

Woody put his hand to the dog, rubbed his scruff, and Hollie pulled back a chair, indicating that Woody should sit. "Take a seat, Woody. You're in time for dessert."

"Oh, no." He put up his hands in protest. "Look, not a big deal, I can come back later."

"You'll do no such thing. Just don't expect great things, however—this working gal doesn't do any home baking these days. But I did stop at a bakery on my way home from work. Or maybe you'd rather have fruit?"

Before Hollie knew it they were sitting around the table, eating brownies and chatting easily. Particularly Jake, who seemed to be in awe of his computer teacher and thought nothing of bombarding him with questions.

"When did you first start working with computers?" Jake asked.

"I started fiddling with them at age six. By nine, I was creating some sophisticated stuff. I once programmed an audio training device for animals, using a pitch not within range of human hearing. It ended up backfiring—it attracted bats. Hundreds of them . . . all hanging from curtain rods in my bedroom."

Jake's eyes behind his glasses grew wide with fascination. Hollie swallowed quickly, the coffee going down the wrong way. She started to cough.

"Are you okay?" he asked with concern.

She nodded, then lifted a napkin to her mouth and swallowed. "What a horrible story."

He grinned broadly. "Yeah, that's what Mom thought, though she didn't voice it quite so nicely. Actually I thought they were fascinating little things. Ever see one of those suckers hang upside down?"

Hollie shook her head. "And I don't want to."

"Do they really suck blood?" Jake asked.

Though the thought of it all was unsettling to Hollie, Jake's eyes shimmered. What was it about sinister creatures that seemed to intrigue boys of all ages?

"Only when the body is warm," Woody answered, in a fine, chilling voice, as he spidered his fingers in Jake's direction. "For instance, when

you're in bed warm and toasty under the blankets."
Now having drawn his audience tightly in, Woody
winked at Hollie as he slackened the reins. "Actually the bats around these parts aren't the vampire
variety, they're strictly fruit-eating. So the fleshiest
thing those sharp teeth are likely to sink into is a
berry."

"Really?" Jake sighed in disappointment.

As Allison and Jake cleared the table, Hollie asked
Woody about himself. Though he downplayed his
accomplishments, as it turned out Eleanor Egan
Woods apparently wasn't the only genius in the
family. Somewhat of an entrepreneur, Woody ran a
small computer consulting business directly out of
his house.

At age twenty-two he had already earned his BA—
double-majoring in math and science—and his master's in computer science, and he was presently
working toward his doctorate. Though he received
a Fulbright for graduate work and could likely
have entered any university in the world, he chose
U. Conn to mollify his mother, who had been frightened at the prospect of being left alone.

"She didn't want strangers with her," he explained, the smile having dimmed from his face.
"She wanted me. And I never was good at refusing
her. Look, I don't play the martyr well. The bottom
line is, I do it because she needs me, and for a lot
of my young life I was totally convinced she was
royalty."

Hollie shook her head, impressed. "All this before
the age of twenty-three . . . not so bad. Between

your responsibilities at home and school, and working at building a business, how do you possibly find time to handle a computer club at Jake's school?''

''Just one afternoon a week.'' He arched thumb and finger like a gun and aimed it at Jake, who was standing at the sink. ''Wednesdays, my friend, in Room 212.''

''Wow, excellent,'' Jake said.

''What about a social life; do you have time to go out?''

''Hey, are you asking me out already?'' He looked at Jake for confirmation. ''Did you hear that too?''

Hollie laughed. ''Stop that. I mean, with a girl your age.''

''Girls my age don't like me.''

''Why not?''

''I'm a nerd, I have cowlicks, a hundred and one reasons I couldn't possibly list.''

''Woody, come on, be serious.''

Chester jumped up on his lap and began to lick his face. Totally unflustered by such sudden friendliness, he shrugged merrily. ''I don't know; ask a girl my age.''

It wasn't until the kids had gone off to their rooms to do homework that Woody said, ''Look at this: I've been here forty-five minutes, and I haven't mentioned my original purpose for stopping over. Raden Locksmith. I saw the truck in your driveway this afternoon. I thought maybe something was wrong.''

Hollie filled him in about the break-in, making it clear she thought Dylan was responsible. Woody was thrown, more than a little reluctant to believe

Dylan would go that far. "In any event, that's why the locksmith," Hollie said. "According to the police, without solid locks I was just about inviting company. At least, company that climbs through windows."

Woody shook his head. "I'm surprised you can joke about it."

"Actually, it's the first time I've come close to anything resembling a joke since it happened."

Woody's beeper sounded—he pulled it out of his pocket, looked at the number, then turned it off and slid it back.

"If you want to make a call," Hollie said, gesturing with her hand to the phone.

He shrugged it away. "It's a client, after hours. It'll wait." Then, "Tell me what else the police had to say."

She went over the entire conversation she'd had with Sergeant Paterson—chewing gum and unsatisfactory results included. She was just about to finish her story when the telephone rang and she jumped nearly off the chair. The next moment Allison called from her room, "I've got it, Mom. It's for me."

Hollie sank back into the chair and Woody looked at her, clearly not sure what to make of her reaction. She began to tell him about the pestering calls, trying to make light of it. But she was doing a poor imitation of light—she looked down at her hands, they were cold and shaking.

"I think I'm losing it," she said.

"What about Call Trace? The cop didn't mention that?"

"No, what is it?"

"It's a new system set up by Southern New England Bell. First you notify the phone company—they set it up and work in conjunction with your local police. Whenever you get a suspicious call, you hang up, then press in a predetermined sequence of numbers to alert them. And in turn, they pull an immediate trace of the call."

"After the connection is broken?"

"Yep, after the fact. Gone are those days when they needed a long connection to get a successful trace. In any event, they'll give the name and address of the caller to the police, and presto: the lady not only finds who the caller is, but she gets her proof."

Hollie shook her head, baffled. "Why didn't Sergeant Paterson mention this?"

"I don't know. It's hard to imagine he wouldn't be aware of the new technology. Maybe he figured a talk with Dylan might end it."

She thought about it, then said, "It's proof of a call, but not necessarily of harassment."

"It's close enough. You say the calls usually come late at night—the time will be recorded. That plus the short connection time and the number of calls received are all indications of their harassing nature. I suggest you contact the phone company and get the particulars."

Twice that night Hollie had a strong urge to call Jeremy and dump it all into his lap. But both times as she went to lift the phone, she resisted. Besides not wanting to admit to needing help, what could Jeremy do? If he were Mike or Jeffrey or Harry, any number of men she knew from the old neighborhood, maybe he would know the right approach to Dylan, a way to push him away with a few tough words. But not Jeremy. With his quick and explosive temper, she couldn't really count on it to stop there. She touched her bruised arm, wondering what Jeremy might do if he were *really* angry at someone.

She flashed her mind to an article she was doing at work, anything to break the line of thought. Finally she turned off her light and laid back, her eyes fixed on the brass fixture overhead and her muscles tensing as she waited for the inevitable ring of the telephone. But after a long period of silence, she felt her muscles begin to loosen. She closed her eyes, took some slow, deep breaths, and was just falling off when she heard the rustling out front. Her first thought was an animal in the bushes. Then when it didn't stop and seemed to be moving, she lifted her head to listen better: she heard a thump at the side of the house.

Her imagination? She got up, peeked in Jake's room, then Allison's room—both children were sound asleep. She walked into the kitchen and saw that the puppy was up and, strangely, walking in tight, compulsive circles. Finally, he pattered to the back door, his ears suddenly perked and growling softly. Whatever noises she had heard, he must have heard them, too.

At a rap at the kitchen window, her insides jumped. She let out a short shriek and her attention focused on the window: pitch blackness. She backed up to the telephone, her gaze not moving. She lifted the receiver and called 911.

"Hollie Ganz, 8 Garden Place, Union. I need the police. Right away, please. There's someone outside my house."

There were no further sounds—mysterious or otherwise—before the police cruiser pulled up in front of her house about five minutes later. She ran to the living room window, pushed aside the draperies. Two officers got out of the cruiser, split up, and using flashlights, each searched around a side of the house. She could hear them talking after searching the backyard, then they came back around to the front and knocked on her door.

The older, obviously more seasoned officer, who introduced himself as Officer Hanks and stood in front of her holding a pen and dime-store note pad, asked the questions. "Did you see anyone?" he asked.

She shook her head. "No, just noises . . ."

Officer Hanks glanced at the silent officer, then back to her. "Can you describe what you heard?"

Was this going to be simply a repeat of her conversations with Sergeant Paterson? "First there was a rustling," she began. "That seemed to come from the front, somewhere in the bushes . . . then something against the side of the house. When I got to the kitchen, I heard a rap on the window. Like someone had knocked on it."

Perhaps it was the freshly painted walls or the cheap room-sized carpet that curled a little at the edges that gave him the clue as he looked around the living room. "You're new in the neighborhood, aren't you?" he concluded correctly.

She nodded, wondering if this was to be the moving man theory Paterson had tried to sell her.

"Ah-hah, what I thought," he said, as though he were proud his hunch had been verified. "What I think we have here is a simple case of nerves. Being in a new location and from what I see . . . alone."

Why had he lowered his voice on that last word, making it sound like a disease? Still he went on.

"You've heard people say, 'Houses talk'? Well the fact is, they do. The hot-water pipes in my house groan and carry on like an old lady. And the squeaks and rattles in the walls could substitute easy for a kindergarten band. My wife used to shake me awake about every fifteen minutes to make me listen to what she believed were ghosts living inside the walls. It's all just a matter of getting familiar with your own particular house sounds."

And do shrinks in blue charge double for evening therapy? *Stop it, Hollie, he's only trying to help. . . .* Should she tell him about Dylan? What difference would it make . . . he hadn't found anything. Besides, it would likely just reaffirm his assessment of her. Dylan must have figured she'd call the police, and had made a quick getaway before they arrived. Or was it like Hanks had said, all her imagination?

She thanked them, closed the door. She forgot to tell them about the dog—surely his behavior had indicated something suspicious. Or was he only reacting to her fear? In any event, by the time Hollie looked in on Chester, he'd climbed back into his furry bed and fallen asleep. Fortunately, the kids had slept through it all.

She went back to her bedroom and pushed the

draperies to the side. Looking out, she saw Roger Spear across the street strolling down the sidewalk. She watched him until he'd disappeared from sight, then let the draperies fall back and got into bed. Her muscles were aching, as though she'd just been through a marathon. She was never one to distort or exaggerate, or for that matter to frighten easily. But that was before—before she thought someone was watching her.

"Hello."

Silence.

"Who's this?"

More silence.

"Hollie, is that you?"

"Yes . . ." A deep breath; then: "I'm sorry, Jeremy, I—"

"Are you crying?"

He sounded concerned, but mostly surprised: the superwoman fallacy put to rest. "No," she said.

"You are."

"I said I'm not. . . ."

"Why're you lying?"

"Don't call me a liar!" she shot back; then: "Okay, dammit, so I'm crying. I have a right to cry once in a while, don't I?"

"Sure, of course—hey, did I say you didn't? What's wrong?"

She sat there, one hand twisting a wet tissue. What could she tell him? Now she didn't know why she'd called him; she certainly didn't want to go into any of the strange things happening around her house.

"Look, I've got an idea, why don't I throw on some clothes, jump in the car, head over there. At this hour, there'll be no traffic. It shouldn't take me but—"

"No, don't, wait!"

"What?"

"I don't want you to come," she said.

"You're not making sense, princess. Why not?"

It didn't make sense, did it? She could get dressed, they could sit in the living room and talk. What would be so wrong with that? "I just don't know," she said.

"Listen, don't make such a fuss over this. You're feeling bad, lonely maybe . . . hey, it happens to the best of us. So I come over, keep you company for a bit. It's real simple . . . basic stuff. No need to make it overly complicated."

Did he sound too eager? If she agreed, wouldn't that put her just where he wanted her? Dependent, letting him take the controls. "I can't run to you every time something goes wrong," she said finally.

"Then something *is* wrong?"

"No, I didn't mean that in the literal sense."

"That kid isn't bothering Allison again, is he?"

"No, it's not that, it's me."

"Yeah, well, this isn't like you."

She took a deep breath, brought her knees up on the bed, hugging them. "You don't know me anymore, Jeremy. Who knows, maybe you never knew me."

Silence, while he was likely trying to figure out what drug she had ingested.

"Look," he said finally, "let me come over. Just

to chitchat . . . about old times, sports, flea markets, whatever. Unless of course you insist on a few hands of rummy. Don't give it a thought, princess, I've been keeping it to a strict three-toothpick betting limit these days. And if you play it right, I supply the toothpicks.''

If ever there was a time she wanted him near her, it was at this moment. But with her palm she brushed more tears away, took a deep breath, and in a voice artificially infused with spirit, she said, ''Nothing's wrong, Jeremy, at least nothing a good sleep won't fix. Will you listen to me? I feel better already. I'm fine, dry-eyed, no more silly blubbering. I'm so sorry I bothered you, I had no right. Put it down to spouse withdrawal, yuk yuk yuk. Okay, not funny. But I didn't mean to do this, Jeremy, really.''

She hung up. She hadn't meant to do that. To talk to him, sure. But never to cry.

CHAPTER
Nine

The next morning things were harried, now with the puppy to feed and walk, then, after breakfast, with barriers to be constructed at the kitchen doorway to keep him from entering the rest of the house while the children were in school.

"I thought the whole purpose was for him to be a watchdog," Allison said, as she pushed the coffee table to the kitchen doorway. She stood up, adjusting the wide black belt on her jumpsuit.

"So far he's only paper-trained. Once he's fully housebroken, he can have the run of the house." Hollie was hurrying to clear the table, put the food away. Glancing at the clock, she decided to put the breakfast dishes in the sink to soak.

"I met a kid named Ricky," Jake said.

"I want you to call me when you get in this afternoon," Hollie said to Allison.

"Okay." Allison stuck another book in her backpack, then slid the strap over one shoulder. "Mom, I met a boy in school, he asked me out."

"He plays chess," Jake said.

Hollie nodded to Jake; then to Allison; "Out where?"

"Actually nowhere, at least not yet. We couldn't get it together on a time. So maybe next weekend."

So casual about it . . . that's good, Hollie supposed. "Why am I only now hearing this?" she asked.

She shrugged. "Barry Connors is his name. He's sort of cute, nice too."

"I can't say I'm sorry about this weekend, though. I don't think I could be too comfortable with you out at night alone."

"I would hardly be alone."

"You know what I mean."

"I know," Allison said. "But I've thought about it a lot . . . how I go out of my way to avoid Dylan. And I'm sick of giving him that kind or power over me! I've decided not to go out of my way to hide from him anymore."

Knowing how much Dylan, the break-in, and everything connected to it and him scared the daylights out of Allison, Hollie had to admire her resolve. She smiled, reached out, touched her soft cheek, and said, "Good for you." Then to Jake, who was feeding Chester toast and strawberry jelly left over from breakfast: "Can I count on you to take the pup for a walk after school?"

"Can't, Mom. I've got computer club with Woody."

"Until what time?"

He shrugged.

"After-school activities usually end about four," Allison said, then: "Don't worry, I'll keep an eye out for him. And I'll take Chester for his walk, too."

"Thanks, honey. Just stay away—" She stopped, then pointed in the opposite direction of Dylan's house. "Go that way. Please. Just to make your mother feel better. And if Dylan should attempt to come near this property, order him off. If he won't leave, call the police."

When Frank Lorenzo spotted Gus Paterson leaving the Phoenix Diner, he pulled into the parking lot and waved him over. Paterson was a team man, a cynic, sometimes a pain in the butt. In fact, Frank had had little use for him when he himself first joined the force. But when some of the rookie righteousness wore away, he noticed that when the stakes got heavy, Paterson did the right thing.

"I didn't see you earlier," Frank said when Paterson got within earshot.

"My shift didn't start till one-thirty. They've got me on some damn rotation schedule. Well, now that you found me, counselor, what can I do for you?"

Frank wore his tan trench coat, unbuttoned, exposing a flowery silk tie. "Listen, you've got a case . . . Ganz, I think it is?" he asked the cop.

"Yeah."

"Did you talk to the kid?"

"Yesterday."

Was he going to make him pick it out piece by piece? "And?" he said finally.

"And like I thought, this lady is making mountains of molehills. Sure, the kid has the hots for this girl, maybe even did some teasing and hassling. But come on, this is how all these kids operate, we're talking everyday stuff here."

As a prosecutor, Frank had a right to meddle in police work, though as a practical matter he seldom did it. And then only with a major case. Right now he could see Paterson's computer tapping away, curious as to why he'd picked this particular one.

"According to the statement I saw in the file, there were two forced entries, one while people were at home."

"That all depends on how you see things," Paterson said. "The first alleged forced entry, the daughter and girlfriend were home baby-sitting the kid brother. So the party happened to end up at the Ganz house. It gets out of control: a little too much booze, the kids get fried chicken on the carpet, panic that they're going to be snagged, maybe even grounded. Now, you tell me, Lorenzo: to wash innocent, aren't these two girls gonna be willing to make up a cock-and-bull story?"

Frank thought about it—yeah, it might have happened that way; then again, it might not have. "And the other incident?"

"I didn't see it, Lorenzo, did you? Nothing was taken. . . . I told her to get better locks on the windows."

The old redistribute-the-blame routine, usually used to dilute and redirect the victim's anger away from the police. "Gee whiz, you're a real helper, aren't you, Gus? What about the chewing gum?"

Paterson crossed his arms, tapped his foot, looked to the heavens: body language designed to bust balls. "Come on, what're you gonna do with that?" he asked.

"Don't try to second-guess me."

Paterson now looked him in the eye. "This is simple stuff, Lorenzo. You don't need a fucking law degree to know it's not worth much. It boils down to his word against hers. And who knows, maybe she doesn't like him and is trying to set him up. Look, I don't mean to be negative, but from what I'm hearing, the mother has severe emotional problems."

"Where'd you hear that?"

"Charlie Bradley."

Frank winced as he put the kid's last name together with Charlie Bradley, the attorney. President of the county bar association, Charlie had a big mouth and narrow mind, both of which pissed Frank off on a fairly regular basis. "This is his kid, huh?"

Paterson nodded, and picking up on his reaction, said, "His wife will vouch for him on this. The Ganz woman came over to complain about the kid. Charlie tries to be friendly, you know, wind her down a little. After all, she's a new neighbor, and a single mother to boot. So in talking to her, he puts his hand on her lower arm, like this." Paterson demonstrated. "All as innocent as that, with the wife sitting about two feet away, watching. And what happens? The lady shits a brick. Just about cries rape."

Having seen Hollie Ganz himself, Frank had no trouble suspecting Charlie's hand was up to no good. But he pushed that annoying thought aside, going back to the original issue. "What did the Bradley kid say to the accusation?"

"What do you think he said? He didn't do any of it. Sure, he likes the girl, wouldn't mind at all getting it on with her, but thems the breaks." Frank thought Paterson sounded a little too glib, figuring he didn't wholly believe the kid's story himself. "Oh, and I shouldn't forget to mention this," the cop went on. "Last night we get a panic call from Mrs. Ganz, someone supposedly in her backyard."

"So?" Frank said.

"Nothing, no one . . . clean." Paterson put his hand to his smooth chin, rubbing it, then in a mocking tone said, "What we have here, counselor, is a person with a very active imagination. Either that or she's one mighty lonely little lady."

"What about the telephone calls? Did you tell her to use Call Trace?"

"No."

Frank could feel his blood starting to warm. "Why not?"

"I figure if it's the kid, maybe my talking would do the trick. You understand, nothing is said on the line . . . it's not like we've got obscenity here."

"No, just harassment."

"Look, lighten up, Frank. I spoke to the kid. If it *is* him, it'll likely end here. No need to make it into more than it is."

"Okay, maybe you're right. I hope so. But now that the kid is forewarned, I want Mrs. Ganz told about the tracing service. Then notify the phone company."

Paterson scratched his head, looked at Frank like he'd grown another head. "Are you serious?"

"I am. And tell them to keep the trace on until we tell them otherwise. If I'm going to attempt to present this to a judge, I want proof positive of these calls.''

"Okay, Frank," Paterson said finally. "I'm gonna assume you've got your reasons to want to take this one on." When Frank didn't volunteer what they might be, he said, "Anything else on your mind?"

"Yeah—pay attention to her complaints." He started to pull away, then stopped. "You handle the phone company, Gus. I'll see that she knows about it."

The computer club had a show of twelve boys and five girls—the best and brightest from grades four through six. And though Jake would have done almost anything to have those kids know that he and Woody were neighbors, he abided by Woody's original introduction and while there, addressed him as Mr. Woodbury.

The club ended at three-thirty, and Jake was wishing it had gone on longer when Woody came up to him.

"Come on, Jake, I'll give you a lift home."

The kids will know now, Jake thought.

"What're you grinning at?"

He gestured with a nod to the other kids. "I bet they're jealous."

"Think so?"

"I know so."

Woody glanced at them walking in a pack, their eyes not leaving him and Jake. As he reached the car, he held his hand high. "Give me five, Jake," he said, and the boy's hand slapped his. Then Woody clasped Jake's hand tightly for all to see.

"How'd we do?" he asked, as they pulled onto the main street.

"Excellent." Every kid there was probably wishing he was Jake. A real turnaround from the usual state of affairs. Since he'd moved to Union, the kids had treated Jake like he was some kind of freak. Except for Ricky, a real good kid, but his mother worked and wouldn't let him hang around with anyone after school.

"It's early; what do you say we hit Friendly's?"

"You mean it?"

Once there, Woody gave the order for two super hot fudge sundaes. "Now, please take a hike," he said to the waitress, his hand waving her away in dismissal. The waitress looked at him as if he were crazy, then walked away, but it didn't faze Woody. Jake liked that about him: he didn't worry about what people thought of him.

"What is it with these people who can't take a little kidding?" Woody said. "I've yet to meet an intelligent person without a keen sense of humor. A definite correlation."

Jake nodded. Woody was talking to him as if he were an equal. It made him feel good. Woody took a straw and stuck it in his water glass, then capped his thumb over it, holding the water in. He lifted the straw, removed his thumb . . . the liquid flowed out.

"Guess what, Woody, Chester's already paper-trained."

He smiled. "I imagine that makes your mom happy. Who came up with the name Chester?"

"We all came up with names, then voted on them. Mine was the one voted in."

"It's a good one—after anyone special?"

"Naw, I just like it."

"What's your dad's name?"

"Jeremy. Why?"

"I don't know, just wondered. Where does he live?"

"He's in Hartford; he's got a two-room apartment at this place called Brandywine Village. I see him Fridays. And he calls a lot to talk. Most times I think it's my mom he wants to talk to."

"Miss him?"

Jake nodded; then, pressing the nosepiece of his eyeglasses closer to his face, he looked at Woody. "Yeah, a lot."

"I know how you feel, my folks were away a lot. My mom off doing concerts or workshops. Dad gave up his contracting company to manage her career, that way he could take care of her. Whenever she had a large block of time free from engagements, they would travel. She loved Europe."

Jake had never known anyone who traveled around big-time like that. A couple of times Mom and Dad had taken vacations—they went to a resort, once even to Las Vegas. Those times, he and Allison stayed with Elaine and Mike. But they had not once gone to Europe. "Wow . . . who used to take care of you?"

"I had a nanny. In fact, Mom found her in Paris.

She was fifteen, didn't have any family, so Mom brought her home to me.''

''What's a nanny do?''

''Takes care of you, teaches you, takes you neat places. Like a mother would do.''

''Your mother must have had to pay her a lot.''

''Why would you think that?''

Jake spread his arms, wondering by the look on Woody's face if he'd said something he shouldn't have said. ''No reason, Woody, just all the stuff that mothers have to do. Well, if you added it up, it would probably cost a whole lot.'' The funny look seemed to fade, and relieved, Jake said, ''I bet you still missed your mom, though.''

Woody puckered up his mouth, then let it smooth out again. ''Yeah, I guess, at first. But you get used to things.''

Jake had a lot of daydreams about his dad and mom, usually all of them ending with their getting back together. But he hadn't talked much about those dreams—at least, until now. ''I doubt I'll ever get used to missing my father. But I might not have to.''

''Why not?''

''Just that maybe my folks will get together again.''

Woody had sort of a doubtful expression on his face. ''Your mom say that?''

''No. But I know my dad still loves her.''

''He tell you?''

Whenever Jake thought about that awful time with his dad and him in the car alone, he could feel a big ache inside him. He looked down at the table so

Woody wouldn't see his face. "Yeah, once," he said. "And while he was telling it, he cried."

"Watch that he doesn't play on your sympathy."

Jake forgot about Woody seeing his sadness and looked up. "What do you mean?"

"There's things in life people have to accept, even when they don't want to. And it's not right to drag others into their despair . . . you know, use the sympathy to move along their cause."

"Charlie, Gus Paterson here."

"How can I be of service, Gus?"

"You can't. But maybe I can help you."

A pause; then: "How's that?"

"I just wanted to let you know. The new neighbor lady is putting a tracer on her phone line."

"Oh?"

"Look, if your kid is not involved, great. I just thought I'd bring it to your attention. This way, if it is your kid, and if my warning didn't make a sufficient dent on him . . . well, look, all I can do is tell you. I'm sure you know what to do."

"Thanks, Gus, I appreciate the call."

Charlie put the phone receiver down, sighing. When would the aggravation end? Hopefully when the kid went off to college. That would be next year, and if all went well it would be Boston College, his alma mater. The last thing he needed with schools about to look over his record was some silly nuisance complaint brought against him in juvenile hall. At the dinner table that night, he brought it up with Dylan.

"Gus Paterson called me today."

"We just saw him, wasn't it yesterday?"

The boy's voice was short and impudent and grating. Charlie couldn't remember: Had it always been that way, or had it shifted sometime when he wasn't paying attention? He picked up a roll, looked around. "Pauline, what about some butter here?" His wife stood up, headed to the kitchen, and Charlie looked at Dylan. "He tells me the lady across the street is putting a tracer on her telephone."

Dylan cut a piece of tenderloin, forked it, stuck it in his mouth. "Good."

"It doesn't bother you?"

He shook his head. "Why should it?"

"You understand, son, even penny-ante shit can stop a college acceptance committee cold. It's not as though you're walking in, showing them dynamite marks or extracurricular activities. . . . Christ, your SATs are barely competitive."

Dylan nodded, chewed on his steak. Pauline walked in with several squares of butter on a plate.

"What'd he want, Charlie?"

"Who's that?"

"Gus Paterson . . . you said he called."

"Oh, yeah. Just looking to pick my pocket again. This time it was their summer camp program, giving poor kids a chance to see what it's about. I sent him a check."

"Really? Isn't that nice."

A crank call came at about ten o'clock while Hollie was in the tub. Allison opened the bathroom door, her voice immediately jumpy.

"Mom, I think Dylan just called . . . one of those hang-ups."

Hollie stood up in the tub, wrapped a towel around her. "I'm coming out now anyway. Do me a favor, honey, put on coffee. Why don't you join me, have cocoa?"

She came out with a towel wrapped around her head, wearing a bulky green terry robe. Just as she entered the kitchen, the phone rang again. She lifted it. "Hello."

Again, "Hello."

She waited, nothing . . . pulled the towel off her head and hung it over the kitchen chair. She broke the connection, then left the receiver dangling. At Woody's suggestion, she had contacted the telephone company earlier in the day, and by tomorrow the trace would be set to go into effect. She looked at Allison.

"By tomorrow we won't need to sit around just getting ourselves upset, we'll be able to do something positive to nail him. Won't that be a welcome change?"

Allison nodded as she carried her cocoa to the living room, then sat on the sofa. Hollie was sinking down beside her, putting her cup on the coffee table, when the house went black.

"Oh, no?" Allison cried.

Hollie got up, made her way to the window. Pulling aside the drapes, she looked out over the neighborhood. The other houses still had their lights.

"It's not the service," she said. "One of our circuit breakers must have kicked in."

"I'm scared."

"No need to be, honey," she said, though she didn't relish the idea of going into the dark cellar. "It's just a matter of throwing the switch." She stood up, feeling her way to the kitchen, Allison tagging along as she opened the junk drawer and began fishing around.

"I'll have the lights back before you know it."

"Why would they go off?"

"I guess we're using too much power."

Silence as they both considered Hollie's answer. The only lights that had been on were the living room and kitchen lights. Maybe Allison's bedroom, too. But none of the three televisions. Not the washer, the dryer, the smaller appliances. She thought about the photograph Jeremy had found in the fuse box, remembering how he'd said he was simply checking it out.

"Suppose he did it," Allison said.

"Who?" Hollie asked, still thinking of Jeremy.

"Dylan, of course."

Now with flashlight in hand, and Chester's furry little body tangling itself between her feet in a frenzy, Hollie reached down, picked him up, and handed him to Allison to calm him down.

"It's not possible. Dylan's not a magician."

"Suppose he's in the house," she whispered.

It was ridiculous, she refused to even consider it. "Stop it, Allison, no one is here." She went to the cellar door and opened it all the way. Hesitating only a moment, she began down, the light beam guiding and casting a shadow on the stair. Her shadow—stretched and distorted. She paused, swallowed hard, then directed the light ahead to the finished room. It must have been the series of events that led to the moment that caused her equilibrium to go out of whack. But when she reached midway and stumbled, everything seemed to circle off-balance. For an instant . . . just an instant, the light beam directed on her office bookshelves made it seem like the wall had moved!

But she caught the railing, steadying herself . . . and steadying her world.

"Mommy?"

Hollie's hands were shaking. She still hadn't taken her eyes from the bookshelves. A play of light, the way the glare had reflected on the wall, then threw her off balance, tripping her . . .

"I'm okay," she said finally.

She moved the light to the hatchway: from where she stood, she could see the bolt was secure. Then, beaming the flashlight back toward the bookshelves, she began down the steps, heading toward them. Finally, standing in front of the bookshelves, she stopped, swallowed hard, and putting her hand flat against the back of the center shelf, pushed. Harder, harder . . .

"What's taking so long?"

Had she actually expected it to move? She pulled her hand away, now feeling foolish. "Just one second, Allison." She lit her way to the circuit box, fingers fumbling, opening it, looking in: The breakers seemed in place. Still she went through each lever, the main breaker included, moving them off, then again on.

"Allison," she called upstairs, "anything?"

"No, nothing."

Hollie took a deep breath, trying to calm herself, but her heart was gunning. Had a noise come from between those boxes, or was she again imagining things?

CHAPTER
Ten

Allison was standing impatiently at the doorway to the cellar when she heard the noises on the back steps, then what sounded like a tapping at the door. She crept toward the kitchen window, her breath stuck somewhere in her throat, and peeked out: she saw the light beam . . . a face, and let out a shriek. But then she recognized the face and sighed: Roger . . . it was only their neighbor, Roger.

She went to the door, opened it a crack. But by the time she could get any words out her mother was right behind her, pushing her aside and shining her flashlight on Roger's face.

"What are you doing here?" Hollie asked, suspiciously.

"Oh, excuse me," he said. "Did I frighten you?"

"Yes, you frightened me!" She opened the door wider. "You frightened us both. What do you want?"

"Well, I was out for my nightly walk when I saw the lights in your house go out. I figured something was wrong and thought maybe you could use help."

"Walking where, in my backyard?"

"No, no, of course not. But I knocked on the front door first, then when no one answered, I thought . . ." His voice trailed off as he stepped into the kitchen.

Hollie stood there, staring at the strange man with the big head and grinning eyes, tempted to take him up on his offer of help. She was so stressed and panicky, she felt helpless fumbling around in the dark.

According to Roger, whom Hollie accompanied back downstairs, her error had been in not pulling the main breaker far enough into the off position, though she was sure she had. When she insisted, Roger thought perhaps she hadn't held it there long enough, which she supposed was possible.

But why had it short-circuited to begin with? "No particular reason is necessary," Roger said. "These things can get temperamental and testy with age."

Fifteen minutes later the electricity was in order and Roger was gone. Hoping to ease the tension by getting a good night's sleep, Hollie hung up the phone in the kitchen but purposely left the receiver in the bedroom off the hook.

So when she was startled awake by the sound of ringing, she shot up in bed, her eyes immediately going to the receiver, lying exactly where she'd left it on the nightstand. Though it couldn't have been more than seconds, it seemed like minutes before her brain connected the ringing in her ears to the doorbell. She got up, rushed to the front room window, and looked out: the police?

She opened the door to Gus Paterson.

"You okay?" he asked.

She nodded. "Why?"

"You take the phone off the hook?"

"Yes, I—"

Though he didn't say so, *annoyed* was clearly the operative word as he pushed the piece of paper into Hollie's hand.

"Your husband's number . . . Call the guy, he's worried. Something about you being overcome with noxious gases . . . or alternatively, a psychotic breaking in, keeping you and the children as prisoners."

He started to go, then turned back. "What is it—the whole family this way?"

She closed the door, looked at the paper with Jeremy's phone number written on it, then began to laugh . . . harder and harder. Even when she realized the children were standing there, listening and watching her, she couldn't stop.

"Did you really say that to the police?" she was asking Jeremy a few minutes later.

"What's that?"

"About poison gases . . . a psychotic holding us prisoners?"

"So I admit, I got a little carried away. But I *was* worried when I kept coming up with busy signals . . . three hours of it. And after talking to you last night, and the weird mood you were in then, well, I wasn't quite sure what to think."

"Still, I'd say you took a major leap." And wasn't she just a tiny bit relieved, even grateful, that there was someone out there who would worry enough to do that?

"Maybe," he said. "But when I checked with the operator, she said the phone was off the hook. I've never known you to do that. I'll tell you one thing: those cops out your way need to have a bonfire put under their behinds. I had to threaten to go to the papers, call the mayor. What kind of town do you live in?"

"I'm beginning to wonder. . . ."

"What's this I hear . . . doubts?"

Think it or not, she shouldn't have let that slip. Now she tried her best to retrieve it. "No doubts, forget it. And don't ever pull a stunt like that again." She paused, waiting for an answer. "Jeremy, did you hear what I said?"

"I hear you. . . . What if it's true?"

"What's true?" she asked, not quite following.

"That you or the kids are in trouble."

She paused—was she being a fool to let him bait her like this? "Are you saying that to frighten me?"

"Me saying it frightens you? Since when?"

"Since now."

"Something is going on; tell me."

"Nothing."

"Why'd you take the phone off the hook?"

"It was done inadvertently."

"You don't do things inadvertently, Hollie. I think you're holding back on me."

She sighed. "Think whatever you want. Look, what was it you wanted?"

"Wanted?"

"You tried to reach me for three hours, I assume for a reason."

"Actually, there was. I made my first sale, Hollie, a twenty-five-thousand-dollar annuity. Not so bad, with the market being so goddamned flighty."

"That's great, Jeremy," she said, making an effort to sound enthusiastic. "Really."

"I thought maybe we could celebrate. No big deal, just a quiet dinner in town—maybe DJ's. We could meet there if you'd rather the kids didn't know." DJ's was a tiny seafood place with ambience, a long-time favorite of theirs.

"It's not a good idea. I'm sorry," she said, trying not to picture the look of dejection she knew was on his face. What was it about him, that he could still make her feel guilty?

"Dammit, Hollie, when *will* it be a good idea? I've tried to back off, to do it your way, give you time to put aside the anger. But I'm getting fucking tired of sitting around like a prize schmuck, waiting!" The fury that had so suddenly leapt out, just as suddenly slid back in the shadows. "I can't be without you, princess. I just can't. . . ."

She broke the connection.

Just about to eat breakfast the next morning, Allison jumped up, suddenly remembering. She headed to the counter, brought back a slip of paper, and handed it to Hollie. "Sorry, I forgot. I took it yesterday before you got home."

The names were Lois Green and Frank Lorenzo, and there was a phone number beneath. Hollie looked at Allison, who was now buttering her toast. "Who are they?"

"All I know is Frank Lorenzo is a lawyer. The secretary, Lois, the one who called, said it's important."

She speculated on why a lawyer from Union might call her, and came up with only one explanation: Charlie Bradley's crony, looking to frighten her away. The attorney was tied up in court when she tried the number at nine o'clock, but according to his secretary he had from three to four-thirty free on his calendar. Could she meet with him within that period?

"I don't understand, what—"

"Frank Lorenzo is the state's attorney for Suffolk. It's about the Bradley complaint."

Considering the importance of such a meeting, she asked Harvey Boynton to let her off at three forty-five with the stipulation that she bring home work to do on the weekend. And though she was encouraged when she learned that Frank Lorenzo was a prosecutor, by the time she got to his private law office she was sure she had misinterpreted his motive. After all, Charlie Bradley was a local attorney—why not a friend of the prosecutor?

That's why when Lois Green showed Hollie into Frank Lorenzo's office and stepped out, the first thing she said was, "If you asked me here to withdraw the complaint, forget it."

He stood, gesturing to an easy chair near his desk, and as she took it she examined him. It wasn't his clothes that were wrong, she decided—in fact, they were fine. But he wore the gray double-breasted suit with a peak lapel with such burly carelessness, it nearly sabotaged the design. He was wide and muscular and tall, and his darkness was startling against a smile that—despite her brash introduction—remained on his face.

"Didn't Lois explain?" he asked.

"She said you were the prosecutor, and it concerned my complaint against Dylan Bradley."

"Right," he said, as he sat down. "Then why would I ask you to drop your complaint?"

"Then you're not?" She stopped, sighed, feeling foolish. "In that case, forgive me. The thing is, I was under the impression the police weren't taking my complaints seriously."

"They're not, and I'm not sure I am either. Kids tend to tease other kids. It's mean, but in most cases harmless. Usually the best way to stop it is to ignore it."

"Those were my sentiments . . . at the beginning. However, it's not gone away."

"Where're you from?"

"Bloomfield."

"This ever happen in Bloomfield?"

"What you mean is, am I a chronic complainer?"

Her bluntness threw him, but he liked it. Recovering almost immediately, he said, "Okay, you're right. These are things I need to know. Are you?"

"This is the first official complaint, Mr. Lorenzo, but then again, I've just moved to Union. Surely given more time, I'll have no trouble coming up with more trivial problems."

"I'm trying to help you," he said finally. "You're not making it easy."

"Sorry, but so far your help sounds loaded with skepticism, pretty much the same tune the police have been playing for me."

She's on target, Lorenzo thought, particularly when it comes to the police. A lot of attitude naturally develops after handling enough of these kinds of cases. Most of them involving over-reactors, neurotics, one neighbor against another, neither willing to give an inch. But she didn't seem to fit any of those categories. "Do we have any witnesses willing to testify to the allegations?"

She sat forward, her defensiveness lessening with his question. "I have a neighbor who stepped in when Dylan was being a nuisance with his car, moving it so my daughter Allison was unable to cross the street. This same neighbor came over to break it up when Dylan and his friends invaded my house. But from what I understand, the kids scattered before he got inside. And then we have those sticks of gum . . . Allison says he's always chewing gum. But the sergeant explained it was only circumstantial, not worth much."

"It's a lot better than nothing, but true—not enough in itself to convince a judge. But if it were a part of a series of circumstances, who knows? Circumstantial evidence—if overwhelming—can be as compelling as scientific evidence."

"Really?" she said.

Clearly encouraged, she smiled, and he liked how it looked. He hadn't meant to make nailing this bastard sound easy, because it wasn't. But he wasn't paying her lip service either. He had every intention of trying to get at whoever was bothering her and her kids.

"Well, I really hate the thought of doing it, but I was considering talking to some of the other neighbors," she said. "Maybe there was someone who saw him in my yard."

"It certainly couldn't hurt to do that. Are you still receiving those calls?"

"Yes, why?"

"There's a tracing service that—"

"I know," she said, interrupting him. "I spoke to a woman at the telephone company yesterday to arrange it. She said all the information would go to my local police. I gave her Sergeant Paterson's name."

"I'll see that he's aware of it. Understand now, once we've established a pattern in the calls, sufficient to hold up as evidence, you'll be informed of the caller. But not until."

"Okay. Tell me, Mr. Lorenzo, why didn't Sergeant Paterson suggest this? Or shouldn't I bother to ask?"

"Look, don't blame Gus. Kids usually give up on these things, so sometimes the less made of it, the better. And also let me be clear, don't expect much out of this: even if we manage to get sufficient evidence to make a case, subpoena the Bradley kid to court, the works, he's not likely to pull much punishment. Remember, we're talking about a juvenile here, with no criminal record."

"None?"

"Some small stuff, nothing that stayed on the books."

"Is that because his father's a lawyer?"

"I don't know, maybe it's because he had representation. But like I said, we're talking minor infringements, no violence. That doesn't mean he's not a bad apple. A lot of things go unreported: kids too scared to speak up or who don't want to be labeled a squealer. But bad behavior is funny. It has a tendency to do one of two things: it either falls off when the kid gets through adolescence or accelerates. I don't know the kid, but if he's anything like his father, he might not be too likable."

She nodded, looked down at her hands, then at him. "Thank you for believing me. But tell me, Mr. Lorenzo, if you expect so little results, why are we even bothering?"

"Two reasons. First, a hearing on this may shoot fear into the kid. Could be, that's what he needs. Second, if the incidents should get more serious . . ."

She swallowed, looked at him, her blue eyes dark with fear. "Do you expect they will?"

Though he wished he could say, "not a chance," the fact was, these things did occasionally turn violent. He looked away, then stood up, indicating that the meeting was over. "I didn't say it would escalate," he said, hands in pockets, studying the carpet while he walked her to the door. "But of course, it could. And if we see that happening, I want to be able to squash him before your daughter or anyone else gets hurt."

* * *

Naturally it had occurred to her that Dylan's antics could get more serious, even result in hurting someone . . . how could it not have? But to hear the state's attorney suggest it was somehow more frightening. The good news was, someone was finally taking her seriously. Frank Lorenzo was not loud or flamboyant or pushy—still, she'd be willing to bet he'd be terrific in court. She trusted him implicitly, and couldn't imagine a judge or jury not doing the same.

That night as Hollie was scooping ice cream into dessert dishes and telling Allison and Jake about her conversation with the prosecutor, the kitchen window exploded, glass fragments flying everywhere.

One of the small fragments just missed Hollie, but hit and wounded Jake. Jake was stunned—blood began to pour from his cheek. Allison shot up, screaming and crying as she rushed to the open space that was once a window.

"Get away from there!" Hollie demanded, not quite certain if there was more yet to come. Allison pulled back—her shoes crunching pieces of glass— as Hollie reached to a drawer, opened it, and snatched a terry dish towel, then began to apply pressure to Jake's cheek to stop the bleeding. But the cut, close to the left eye, was deep, and the bleeding wouldn't stop and she was becoming frantic.

"Oh, God, I think this is going to need stitches." She seized the phone, realizing that she hadn't a clue as to where the nearest emergency room was, or even the name of a good doctor. How had she been so remiss in not getting a physician recommendation before moving from Bloomfield? She dialed information, got the number of the hospital, and called, requesting directions.

"Just a moment," the woman said, putting her immediately on hold.

"Dammit, she put me on hold!" Hollie cried, glancing nervously toward the gaping hole in her kitchen wall, making them totally vulnerable. She squeezed the phone between her head and shoulder and again lifted the bloodied towel, trying to exert more pressure on the wound.

Jake said, "Call Woody, Mom. Ask him where the hospital is."

Allison was already looking up his number in the little local phone book and found it before the woman came back from hold. And when Hollie did finally reach Woody, a voice like his but more distinct answered.

"Mrs. Woodbury, this is Hollie Ganz from across the street. May I speak to your son?"

And the next thing she knew Woody was on the line, saying, "I'll be right over."

"If you'll just tell me where—" But the line went dead, and in view of her semi-clouded condition at the moment, it wasn't such a bad idea that he drive them to the hospital.

After quickly taking in the condition of the kitchen, Woody examined the short, deep cut while Jake bit down on his lip, determined not to let his teacher see him cry or act in any way like a baby. "I doubt it'll take many stitches to close," Woody said, as he directed everyone to his car, already waiting out front.

"Did you see who it was?" he asked on the way.

Hollie shook her head, seeing Chester sleeping peacefully on the sofa as they left the house. Totally in his own world, she thought; she wondered if he would ever be a watchdog.

Woody glanced at her. "Hollie?"

She jumped, then backtracked to his question. "No, we didn't see anything. We were eating, I had just gotten up to get dessert, and suddenly it exploded."

"I hate him," Allison said.

Once Hollie had conferred with the doctor and given the receptionist at Union Valley the insurance information, she left Woody with Jake in the treatment room and went to a pay phone to call Jeremy. Allison followed after her. Hollie let it ring a dozen times, and was about to hang up when the out-of-breath voice came on the line.

"Jeremy, is that you?"

"Yeah, it's me, just an out-of-shape me. Can't run the same anymore. Is something wrong there?"

"Don't get scared," she said, before briefly telling Jeremy what had happened. "The doctor cleaned the wound, they're stitching it now. It'll only require four or five stitches."

He was immediately concerned. "I'm coming out now."

"It's not necessary, Jeremy, really. He'll be fine. He's been very brave, not fussing once when they cleaned the wound. I hesitated to even call. By the time you get here we'll be on our way home, and with medication Jake'll be ready to sleep. Besides, tomorrow's Friday and you'll be seeing him then.''

A hesitation, like he wanted to insist further. Instead he asked, ''What was thrown at the window?''

The last thing she wanted to hear now was him bashing the town or neighborhood or whatever else he could fault concerning her new life. ''I assume a rock,'' she said, coolly.

''Who did it?''

''I don't know. Wait, Allison's here, let me put her on. See you tomorrow.'' She handed Allison the phone, then went to the phone beside it to call the police.

CHAPTER
Eleven

The doctor had given Jake only a mild painkiller, but as she'd predicted, by the time they were on the way home at nine-thirty, he had fallen asleep in Hollie's arms.

The back door of the house was open and Sergeant Paterson and another officer were already searching the yard when Woody carried Jake inside and put him to bed. Woody then headed home to return the several phone messages that had come in earlier on his beeper.

Allison, tired too, headed straight to her bedroom. Hollie had just begun to sweep up the glass fragments from the kitchen floor when Sergeant Paterson stepped inside. There was a remarkable change in his attitude—she could see it immediately in his expression, then in his voice.

"How's the boy doing?"

"Okay. He's sleeping."

He gestured to the window, blocked off temporarily with cardboard to keep out the autumn night.

"Did you notice anyone around the neighborhood before or after this happened?"

She shook her head. "No, nothing. The children were eating dinner. I had gotten up to get dessert when suddenly it seemed to explode."

"Where were you standing?"

She thought a moment, then pointed to the counter to the right of the window. "About there."

"Then you could see out the window?"

"It was dark. Besides which I don't think I looked."

"Did you or didn't you?"

She stood there, trying to remember. Was there a chance she'd glanced out without realizing it? Finally she shrugged and shook her head.

"Try to backtrack; what exactly were you doing at the time?"

"Scooping ice cream." She laughed, not quite sure what she found so silly. Then she pointed to the half-gallon chocolate ice cream container that was lying in the sink melted. Little shards of glass were mixed in with the brown goop.

"Maybe you saw what hit the window?"

"I don't think so. Why?"

Paterson's mouth tightened as he turned to the window. "It's strange. We can't seem to figure out what broke it. No rocks, balls, heavy objects . . . in the kitchen or on the ground in the area of the window. In fact, nothing larger than a pebble. It doesn't make sense, unless of course the person who did it was up close and banged the window with some long, heavy object . . . or alternatively, came back to get whatever it was."

She wondered if the man ever solved a crime, or was he always too busy fussing about things that didn't seem to make much difference? "Does it really matter?"

"Everything matters," he said.

"Sergeant, if you want to know what was used to break the window, I suggest you question Dylan Bradley. I think he's likely to know."

"I did."

Squatting, she was brushing the glass with a whisk broom into a pan. She stopped, looking at the officer.

"Dylan and his mother were in Boston today . . . all day. They didn't get home until just before we arrived."

Hollie was taken aback. She was still wondering about it as she got ready for bed. They could have been lying—Pauline or her son were hardly above lying. But it wasn't as though she'd seen Dylan do it, so the fact was it could have been anyone. She thought of Jeremy . . . but he was home when she called. Would he have had time to get home? What about Roger? Certainly she had seen him on other occasions out at night. And on that one night, hadn't he even come to her back door?

Or for that matter it could have been a total stranger, an isolated incident. She considered that, then shook her head. She could come up with a slew of ifs and maybes, suppositions to try to shake away the fear, and even buy some of them. But this wasn't one of them.

After the window incident, the police paid her special attention. The cruiser normally assigned to patrol the neighborhood made it a point to pass by her house day and night, and that eased her mind some. Particularly the surveillance during the afternoons, when the kids got home from school.

Jake, returning from school a few afternoons later, had just started toward his house when Woody opened his front door and waved him over. Jake grinned when he spotted him, ran across the street, up the stairs to the doorway.

"Hi, Woody, what're you doing?"

"Actually, looking out for you. I've got some software that might interest you. Game programs, originals, things I've come up with myself. Anyway, I thought you might like some on your PC. I'll show you how they work."

"Really?"

"You wait here, let me get the disk."

Woody went downstairs, leaving the front door open. A pair of women's pink bed slippers were beside the stair landing. Woody's mother's, Jake supposed, remembering Woody telling about her being sick. As soon as he came up from the cellar, they headed across the street.

"See that guy up there?" Jake asked, as they reached the street. Moving his head, he gestured back, indicating the brown house.

Woody glanced back, then, smiling, said, "Oh, you mean ol' Roger?"

"Yeah, him. He's all the time watching me and my sister. My mother, too."

"Want to see a disappearing trick?"

"Yeah, sure."

Woody turned, raised his hand high, waving to Roger in the window. Roger jolted back, disappearing from sight. Woody turned to Jake. "How's that?"

"Excellent," Jake said, laughing. "Do you think it would work if I did it?"

"I don't know. I think it's something you have to practice to get just right."

"Oh." Then as they went up Jake's front walk, he asked, "What kind of games you got, Woody?"

"You name it, and I've thought of it."

They went in the house, greeting Allison as they passed by to get to Jake's bedroom. Woody sat at the computer, booted it up, fed the disk in, then looking over the different options, asked, "Just how scary can you take, my friend?"

"The scarier the better."

Woody put his finger to his chin, rubbing it, like he couldn't quite decide which ones to give him. "I'm just wondering," he said. "Maybe your mother would rather I kept it sort of mild."

"Come on, Woody, she won't know. Besides, what's so bad, it's only a game."

Woody looked at him, then smiled. "Okay, tell me—ever have a Mister Potatohead?"

"Yeah, sure, who hasn't?"

"Well, I know you never had one like this."

Woody keyed in a couple of letters and a screen opened up to a dozen sections, each section a different part of the anatomy.

"Okay, let's start with faces." He keyed in again—this time the screen opened to hundreds of faces:

animal, human, all different sizes and stages of growth.

"Oh, wow! You mean you make up your own person?"

"Now you're catching on. Here, let me do a quick one for you so you can get a grasp of the possibilities." Jake sat there in awe, watching Woody open and close windows, manipulate objects on the screen, and within five minutes, combine animal and human to form a wonderfully grisly horned creation.

Jake stared, amazed, at the creature that was moving along the screen. So real, even down to the clapping of the hooves. "Geez," he whispered almost to himself. "Will you look at that!"

The door opened—Allison stepped inside. "Anyone want a snack? There's pears and— Ooo," she said, pointing to the monitor and starting to come closer, "what is that ugly-looking—"

Woody pressed a key, blanking the screen, and Jake said, "Get out! Can't you see we're playing a game?"

"Fine, creep . . . play," Allison said. "If you get hungry, feed yourself. Not you, Woody. If you want something, let me know." She closed the door.

Jake sighed. "Whew, that was close. She probably would have puked if she really got a good look." He tapped the key, bringing the creature back to the screen. . . .

"Well, what do you say, Jake, does that thing look as lonely to you as it does to me? I say it's time you design him a playmate."

* * *

A week or so later on a Friday night, Jeremy didn't show. Not until nine o'clock did Hollie go to the window where Jake was looking out and suggest he and Allison have something to eat. She stroked his forehead, examining the little red line left from the stitches. So close to his eye, she thought, shuddering.

"I'm sure he has a good reason," Hollie said. "No doubt he'll call tomorrow to tell you what it is."

"If he wasn't planning to show, the least he could have done was let us know in advance," Allison said, thinking of the trouble Barry had gone to to switch his work schedule so he'd be able to take her out Saturday night rather than Friday.

Allison made a frozen pizza for her and Jake, then went into her bedroom to call Toby, who was quickly becoming her new best friend. But when Toby's line stayed busy she called Chelsea.

When she had first told Chelsea about the incident with the smashed window, her friend squealed in disbelief, making it seem more exciting than horrible. But now her attitude was changed. "I think you'd better get out of that neighborhood," she said.

"Why?"

"It's obvious. It's like you don't know what to expect next." She paused, sighed. "Allison, I told Gracie about what happened the night I slept over, and, well, you'll never guess what happened yesterday."

"What?"

"She was talking on the phone to Linda Saperstein, and telling her about it. Well, Gracie's mother just so happened to have her radar signals tuned."

"Oh no, I hope this isn't what I think. . . ."

"It is. Grace's mother called my mother and she went nuts. Now I'm not allowed to even visit."

"Ever?"

The kids were asleep by ten-thirty o'clock—no crank calls. Hollie was irritated that Jeremy hadn't come by for the kids. Thinking back, the past week he had seemed distant, only calling the children twice, and neither time asking for her. Again she thought about the smashed window. Not that Jeremy would have done it with the idea of hurting any of them, of course. But what if he was just looking to undermine her confidence? And the next moment she was furious at herself for even considering such a thing.

Allison had called his apartment a half-dozen times that night, getting no answer. Maybe work-related. *Stop speculating, Hollie, it's not getting you anywhere.*

After taking a short walk outdoors with Chester—always on the lookout not to run accidentally into Roger Spear—Hollie took a hot bath. She wrapped a towel around her head and climbed into her warm terry robe. Tying it at the waist, she took a paperback from her room, settling herself with it on the sofa. She didn't look up again until midnight, when a car horn honked. Pulling the towel off her head, she shook her curls free and rushed to the window: a car—headlights still on bright—was parked behind her Toyota, and someone was getting out, coming up the flagstone walkway. Jeremy?

She went to the door, opened it before he'd even reached the step.

Keeping her voice low, she said, "How about some consideration for the neighbors?"

"Let me see . . . Was that a book or movie . . . or maybe a TV sitcom?" he said, louder than necessary.

"Shhh, be quiet!" He was uncombed, unshaven, and disheveled. "Have you been drinking?"

He stood tall, one long arm raised above his head. "Fine, and how are you?"

He apparently hadn't given the children a second thought. "The kids waited for you," she said. "Jake was crushed."

"I don't know," he said, not responding to what she said, "What're *you* doing for Halloween?"

She sighed, folded her arms at her chest. There was no use getting angry, or even trying to talk. He was in no condition to listen, let alone care. "It's late, Jeremy, what do you want?"

"And here I thought you'd never ask." He pushed back the door, stepped inside, went toward her. The determination in his eyes made her uncomfortable. She backed up, and she could hear Chester beginning a low growl.

"I think you'd better leave."

He came forward, wrapped his arms around her, then buried his face in her neck.

"Stop it, Jeremy," she said, shoving and pushing and trying not to give in to her growing panic. Chester, now excited, began to yelp and nip at the cuff of Jeremy's pants leg. Finally, using all the power she had in her, she pulled free. Taking a couple of long, deep breaths, she cried, "What's gotten into you?"

His features pulled so tight, he was nearly unrecognizable. "How much do you expect me to take? Don't you think I can hear the fear and desperation in your voice when I talk to you? Some stranger throws a rock through your window, hits one of the kids—what the fuck is going on around here?"

Her heart pounded in her eardrums—she needed him to back up, to give her space. "Jeremy, that was weeks ago. Besides, these things happen."

"Yeah? Not where I come from. And the stupid part is, there's no reason for you to be scared and alone." He stretched out his arms, his hands open and pleading. "Let me stay here, take care of you and the kids, Hollie." He pointed toward the bedrooms. "I'm still your husband, the father of those kids in there. So okay, I screwed up big-time, I'm not saying otherwise. But if we try, we can get through this. We did it once before, didn't we? Christ, I love you so much. . . ."

He must have seen in Hollie a flicker of something out of the past, or maybe just sadness for his pain. But whatever it was, he took it to mean more. Suddenly he took hold of the terry rope around her waist, and though she fought to dislodge his hands, he managed to untie it. Her robe parted, but before his hands could come near her again, she yanked the robe together and held it with shaking hands.

"Damn you, don't you dare!" she shouted. But he moved closer, backing her against the wall.

Just as his hands clamped over her shoulders, a voice shouted, "Hey, what's going on?" Woody, who was standing outside the screen door, stepped inside. He looked from Hollie to Jeremy, then turning, he pointed to the door. "Get out!"

"And who the fuck might you be?" Jeremy asked, as he walked toward him.

"He's a friend of mine," Hollie began, but she didn't like the look on Jeremy's face. "Jeremy, don't . . . I mean it, don't you dare. . . ." But it was too late. He had already thrown a punch that startled Woody and knocked him to the floor.

"You jerk!" she yelled at him, nearly in tears. "How could you?" She ran to Woody, who, despite one hand clasping his jaw, was already on his way up to confront Jeremy again.

She moved in front of him, stopping him. "Get out of here, Jeremy. Now!"

At a knock at the door, Hollie looked over to see a police officer standing there. A white cruiser with a red spinning light on the roof was out front.

If Woody had asked to press charges against Jeremy, Hollie would have understood, but he didn't. In fact, he was the one to urge the police to let him go—and none too soon for Jeremy: by that time, the children had gotten up and were watching. And though they didn't know exactly what had gone on earlier, they knew their father had struck a man three inches shorter and twenty-five pounds lighter, and apparently for no reason. A person who they liked.

Once the police had identified the players and were assured no one was seriously hurt, they insisted that Jeremy—who was by then spouting insane accusations about Woody and Hollie—take a sobriety test. He passed, but barely, and after taking him to the diner for a cup of black coffee, they escorted his car to the turnpike.

Hollie applied an ice-bag to Woody's jaw, and it was a full hour after he had gone before Hollie could finally stop trembling. She thought up all the excuses for Jeremy she could possibly think of, but still there was no excuse for what had just happened. How far would he have gone if Woody hadn't come over? Would he have hit her again, beaten her . . . for God's sake, would he have raped her? Obviously he had no trouble hauling off and hitting a perfect stranger.

All night long she had recurrent nightmares: hundreds of faceless creatures with long rubber arms and hands and fingers reaching out to feed on her and the children. With a long sharp knife, she would swipe at the hands, sticking them and slicing them away. Only to look up to see new hands appearing. Upon entering the kitchen the next morning, she found that both Allison and Jake were up early, ready to conduct their own inquisition.

"Why did Daddy hit Woody?" Jake wanted to know.

Hollie poured his juice. "I don't know. He got angry just seeing him here."

"Was Woody here when he came?" Allison asked.

"No, likely he heard the car horn . . . along with the rest of the neighborhood. Your father blasted the horn when he pulled up. He'd had a little too much to drink."

"Yeah, but the police let him drive," Jake said, stating a fact rather than defending him.

She nodded. "Well, anyway, Woody must have thought it was Dylan outside. So he rushed over."

"Did Daddy say why he didn't come to take us to dinner last night?" Jake asked.

Hollie shook her head. "We never did get that far, honey. But I'm sure he'll call and tell you himself."

"What about the police?" Allison said. "Why were they here?"

"You remember the police surveillance? Well, I imagine when they drove by, they heard the commotion."

"What commotion?"

"For one, me yelling at your father."

"Why did Daddy bother to come here so late after he missed our visit?" Allison asked.

And though she wanted to scream by now, Hollie shrugged and said, "I gather he wasn't feeling particularly good."

"You mean, sad?" Jake asked. "Did he say he wanted to come back to us?"

Hollie swallowed hard, then nodded her head. "Well, something like that," she said. Mercifully, the questions seemed to drop off, and Hollie was relieved.

This time it was Gus Paterson who initiated the talk with Frank Lorenzo. When he saw him at the coffee urn on Saturday, he headed over, picked a styrofoam cup off the stack, and tapped his shoulder.

"Hey, counselor," he said. "Since when are you working the weekend shift?"

"Just a couple of hours . . . some paperwork."

Having had time to think about it, Gus concluded that Frank's interest in the Ganz case was personal. Not that that was hard to imagine, with the Ganz lady being such a looker. But despite a run of women in and out of Frank's life through the years, Gus had never known him to mix business with pleasure. He figured it was one of those silly self-imposed rules people make for themselves.

"Still interested in that Ganz case?" he asked.

Frank looked up right away, eliminating the need for an answer. "A big to-do over there last night," Paterson said. "About midnight. It made me start wondering: maybe the lady isn't nuts after all; maybe what it is, she makes other people nuts."

Gus spotted the inward cringe. Frank turned to him, the coffee cup now filled and the initial reaction well covered. "Okay, you've got me hooked. Is there more?"

"Marks and Gray were on cruiser duty in the Garden Place area, keeping a special eye out for our little lady, of course. Well, Marks spots a car with headlights on in the driveway. Being that it's late, he figures they ought to stop, check it out.

"Well, they walk in on a fight. It seems the husband's there—soon to be ex-husband, whatever—and the boyfriend/neighbor. And then there's some damn puppy yapping at everyone's heels. The husband—who according to a sobriety test was millimeters from legal intoxication—hauls off, clocks the boyfriend. And there she is, refereeing this fight in some skimpy robe, nothing under it.''

''How do you know nothing was under it?''

''Some things you can tell, Lorenzo. You know, you ought to get out more.''

''Are you through?''

Paterson shrugged. ''Just wanted you to know what type of lady you're dealing with. She may look like the virgin snow, but not everything is what it looks like. Which might lead you to ask, how reliable is she?''

''I'll keep your warning in mind, Paterson. Meanwhile, have you found out who or what was responsible for breaking that window?''

''No. I'll tell you, it's the strangest son-of-a-bitch thing. I talked to the neighbors, back and sides. Nothing.''

''Well, keep at it. Meanwhile, save the bullshit except where it pertains to the case.''

He began to walk off, but Paterson reached out, stopping him. ''You know, Frank, actually this business with the husband might be more relevant than we think.''

''In what way?''

''Well, we know we've got a jealous husband to add to the equation. And not necessarily strung too well either, judging by that bizarre phone call he made to the station the night he couldn't reach her. So who's to say he wasn't the one responsible for that window, maybe even other things?''

Lorenzo thought about it. ''The motive being to scare her back?''

''Exactly.''

Frank thought about it. "I don't know, we have only a few of those phone calls, and so far it's the kid every time. I see a pattern developing: a few more calls, and we've got him dead to rights. And with that, along with the friends or neighbors testifying to some of the other harassment, I'd say the chewing gum dropped in the girl's bedroom is beginning to look better." He shook his head. "Not that I'd mind having another real solid piece of evidence."

"Look, before you fry the kid, give me time to concentrate my efforts on the husband."

CHAPTER
Twelve

Though dreading it, Hollie decided today was as good a day as any to introduce herself to more neighbors and question them about Dylan. And with all the stress and mixed emotions resulting from the night before, if the visits did nothing else they would keep her mind focused on something else.

Roger, overjoyed at her unexpected visit, took her by the arm like an adored child and ushered her into the living room to meet his sister. Margaret Spear, a woman well into her seventies, was wrinkly and gray, with sharp eyes that didn't seem to view Hollie anywhere near as kindly as those of her brother. Still she was gracious, and as the older sibling, took immediate charge.

"How nice it is to have company," Margaret said, insisting on Hollie's having tea with them in the formal sitting room. She put a plate of homemade butter cookies in the center of the dark wood table. "Isn't it, Roger?"

Roger nodded and then, taking two cookies off the platter, put them on Hollie's plate. Finally, choosing the seat directly across from her, he sat down.

Again the large, high-ceilinged rooms, along with the detailed woodwork, the stone-walled fireplaces, and the elegant furniture made Hollie's plain little house seem entirely inappropriate by comparison. This house had the feel, smell, and appearance of age, though: the mustiness, the lace doilies on the chairs, the tiny twelve-inch black-and-white Philco television—surely a collector's item.

"I've been meaning to get over sooner," Hollie said, trying to ignore Roger's eyes on her.

"Well, I'm sure my brother has told you, I don't get out much. Weekly grocery shopping and Bible meetings twice a month. Roger drives me, of course." Hollie nodded, remembering the old model Chevy Nova sitting in the driveway. "Well, what do you think of our neighborhood?"

"It's lovely; such beautiful old trees . . . and of course the large parcels of land. When I first spotted Garden Place from Ashmore, it looked like an oasis."

"Yes, quite an interesting way to put it. But of course, it was designed with the eye in mind. Sam Egan wasn't one of those types to throw up a bunch of lookalike houses. He had style, imagination, some people said genius. And then of course, he was intending to live here himself."

"Egan . . . that's Woody's mother's maiden name. Any relation?" she asked.

"Well yes, of course, Sam was Eleanor's father. But then I thought you would have known that."

Hollie noticed a little smile, or was it a smirk on

Margaret's face? That kind of silly one-upmanship a person can feel when taking another by surprise.

"Oh, yes, Woody's granddaddy literally dug the street out of the woods. Then, unlike other builders who spoil the landscape, Sam left most of the trees and greenery intact. Instead of plowing through them, he built around them."

Hollie cleared her throat and went on. "As lovely as the neighborhood is, I haven't really been able to enjoy it as much as I'd like." While Roger looked disheartened at that, Margaret simply looked curious. "You know the Bradleys, of course."

Margaret nodded. "Oh my, yes. Edna, Charlie's mother, and I have been neighbors more than forty years. In fact, other than myself, hers and Woody's family are the only original owners."

There were strong ties there. But remembering Roger's silent tirade about Charlie Bradley that day in her front yard, Hollie had expected a bit more of a reaction from him. She looked at him, but now he looked away.

"Yes," Margaret went on, "it used to be Edna, her husband Mortimer, and their three children. Mortimer died early on of a heart attack, and the children of course moved on. Charlie was always Edna's favorite. Once he finished his education, she sort of coerced him back . . . and ended up giving him the house."

"I see. Well, Dylan—Edna's grandson?—I understand he's quite a handful."

"Most boys his age are, I suppose. Not being married, I never had children . . . never wanted them, and from the trouble I see they often turn out to be, I'm not for a moment sorry."

Hollie nodded, not offering argument. Finally she said, "I thought perhaps you'd seen Dylan hanging around on my property . . . while the children or I were out? Or maybe at night?" she said, directing the question to Roger.

He shook his head ruefully, as though he wished he could help more. "Of course I have seen Charlie." Hollie could feel her breath catch deep in her lungs. Charlie Bradley . . . in her yard? Meanwhile Margaret gave her brother a scolding look, and his shoulder a nudge, and Roger quickly went on to clarify. "I didn't mean in your yard . . . anything like that. No, no, just passing by."

"Charlie's always been one for early-morning exercise, you know," Margaret put in. "So it wouldn't be unusual to see him jogging by at dawn."

Hollie's breathing came easier. Surely jogging past her house was innocent enough, even for Charlie Bradley. Besides, what she ought to be asking Roger was, what was he doing up at sunrise staring out the window, watching her house? *What is your problem, anyway? Why are you, a decent-seeming man, wasting your life away at a window?*

"Roger's one of those early retirees," Margaret said, seeming to scoop right into Hollie's mind. "And why not? Certainly he's worked long and hard through the years. Supporting his little family, never once refusing them a thing. And having built single-handedly a quite successful real estate firm."

"Really, which one is that?" she asked, wondering how someone so mild-tempered and lacking in confidence had managed to build *any* business.

"Sampson Realty."

"Really, that's where I—"

"We know, dear. Kathryn told us." Hollie must have had a baffled expression on her face, because Margaret absolutely delighted in telling her, "Kathryn is my niece, Roger's daughter."

So Kathryn Morrison's maiden name was Spear. She remembered her mentioning that she had spent a lot of time around Garden Place as a child. Her parents' ugly divorce. Apparently Roger wasn't as mild-tempered as he seemed.

Hollie thought about all the interconnections. Edna Bradley, a longtime friend and neighbor of Margaret's; Sam Egan, Woody's grandfather who was responsible for building the entire street. Kathy Morrison, the realtor, Roger's daughter. And though according to Margaret most of the others were late-comers, there seemed something incestuous about the neighborhood.

She felt as though she were trying to penetrate a stone wall, but still she knocked on other doors: the Mayberrys, the Larsons, the Freemans, the Haggertys, all middle-aged people who looked at her rather oddly and were apparently too busy to ask her inside.

But if Barbara Wingate, owner of The Chiropractors' Institute, had any qualms about her, she was better able to hide them. As soon as Barbara brought up the institute, Hollie remembered the detached yellow-brick building in the shopping plaza. Barbara was short, husky, with cropped, partially gray hair and a direct and refreshing manner. She greeted Hollie with a handshake and invited her in.

"I knew someone moved in next door," she said, showing Hollie to a seat. "And I ought to have taken the initiative to come over and introduce myself. But isn't it terrible how there's always so little time for what you ought to be doing? You'll find we're not a very friendly bunch around here, but on the plus side, we're not a bad bunch either. In any event, Hollie—and do call me Barbara—welcome."

"Thank you." She shook her head, laughed. "It's funny, you're one of the few people in the neighborhood who hasn't gawked at me as though I had slipped on the wrong head."

"Well yes, of course." She paused a beat before asking, "You mean to say, they didn't say why?"

Hollie sat forward. "You mean to say, there's actually a reason?"

"But of course. You look so much like Nina." When the name didn't register immediately, Barbara clarified. "Nina Richards, the woman who lived in your house."

Hollie thought back to the photograph Jeremy and Jake had found in the cellar. "Then they weren't just teasing me," she said, almost to herself.

"Excuse me?"

Hollie shook her head, somewhat flustered, then explained, "My son and his father found an old snapshot down in the cellar. It was scribbled over, so it couldn't be made out all that well. But they insisted there was a resemblance between me and the woman. And after looking at it later myself, I guess I saw some too."

Barbara smiled, and her face softened. "So much so, you might have been mistaken for her. Surely for a sister."

"Then it *is* odd that no one mentioned it."

"Coincidences tend to make people uncomfortable."

"Coincidences?"

"You being the one to move in there, of course."

"Oh yes, of course." She thought more about it. "I remember the realtor mentioning that the woman baby-sat. In the cellar there's a playroom; I ought to say there *was* a playroom. I've since made it into my office."

Barbara nodded. "I never had children myself, but from the neighborhood grapevine, I gathered the kids adored her. She had a wonderful rapport with them, and in the nice weather she'd take them on outings. I suspect she cared for all the kids on the block at one time or another. Of course, they're gone now."

"Was Dylan Bradley one of those children?"

"Oh sure, he was."

"Then they're not gone, at least not all. Actually, the reason I'm here is Dylan. I'm having some problems. . . ."

She shook her head. "Say no more. This must have something to do with the broken window."

"How did you know?"

"A police officer came around not long ago, asking questions. And as I told him, I didn't hear or see anything. Are you implying it's Dylan who broke it?''

"He's done other things."

She shook her head, sat forward with her arms resting on her thick thighs. "Well, he was always a hyperactive squirt. But probably no more a pain in the butt than the other kids who grew up around here. He did his share of fighting, skipping school . . . and as I recall, a few years back, there was talk of him in a drug rehab program. Just another kid who needs time to socialize, or should I say civilize?

"I've come to the conclusion as I gain years and wisdom—in that order—that most kids will be okay if they and those around them can survive long enough for them to reach adulthood without any major screw-ups happening along the way."

"Then you think it's all a matter of chance," Hollie said, starting to stand.

"Scary, but pretty much my philosophy," she said, getting up as well.

Finally home, her head aching, Hollie passed Allison's empty bedroom, heading for her own. Despite some second thoughts, she had let Allison go to the shopping plaza with Toby. But now hearing two voices in Jake's room, she stopped to open the door: Woody—his face a mess—was sitting beside Jake at the computer, piloting a state-of-the-art airplane on the monitor. Seeing her, Woody smiled, though it looked like it hurt him to do so, and handed the controls to Jake.

"You take over and land it," he said. "I need some time with your mother, okay?"

Jake look displeased at her interruption.

She led Woody into the kitchen, then turned and gently touched the bruise and swelling put there the night before. And as she did, felt that same sickness. "Does it still hurt?"

"No, it's okay."

And though she had said it a dozen times the night before, she couldn't stop herself from saying it again. "I'm sorry, Woody. I'm so furious at Jeremy, it hurts to think about it. Here you were coming to my rescue, and you end up hurt."

He raised his hands, shaking his head. "Hey, it's okay, honest. First off, like I said last night, you have nothing to be sorry about. So please hammer that into your head so you won't forget it. What I want to know is, how *you're* doing."

"Me?" She smiled, shrugged. "Physically, I'm fine."

"And emotionally?"

She did one of those pressed-on smiles, then turned to the sink to take a glass of water. Turning back finally to Woody, she said, "Let's not go into that."

"Stop punishing yourself." Then, in a lighter tone: "And to look at the humorous side: what about that business of your ex-husband taking me for a boyfriend?"

She shook her head, looking down, mortified at the mention of that. Grasping for another subject, she said, "Woody, did you know the woman who used to live here—Nina Richards?"

"Of course," he said. "I was one of the kids she baby-sat here most afternoons. In fact, my parents were the ones who brought Nina over from France. For her first few years in this country, she was my nanny.''

Suddenly, Woody took the water glass from Hollie's hand and set it on the counter. Without warning, he pulled her into his arms, his lips pressing hard onto hers, and kissed her.

Stunned, it took her a few moments to recover enough to push him away. As she did she stumbled, knocking into Chester and making him squeal. Looking toward the hallway—thank God Jake hadn't seen!—she demanded of Woody, ''What's gotten into you?''

''I care about you. . . .'' he began.

Sure you do, because I remind you of your nanny, she thought. For heaven's sake, it was straight out of a beginners' psychology textbook, and she almost started to say as much. But she held her tongue— after all, he was young and vulnerable and probably inexperienced in such things. She certainly didn't want to treat him or the situation callously. So, with the puppy now scratching at the door, she said, ''Let's go outside where we can talk, Woody. Okay?''

She opened the door, and the puppy barreled out toward the side of the house. Once they'd caught up to him, Hollie stopped and faced Woody. ''It's not that I don't care for you—I do. But as a neighbor, a friend.''

''No, Hollie, you're wrong. That wasn't the way a friend kisses another friend.''

She shook her head, looked at the ground, then at him. Finally she said, ''This is silly, Woody. You don't even know me . . . at least not in that way. Love isn't the same thing as attraction, or even caring."

"Don't patronize me. Surely I ought to know how I feel."

She swallowed hard. Why was he doing this? It seemed as though his eyes were pleading with her.

"Woody, I'm sorry. This is my fault, I shouldn't have let this—"

"*This?* What does 'this' mean?"

It was the first time she had ever heard his voice rise in anger, and she drew back. Not that she didn't in some peculiar way feel she'd had it coming: being inexperienced and vulnerable, he might have misinterpreted something she'd said or done . . . or even misunderstood her delay in ending the kiss. Now she could see his distress as he stared at the ground. "Please forgive me, Woody."

He kicked the grass with his sneaker. "Is it your husband, are you going back to him?"

She shook her head. "No, it's not that at all."

Suddenly his beeper sounded. He stuck his hand in his pocket, turned it off.

"Aren't you going to see?"

"Just business," he said, heading off with his head lowered.

Hollie could have tried to call him back, but that would only have humiliated him more. Besides, what else could she have said to him? Instead she scooped up Chester, who began to bark and wiggle to get free. Then, seeing Roger watching from his window, she hurried indoors. Her headache was now pounding worse than ever.

She took two Advils, lay down on the bed, and started to think. Nina Richards, first Woody's nanny, then the neighborhood baby-sitter . . . and her apparent lookalike. Certainly an odd coincidence. Then another disturbing thought: the way Roger fawned over her and ogled her. Was that because he too had had a crush on Nina?

She remembered his referring to "the other one" that night he came to the house—apparently meaning Nina. "Alone, high-spirited," he had said, "but look what happened to her." But nothing did happen to her, so why had he said it? To scare her?

Suddenly she thought of Allison, not yet home. She glanced at the alarm clock at her bedside: four o'clock. Shouldn't she be done shopping by now and home already? Hollie turned over, her hands squeezing the pillow's edges. She couldn't continue to live in this panic state, she just couldn't.

Gratefully, the painkillers worked, and when they did it was like she had been knocked unconscious. She didn't open her eyes again until Allison was sitting beside her, holding up a bright blue turtleneck sweater for her to see.

"Do you like it, Mom? Won't it look excellent with my stone-washed jeans?"

Hollie opened her eyes, got her bearings, then sat up, noticing the rumpled top sheet down around her feet. "It's lovely," she said, untangling it and pulling it up. "When did you get home?"

Allison's cheeks were flushed with excitement—Hollie hadn't seen her look so happy since before the move. "About an hour and a half ago. I didn't want to wake you, you looked too peaceful, but it's almost seven. I made hot dogs—Jake scarfed three, which leaves you only one. Don't feel too bad about it, though. Sitting out on the plate that long, it looks pretty gross."

Hollie made a face, then put her feet to the floor. "Well, thanks for the thought. I take it you had no trouble this afternoon?"

"None. . . ."

"What time is Barry coming for you?"

"Seven-thirty. The movie starts at eight-fifteen."

"Who's driving?"

A loud sigh; then: "Didn't we go over this already?"

Hollie stood her ground, not willing to be intimidated by her daughter. "Try it again."

"His sister's boyfriend; he's nineteen."

"What does he do?"

"I don't know, Mom, maybe he's a brain surgeon."

Hollie stared at her for a moment, trying but not able to appreciate the comedy. "Okay, don't make fun. These days it's not easy being your mother."

"We'll be fine."

When Barry came, Hollie might not have been as tactful as she ought to have been, but it didn't seem to bother him. Apparently he knew about the trouble with Dylan and felt confident despite it.

"My sister and her boyfriend will be dropping us off at the Twin Plex," he said. "Then they'll meet us later at Major's. That's a restaurant about two blocks from the theater. And it's a real good area.''

A good area—wasn't Garden Place a "good area"? However, there were older kids watching out for them—certainly that was a plus. Other adults around, too. And what else could she do?

"Can I call Woody, ask him over?" Jake asked, as soon as the kids' car had pulled away.

"No, not tonight, Jake."

"Why not?"

"Because I said so."

He frowned. "Allison gets to have friends over."

"Jake, Allison is older. Besides, Woody is an adult, he has things to do."

"I bet he's not doing anything. Just let me call and ask."

He started to lift the phone, but she put her hand over his. "I said no."

He screwed up his face, waving his arms around. "But why?"

"Damn it, Jake, for once just accept what I say!"

Jake stomped off to his bedroom, and Jeremy's telephone call came soon after. Just hearing his voice infuriated her, made her wonder again what might have happened last night if Woody hadn't come. Almost as soon as she picked up, Jeremy said, "Wait, don't call Jake yet. I want to talk to you."

"We have nothing to say."

"About last night."

"You made a fool of yourself . . . of me."

"I thought maybe he was a boyfriend."

"And if he was?"

"Is he?"

"That's not the point, Jeremy. You had no right."

"Is he?"

She pulled the receiver from her ear. "Jake, it's for you!" she called. "Your father."

Jake came into the kitchen, lifted the phone. Short, vague answers, a monotone voice. When he got off a few minutes later, Hollie asked, "What's wrong, honey?"

"Nothing."

"What did Daddy say?"

He shrugged. "He said he was sorry about not showing up or calling last night."

"Well?"

"Sorry doesn't always fix everything." And before she could think of what wise thing to counter with, he ran back to his bedroom, no doubt still angry at her, too.

CHAPTER
Thirteen

At loose ends, but remembering her promise to Harvey Boynton to put in some work at home this weekend, Hollie got the research file on the next article from her bedroom and headed downstairs. Chester—for the first time able to handle the steep stairs—followed after her, and Hollie, never quite managing to be comfortable downstairs alone, truly appreciated the puppy's company.

She worked quite a while, interrupted only occasionally by house noise and Chester jetting to one corner or another trying to catch the sound. She wondered briefly if there were mice, but then, upsetting herself with just the idea of it, crossed it off her mind.

She was well into the article by the time she decided she would call it quits for the evening. She saved, printed, slipped the hard copy into the folder, this time to take upstairs. She looked at the books lining the built-in shelves, some of them from when she was a child herself. She went over to the shelves, and laying both hands against the back, pushed.

They didn't move, of course. She shook her head, again feeling foolish.

She backed up, sat on the edge of her desk. Feet up on the edge of it, knees clasped, she looked around the room, her gaze stopping a moment at the little compartment near the floor where she had found the mutilated kitten. She shuddered and tilted her head up, and as she did she noticed on the white inside of the light fixture a small brass disk. She got on her knees, looking closer: a tiny hole in the center of it. Was it ornamental? She stood on the desk, reached up, touched the smooth surface. Then, because of the heat emanating from the bulb above it, she pulled back.

She got off the desk and picked up Chester and the file, ashamed of her increasing paranoia.

His mother was busy working in the cellar when Jake walked out the front door. Sure enough, Roger was spying, but Jake wasn't about to let it bother him. He glanced over to Dylan's house—no one was around there. Finally he headed across to Woody's. Mom had said Jake couldn't call or invite Woody over, but she hadn't said a thing about going to see him.

Jake knocked on his door four times—he knew Woody was home, because he had first peeked in the garage window to see if his car was there. While standing on the stoop, he looked through the narrow opening of the large draped window to his left. The living room was big and fancy and spooky: lots of dark wood armchairs with clawed feet and silky prints, a shiny grand piano, and a big stone fireplace with brass andirons so clean they looked unused.

China cups and saucers and figurines lined the wide mantel, with two tall matching brass urns on either side. Suddenly the door burst open, bringing Jake's attention back. But to his surprise, the person looking at him wasn't Woody.

She was standing there, a half-dozen fancy silver necklaces dangling down her red dress. Maybe it was just the surprise of seeing her, or the long gray frizzled curls, clipped with sparkly barrettes, or the way her fingers looked all gnarled and disjointed and weird. But when Jake went to open his mouth to ask for Woody, the words wouldn't come out. Instead he turned and ran. But he wasn't home a few minutes before the phone rang.

"Why'd you leave?" Woody asked.

"How'd you know it was me?" Jake asked, feeling dumb and mad at himself all at once.

"Mom said it was a little kid with big glasses. Listen, Jake, she may look like something that bites, even sound it at times, but she doesn't. Of course when I was a kid, I wasn't always sure of that either."

"Yeah, really?" Jake said, Woody's admission somehow making him feel less dumb.

"Really. So, what did you want?"

"I wanted to ask you to come over, but my mom said I couldn't. Why is she mad?" He stopped for a moment, his attention momentarily drawn to the low, deep sobs coming from Woody's side of the connection. "Hey, Woody, is that your mother?"

"Tonight's a bad night."

"What do you mean?"

"Her arthritis. She took medication, but sometimes it takes time to kick in."

Now feeling even more guilty for having run out like that, Jake wondered if he ought to say he was sorry to Woody. But just like with Daddy, sometimes the word was so little it seemed almost silly.

"So, Jake, what was it you wanted to ask?"

"I wanted to know why my mom's mad at you."

"Did you ask her?"

"She wouldn't say."

A long pause, where Jake could almost hear Woody thinking about what to tell him. Finally he said, "It has to do with last night."

"You mean, my father hitting you?"

"Your mom's a little nervous about going against him. The thing is, your old man has a temper—a short fuse, they call it. Am I right so far?"

"Yeah, I guess."

"So, your mom tries not to get him angry."

"You think she's scared of him?"

"I don't think, I know." The last part was quick and flat, as though it had come out on its own and he was sorry it had. "Listen, Jake," he said, "this is heavy stuff for a kid, and I had no business even starting it. Just forget I opened my mouth. Okay?"

"I can't now, Woody." Jake said. After a little while without hearing Woody answer, he said, "It's okay to tell me, honest. I'm not such a little kid as you think."

"Hey, come on, did I say that?" Then, without Jake even needing to answer, Woody sighed.

"Okay. Can I count on your discretion? In other words, can you keep it to yourself?"

"Swear to God, hope to die."

"All right. Now let me preface this by saying, women—even the best of them—are often hard to understand. They play this game called Charades. It's sort of like telling you only what they decide you ought to know. Your mom puts on a fairly good performance for you kids: strong, able, liberated lady . . . can do it alone. But as great as that would be, it's not always that simple. Maybe you've noticed from this business with Dylan. She'd love you to believe she's got a handle on it all. But she doesn't."

"But what does that have to do with her being scared of my dad?"

"You don't know?"

"I know he loses money. And he fights sometimes. She really hates that."

"What about those times when his temper gets out of hand and he hits her?"

"No, sir! If that happened, I would of heard . . . or seen something."

As another long silence stretched, Jake began to remember marks—once on his mother's cheek, another on her wrist. When Allison asked what had happened, none of the stories Mom had come up with mentioned their father.

"Look, maybe you didn't see them because you didn't want to see them," Woody said gently. "Besides, I'm sure your mother did her best to keep it hidden. You and Allison are probably the last two people she'd want to know about it."

A couple of deep shaky breaths. All the memories

he had of his mom and dad together seemed to crop up at once, all bumping into one another and fighting to get his attention.

"Jake?"

"Yeah."

"You okay?"

"Yeah."

On weekends, his mom usually let him stay up as late as he wanted, but he rarely made it past eleven o'clock. Now it was almost midnight when mom tiptoed into his room and found him lying on the blanket, wide awake and staring down at his pillow. Ever since he talked to Woody his mind wouldn't stay still—it kept circling and circling around Daddy. She sat on the edge of his mattress and said softly, "Let's talk about it."

He shook his head, not even looking up.

"Is this about me not letting you ask Woody over?"

"Uh-uh." She waited a few moments, but when he didn't say anything else she said, "Then I might be able to consider this just a general, overall funk?"

He shrugged his shoulders, his face kind of saying "Maybe."

"Oh." She put her hand on the back of his neck, rubbing. He usually loved the shivery way that made him feel, but tonight he didn't even like it. "You know, with all this bad stuff happening around here—add to that moving and my new job—well, it hasn't given us a lot of time together, has it? I know you haven't complained, and I appreciate that. But I also know how rough it's been on you."

"I'm okay, Mom, don't worry about me."

"Well, you know how mothers are, they worry naturally—it's sort of built in to the job. The thing is, I don't want you being scared about what's going on—granted, it's easier said than done. But the thing is, now we've got a prosecutor on our side, and he and the police are determined to catch the person bothering us. And once they do, Jake, we're going to nail that person to the wall. And we're going to do it in court." She leaned over and kissed his cheek, then stood up.

It wasn't until she'd left the room and shut the door that his tears started to come—wetting his pillow and sheet and smearing up his glasses so that he couldn't even see out of them. Mommy had no idea that the one who might end up getting nailed was Daddy.

Eight-year-olds have no business being sad, Hollie thought. Cranky, irritable, annoying, fine—but never sad. If only he would confide in her, but it was always Jeremy he sought out when he was troubled. She went into the living room, picked up the puppy, and cradled him—though he was a moody little pup, tonight he seemed eager to be held. She looked at her watch: eleven forty-five; the movie would have been out for at least an hour. By now the kids were safely at the restaurant, having met up with Barry's sister and her boyfriend.

The phone rang. She lowered Chester to the floor and put the receiver to her ear.

"Hello."

"Mom, don't get scared."

"Oh, God, what? Dylan?"

"Yes, but I'm okay."

"Where are you?"

"The emergency room at Union Valley. Mommy, it's Barry."

It was only a broken nose, brought on by a sound whack. The doctor in the emergency room had to pack Barry's nose to stop the bleeding. Dylan, along with three friends, had spotted Allison and Barry from where they sat a half-dozen rows in back of them in the movie theater.

"Either that, or they followed you there," Hollie said.

"I never thought of that," Allison said, still sounding a little stunned. "I haven't had a chance to think. I was just so scared when I saw all that blood coming from Barry's nose, and we couldn't stop it. And the worst of it was knowing it was my fault."

Hollie sat, took Allison's hand in hers, and drew her down beside her. "You mustn't blame yourself."

"If not for me, none of this would have happened."

"Correction. If not for *Dylan*, none of this would have happened. Tell me, honey."

"It started with them bouncing popcorn off Barry's head. When Barry turned, saw who was doing it, he told them to quit it or he'd call for an usher."

"And they didn't, of course."

She shook her head, her eyes darkening with anger as she thought about it. "They thought it was a joke, just like they think everything is one big joke. They were saying stuff to humiliate him . . . calling him wimp, metal-mouth, gayboy. And then of course me . . . They said I was his tight-assed little virgin. Then one of the kids squirted him with an orange drink, getting it in his hair."

"Those pigs."

"Barry finally got up to get an usher, and Dylan stuck his leg out in the aisle to trip him. He fell, and his nose slammed against the bottom part of a seat."

Hollie sighed, shook her head. "What did Barry's parents say about all this?"

"Nothing, neither were home. He lives with his mother, and she's in Boston for the weekend. His sister didn't look at it like a major deal, though. She said those things happen between kids. She just warned him to steer clear of Dylan."

"Not so easy to do—at least not for you it wasn't. Does she know Dylan?"

"She knows who he is from when she went to Union High. She thought he was a jerk."

At one-thirty—after both kids were asleep—a crank call came, only the fourth since the trace had begun. And though it jarred her as always, she welcomed it. She broke the connection, worked the code numbers, then hung up. Somewhere out there, Dylan's telephone number was being spit out by one computer and swallowed by another—to hopefully end up as evidence in a file on the prosecutor's desk.

The next weeks were difficult: though the phone calls were at a minimum, the harassment seemed to come full-force. At night alone was the most nerve-racking of all. Several times she was certain someone was walking around the house, but each time, trembling and close to panic, accompanied by a sharp kitchen knife and Chester—sometimes frantic, sometimes indifferent—she'd go from room to room, even to the basement. But the noise always seemed one step ahead of her.

Other times the noise seemed to come from outside. Twice again she called the police. But they found nothing, not even a footprint in the soil surrounding the shrubbery. Once she willed herself not to call: she sat on the kitchen stool next to the telephone with her hand barely touching the receiver. She woke in that same position at dawn, sore and stiff, but with the noises gone.

Though the police—and ultimately Elaine too—believed they were typical house noises or a product of an over-stressed and anxious woman, she wasn't convinced. At times she agonized silently, wondering if she was losing her mind, while at other times she was firmly convinced someone was getting in and out of her house, deliberately tormenting her. It was a tossup as to which scenario terrified her more.

One Thursday night when she and the children had returned home from shopping, they found an uncapped jar of live insects—big black water bugs, grasshoppers, spiders, flying ants—sitting on the living room carpet. A couple of dozen, already free, were crawling on the ceiling, the walls, the woodwork. She froze, and it was Jake and Allison who finally began to retrieve them. Then, horrified that she had let her fear paralyze her, she forced herself to help them gather the last of the insects.

Who knew she was so frightened of insects? Jeremy, of course. But then again, that wasn't a fair test—weren't lots of people squeamish about insects?

Her relationship with Jeremy, which when they had first separated was amicable, now, only a few months later, had deteriorated miserably. Since that drunken Friday night, Jeremy had seemed to duck out of sight. Though he kept in touch by phoning the children occasionally, the calls were brief and cool, with no one able to find much to say. He had begun to beg off from his regular visits, always with a different excuse, and the kids seemed relieved not to have to go.

Since Allison's only opportunity to date was weekends, and Barry usually worked Saturday nights, she liked being able to spend Friday nights with him. But even then, it wasn't as she would have liked it: with the constant threat of Dylan, Hollie insisted they be chaperoned or hang out at his or her house. Once they double-dated with Barry's sister and boyfriend.

Jake's reasons for not wanting to visit with his father were less clear: though initially upset over Jeremy hitting Woody, that surely would have died out were it not for Jeremy's pouting and apparent lack of interest.

Hollie was distressed to learn from Elaine that Jeremy had had a setback—in the form of a marathon poker game. Which made her wonder if he still had his job at Travelers. Which led her to wonder next: could he be spending some of his spare time prowling around their neighborhood?

It was late November. Though Elaine and Mike had asked Hollie and the kids to join them and their large extended family for Thanksgiving, she had refused, not much in the mood to be around a lot of people. The weather unseasonably warm, the Ganzes spent a quiet if lonely Thanksgiving at home. The following Monday, Hollie was surprised by Jeremy's call at work. "What are you pulling?" he began.

"Translate, please."

"Don't pretend ignorance. Wasn't turning the kids against me enough to satisfy you?"

She couldn't believe what she was hearing—not after these weeks of his ignoring the children. She turned her chair so that she faced the window, and tried to keep the anger in her voice from carrying across the hall. "I don't believe this. . . . No, no, wait, I change my mind. Jeremy, the plow-master: it gets too deep, shovel it on someone else. Well, you're not dumping this on me. Keeping a good relationship between you and the children is your responsibility, not mine."

"That might be a lot easier without you always looking to cut me down."

"I don't know what you're talking about. I go out of my way not to belittle you to them."

"Maybe it's what they overhear you tell other people."

She considered it a moment: had she discussed

Jeremy with someone? No. In fact, even when Elaine brought it up, which she did often, Hollie tended to cut her off. Her hand tightened around the receiver. "I haven't the faintest idea what—"

"You've been having some trouble—police trouble?"

Now she *really* wondered who he had been talking to. "Some . . . Why?"

"What kind?"

"Well, you know about the broken window. . . ."

"And you think *I* broke it?"

She had never mentioned her occasional nagging suspicions about Jeremy to anyone, not even Elaine. "Why would you even suggest that?"

"You've got a cop out there making inquiries about me."

Was that possible? "That's not true, it can't be. What kind of inquiries?"

"He's talked to my landlord, a couple of our old neighbors, Marshall Finnigan." Marshall had known Jeremy since college days and had even worked for him while he was in business. "I ran into Marshall yesterday," he said. "And according to him, a Union cop came to visit at his home a week ago. He wanted to hear all about my temper. And he wanted to know if I'd ever gotten violent with you."

She had told no one about that. The police must have been operating on what they saw the night Jeremy got drunk. If she could only defuse some of the tension between her and Jeremy. She took a deep breath, then before she even had time to think it fully through, said, "Come to dinner tonight."

A long pause—he was clearly bewildered by the invitation. "Why?"

"I'm not sure. Maybe it'll give you and the children a chance to get it together."

"Are you going to tell me what the police business is about?"

"Yes," she said. "I'll tell you."

As soon as she'd put down the telephone, she called the house. It took about twelve rings before Jake answered—out of breath, as though he'd been running.

"Hi, honey, where were you?" she asked.

"Out."

"Doing what?"

"Me and Allison are outside looking for Chester."

"What happened? Did you let him out unleashed?"

"Uh-uh. Allison said she didn't see him when she got home from school. She looked for him to let him out. Now she thinks maybe he snuck out the door when she first came in."

"Well, tell her not to be too concerned. By now Chester should be able to find his way home. Listen, honey, I need a big favor, how about it?"

"Yeah, sure."

"There's a package of chicken in the cellar freezer, second shelf from the top. Take it out to defrost."

"Okay."

She almost told him Jeremy was coming to dinner before she hung up, but changed her mind. Let it be a surprise. She really wanted the kids and Jeremy to come to better terms; Jake in particular, who more than ever probably needed Jeremy's attention. Listening to Jeremy today, she wondered if he wasn't finally surfacing, accepting how it was between them. And if that was so, then maybe they would be able to talk openly about the children, come to a tolerable understanding.

When she came up to Garden Place, it was already turning dark. She saw Jake, Allison, and Woody in their parkas and hats, walking, then Woody headed for home and Allison and Jake continued on to the house. She followed the kids into the driveway and got out of the car. "I take it you haven't found Chester."

"No," Allison said. "We looked everywhere. Woody even helped. We went all the way down Ashmore. Jake thinks maybe someone saw him and took him in."

She hoped Jake was wrong, that the pup hadn't been prevented from getting home. On the other hand, if he couldn't find his way, it would surely be too cold for him out overnight. "I suppose that's possible," she said. "Let's hold off a bit, see what happens. If he doesn't turn up by the time dinner's done, we'll contact the animal shelter to see if someone's turned him in. By the way, did you look carefully through the bedrooms, the closets? Twice before, I snagged him in my closet chewing on my shoes."

They all went inside, the kids heading to the bedrooms, she to the kitchen. As she took off her coat and tossed it temporarily over the back of a chair, she looked on the counter—no chicken defrosting. "Where's the chicken?" she called out.

"What chicken?" Allison said. Jake's silence was telling.

"Jake, please say you didn't forget."

A small voice finally. "Sorry . . ."

She sighed. It wasn't until she noticed the door to the cellar ajar that she even thought of it. Though she'd never seen Chester go downstairs alone, ever since he'd mastered the stairs he loved to follow after her. She went down four steps and looked into the cellar.

"Chester? Here, boy."

The first thought of anything wrong was when she saw the half-dozen packages—chicken, fish, pizza, vegetables—lying in a puddle on the floor in front of the freezer. Defrosted. Who would have . . . ?

She went down the remaining steps and began walking toward it, not quite sure what was propelling her. Stepping over the spoils, she finally took hold of the freezer's chrome handle and opened the door. She flew back like a balloon expelled of wind. Her mouth dropped, her hands sprang up to cover it: Chester was lying on the empty shelf . . .

Frozen.

CHAPTER
Fourteen

She must have screamed, because she heard the footsteps of the children overhead come to the doorway.

"Don't come down here!" she shouted, her eyes riveted on the corpse.

"But why—" Jake began.

"Because I said!"

"Mommy, what is it?" Allison's voice was now quavering. "If we can't come down, then you come up."

Hollie tried to move, to pull her eyes away, but couldn't.

"Ohmygosh, something happened to Chester, didn't it?" Allison cried. Jake started to whimper.

"One of you please . . . go get Woody," Hollie said finally.

She couldn't remember another thing, not until she sensed someone come toward her, follow her eyes. . . . Finally she felt arms. She sank into those arms, letting them shelter her. She felt her head being forced to turn away, then she was led upstairs.

It was Woody who broke the news to the kids, and it was he who helped her comfort them before they went off to their bedrooms. She—finally able to control the shaking in her voice and hands—called the police, something she supposed she should have done fifteen minutes earlier. Back on the sofa next to Woody, he took her hand in his hand . . . and that's when Jeremy walked in. He started to say something, but changing his mind, he turned to go.

She disentangled her hand from Woody's and leapt up. "Wait, Jeremy, don't go! I need to talk to you."

He stopped, turned, looked at Woody.

Jake and Allison started to come from their bedrooms and Hollie, seeing them, waved them back. "Please give us some time alone." Silently, she implored Woody to get up.

He looked at her, then Jeremy. "No problem, I'll wait in the kitchen," he said.

And she knew he was remembering what he'd seen the last time Jeremy was there. But Jeremy was drunk that night—besides, that was then. "No, please. I invited Jeremy here. We need to talk alone." Woody hesitated, then stood up and headed to the door. "Woody, thank you again for coming."

Jeremy watched Woody until he'd reached the street, then turning to Hollie, said, "Just what is it you see in that little motherfucker?"

When he came out with those kinds of remarks, it exasperated her, made her want to do anything but talk to him. "Stop it! Why do you have to put someone down in order to lift yourself?"

"Is that what I do?"

Though his slacks and shirt seemed clean enough, they looked as though they'd been slept in. Deep ridges she hadn't noticed before cut into his forehead. He looked older . . . tired. "That's what you're doing now," she said, trying to be calm. "Woody is kind and caring . . . that's what I see. He's been a good neighbor . . . that's it."

"Yeah? How clear have you made that to him?"

Tears began down her cheeks. She took a fresh tissue, brushed them away.

He looked at her a moment, then sighed. "Okay, are you going to tell me what's wrong?"

She nodded, and he took the chair across from her and sat. "Go on, I'm waiting."

She cleared her throat, then hesitantly began. "You remember Dylan . . ."

"The kid who bothered Allison?"

She nodded. "Well, that's what seemed to start it all."

"All?"

"Late-night calls, no one there, odd noises like someone's in the house, Allison's bedroom broken into, the kitchen window smashed, a jar of insects left in the living room. Things like that. Constant harassment." She was watching Jeremy's face closely, thinking that if he had anything to do with any of these things, it would surely show.

"I don't get it. Did Dylan do these things?"

She nodded, and her voice was trembling. "Yes, I think he did. I mean, everything points to him. We know for a fact he's made macho bets with respect to Allison, and one night when the kids were alone he and his friends pushed their way in the house. And then tonight . . .''

"What about tonight?"

She swallowed hard, then looked directly into Jeremy's eyes. "I found the dog in the freezer."

He drew in his breath. "I don't get it," he said. "How would this Dylan kid get in?"

"Well, the first time the police said I needed better window locks . . . so I got them. The time with the insects, I don't know."

"What did the police say?"

She shrugged. "As far as I know, they never determined it. And as for the other times, I don't know that anyone really got in. . . . It just seemed that way."

He stood up and put his hands in his slacks pockets. He looked at her, moved around some, then inched closer. "So you're saying maybe you're just hearing things?"

"No, I'm not saying that."

"Then what?"

She felt like he was trying to manipulate her, get her to say or admit to things she didn't want to. She rose and distanced herself from him. "Whatever it is you're trying to do, Jeremy, stop it!"

"I'm just trying to figure out which will happen first: the kids or you get seriously hurt, or you crack. Anyone who would stick a dog in a freezer has a severe problem, Hollie. Surely you'll admit to that."

"So what are you saying?"

"I'm saying, get the fuck out of here."

"What about the house? It's all the kids and I have."

"There's my place."

"You know that's out of the question, Jeremy. Besides," she said, "should I let a seventeen-year-old boy control me and the children, run us out of town, wreck our lives?" She caught her breath, and her eyes zeroed in on his. "Or for that matter, should I let *anyone* do that?"

If she was waiting for a response, she got none. He just headed for the door. "Where're you going?" she shouted, but by the time she reached the door he was already in his car. "Jeremy, stay out of this!"

He drove to Dylan's house. She stood there in the driveway—no coat, her arms wrapped over her chest, the kids now beside her, watching. She saw him bang on the Bradleys' door. She looked up and down the street for the police. What was taking them so long?

Pauline came to the door, and after what seemed like only a few words to Pauline, Jeremy headed back to his car. Apparently neither Charlie nor Dylan was at home. Hollie felt a shiver of dread as she watched Jeremy back out into the street and drive away from Garden Place.

It was Gus Paterson and Hanks who finally responded to Hollie's call. While the sergeant investigated, Hollie called the prosecutor's office and got his answering service. She left a message, asking him to call. But within fifteen minutes Frank Lorenzo was at her front door. Hollie was relieved and surprised to see him standing there.

"You said trouble. What kind?" He stepped inside, looked around the living room, then back at her.

"In the cellar," she said. "Someone killed the dog."

He flinched, then moving into the kitchen, pointed toward the open door.

"Yes, but wait." She put her hand on his shoulder, turning him. "Frank, I need to know. Who's making the calls?"

"Dylan Bradley."

Not Jeremy; gratefully, not Jeremy. But now she was furious. She wanted to make Dylan pay. For the pain and fear and false suspicions. "Let's prosecute, Frank. Now."

According to Paterson, there were lacerations on the dog's head and blood smeared on one of the cellar walls. "You think someone smashed him against the wall?" she asked. Arms folded, Hollie stood high on the stairway, not yet ready to fully enter the cellar.

Paterson looked at Frank, then her. "From the position of the marks, Mrs. Ganz, it looks more like the dog butted himself against the wall. Has he ever done anything like that?"

Sure, Chester was high-strung, temperamental, but to intentionally injure himself . . . ? No way. She looked at Paterson, wondering why he would have come up with such a suggestion. "And I suppose he got up and walked into the freezer, too?"

Now the sergeant blanched, and Frank picked up. "Obviously, there was someone involved in this.

And that someone likely came in through the bulk-head."

"That's impossible," Hollie said. "It was locked." Frank went over and examined the lock, and by his immediate expression of affirmation, not for the first time. "Frank, I always keep it locked."

"Look, Hollie, Gus found it unlocked, not even a sign that it had been tampered with. Maybe one of the kids was downstairs, opened it, then forgot about it. In any event, let's begin here. Gus is going to question the neighbors to see if anyone was spotted in the yard."

"And if not?"

He climbed partway up, meeting her, placing his hand on her shoulder, then walking her up with him. Once in the kitchen, he sat her at the table. "We're going to have to go ahead either way. Like you, as far as I'm concerned he's gone way beyond the limit. We're just going to have to hope we've established sufficient circumstantial evidence to convince a judge."

Jeremy called soon after Frank and the police had left.

"Okay, start packing, princess, I found you and the kids a place," he said.

"What are you talking about?"

"I'm talking about getting you out of there." She recognized the take-charge sound in his voice. "I found a nice apartment in Manchester. Decent rent, a nice backyard, close to schools, and not far from your work. The owner who lives upstairs is a real nice old lady, used to be a client when I was—"

"Jeremy, wait, stop! Why would you do that?"

"Because you haven't."

"What is it, weren't you listening to me at all? I'm not going, at least not now. If I go it'll be walking, not running. Besides, I spoke to the prosecutor—Dylan is getting served papers tomorrow."

"You can still go ahead with—"

"No, Jeremy!" She paused, disliking the bite in her voice. Take charge or not, he was only trying to help. Her voice was calmer, more composed when she said, "I was watching you with Pauline Bradley . . . so were the children."

"Then you must feel good knowing Dylan's ass is still intact."

"Jeremy, violence only creates more violence," she said, remembering vividly how badly she had wanted to hurt Jeremy after he'd hit her. And if something had been there handy at the time, something heavy she might have gotten him with, would she have?

A long silence . . . Jeremy likely picking up the gist of her thoughts. "Look, Hollie," he said finally, "I want you and the kids out of there."

"I do believe you mean to help, I really do. But tell the lady thanks, but no."

A sigh; then: "See you around."

"Jeremy, wait. What's going on with you and Jake?"

"I don't know. Best I can tell, he's angry."

"Have you asked him about it?"

"Look, I'm not good at this parenting thing. At least, not alone."

"What does that mean? Sorry, Jeremy—you're

fourteen years and two births too late for qualifications and second thoughts. If you're not good at it alone, practice and get good. Please—''

He hung up. So did she.

She lay in front of the television until one in the morning, wide awake, her eyes going first to the door, then the window, and back again. Unable to shake the feeling that someone was watching.

CHAPTER
Fifteen

Frank Lorenzo phoned Hollie the day after, asking her to come by his office at her lunchtime. "I wanted to talk about the case," he said, worried at how tired she looked.

"That's all I can think about these days. I suppose I might as well talk about it."

He nodded, remembering what a nice smile she had. Unfortunately, she hadn't much opportunity these days to use it. "How are your kids taking it?"

"I don't know. How does one take that kind of thing? We hadn't had the puppy for very long, but still it's amazing how quickly you become attached."

Losing a pet was hard, particularly on a kid who usually loved without restraint. It wasn't until the kid experienced a death that those barriers against being hurt went up. "As a kid I had an Irish setter," Frank said. "He got hit by a bus. I wouldn't let my parents get another dog . . . I was afraid to get attached again. Maybe they ought to have insisted. Who knows? Perhaps when this is over you'll decide to get another."

"Will it be over?"

He gazed at her a little longer than necessary. "It will, trust me." Then focusing his attention on the file, he said, "You might be interested to know, the complaint's been drawn and, as promised, it and the summons will be served today."

"Good."

It was an odd question to ask at this stage of the game, but in light of the skimpy evidence he'd picked up on Dylan, it was one he had to ask. "Aside from Dylan, can you think of anyone, anyone at all, who'd want to hurt you or Allison?"

She sat forward in her chair. "No, absolutely not. But I don't under—"

"Hollie, Gus Paterson isn't convinced that Dylan is solely responsible."

Her eyes reflected confusion as she tripped over her next words. "I'm aware that you investigated my husband, Frank. But now that we know about the telephone calls being from Dylan . . . well, I just assumed it was settled."

"No, you're right, at least it would seem so. And I hope you understand why we had to investigate him. It wasn't something we could overlook. I mean, being that you're in the process of a divorce . . ."

She nodded as though it were a question, and he went on. "Well, you know how it is, a lot of guys freak out. They want their wives back, and think that maybe if they scare them enough . . . Well, you get the idea. In any event, we thought he might be one of those.''

''And now?''

''We have no case against him, if that's what you're asking.''

Was he mistaken, or did she look overly relieved? ''Hollie, did you suspect—'' he began.

But she shut him off quickly. ''No, no, of course not. For goodness sake, what kind of man would do that to his own children? It just gets so crazy you find yourself suspicious and unsure of everyone you know. Without rhyme or reason.''

As the conversation went along, she thought about Roger with his nightly walks and window-watching, and all the other neighborhood oddities. ''What about you,'' she said to Frank, ''do you have doubts about Dylan being the one?''

''There are always reservations. That's why we have judges and juries to hopefully lend an objective ear . . . and come up with a rational decision. But I believe Dylan is our guy. We have the phone calls. In addition, he's been observed harassing Allison.'' He picked up a pen and on a yellow pad scribbled something she couldn't make out.

''We're going to ask the court not only to believe that evidence,'' he said looking up, ''but to draw inferences from it. That's called circumstantial evidence . . . just like the chewing gum. Anyone might have dropped it, but put together with the other things pointing to Dylan, well . . . Got it?''

Though she nodded, she must have looked skeptical, because he said, "And do I want to go in with a lot more substantial proof? Sure. But we've got what we've got—and in view of what happened last night, I don't think we ought to wait longer. So the question is, what do we have a chance of proving?"

"Meaning?"

"We won't use the broken window incident."

She thought about it. Though she believed Dylan was somehow in back of all the cruel harassment—including the broken window—she understood Frank's dilemma. He not only had no proof of it, but he was up against Dylan's alibi, the claim that he was out of town. "Okay, if you think it's weak."

"I do. This is an instance where I *don't* think he did it. His mother's statement—"

"For the record, I think Pauline Bradley wouldn't think twice about lying for either her husband or son."

"Look, Hollie, maybe you're right. But we checked this ourselves. He *was* in Boston that day, he had an interview and tour at Boston College which began at two and ended at four. Now it's true, we don't know for certain the time he arrived home, but consider the traffic at that hour. Add that to the mother's statement—according to her, they stopped for dinner at a HoJo's on the road and didn't arrive home until after seven. I think a judge would buy that with no difficulty."

"Did you ever consider that Dylan might have had one of his friends do it for him?"

"Yes, but I don't like it, I don't think it fits. And what I don't like, I have problems selling."

She could see he was trying to see it objectively—something she had to force herself to do.

"Also, I won't allege those night noises."

He was doubting her, now. And why shouldn't he—didn't she at times doubt herself? "You think I imagined it?"

"I'm not saying that," Frank said. "It's what the other side will say. The bottom line is, the police turned up nothing. And what we don't need are unfounded accusations that might paint you as frightened and neurotic."

Then he leaned forward, his eyebrows drawn together. "Listen to me, Hollie, I'm trying to put forth the best case I can. I want this garbage to end for you." He was so close, she could smell his cologne. She twisted back in her chair, feeling as though she'd been thrown a fast ball.

"With respect to the other incidents," he went on, "we'll have Allison's testimony—naturally I'll need to prepare her. Also, I'd like to use Allison's boyfriend—he can attest to the harassment in the movie theater. Then the girlfriend, Chelsea . . ."

"Let's forget Chelsea."

"Why?"

"I doubt her mother will let her. She's already forbid her to come to Union to visit."

A sigh, a tap on the file with the tip of his pencil.

"I would have liked corroborating testimony on that incident. It's the one opportunity to show trespassing. If the judge buys that, he's apt to buy similar allegations."

"I'll be glad to call Chelsea's mother and try to persuade her, but when it comes to her daughter . . . Well, let's just say she can be a stubborn woman."

"What about this neighbor, Leon Woodbury? Will he testify?"

She grimaced, hating the idea of having to pull Woody into this too. "I'll need to ask, of course, but I'm fairly sure he'll agree to help. You said we could do this quick—how quick?"

"I've set it for a week from Tuesday."

Remembering their last conversation about Dylan, about the minuscule punishment he would likely get, she now asked, "What about trying Dylan as an adult?"

He sat back in his chair, tipping it back. "Forget it."

"Why?"

"Because he's seventeen, because he has no prior record." Frank looked up—as he did, she noticed his jaw tighten. "And because his father's an attorney and every judge in the district knows Charlie Bradley."

She sat forward, placing both palms down on his desk. "Are you saying the judge will be partial?"

"I'm saying he'll give him every benefit of the doubt." His chair tilted forward, bringing him in closer to her. And in a voice extraordinarily gentle, he said, "Leave it to me, Hollie. Okay?"

For an hour after she'd left, Frank sat at his desk, going over her case and getting angrier. Single women with kids were targets for sickos—it was something he worried about with increasing regularity with respect to his sister-in-law and niece, living alone in a big city. Finally he sat back and closed his eyes. Was it possible Gus Paterson was right, that maybe Hollie was holding out or missing something?

According to her, Allison had no enemies and neither did she; so where did that leave the unresolved issue of the broken kitchen window? If not Dylan, then who? A vandal simply passing through, smashing a window strictly to get his jollies? Quite a coincidence, particularly in a neighborhood like Garden Place. Or maybe the husband, but that too seemed a dead end. Though Gus had questioned the neighbors, showing a picture of Jeremy Ganz from the motor vehicle files, no one recognized him.

And why couldn't they come up with the object used? Hollie Ganz had been standing right at the counter; surely she would have seen if someone came up close enough to strike the window. And sure, someone could have thrown an object, come back to retrieve it. But then the question, why? Why risk getting caught just to retrieve what . . . a lousy rock?

Damn it, there was something odd about it he didn't like, and he particularly didn't like being pressured into going to court before the issues were clear. But he could no longer wait. Not when someone had gone so far as to kill the family pet.

Hollie didn't call Woody until after the kids were in bed, which was later than usual—when Allison learned she'd be the major witness at the hearing, she became upset and anxious. But Hollie didn't realize *how* late until Woody's mother picked up. Her voice was hoarse, as though she might have been asleep.

"Oh dear, I'm sorry, did I wake you?"

Though she didn't respond, Hollie was remembering the time she'd seen Eleanor Woods perform. "This is Hollie Ganz," she said, "from across the street? Now that I have you on the line, may I tell you how much I enjoyed your—"

"I'll get Leon." The voice cut Hollie off, along with her intended compliment.

When Woody came on, sounding a little spaced himself, she apologized for the hour.

"Forget it. What's wrong?"

"No, nothing. I just wanted to ask you . . ."

"Ask."

"Could you testify at Dylan's hearing?"

"What do you want me to testify to?"

"Simply the truth."

The next call was to Jeremy, to give him the date of the hearing. But despite the late hour, there was no answer.

In school the next day, Allison was morose: bad enough she had to take an oath, sit up on the stand and tell the entire horrible and embarrassing story to a strange judge while Dylan would be sitting there, staring daggers at her. But to ask Barry to do it too? And to hear Toby tell it, it didn't make her feel better.

"Poor Barry," Toby groaned. "Damned if he does, damned if he doesn't."

"That's not true. If he doesn't want to do it, I'll understand."

"Oh yeah, sure."

"No, I mean it. I wish I didn't have to do it myself."

"Then why are you?"

"Toby, shut up."

"I only meant—"

"You only meant to bug me—why do you do that? Sure, I hate to have to do this, but if I don't Dylan's going to get away with this. And I refuse to be scared off. Have you forgotten all he's done. Broken into my house, played with my personal things, smashed our window, put bugs in our living room, tortured me and my mother and brother . . . and now actually killed our dog!"

"I've got to say, Allison, of all the things he's done, killing a dog is pretty sick. He must be in bad need of a shrink."

"I only hope the judge puts him away."

"Do you think he will?"

She shrugged. "He might not even go to jail."

"Then what's the point?"

"Because it's got to *stop*."

"Yeah . . . I guess if nothing else, it ought to convince him it's time to quit. Wouldn't you just love to see his face when he gets handed those papers?"

Woody had come over after school, something he did often these days, and though he would never say so, Jake and Allison knew it was to check up on them. Not that Jake ever minded Woody coming over. He now sat by as his friend showed him through another software program. When he was through, he said, "Are you going to testify at Dylan's trial, Woody?"

"Sure, of course."

"What about my dad, you don't think it's him doing this stuff?"

Woody turned to Jake. "To be honest, Jake, I'm not sure what to think. So I figure the best thing to do is to leave it up to your mom to do what she thinks is right."

Jake studied him for a few minutes, then asked, "You really like my mom, don't you, Woody?"

"Yeah, I guess I do." Then, looking a little embarrassed: "How can you tell?"

"The way you look at her, I guess."

Woody nodded; then, in the silence following, he turned back to the computer screen. "Want to see something neat?"

"Sure."

Woody opened the Mister Potatohead program, then held up a finger and said, "Between you and me only. Okay?"

"Hey, Woody, you know I can keep a secret. But I've seen all this already."

"Ah, you only think so, my friend. You've heard of codes, right?"

"Sure, but—" Jake stopped as Woody logged in a code word so fast he couldn't catch it. And what opened onto the screen made him gasp and forget whatever it was he'd been saying.

"Well, what do you think?"

The figure on the screen was a woman, about four

inches tall—blond hair, curly and nearly to her shoulders. She had blue eyes, a narrow nose, full lips. Jake followed the character's movement along the screen, her movement uncannily familiar. He finally looked at Woody. "Is that my mom?"

"I don't know. It sure looks like her though, doesn't it?" Jake's attention went back to the screen while Woody explained. "You're a hacker, Jake, you know the potential is limitless. For instance, soon movies, the ballet, opera, symphony, spectator sports will all be computer-based. There'll be no need for actors, singers, dancers, musicians, athletes. We'll create it all ourselves. Or recreate what already exists. All we'll need are damn good scriptwriters. And hopefully that'll be people like you and me, Jake."

"Are you going to show her?"

"Your mom? Sure. Why not? When the time is better, of course. Right now though she's got her hands full dealing with this miserable court case."

Jake stared as Woody began to manipulate the screen. The woman who was the replica of his mother was now in a bedroom, standing in front of a mirror.

"Want to see her do something? She talks, plays, eats, works, changes clothes, there's even a little bed where she lies down and— Tell you what, why don't I just click the option and—"

"Uh-uh, I don't want to see now."

Woody looked a little surprised, but he didn't push. "It's your call, Jake. Well, I guess you see what I mean, though?"

"What?"

Woody tapped the computer with his fingers. "The incredible potential in these things."

Jake nodded; he was feeling a little funny. Like the room had suddenly grown too hot and stuffy, and needed more air pumped in. He got up, went to the window and opened it, letting the cold inside.

From work, Hollie called Elaine to tell her about the court date.

"If you need moral support, let me know now. I'll close off that day on my calendar."

"Thanks, I appreciate the offer, but in some ways this part will be the easiest, at least the most satisfying. Finally someplace to dump all this frustration and anger. Not that I expect the kid's going to boil and bubble, but at least he'll be punished."

"When's the hearing?"

"A week from Tuesday . . . Which reminds me, I've yet to tell Harvey."

"Oh yes, Harvey, our adoring camper."

"Not so adoring yesterday. He didn't say much, but he wasn't at all happy with my being late from lunch: my appointment with the prosecutor ran longer than expected. I really don't know what to do about it other than apologize, which I do on a regular basis these days. The problem is, it's not over yet."

"I hate to say this, but I'm beginning to see an unpleasant trend unfolding here: your dealings and transactions with males of late have not been too positive."

Hollie thought about the statement on the way

home that night. . . . Not completely true. There was Frank Lorenzo. He seemed a bit too conservative, and his bluntness was sometimes startling. But she trusted him. . . .

CHAPTER
Sixteen

When she got home, she was greeted from the other rooms: Allison in her bedroom, likely on the telephone, and Jake—who lately had shown little interest in his hamster—in the bathroom reluctantly cleaning Popeye's cage.

She took the mail that had been lying on the credenza and headed with it to the kitchen. It was when she opened the telephone bill and saw the pages of long-distance charges that she drew in her breath. She ran her eyes down to the last page total.

"Allison!"

Apparently not on the phone, but waiting on the sidelines to be summoned, she came in immediately, her face acknowledging that she knew.

Hollie handed her the bill. "Look at it."

She took it, looked, then her mouth opened wide and she looked at Hollie. "Ohmygosh. I'm sorry."

Hollie dug her hands into her hips and stared at her daughter. "That's it? You're sorry? You disobeyed . . . deliberately!"

Allison's eyes were big and pleading. "I needed to talk to her."

"Don't you dare give me excuses! I've tried to be fair with you, allowing you three long-distance calls a week. Believe me, other mothers on my salary wouldn't have been nearly as generous!" She took off her jacket and tossed it on the kitchen chair. Then, as though suddenly putting two and two together, she said, "How long have you been doing this?"

Allison took a deep breath before she answered. "Since September, but not so much then."

"In other words, because you got away without my noticing, you got bolder, is that it?"

She shrugged, her eyes downcast. "I didn't think it would be so much."

"You didn't think . . . and that's because you didn't want to think. You wanted what you wanted and you took it! Why does that remind me so of your father?"

In the ensuing silence, Jake's face peeked into the hallway. She shouldn't have said that. . . .

"Damn it, Allison," Hollie said, on the verge of tears herself, "who's going to pay this?"

Allison ran to her room . . . and Hollie sank into a kitchen chair. A phone bill of five hundred and twenty dollars—more money than she netted in a week. And Jeremy, with all his fine intentions, so far hadn't sent her a dime.

The county sheriff asked for Dylan Bradley. When Dylan said, "That's me," the man quickly handed him an envelope, then disappeared. Charlie Bradley had been standing behind him, watching the process. Dylan shut the door, turned and stared at the envelope in his hands. Before he had a chance to find out what was in it, Charlie stepped up and snapped it from his hand. He ripped it open, removing a complaint and summons.

"I don't believe it," Charlie said, shaking his head while he read. Then, his face going from puzzlement to anger, he looked at Dylan and shouted, "How is it possible to have gotten a son so goddamned stupid?"

Pauline came rushing in. "What's going on?"

"Shut up!" Charlie shouted, and she withdrew as though kicked.

"What?" Dylan said, taking the complaint from his father. He read it, then tossed it to the floor.

"It's a fuckin' lie!"

"Are they going to allege crank calls with no proof? You knew about the trace. Could I have made it clearer?"

Dylan swung his arms through the air, then brought them in. "I said it's a fuckin' lie! A setup!"

"What about the other allegations?" Charlie said, picking the complaint from the floor with one hand and slapping it with the other. "What are those about?"

"Nothing, I don't know!"

"You're telling me this little girl and her mother are making it all up? They've fabricated this entire story?"

Dylan stuck his hands in his pockets, stared at the gray tile entryway. Pauline had crept back into the room. She looked from Charlie to Dylan, her hands and arms fluttering like wings. Charlie looked at Dylan.

"You dumb little bastard!" He sighed; then, folding the complaint, he stuck it in his shirt pocket. He picked up a man's black umbrella from the stand near the door and poked the base of it into Dylan's chest.

"Tomorrow, four o'clock sharp at my office. Be there!"

When Hollie peeked into Allison's room later, she found her still awake. She kneeled at her bed. "I'm sorry, honey."

Allison began to sob, and Hollie put her arms around her, crawling in beside her.

"Oh, please, honey, don't cry. This will be over soon, and we'll be able to get on with our lives, to deal with things rationally. Just hold on a little while longer." She paused; then, in an attempt to see a smile come onto Allison's face, she said, "And won't it be nice to go on a date without a chaperone?"

It didn't work. More tears started to come. Hollie touched her chin, raised it.

"Come on, I didn't mean to attack you earlier. And that remark about your father, I was just feeling stressed and angry and—"

"It's not just that, Mom. There's more."

More . . . Was she ready to hear more? She took a deep breath, then waited.

"Barry's sister convinced his mother not to let him testify."

"Why?"

Allison shrugged. "She doesn't think he should be a squealer."

She tried her best to assure Allison that they would do fine without Barry's testimony, but the crux of it now was her daughter's heart. Would this break them up?

She wished she could think of something smart and encouraging to say to make her feel better, but there weren't any right words.

Chelsea was fighting back—not an easy thing to fight Fran Grant, either. When Hollie phoned Fran yesterday, she said Chelsea testifying was out of the question. However, according to Allison, Chelsea was still working on her.

The telephone rang at two in the morning. This time it took her by surprise—the hour not fitting the usual pattern. For an instant she thought it might be an emergency call from Palm Beach saying one or the other of her parents was sick. But no, gratefully, it was only Dylan. To think he'd just been served the papers . . . and the nasty little bastard still had the balls to—

Suddenly she heard a scream. She shot up in bed. *Jake?*

She stood up, ran into Jake's room—he was crying, pounding his fists into the pillow. She knelt down, gently turned him over, and shook him awake, then ran her fingers over his damp forehead.

"Honey, it's okay," she said.

For a few moments his eyes adjusted, then he looked at her.

"Was it a bad dream?" she asked.

"I guess."

"Want to talk about it?"

"Uh-uh. Mommy, where's Daddy?"

"I imagine at his apartment, honey. Why?"

He shook his head. "Can I call him?"

"Now? Jake, it's after two."

"I know, but—"

"Why don't you call him first thing in the morning? Before he leaves for work?"

"Can't, he leaves too early."

Jake apparently knew more about Jeremy's schedule than she. "How about after school then? I'm sure he won't mind you calling him at his work."

He nodded; then: "Mommy, did Daddy ever hit you?"

She could feel herself suddenly warm. . . . She swallowed hard. "Why would you ask such a thing?"

"I just need to know."

Hollie took a long deep breath, then shook her head. It was the first time she had ever lied to one of her children, and she hated the way it made her feel. *Never again, Jeremy. Never.*

Finally satisfied, he let her kiss him good night, and she headed back to her bedroom. Bad dreams? Unusual for Jake. In fact, she could count the nightmares he'd had on one hand.

On the positive side, if there was such a thing, whatever had made him upset with his father earlier seemed no longer to exist. Apparently, Jeremy was forgiven.

* * *

Allison was both surprised and disappointed when Barry didn't show up as usual at her locker after school. Though her immediate reaction the night before to the news of him not testifying was as upsetting as Toby had predicted, she had tried to hide it. Toby waited with her at the lockers, but when Barry still didn't show five minutes after the last bell had sounded, they headed toward the front door.

"Why do you think?" Allison said.

"It's obvious. He's let you down, and he's embarrassed."

"I wish he wouldn't feel that."

"How can he help it? You might not have admitted it to him, but you feel let down."

"Well, if I do, it's my problem. I have no right to expect so much of a friend. Especially one who lives and goes to school here. Remember, the whole school is going to hear about this."

When they reached the corner, they split: Toby heading toward her father's bakery to work, and Allison heading up Clayborne, a side street that cut to Ashmore.

Toby was some five hundred feet away when, for no particular reason, she turned and saw what looked to be a blue Torino turn up Clayborne. Dylan's car? Now having been served court papers, would he be so daring as to bother Allison again?

Toby stopped to watch the car, capping her hand like a visor over her eyes as it headed farther up the street. By the time it stopped and two guys got out, it was so far away, she couldn't really tell who they were. But she did see them go toward a girl, likely

Allison. And the next thing she knew, all three were getting into the car.

Allison had been so deep in thought she hadn't even heard the car come up the street . . . or been aware of anything until she heard the car doors open, then rapid footsteps coming up from behind. But by then it was too late to escape them. Though she'd started to run, the hands were able to grab her with ease.

They dragged her to the car and pushed her into the backseat, Dylan following after her and slamming his door. Ray got into the driver's seat and accelerated so hard, the tires squealed. The windows were closed, the doors were closed, Dylan was holding her down on the backseat: her screams were useless.

"Quiet!" Dylan kept saying to her—his mouth up so close she could smell his Juicy Fruit breath. But useless or not, the screams wouldn't stop coming.

"Come on, no one's going to hurt you, babe. I need to talk to you, that's all."

"She's going nuts! Maybe you'd better let her go!" she heard Ray shout over her screams.

"Come on, damn it, stop it!" Dylan shouted even louder, then stuffed one of his gloves into Allison's mouth. And at last, the screaming stopped.

It was Harvey who came to fetch Hollie—and not looking at all pleased about it. "I have a personal call for you in my office," he said. "I don't know how it got to me. I tried to redirect it to your extension, but couldn't get the switchboard."

She swung her chair around—her limbs getting weak as she waited for more.

"Some young girl—"

Not Allison. She would have called her extension direct. Hollie hurried to Harvey's office and picked up the phone.

"Hello, Hollie Ganz here."

"Mrs. Ganz, this is Toby Cramer. We never met, but I'm Allison's friend."

"Yes, of course."

"At first I couldn't remember where you worked, then when I finally did remember . . . Well, that place is so big, and I had no idea which department."

Hollie was tapping her fingers impatiently against the phone. "Please, Toby. What is it?"

"Well, I don't mean to scare you. Actually, I'm not even sure anything is wrong. I tried to call Allison at home as soon as I got to my father's bakery, but there wasn't an answer. I tried twice since . . . and still no answer."

Hollie looked at her watch. It *would* mean she was late getting home, by at least twenty minutes. But she could have decided to go and meet Jake partway.

"I don't understand. Why would that—"

"There's more, Mrs. Ganz. This is the part I'm not sure of. I saw what looked like Dylan's car go up Clayborne—"

"Clayborne?"

"The street Allison sometimes takes home. It's a side street that cuts onto Ashmore." Toby told Hollie about the car, and the girl she thought was Allison.

The first thing Hollie did was call the house. It rang eight times with no answer. Then she called Woody, who picked up almost immediately.

"Woody, have you seen Allison?" Though she was trying not to sound panicky, her voice betrayed her.

"No," he said. "But I haven't looked either."

"Can you?"

"Sure, what's wrong?"

"Just go to the door, take a look up the street. Maybe she went to meet Jake."

He came back to the phone seconds later. "No, I don't see her. What's happening?"

She explained quickly, then hung up. Rather than deal with the police, she phoned Frank. He would know what to do. Lois, his secretary, put her right through.

"Frank, he took her!"

"Wait, what . . . are we talking about Allison?"

"Yes. Allison's girlfriend called me at work. She saw Dylan's car go up the street a little bit after Allison. Then she saw two boys get out of the car and force a girl inside. I'm sure—"

"Where, when?"

"Clayborne. After school. I don't know what time. . . . " She stopped, glanced at her watch, feeling as though her brain had been shaken up and needed clearing. "That would have been about thirty-five minutes ago," she said finally.

"Did the girlfriend have any idea where they were heading?"

"No, that's all she could tell me. What are we going to do?"

"Have you tried the house?"

"Yes. She would normally be home by now, but she isn't. I even called a neighbor. Do you want me to call the police, or—"

"I'll handle that end," he said, his voice calm and controlled. "Hollie, just hold tight. I promise you, we'll find them."

"But he might have taken her anyplace. Where do you begin? And why do you suppose he did this? I mean, to pull this now, after he's been served!"

"I don't know. Why a kid deep in hot water turns the flame higher is beyond me. But I'm going to find out. Listen, where will I be able to reach you?"

She took a deep breath as her mind raced ahead further. Finally it slowed enough to give an answer to his question. "Home. I'm heading there now."

Harvey, having sat there all the while listening to the conversations, didn't say a word. And that was good, because she wasn't about to listen to him. She got her coat and scarf and purse, ran to the parking lot. Was Dylan even more out of control than she'd thought? By taking him to court, had she put her daughter in even greater danger?

Jeremy . . . As soon as she got home, she'd call Jeremy.

Allison had stopped screaming, but not kicking or squirming, not until Dylan finally set her free. The door opened in front of a park bench, and he tossed out her purse. Then, telling Ray to move it, he slammed the door shut. With a squeal of brakes, the car sped off.

Now she studied the unfamiliar surroundings: a small park, maybe the size of a football field, and open, except for a woodsy area near the playground. A white marble fountain stood next to a granite statue of a man on a horse.

Several people walked down the tarred path that cut past her and through the park. But if they noticed anything unusual, they said nothing: maybe she didn't look as awful as she felt. But she was tired and cold, her legs and arms were sore, her mouth dry from the gag. Finally she got up, walked to the fountain, and scooped water into her hands to drink. The taste of the leather glove washed away, she started for the street.

She couldn't be far from home. They hadn't been in the car that long—at least it hadn't seemed so. She had just reached the corner and decided to head to a CVS across the way when she looked up and saw Woody's car. Then he was getting out and heading toward her.

She ran into his waiting arms. Finally safe, she could cry.

CHAPTER
Seventeen

Hollie called Jeremy at Travelers, only to learn he'd been absent from work for two days—according to his secretary, out with a flu. Hollie rang his apartment, but he wasn't home. *Right, Jeremy, some flu.* Finally too tense to sit still, she went outdoors, pacing back and forth in front of the house. Roger was sitting at his window across the street, looking more curious than usual, and a cruiser that hadn't been there earlier was now parked at the Bradley house.

Should she stay put, wait? She had told Frank she'd be at home if he needed her, but standing here helplessly, doing nothing, was too maddening. Just as she was about to head for her Toyota, Woody pulled up in front, and Allison opened the door and got out. Tears dry on her face, but Hollie still could see by her expression that she was okay. Relief rushed through her, almost dizzying her.

Once they were in the house with Allison sitting beside her on the sofa, she asked, ''What did he do, honey?''

She shook her head, swallowed hard. "Nothing really."

"Tell me about it."

"It was Ray and Dylan. They forced me inside the car, then Ray drove . . . while Dylan was in back with me."

"What did he want?"

"I don't know, he said he wanted to talk. But he had me lying down, and he wouldn't let me up. I kept thinking about that bet he made, remember?"

Hollie nodded. "How did you get away from him?"

"That's the weird thing, I didn't really. I was so scared and screaming and fighting, I think it freaked Ray. He kept telling Dylan that I was acting too nuts and maybe they ought to let me go. Dylan let me out near some park bench; I don't even know where I was."

Hollie hugged her again, then stood up and hugged Woody. As she drew back she said, "Thank you, Woody. I didn't even know you were going out after her."

"Why're you home, Mom?" Jake said, coming in the door.

Allison looked at her mother with sudden realization. "What *are* you doing home?"

"Toby called me; she thought she'd seen Dylan get you into the car. Speaking of which," she said, raising a hand, "let me call Frank. The police are all over town looking for you."

Allison's voice was wary as she said, "This isn't going to be in the papers, is it?"

"I don't know, I didn't think about it."

"Where'd he take you?" Jake asked.

"Come on," Woody said, taking hold of Jake's arm. "I'll tell you in the kitchen."

But he pulled back. "No, I want to hear from Allison."

"Jake, please," Hollie said, "your sister will talk about it later. Just give her some space now."

He sighed. "Okay. Can I call Daddy now?"

"No, I have to use the phone. Later."

"But you said!"

"Jake, please. Right now this is priority. Besides, Daddy's not at work or at home, I've already tried."

Hollie picked up the receiver, then turned to Woody, who was trying—none too successfully—to get Jake interested in the two-scoop ice cream sodas he was making them.

"Where did you find her, Woody?"

"A little park on the south side. Dugan Square."

"How did you happen to look there?"

He shrugged. "Just figured it as a good bet."

Fortunately, Woody knew the area and the kids—apparently a popular locale for hanging out.

Frank Lorenzo was just about to call when Hollie reached him and said Allison was home and unhurt. The police had picked up Dylan and Ray Anderson outside the Pizza Palace only ten minutes earlier; the boys admitted to having had Allison in the car, then leaving her off at Dugan Square. Now, relieved by the information that the girl was home safe, the prosecutor would call off the cruisers still out searching in the park and surrounding areas.

"What else did the boys admit?" Hollie asked,

wanting to know if they gave any reason for doing such a thing.

"Nothing. According to the report I got, they were pretty scared. Dylan decided he'd better shut up until he talked to counsel. The other kid followed his lead. I've had them both detained at headquarters for an arraignment in front of a juvenile court judge, which will be at seven tonight. Can you be there with Allison?"

She was relieved and grateful that he was moving on this right away. "Yes, of course."

"Good. How's she doing?"

"Still shaken, but she'll be okay. She was found right away. Thanks to Woody."

"Woody?"

"Leon Woodbury, my neighbor. When I called earlier to ask if he'd spotted her after school, he went out looking and found her outside the park."

"I see," he said, his voice somewhat puzzled. But then, moving on: "Well, that *was* lucky, wasn't it? Maybe he ought to come tonight, I might be able to use him."

Next, Allison called Toby.

"I'm still alive," Allison said. "Thanks for worrying, and thanks for calling my mom."

"What'd he do?"

"Well, for one he kept me down in the car. I went wild, though, so he finally dumped me at some park."

"What was the purpose?"

"I guess to scare me. Well, they ought to be as happy as pigs in garbage, 'cause it worked."

"What's going to happen to them?"

"I don't know yet. We go before a judge tonight, but I think it's going to get postponed, then heard with all the other stuff next week."

"Oh."

A sigh; then: "I'd better go; I still feel a little spacey."

"Yeah, well, listen, before you go. I was thinking. . . . Look, if you need me . . . I mean, it wasn't possible to really see who was in the car, or even to be sure it was you they were taking. I just figured because it looked like Dylan's car, then I knew you went up that way. Anyway, if it'll do anything for your case, I'd be willing to testify."

Allison hung up, thinking it weird that in the midst of all this hell and misery, she'd found a friend.

Because they were minors, both boys were kept out of a cell. Instead they were locked in separate small rooms off the precinct corridors, the rooms used for questioning suspects. Ray's parents—outraged at what had transpired—immediately put the blame on Dylan. So when Charlie Bradley arrived after finishing a tedious deposition in Hartford and kindly offered his services free to the Andersons, they made it clear they would rather take their chances, *pro se*.

It wasn't until Charlie was let into the room with Dylan that his amiable facade broke down. Dylan, spotting it, went immediately to the one barred window and looked out.

"I ask you to be at my office so we can come up

with a somewhat reasonable defense, so what do you do instead? You go out and fuck things up more."

Silence.

"Say something! What's going on in that brainless barrel your mother calls a head?"

Dylan, one hand balled in a fist, punched the wall. His head nodded like a seesaw. "I thought it would help."

"You thought abducting the girl off the street, scaring the shit out of her, would help your case? Go ahead, tell me more about it—maybe you're a natural strategist and I'm just a plodder too simple-minded to grasp the concept."

"I wanted to get her to listen!"

"To what, your threats?"

He turned, finally facing his father. "I wanted to find out why she's setting me up."

"Cut the crap! I'm not your mother or one of your dumb-assed girlfriends. I'm not impressed by your fancy hairdo or your jeweled earlobe. As spellbinding as you might be to some, I manage to hold my own. What I want here is the simple truth! Are you or are you not capable of giving it to me?"

Dylan put his hand to his head, rubbing his crown nervously. "Okay," he said. "I did hassle her some. But I didn't break into her room, break windows, any of that stuff. And I didn't make any phone calls."

"I looked through the police file this morning, dammit. They've got you dead to rights."

"It's a lie."

Charlie took a vial out of his pocket and emptied

two antacid pills into his palm. Tossing them into his mouth, he tilted his head back to swallow. He then went to Dylan, lifted him by the scruff of the collar, and dragged him to the straight-backed chair in the center of the room. With his hands pressing heavily on his son's shoulders, he sat him down.

"Stay there, shut up, and listen as carefully as you know how. I'll tell you what you did, and what you did not do. I'll even provide you with the reasons, how's that? Then it's in your ball park: if you don't want to end up in some fucking reform school till you're eighteen, ruin your chances of college or a career, you'll get what I tell you down so pat you'll be able to mouth it in your sleep!"

Judge Linwood Crosby was a sharp-witted old-timer, whose lethargic demeanor fooled many a citizen into thinking he had long ago lost interest in the case at hand, only to have him come up with a sound and reasonable ruling. Dylan pleaded innocent, and Charlie Bradley made a motion to mark up the fiasco to be heard with the other complaints already on the calendar for the next week.

"Your honor," Frank Lorenzo said, looking big and brawny and slightly rumpled. "I have no difficulty with that. However, I ask that in light of the cruel and unrelenting harassment of Allison Ganz and her mother and eight-year-old brother, the defendant be held in custody by the juvenile authorities until such time as the case is heard."

Charlie Bradley jumped to his feet.

"That's outrageous! This young man is a senior at Union High School, has taken his SATs, in fact, has scored remarkably well. Upon graduation in June, he plans to attend college in Boston. In addition, he has no juvenile record to warrant such an extreme and unusual remedy. What we have here, your honor, and what I intend to show at the hearing, is a series of misunderstandings between two fine young people.'' He stretched his arm toward the prosecutor. "I suggest my brother here is not seeing things as clearly as he ought to. Perhaps a little burnout, Mr. Lorenzo?''

"I object,'' Frank said, faking anger, then looked up to Crosby, who was sitting with an elbow on the desk, his chin cupped in his hand and his eyes partially closed.

"Cut it, Charlie,'' the judge said without changing his pose.

Lorenzo took back the floor. "For three months this seventeen-year-old defendant has gone out of his way to make life hell for this fourteen-year-old girl, her working mother, and younger brother. Who, I may add, are a single-parent unit, newcomers to the town of Union.'' He purposely stopped to direct the judge's attention to Hollie. "In fact, people in these difficult circumstances are particularly vulnerable, so much so, that if one were searching for the perfect people to victimize, they might well be the choice.''

"Objection! What is this, Intro to Sociology?''

"Overruled.''

"Served with a harassment complaint just yesterday, the defendant suddenly escalates his behavior, actually *abducting* the girl right off the street coming home from school. Which shows me, your honor, that this boy has no regard for the law."

"This afternoon was a total misunderstanding," Charlie Bradley said. "He had no intention of abducting anyone. In fact, he was under the impression the girl wanted to talk to him."

Frank looked over at Woody. "Maybe you'd like to hear from the young man who found Allison after the abduction, your honor. To have him relate to you how terrorized this girl was."

"I object!" Charlie shouted. "This isn't an evidential hearing!"

Crosby put up his hands. "Okay, enough. We have agreed to consolidate this issue with the others, and all evidence will be brought at that time." Then, addressing both attorneys and clients, he said, "In the meantime, let me just say I do not view these complaints as minor or unimportant: no person need live in fear of another. And if it's happening in my jurisdiction, you may rest assured that it will not continue.

"Still we must be fair to both parties. This lad has no prior record, and he claims to be innocent or, at most, misunderstood. So I must give him the benefit of the doubt. He will be sent home in the custody of his father to await hearing."

"Then I must at least insist on a restraining order!" Frank shouted.

And before Charlie could argue the issue, Crosby made up his mind. "Okay, you've got it," he said. He looked at Dylan, who had been sitting stiff and silent, not once being so bold as to look in the direction of Allison or Hollie. "Young man, you are

not to speak to or go within fifty feet of the com-
plainant, Allison Ganz, her home and/or her family,
until further notice. Do you understand?''

Dylan nodded; then, jolted by his father's finger
sticking in his rib cage, he jumped to his feet.

"Uh, yes, your honor.''

Crosby wagged his finger. ''And I warn you, son,
don't buck me on this.''

In lieu of a hearing and at his parents' plea, Frank
Lorenzo was willing to strike a deal with Ray Anderson: twenty hours of community service for his
part in Allison's abduction. Hollie sent the children
with Woody on ahead to the lobby, and took her car
keys from her purse as she waited for Frank to pack
up. He lifted a soft leather briefcase from the floor
and tucked the Bradley file, two loose documents,
and a yellow note pad inside. Together they walked
from the now empty courtroom. ''We got what we
wanted,'' he said.

"It sounded like you wanted more.''

"I was after a restraining order—no more, no less.
Charlie Bradley was right, my other suggestion was
outrageous. But at least it got the judge in the right
frame of mind. The important part is, Dylan Bradley
is barred from going near Allison.''

She still felt a little ambiguous about that. ''Do
you think he'll obey?''

"I think so, he looked scared to me. What do you
think?'' he asked, putting his hand on her elbow,
stopping her, his concerned eyes looking into hers.

"Yes, I guess he did.''

"Trust me, Crosby doesn't take well to violation

of an order, particularly one he's issued. And I think Charlie Bradley will go out of his way to get that across to his son.''

She thought about his statement to the judge, how exposed it had made her feel. ''You used the fact that I'm a single mother to try to get the judge's sympathy.''

''It's true, isn't it?''

''Yes, but—'' The car keys slipped from her hand, and together they stooped down, nearly butting heads . . . and when they started to laugh, locking gazes. She finally broke contact, and feeling a little rattled, took the keys and hurried to the lobby.

In the courtroom, Woody's beeper had gone off a number of times. Each time he'd looked at it, turned it off, reset. Allison had been jumpy throughout the whole proceeding, sneaking looks at Dylan a couple of times, then turning away. Now on the way home Allison—like Jake, who hadn't been able to reach Jeremy before leaving for court—was silent and grim.

When Hollie suggested they pick up a video movie on the way home, they agreed halfheartedly. She detoured to the Fieldstone Plaza, letting them out at the video store. At least it was a way for them to take their minds off themselves—off Jeremy's absence, Dylan, the upcoming trial, Barry. She sighed: the list was forever growing.

Woody sat next to her in the front seat. His beeper went off again. Again he checked the number, clicked off, and reset.

''Sounds like a lot of business coming in,'' Hollie said. ''If you need to do a callback, I spotted a phone near the A&P. If the kids get back, I don't mind waiting.''

He shook his head. "What did you and the prosecutor talk about?"

Though it was likely an innocent question, she felt awkward answering it. "The case," she said. "He was pleased about the restraining order. So was I."

"Do you think it will work?"

"He thinks so. I hope he's right. Actually, it's a relief to have him taking over on this."

Woody smiled, put his hands in his blue parka pockets. "He likes you, you know."

She turned toward him, recalling when he'd tried to kiss her. And wondering now if he perhaps still carried that little-boy crush. "What . . . who?"

"The prosecutor."

"Frank Lorenzo?"

He nodded. "I can tell by the way he looks at you."

This was a conversation she didn't want to be having—certainly not with Woody. "Tell me, why are we talking about this?"

"I just thought I'd mention it. A single mother has to watch out: she's a perfect victim."

Okay, he was teasing her . . . this she could deal with. She smiled at him. "Oh, that. I hated when he did that."

"Why? It's true, isn't it?"

She didn't answer. "I wonder what's taking the kids so long."

"What, you don't want to talk to me?"

"Stop it, Woody."

"Stop what?"

"I don't know, playing this funny little game with me. It makes me uncomfortable."

"Then shall we put the stops on your game, too? You know it's my mother always calling, don't you?"

She sighed, shrugged. "I'm sorry, I didn't want to pry."

But now that he had pushed her into asking, it led to a continued conversation back at the house while the kids watched the video in Allison's room on the VCR.

"What do you suggest I do?" he asked her.

And she wanted to help him. Hadn't he helped her enough times? But it was difficult to advise someone on such a personal decision. What should she suggest, that he pack up and abandon his invalid mother? He hadn't done that when it came to his schooling, at a time when he'd had a perfectly legitimate reason to do so.

"I don't know, really. Maybe if you talked to her. If you could just get her to understand that you're no longer a little kid. It's a difficult thing to let go of children. Especially, I would imagine, in your mother's case—her being an invalid and frightened of being left alone."

"Ironically, she had little use for me when I was young. Mostly I was in the way. It wasn't until later on, when she realized I was all she had left, that she became so clutching and demanding and possessive. It's not easy to live with."

Hollie nodded. "Well, if there's ever anything I can do—talk to her, whatever, just ask." And she meant it, even though she was relieved when he finally left and she could fall into bed. She was drained, physically and emotionally.

Though Allison had watched the entire movie, if someone had asked her to describe the plot she would have failed miserably. Now, lying in bed with the lights out, her mind was still whirling around and around the same circle.

It started with that afternoon, how monstrous Dylan had looked, so huge and strong . . . and evil. Him above her, with absolute control of what was to happen. At any moment his hands could have begun to touch her, fumble with her clothes. . . . And then her thoughts would shift to the courtroom that night: Dylan sitting at the long wooden table beside his father.

Looking suddenly so small, as though he'd shrunk. How had that happened?

CHAPTER
Eighteen

Though the next few days were stressful, it was clearly the stress of anticipation. The restraining order the judge had imposed on Dylan did indeed work its magic. Though Allison spotted Dylan several times in school watching from a distance, whenever their glances met he was quick to turn away.

Miraculously, Fran Grant agreed to let Chelsea testify, providing she be the first to take the stand so Fran could whisk her back to school. And though Toby hadn't seen a great deal the afternoon of the abduction, she had seen enough to come to the correct conclusion. So Frank took her up on her offer to testify.

Allison hadn't heard at all from Barry, and now when they passed each other between first and second period he made it a point to direct his attention elsewhere. But after a good deal of stalling and deliberation, Allison got the guts to go up to him in the corridor and take hold of his sleeve, stopping him.

"Can we talk a minute?"

"I have class," he said.

Now that she'd started this, she wasn't going to let him go that easily. "I know; me too," she said.

They went to the wall, away from the traffic.

"Okay, what is it?" he asked, as though it were the last thing he wanted to know.

"I just wanted to tell you not to feel so bad."

"Yeah, sure," he mumbled under his breath.

"I mean it, really. This is my fight, not yours."

He finally looked at her directly. "But I should have—"

"No, that's not so. People need to decide what's right for them, then do it."

"You're not mad?"

She shook her head, then they talked for a couple of minutes before they parted. She'd meant it: she wasn't mad, she even understood what had made him back off. But she didn't suppose she could ever feel the same about him either.

She began to think: Maybe that's a little the way Mom feels about Dad.

Jake was still unable to reach Jeremy by Friday, and when he failed to show Friday night without even a telephone call, Hollie became concerned. Though she called Elaine and Mike, as well as Jeremy's cousin Larry in New Britain and a half-dozen of his friends, no one had seen or heard from him in days. So did that mean he was out on some gambling binge?

Later, Woody stopped over with a list of points he thought might be helpful to Frank with respect to his testimony. She thanked him, promised to pass the paper on to Frank, and they got to talking about the upcoming hearing. That's when she voiced her concern about not being able to reach Jeremy to give him the date.

"Why the pull toward him?" he asked.

"I don't know, it's just . . . where is he?"

"What difference does it make? I thought it was over between you?"

"It is, but that doesn't mean I want to see him fall on his face."

A long silence; then: "I think what it is, is you're feeling particularly insecure, thinking you can't handle this court business without him. Well, you're wrong. You have friends to rely on . . . and yourself. Which in itself is enough."

"You know just what to say, don't you?"

"Naturally. I took a stroking course as an undergrad."

She smiled. "Speaking of which, how is school coming? You never mention."

"Nothing to mention. My thesis is nearly complete."

"Really, what on?"

"Computer capability and practical application in the twenty-first century. Big time futuristic stuff."

"Oh, I like that. What sort of thing are we talking about? And please don't say you've now come up with a practical application for your bat attractor."

"What about a device with a chip the size of a pinhead, able to, let's say, be planted in a pinky ring? You point the finger, and it picks up voices up to two hundred yards away."

"What's to stop interference?"

"Like a radio. You've got a direct line of waves, programmed to bounce off the sound and frequency of a voice."

It all sounded great—that is, until some of the negatives came to mind. "Then you could, let's say, point across the street and listen to a conversation?"

He sat back, his hands clasped behind his head, looking at her, grinning.

"But you can't . . . I mean you don't?"

He shook his head, laughed. "Got you nervous there for a minute, didn't I?"

She threw a couch pillow at him. "You did . . . and yes, Woody, you are certifiably nuts."

He laughed while she got up, went to the kitchen, and put on coffee.

"Woody?"

"Still here."

"Why is it you never mentioned it was your grandfather who built Garden Place?"

"No reason. It just never came up. According to Mom, Grandpa got the land for a song and made himself a quickie fortune developing it. Dad married into the business, but not until years later. So okay, who's been squealing?"

"Margaret Spear. I spoke to her a while back, trying to find out if she ever saw Dylan around my house when no one was home."

"Margaret wouldn't admit it if she had."

"You don't think so?"

"Margaret's longtime friends with Edna Bradley."

"So she mentioned. Tell me something, what's the scoop on brother Roger?"

"What do you mean?"

"Just that he's so young . . . at least to be sitting all day, looking out a window."

"The useless bum is likely looking to catch a glimpse of you."

She immediately remembered her thought about him having a crush on Nina. "Why would you say that?" she asked.

"Don't ask why, just take my word for it."

"Has it anything to do with me looking like Nina Richards?"

No movement, but she noticed a pulse beat at the side of his slender neck.

"Well, yeah, sure, there is a resemblance. Not a big deal, though." He shook his head. "I mean, you didn't know her, so—"

The phone rang. It was Frank Lorenzo, checking to see how the restraining order was holding up. He wanted to make an appointment to see Hollie and Allison in his office Monday. Unfortunately, it would mean taking more time off work and school. Reading her concern, Frank suggested an evening appointment.

When she got off the phone, Woody was in a less open mood, so they never did get back to his thesis, Roger, or the baby-sitter. But apparently his beeper had gone off in the interim and he had to go. Clearly he wasn't making much headway with his mother.

In rolled shirtsleeves, necktie long gone, and tilting backward on a straight-back chair, Frank Lorenzo finally looked comfortable. And so right, Hollie thought, wondering for a moment how he'd look in jeans, outdoors, away from all this trouble. She sat quietly by for nearly an hour and listened while Frank prepared Allison for the hearing.

"Will many people be there?" Allison asked when they were finally through.

"Not unless you invite them."

Allison's hand went to her chest. "*Me*, invite them! You're kidding, right?"

He looked at Hollie, smiling, and winked, then said to Allison, "The judge, a clerk, two lawyers, a few witnesses, and the involved parties. That's it."

"No jury?"

"None."

Allison, trying out the term for size, said, "I'm an 'involved party'?"

"Right."

"How long will it take?"

"A half a day, maybe a little longer. Your testimony will take anywhere up to two hours. Just remember, stick to the truth, and tell it simply. That way you won't have to worry about getting tripped by the other side."

She took a deep breath, and taking a last faltering shot, said, "You know, I was thinking. . . . Well, the restraining order is working so well . . . If we could keep it up, we wouldn't have to go through with any of this."

"Trying to put me out of a job, is that it?"

Hollie, who until now had kept quiet, sat forward. "Try to think of it as a learning experience, Allison. Once you're done, you'll know all about court procedure."

"That would be nice if I wanted to be a lawyer,"

Allison said, then turned to Frank. "Would you be-lieve she used that line on Jake to get him to the dentist?" But before Frank could react, she said, her eyes on her mother, "If I were you, Frank, I'd watch out for her."

Though Jake pleaded valiantly for Hollie to let him stay out of school to attend the hearing, in light of recent events she thought he'd be better off in school. In addition to the nightmares over the last few days, she'd noticed a behavioral change: he seemed distant, unhappy, not even interested in his computer. All since he'd been trying without suc-cess to reach Jeremy. She had tried to talk to him but with no success. Even Woody was unable to bring Jake out of his funk.

But the evening before the hearing, after seeing Jake again try to reach Jeremy, she went over to him and sat him down. "Jake, can't you tell me what's wrong?"

He shrugged. "There isn't anything to tell."

"I can see something is bothering you. And I un-derstand that you want to talk about it to Daddy. But since he's not here, why don't you tell me in-stead?"

He shook his head, then pushed up his sinking glasses.

"Honey, I might be able to help."

He looked at her, hesitating, for a moment consid-ering it, but then suddenly his voice rose in anger: "I told you, it's nothing. Leave me alone!" He got up and stalked off to his room.

Before she and Allison and Woody left for court

the next morning, Hollie made one last-ditch effort to reach Jeremy at his apartment. But still no answer.

What could he be doing? It wasn't like him to disappear totally with no word. At least not since the last year or two of their marriage, when his gambling was at its worst. Could he have slid all the way back down into the hole of his addiction?

The court case didn't begin until nine, but by eight-thirty Frank Lorenzo had already met with each of the other three witnesses. Woody was dressed in suit and tie, looking like a businessman but lacking that calm, joking, confident exterior Hollie was used to seeing. Clearly he too was dreading taking the stand.

Both she and Allison were stunned momentarily when they saw Dylan walk into the courtroom: gray slacks, a dark blue suit jacket and paisley tie—and a brand-new haircut that revealed that he was minus his gold earring. He sat straight, tall, and grave beside his father at the defendants' table. Nails cleaned and buffed, hands scrubbed and folded neatly in front of him, no gum-chewing, he looked every bit the collegian he was masquerading as. Hollie wondered if the judge would notice the inconsistency between his last week's appearance and today's. Or if in fact appearance made a difference at all.

Chelsea did fine, her testimony succinct and unflustered. Though Charlie Bradley tried his best to twist her words to make it seem like she and Allison had indeed invited Dylan and his friends into the house, Chelsea didn't give an inch.

It was midway into her cross-examination when Hollie turned, looked to the back of the courtroom, and saw a boy and girl about Dylan's age. Though she couldn't place them, both looked familiar. Sitting in front of them, to Hollie's surprise, were Margaret Spear and her brother, Roger. Were they there to gape, to snoop?

She sat forward, reached a little to the table in front where Allison and Frank were sitting side by side; tapped Frank's shoulder and he tilted his head back to listen.

"Two of the people in the back row are my neighbors," Hollie said. "Margaret Spear and her brother. Have you any idea what they're doing here?"

He glanced quickly; then: "The lady's their witness."

"Witness to what?"

"Dylan's character."

Hollie nodded, sat back. What did Margaret know about Dylan's character? Likely nothing. Just professional busybodies, there to see what they couldn't see today from their window. Her palms were warm and damp. Just being aware that Roger was sitting there, she could now feel his eyes on her back.

Toby's testimony was short and to the point, and since she couldn't testify that she'd actually witnessed a struggle between Allison and the boys, the defense surrendered its right to cross-examine. Unfortunately, Woody's testimony didn't go as well. Most of what he said was objected to as hearsay, even going back to the evening Dylan and his friends had forced entrance to their house.

"Did you see what transpired between the young-sters that night, what led up to the defendant and his friends entering the Ganzes' house?" Charlie asked.

"No, but—"

"In fact, did you see the defendant or his friends inside the house at all?"

"I saw the pigsty they left behind. There were greasy fries, chicken bones, and beer cans."

"Objection!" Charlie shouted followed by a noisy sigh and roll of eyes—basic lawyering moves meant to imply annoyance.

Finally, the judge cut in. "Mr. Woodbury, I ask that you restrict your answers to the questions be-fore you. Understand, please, the mere fact that you saw damage or what you construed to be damage does not speak to the crucial questions: for example, the intent. Was the act willful and malicious or ac-cidental . . . and even more important, who was re-sponsible?"

"Well, surely you don't think—"

Crosby banged his gavel, for the first time that morning showing his temper.

"Young man, this is not up for discussion!"

Although Allison's voice was so soft that at times it was necessary for her to repeat herself to be heard, she testified to the episodes clearly and accurately. Charlie Bradley did little to knock holes in her de-tails, and in fact didn't lean on her as much as he might have.

Hollie's testimony on the lateness and frequency of the phone calls was followed by Frank Lorenzo's putting into evidence Southern New England's telephone record affidavit. And since the prosecution was not using either the broken window incident or the noises Hollie frequently heard at night, her examination was completed in less that ten minutes.

However, then came the cross-examination . . . and to her surprise it was Charlie Bradley who brought up the broken window.

"Mrs. Ganz, I direct your attention to Thursday, October 3, at about seven P.M. In your own words, can you describe to the court what happened that evening?"

"Objection!" Frank said. "The incident he's referring to was not mentioned anywhere in the complaint, and has nothing at all to do with this case."

"On the contrary, your honor, it seems this little family is being harassed. What isn't evident is who the harasser is. If in fact there are similar incidents taking place in this household, it would be absurd to assume they have no bearing. Each is part of the whole and must be included in today's hearing."

"Overruled," the judge said, and the question was again put before Hollie.

She swallowed hard. "You're referring, of course, to the broken window."

He nodded. "Please tell the court about it."

Once she had completed the story, he said, "Mrs. Ganz, who was responsible for breaking your kitchen window?"

Again Frank was up on his feet. "I object! The witness couldn't possibly be asked to speculate—"

"I'll modify the question," Charlie said; then again to Hollie: "When the police officer questioned you later that evening about the window, who did you say was responsible?''

''I didn't. But I did say if he wanted to find out who did it, he ought to ask Dylan.''

''Implying Dylan Bradley was responsible.''

She took a deep breath. ''I believed he was.''

''And was he?''

''I don't know. Apparently, the police think not.''

Charlie Bradley went on to tell about the airtight alibi Dylan had for the time of the incident, entering into evidence an affidavit from a Boston College counselor who, after interviewing Dylan, had showed him and his mother around the twenty-acre campus until five o'clock.

Next was entered a stamped car receipt from the Connecticut Turnpike Authority showing that on that same date Pauline Bradley's car had exited the turnpike at Exit 28—Union, which would have her entering the city proper at precisely seven-twenty P.M.

That was followed by a five-minute recess. Then, with Hollie on the stand again, the defense went through the numerous times she had been panicked by unexplained noises, and the four times she'd actually called the Union police, only to have them search the entire yard and area to find nothing.

''I understand you have only recently separated from your husband, Mrs. Ganz. Am I correct?''

''Objection, not relevant!'' Frank said.

''On the contrary,'' Charlie said. ''This speaks directly to this lady's questionable state of mind. And in this particular type of complaint, it is quite relevant.''

''I'm going to allow it,'' Crosby said.

Charlie repeated the question, and Hollie affirmed that she had only recently separated.

"May I ask how long were you married, Mrs. Ganz?"

"Fifteen years."

"That's quite a long time, Mrs. Ganz. And before that, did you live alone?"

"I lived on campus. The University of Connecticut."

"A private room?"

"I had two roommates."

"I see. And before attending college, whom did you live with then?"

"My parents."

"During your marriage, was Mr. Ganz routinely away from home, perhaps on business trips?"

She shook her head. "No."

Charlie nodded. "How often would you estimate he was away from home in a year, for any reason? One night, two nights, ten nights, maybe twenty nights?"

"Objection," Frank said again.

Crosby looked at Charlie. "Get to the point, or I'm going to rule out this line of questioning."

And then in a syrupy voice that made Hollie want to gag, Charlie said to her, "The truth is, you're not used to being alone at all—that is, without a man. Isn't that correct, Mrs. Ganz?"

Silence. Shouldn't Frank Lorenzo be jumping to her defense just about now? She looked at him—the irritation in his face showed her there was nothing he could do.

"I'm waiting. Please answer the question, Mrs. Ganz."

She nodded her head finally. "Yes, that's true," she said.

CHAPTER
Nineteen

Seeing how devastated Hollie was following her testimony, Frank suggested they talk, over lunch.

"Charlie Bradley made me look neurotic, like some sad soul afraid of her own shadow," she said to Frank.

He nodded, sighed. "Their tactic is to make you look like you're part of the problem. Sure, they're willing to concede the minor details—Dylan being a naughty boy—just as long as they move the focus onto you as the over-reactor."

She looked at Frank, trying to see if he was becoming convinced of that too. But there was no sign of it, neither in his voice nor expression. She sighed wearily. "And by bringing up everything they know darn well we can't prove, they're doing a good job of it. It's all blowing up in our faces, isn't it?"

He leaned in closer to her. "Look, they're trying to muddy the waters, complicate things, that's their job. But the judge isn't a fool. We have them on the telephone calls, and Allison's testimony was excellent. Notice Charlie didn't bother to trounce her."

"I did notice, why?"

"She was clearly vulnerable. The judge liked her."

Hollie shook her head. "It's all really a play, isn't it? Who can stage the best case."

He nodded, looking at the table and then back at her. "I'd be a liar to say it didn't enter the picture."

But either Hollie's script was badly written, or as a character she didn't quite fit the part. The mere mention of those night noises had crushed her credibility, making her look silly and pathetic and lonesome.

When in fact there *were* noises. . . .

Dylan took the stand after lunch. His role was to come across as bewildered yet confident, and he was apparently well rehearsed. Of the answers Hollie could be certain of, seventy-five percent were outright lies. First Charlie had Dylan point out Allison in her seat. Then, as a sensitive adult might address a precocious youth, he delicately asked him how he felt about her.

"I like her," Dylan said. "I liked her since the day I met her. Somehow, I don't know how, I've led her to believe otherwise. But if I'm in any way responsible—"

"Objection," Lorenzo said. "Unresponsive."

Silence from the bench . . .

"Your honor?" Frank said, drawing Crosby's attention back to what was at hand.

"Don't offer up things on your own," the judge instructed Dylan.

Charlie Bradley continued. "Can you tell the court how you first met this girl?"

"Sure . . . at school, in the cafeteria. I realized she was new—she looked nervous and alone—and I had never seen her before. So I thought I'd be friendly. I went up to her and started talking."

"Did she respond to your friendliness?"

"Oh yeah, sure. In fact, she seemed happy. It's hard being at a new school, not knowing anyone. The next few days she'd smile when we saw each other in the halls. Twice she walked up to me and started a conversation."

Hollie heard Allison draw in her breath.

"We had the same lunch period every day," Dylan added. "I asked her to sit with me—me and my senior friends sat together—but being a freshman, she felt shy about joining us. I tried to convince her that she was being silly, but she was stubborn about it. Anyway, we got in the habit of talking right after lunch."

"What did you talk about?"

He shrugged. "Stuff kids talk about. Concerts, movies, classes, other kids. When she told me she lived on the same street as me, I was surprised. I hadn't known."

Clearly pleased with the way the testimony was going, Charlie stepped back, and for all but the questions, gave the stage over to Dylan. "Did you ever ask her out?"

"After a few days or so, I did. And she put me off. She said she'd really like to go but her mom was real strict, so she'd have to check, then let me know."

"And did she?"

"No, not really. She just started to act cool toward

me. I had no idea why. All of a sudden she was avoiding me like she was afraid of me . . . it was weird."

"Did you ask her why?"

"I tried. I thought maybe I did something to upset her without knowing. But at school, no matter what I did, she refused to look at me. I talked, joked, I suppose even teased her a little, hoping that would bring her around."

"But it didn't?"

"No, sir."

"So then I assume you quit."

He shook his head. "I couldn't stop just like that, not without knowing. One minute she liked me, the next, she hated me. It was too crazy."

"Leon Woodbury testified earlier that one Friday afternoon he saw you move your car back and forth on the street, positioning it in such a way that Allison couldn't cross the street to get home. Would you say that was an accurate description of what happened?"

Dylan looked down at his hands, then finally, with a deep sigh, faced his father. "Yeah, I guess it is. Leon came out, told me to get lost . . . and I did. I know it looked bad, but I swear to God, I only wanted to get Allison to talk to me."

"Did you ever phone her during the day?"

He nodded. "Several times."

"Describe those conversations."

"At first she seemed scared to talk to me, like maybe she'd get caught and be in trouble. Then one day she loosened up and admitted how much she liked me."

Allison's back stiffened and Hollie sat forward, rested a hand on her daughter's shoulder.

"Really? Then she finally agreed to go out with you?"

"No."

"I don't understand. Why not?"

"Because her mother wouldn't let her."

"You mean, she didn't let her date?"

"No, that wasn't it. She dated all right. She just wouldn't let her date me."

"Wait, let me get this clear. Did her mother know you?"

He shook his head. "I couldn't figure it . . . other than maybe she'd seen me on the street."

Charlie, putting on a face long with sympathy, walked to the stand. "So that was the end of it?"

"Well, not quite. That's when she told me about her mother going out that Saturday night. Allison said she was having a friend stay overnight, and why didn't I come and bring along a few of my friends."

"She actually asked you?"

"How else would I have known her mother was going out?"

"Objection, unresponsive!"

"Sustained."

"Dylan, we've heard testimony here saying you forced your way inside the house. Is that true?"

A pause; then: "I thought about that later . . . and I suppose it might have seemed so to someone who didn't know."

"Please clarify."

"Well, suddenly she made out like she hadn't

even asked me, like she had no idea of what I was doing there. At first I thought she was fooling around. I mean, it didn't make sense. What kind of emotionally unstable kid would play a game like that?''

''Objection! He's hardly qualified to comment on anyone's emotional stability,'' Frank said, clearly angry.

''Sustained.''

''Okay,'' Dylan said. ''It's just that I didn't believe she was actually serious about me leaving . . . that is, not until I saw Leon Woodbury come up the front walk.''

At that point Allison stood up, accidentally knocking over her chair as she fled the courtroom. Frank Lorenzo leapt forward, asked for a recess . . . and Hollie rushed out after Allison.

Hollie found her in the bathroom, in the process of vomiting up her lunch. Finally, Allison's stomach empty, if not yet settled, she sat on a straight-back wooden chair in the stark, white-tiled bathroom as Hollie applied damp paper towels to her forehead.

''All those lies,'' Allison said. ''I just can't believe he would lie like that.''

''Considering who he is, what he's done, maybe it shouldn't surprise you.''

''I know. But doesn't his father know he's lying?''

''I'm sure he does, honey.''

Her hands came up, shaking in protest. ''Then I don't understand! I mean, he's not just a father, he's a lawyer, too. Shouldn't he be trying to get at the truth?''

"He's just trying to get Dylan off any which way he can." And to make matters worse, he was surprisingly skilled at what he did. But that it was so, didn't make it less appalling.

Though the recess lasted fifteen minutes, in retrospect it was not nearly long enough. Not now that Hollie felt her own head on the chopping block.

Dylan had taken the stand again, and Charlie had asked, rather nonchalantly, "Oh, by the way, Dylan, did you ever find out why Allison's mother wouldn't let her date you?"

He bent his head, looked at his shoes.

"I know this isn't easy for you to talk about, but I'm afraid it's necessary. Now, I repeat, did you ever find out why Hollie Ganz wouldn't let her daughter date you?"

He straightened up, sat back, took a deep breath, then looked at his father. "Yes, sir," he said finally.

"Tell the court, please."

"She wanted me for herself."

This time it was Hollie's turn to gasp as Frank Lorenzo stood up and objected vehemently. Both attorneys approached the bench, arguing so quietly she could barely hear, but she could feel eyes on her: Margaret's, Roger's . . . even Woody's.

But no matter how fiercely Frank fought, he had apparently lost. When they came back to the bench Charlie was beaming, and he turned to Dylan to resume questioning.

Hollie listened as Dylan told how Hollie had telephoned him—he was naturally surprised out of his mind—and asked him to meet her. She suggested a roadside bar, he counter-suggested a local diner. They met that evening at the diner, only to have Hollie stamp off furiously five minutes after her arrival. According to Dylan's testimony, angry because he had rebuffed her advances.

And according to the two nameless youths who'd been sitting in the rear of the courtroom, who Hollie now recalled as the couple in the diner that evening, Hollie had supposedly made a big issue of telling Dylan how good-looking he was.

"Also," the girl said, "She wanted Dylan to do something, and he wouldn't. I couldn't tell what it was, exactly. It wasn't as though I was trying to listen."

Though Hollie wanted to get out of there, she still had to sit and listen to the cross-examination—Dylan stuck hard and fast to all his lies. Then Margaret Spear's testimony highlighted the night Jeremy was drinking and making such a ruckus that the police had to come. And how at nearly one o'clock that morning, when Margaret—who regularly was up with bouts of insomnia—just happened to glance out her front window, she had spotted Woody, clothes disheveled, leaving the Ganz house to go home.

"Objection!" the prosecution shouted! Margaret stood up, and in a thin voice shrieked, "The woman is a harlot!"

"Your honor, I insist you tell this woman to shut her mouth!" Frank shouted.

Again both attorneys marched to the bench. This time the State won. Margaret's testimony ended, she was dismissed. Hollie wanted to grab Allison, get out of the courthouse, and run. But she had to sit and listen to the judge make his ruling.

"In large part what we have here are misunderstandings: a headstrong young man smitten by a young lady. In an attempt to win her favor, his brazen behavior causes both her and her mother undue anxiety and grief. However, the court is then asked to find the young man's arrogance a natural and clear path to other actions of a more serious nature. It is my opinion that the prosecution has not presented sufficient evidence to warrant such a finding."

Charlie's eyes registered relief, and the judge went on:

"That is not to imply that defendant's behavior has been proper, or even acceptable to this court. Clearly some force was employed to get the young lady in the defendant's car. And no matter how well-intentioned the motive, such methods are considered callous and unlawful. What perhaps infuriates me most are the consistent late-night calls, a cruel and childish and vengeful act."

Then, looking directly at Dylan, he said, "Life does not always spin perfectly or even fairly. But if all persons chose to solve their dissatisfactions and perceived inequities by a display of temper, there would be anarchy—which, when we look to our larger cities, we see evidenced today. But not in my town, young man!"

He pointed his finger. "I do not want Allison Ganz or anyone in her family needled or harassed by you again. Do I make myself clear?"

A pause as Charlie kicked Dylan in the ankle. "Yes, your honor," Dylan said.

"In fact, I want their names stricken from your vocabulary. To that end, I extend the restraining order for a ninety-day period, at which time I will assume that any overactive hormones not presently in check, will be. Be assured also, if there is any infringement of this order, I shall not hesitate to issue immediate and severe sanctions."

Crosby banged his gavel. "Dismissed. Everyone go home."

A continued restraining order, a slap on the hand as Frank Lorenzo had tried to warn her, and that was justice. For his more minor part in Allison's abduction, Ray Anderson got twenty hours of community service—a harsher penalty than Dylan's!

Frank asked Hollie to go with him downstairs to the prosecutor's office before leaving. Though neither of them spoke on the way down, the tension between them left little room to doubt how she was feeling. He felt so damned inept—Charlie had snipped her into a dozen little pieces and he was able to do nothing but sit by and watch. One of the reasons not to get involved with a client. *Involved? Who, me? No way, only about up to my earlobes.*

Once in the office, he had her take a chair. While he pulled at the damned tie choking his neck, he perched on the corner of his desk, leaning toward her. "Look, I want you to try to forget that little bit of dirt-smearing that went down in there. No one paid much attention to it, least of all the judge."

"Sure, just a part of the damn play," she said, her voice just about spitting nails.

"Charlie is not known for his scrupulous methods. Most attorneys wouldn't have taken that tack."

"Well, why not? It paid off, didn't it?"

"Not totally. We did get—"

The door opened—it was Leon Woodbury.

"Hollie, you need to get something into your stomach. You've been operating on straight caffeine all day. And Allison is getting antsy, she's been through a rough time. How much longer do you think?" he said, looking at Frank.

Frank caught Hollie's reaction, which seemed almost as surprised as his own. But looking back to the kid, he said, "Give us about five more minutes."

"Okay, Woody?" Hollie asked. The kid didn't look particularly satisfied with it, but he nodded and shut the Plexiglas-paneled door. Not bothering to even step away from it, Frank noticed.

But he turned his attention back to her. "Well, as I was about to say, we did manage to get the continuance of the restraining order, and that's not exactly nothing. Dylan paid strict attention to it before, so there's no reason to believe he won't do so again."

"He doesn't have a hearing facing him now."

Frank reached down and took her hands in his—they felt cold. "Listen to me, Hollie. If he disobeys it, I'll go straight in on a contempt charge."

She sighed, sounding drained. And even worse, sounding beaten. "Frank, I appreciate how hard you've worked. . . ."

"But?"

She shook her head. "It wasn't your fault. I don't want you to think that for even a mom—"

The door opened—again the kid, this time his voice not hiding his annoyance.

"Hollie, this isn't fair to Allison. Are we almost done here?"

Less surprised, but maybe more confused, Hollie looked at him and said, "Woody, I'll be right out. Would you please tell her that?"

When the door closed this time, Frank said, "Look, do me a favor—tell the kid to go ahead. I'll take you and Allison."

She shook her head. "No. It's my car. He's right, though, this is selfish of me. Allison is probably an emotional wreck." She stood, and before he knew it had happened, she'd leaned over and kissed his cheek. "Thank you, Frank, for everything." Then she rushed toward the door.

"Wait a second!" He reached over, opened his top desk drawer, and pulled out a business card. Taking a pen from his pocket, he wrote on the back. "My home number," he said, stepping forward and handing it to her. "Call me if you need me. Any time, don't hesitate." Oh, great—she looked about ready to lie down and die, and what was he offering her as comfort? A god-damned telephone number.

She took the card and slid it into the change compartment of her purse.

"Hollie, I know it's none of my business, but indulge me?" She waited, and he gestured to the kid whose shadow showed through the door's glass insert.

"Who is he?"

"I'm not sure what you mean."

There was no easy way to ask it, so he dove in. "Are you two involved?"

"What's this, finding yourself buying into some of that testimony, Frank? No, we're not—at least not in any other way than as friends."

It was still early enough that Frank could have gone back to his other office, but instead he drove toward home. He felt drained—angry, too, but not quite sure at what: Charlie Bradley, Dylan, the outcome of the trial . . . or maybe at his failure to get rid of the fear in her eyes.

And that annoying kid, Leon—the way he had stood outside the door, sticking his face in, pressing her to hurry. Like he owned her.

CHAPTER
Twenty

She was driving too fast, so much so that Allison asked her to slow down and Woody reached over her shoulder and pressed down the lock button on her door.

One of her hands flew off the wheel, circling for emphasis. "Maybe I ought to be grateful the judge chose to ignore the diner incident. Who knows, he might have found me guilty of corrupting a minor."

"It was a lie, right?" Woody said.

She turned, glaring at him. "Need you ask?"

"Look, I didn't mean it to come out that way. I just meant I didn't understand—"

Hollie shook her head. "No, Woody, don't apologize. That's just my frustration talking. What happened is, I called and set up a meeting with Dylan to ask him to leave Allison alone. What a nitwit I was to think it might work!"

"Stop kicking yourself. It's not easy to—"

"Please—if I hear that 'poor single mother' routine one more time, I'll vomit." She went through a

stop sign, squealing to a sudden stop less than a foot
from a crossing car.

"Watch it!" Allison shouted from the backseat.

Hollie took a deep breath, avoided the hateful
stare of the other driver, then proceeded with care.
She didn't say another word until she'd pulled into
their driveway.

"Again, Woody, thank you for testifying," she
said as she got out of the car.

"Uh-uh. I'm afraid there'll be no dismissing your
good buddy that easily. I'm not going anywhere—at
least not while you're stuck in this frame of mind."

"No, please go home. I plan to be rotten company," she said, again not quite understanding his
need to take care of her.

"Forget it, I'm staying."

She sighed, too tired and irritable to argue more,
and escaped into the house, to her bedroom, closing
the door behind her. She fell onto the bed, leaning
on her elbows, staring at the pillow . . . then turning
her head to look to the closet, around the room. Always that feeling, that fear that she wasn't alone.
Well, so much for justice. Jeremy was right. She had
to get out of there.

She reached out, brought the phone onto her bed,
dialed Jeremy's number. She let it ring several times,
hung up, called information, and got the number of
the Travelers Insurance company. She asked for Jeremy's department, then him.

"Sorry, he's not in."

"When do you expect him?"

"Who is this?"

"Hollie Ganz . . . his wife."

A hesitation; then: "Why don't I let you speak to his supervisor?" Within a few minutes a Mr. Hendricks was on the telephone, and she introduced herself.

"We're separated, and I've been trying to reach him regarding the children. I don't mean to be so blunt, but he does still work there, doesn't he?"

"Mrs. Ganz, the last time I spoke to Jeremy was about a week ago. He said he had the flu. In fact, he left me a number where he could be reached if necessary."

"Oh?"

"A friend's house. We called that number the other day ourselves when some time had elapsed and we hadn't heard from him. But all we got was an answering machine."

"Can I have the number?"

He hesitated a moment before he said, "I don't suppose it could hurt." He gave her a West Hartford exchange, and when Hollie reached it she got the same answering machine. The woman introduced herself as Lenore; Hollie left no message. Instead she put down the phone and just as she did, Woody opened the door.

She was about to say something about knocking, but wasn't up to dealing with etiquette. He was carrying a tray with a bowl of soup and Saltines. She wasn't hungry, but said nothing as he placed the tray on her bedside stand.

"Who were you calling?" he asked.

"Jeremy."

His head tilted toward his shoulder and he sighed, as though he didn't approve. "Why?"

Dammit, what was going on with him? But then again the whole court episode had been hard on everyone, not just her. So, trying not to let her anger take over, she said, "I need to discuss something with him. Besides which, I'm worried about him."

"Because he hasn't called?"

"He's not been at work either."

"He must be heavy into gambling."

"Woody, would you please—" she began, then stopped. "How do you know about his gambling?"

"I think you told me once. Or maybe it was Jake."

She nodded. "Look, I'd rather not discuss this. And if you'll excuse me please, I have another call to make."

He nodded, gesturing to the food. "How about trying some of this soup?"

"Why don't you just leave it?" she said, trying to dismiss him nicely. "Maybe later. Thank you," she added, as he closed the door behind him.

Her hands fisted, and she drew them up alongside her face. *Thank you, thank you, thank you.* Could she bear to say it one more time without screaming it? *Just back off, Woody, please. Go home and let me gut it out myself.*

Her next call was to Sampson Realty. A secretary came on, but the brokers were either out showing properties or gone for the day, including the owner, Kathy Morrison.

"Can you leave a message for Kathy?" Hollie asked.

"Sure, go ahead."

"This is Hollie Ganz. Not too long ago I purchased a house through her."

"Oh yes, I remember. You're the one who bought 8 Garden Place, right?"

"Yes, that's right."

"How do you like it there?"

"Well, that's why I'm calling, I'm putting the house back on the market."

"You're kidding. You've been there what . . . only a few months? I hope there weren't any problems with—"

"Not with the house. Personal problems."

"I see. Well, I'll be sure to leave the message for Kathy. I'm sure she'll get back to you first thing tomorrow."

Hollie put down the receiver, wondering if maybe she wasn't making a mistake putting the listing back in the hands of Sampson Realty, despite their being familiar with the property. No doubt before the night was out, her nosy neighbors would know of her intention to sell.

She shook her head, sighed. At this point, did she really care?

She told Woody when he came to pick up the tray with the soup she hadn't touched.

"Sit down, Woody," she said, indicating a chair.

He pulled a chair closer to her bed, turned it around, and sat. "Does this mean you're feeling better?"

"I'm putting the house on the market."

"Whoa, wait, hold on!" he said, his jaw dropping and his expression growing deeply serious. "You're talking about as in selling?"

She nodded.

A little vein in his neck began to throb. "But why?"

"Woody, the court case is over and done with. We all had our say, the judge spoke his piece. And don't ask me to explain it because I can't, but I'm more terrified than ever."

"What about me?"

Now it was her turn to be surprised. What exactly did he expect her to say? "We're friends," she said finally. "Surely that won't need to change."

"But you can rely on me."

"I have, far more than I had a right to. And still it's not enough. Let me tell you something. From the beginning, this house unnerved me: a paper would disappear, then turn up elsewhere. . . . Not a day goes by that I don't feel as though I'm being watched, and even the behavior of the animals has been odd. I'm not trying to pass myself off as an expert on animals certainly, but even Jake would complain how his hamster didn't seem the same.

"Maybe I'm imagining these things, or at least exaggerating. But I surely didn't invent an entire list of complaints for the police, or for that matter for anyone. It's enough I have to wonder about my own sanity, I don't need others to wonder too." Woody started to protest but she didn't let him get a word in.

"Oh, I thought I'd get over it, naturally, once justice was properly served. But it didn't work out that way. And thanks to Dylan and all the stress and anger and fear associated with him, I've got to get out of this house."

Shaking his head, Woody stood up. "I won't let you. I can't."

"I've already decided."

She was getting annoyed and impatient, feeling as though she were dealing with a child who refused to understand what he didn't want to understand. Woody stared down at the floor, and she found herself wishing he'd leave.

Finally he seemed to accept it. His teeth chewed his lower lip, leaving indentations; the sole of his shoe tapped the floor, and he asked, "When? When will you go?"

"I haven't decided yet. I would have liked to wait to sell the house, to get my money out, but I don't know that I can." She slipped on her shoes and stood up. "It's time I tell the children."

Suddenly he pulled her toward him and wrapped his arms around her, and for a moment she could do nothing. Finally, her muscles beginning to work, she pushed him away, but he held tighter.

"Don't go," he said. "Please, Hollie, say you won't go."

"Stop it, Woody!" she insisted. Managing to disentangle herself, she backed toward the door, looking at him. His behavior was frightening her.

But he shook his head, lifted his hands to immediately appease her. "Sorry, I . . . didn't mean to get that emotional about it. Just don't be angry with me, okay?"

"I'm not," she said, and she supposed she wasn't

really. But she was tired and tense and frustrated, and didn't have the patience to deal with him any further. "Look," she said, trying desperately to relax and to convey a kinder attitude, "why don't you go home for now? I think we both need a break."

Frank had picked up a meatball sandwich on the way home. As he ate, his mind went over the day's testimony, getting annoyed every time he thought of Leon Woodbury, aka Woody, and that little manipulation of Hollie he'd witnessed at the courthouse. He wasn't any expert on relationships, but it seemed like a lot of possessiveness for a neighborly friendship.

Did she even realize it? Maybe so, and for all he knew, she liked it. Sure he was young—twenty-one, twenty-two tops, but not exactly a dummy. Frank thought back to the kid qualifying himself on the stand, saying he ran a computer consulting business, was close to getting a doctorate . . . math, computer science.

If it was all true it *was* pretty impressive, extraordinary, really. Just out of curiosity, Frank got up, went to the yellow pages, and looked up computer consulting. Woodbury's name wasn't there. In fact there were only three listings in the area, all of which Frank called: none had any affiliation with Leon Woodbury. He then tried the larger Hartford phone book—still no luck. Finally he called information: no business number. Though there was a private phone listing on Garden Road for the kid, it was unpublished.

Now he was getting even more curious. Why

would he have said there was a business if there wasn't . . . perhaps to impress Hollie? Was he even a graduate student, or was that just more bullshit? He looked at his watch—the Registrar's Office at the University of Connecticut was surely closed, and though Frank knew a professor from the Business department, he had unfortunately retired recently and gone west. Frank dropped the receiver, went for a beer. So maybe the kid wasn't all he pretended to be, so what? But to *lie* on the stand . . .

He sighed, went back to the phone, this time going through his address book until he came to the name Alan Gray: friend, computer specialist, and even better, a Massachusetts Institute of Technology professor for at least ten years. Surely he could steer Frank to someone at U. Conn.

"Are we going back to live with Daddy?" Jake asked, when Hollie told them about selling the house.

She shook her head. "No, we're going to find another place, is all. In fact, Daddy mentioned a place he knew was available in Manchester. Maybe I can—"

"You mean he called?" Jake said, excited.

She shook her head, took a deep breath. "No, I wish. I still haven't been able to reach him. Though I now have another number . . . Well anyway, I'll try him again later."

"Would we move right away?" Allison asked.

"It depends."

"On Dylan?"

"I suppose, somewhat. Don't misunderstand, I

want out of here one way or another, but I guess I could hold off a few weeks if Dylan abided by the restraining order. I'm just so angry that he was allowed to get away with it all.''

''It wouldn't have been so awful if he hadn't turned everything around,'' Allison said. ''Telling all those lies. Making it like he was innocent and we were the ones guilty.''

Hollie nodded, took one hand of Allison's, one of Jake's.

''Let's try to get this out of our minds. We tried our best, did the right thing by taking it to court, and . . .'' She shrugged. ''What can I say? Sometimes the system doesn't work as fairly as it should. But it's time for us to move ahead.''

Allison, ecstatic with the news, got Hollie's permission to make a toll call to Chelsea. After ten minutes with her, she called Toby. She was on the phone nearly three hours in all, not even giving Hollie a chance to call Elaine.

It would have been funny if it weren't so freaking sick . . . a twenty-two-year-old actually having to go through such machinations to avoid his own mother in his own house. The incessant questioning, the accusations and judgments, followed by the force-fed guilt trips. Always the fight to win control. When did a son get the right to be free, to take charge of his own life?

Woody closed the front door quietly after coming in, careful so as not to disturb his mother. Whenever she got on his case; no matter what he was doing, or how important, his brain would shut down, be put on immediate hold.

But no such luck, she must have been listening for him.

"How did it all go?"

He shrugged, pulled off his tie, unbuttoned his shirt. And worse still, did he need more yipping and yapping about the hearing? But ever the subservient and obedient son, he answered her sweetly. "Not as well as we had hoped."

"She's leaving, isn't she?"

He jerked his head, stared. "Who told you that?"

She smiled. "Mothers know what goes on in their children's heads. They can read it right off their faces. It's better this way, Leon. Wait, you'll see once she's left. Let her find herself a real man, one that can give her the love and attention she requires, one who can really protect her. A man like your father."

He remembered well the amount of attention his mother had required, but she had wanted it always from his father, not him. And Father, fully aware of who held the riches, the whole construction business, kit and caboodle, yielded to her wishes. But it was easier then. That was when Mother had been beautiful and accomplished and sought after by strangers. Once that had ended, he'd handed her back to Leon . . . while he went off with the other men to lust after the one woman that belonged to Leon.

Where was your handsome, strong, attentive husband after you got sick? he thought, but didn't say it. Why did he always put himself through this?

"She doesn't love you, she never will. She'll use

you like some poor lovesick, wingless freak. Certainly not the way a woman should look at a real man.''

Sarcastic and cruel, and always so close to the jugular, like she was crawling inside him, watching and listening. If not for the coded entry to all his audiovisual operations, he might well have believed she pulled her information right off his computer. But no, her targeted gibes were simply good guesses, coupled with a mother's sixth sense.

The fact remained, Hollie didn't love him enough—at least, not yet, not with the same intensity he felt. And though he had been ready and willing to give her as much time as she needed to reach the level of devotion he required, time was quickly running out.

It was after nine o'clock when Hollie finally called Jeremy's apartment. When there was no answer, she called Lenore. The phone was picked up on the second ring.

"This is Hollie Ganz," she said. "Is Jeremy there?"

"No, he's not." A pause, while Hollie couldn't help but wonder what her relationship with Jeremy was. "Did Jeremy give you my number?" she asked.

"Actually, he didn't. I got it from his work."

"Oh, I see."

"I've been trying to get in touch with him. When I called his office yesterday, they gave me a number Jeremy left with them—which was yours. According to his supervisor, he called in sick last week and hasn't been heard from since. They've attempted to reach him, but—''

''I know, there was a message left for him on my answering machine a couple of days ago. I tried to—'' She stopped; then: ''Listen, Hollie, I don't know what Jeremy's told you about me.''

''Actually, not a thing. But that's all right. I mean, he's not required to.''

''Well, it's not what you're likely thinking. I'm Jeremy's neighbor, the apartment above his. He's been great . . . you know, helping me move a couple of pieces of furniture, taking in a package for me, things like that. Anyway, we've become friends.''

''This isn't necessary.'' Though she meant it, she really did, did she say it because she was just a little scared to find out what there was to the friendship?

''But it is. I mean, we *are* just friends. And hearing the way he's always going on about you, I would hate for you to think otherwise. Anyway, he had a bad case of the flu, running a 102 temp, and like I said, he'd been a real sweetheart. Well, I was off the next few days—I'm a stewardess with a wacky schedule—so I insisted he hole up at my place and let me look after him.''

''Then you're saying he's left?''

''Yes, the next night. He was feeling better—in fact, it was my impression he was going to work the next day. And when the message came in for him, I tried to reach him . . . actually, several times. I even went downstairs twice, knocked on his door.

That's why you threw me when you said you were looking for him.''

''I don't understand.''

''Well, him disappearing like that. When I couldn't locate him, I figured it had to mean he'd gone back with you.''

Disappearing? The woman hardly knew Jeremy. And she more than likely didn't know about his gambling.

''Well?'' Jake said, coming up behind her in a T-shirt and an odd pair of pajama bottoms.

She jumped, her hand going to her chest. ''What are you doing out of bed?'' Looking at him more closely, she said, ''You were listening in, weren't you?''

''Where's Daddy?'' he said, ignoring her accusation.

''I don't know,'' she said, hating to have to tell him that.

''Who were you asking?''

''A friend of his.''

She had already seen the change in his expression before he asked, ''A lady friend?''

''Yes.'' His eyes were wet, and she stooped down, taking him in her arms. ''It's okay, Jake.''

''It's not,'' he said. ''*You're* supposed to be his lady.''

She sighed. ''Come, you,'' she said, lifting him and carrying him back to bed. She tucked him in, then kissed his forehead.

''Mommy . . . what if something happened?''

''What do you mean?''

"If he's hurt and he can't get to a phone . . . and that's why he isn't calling?"

"Jake, you know Daddy, he can take care of himself." She had thought it when she spoke to Lenore, and she still thought it: the only explanation for Jeremy's absence was a run of poker games. But Jake's tears refused to let up. "Tell you what," she said finally. "Suppose tomorrow I go see if I can find him?"

Frank was on the right track. Alan Gray knew two professors in the computer science department at U. Conn, and he gave him both names. One was on sabbatical, but Professor Gardo, who, as it turned out, had had Woody as an undergraduate for a computer/biology course, was reachable at his home.

"Though I'm not aware of him operating his own business," Gardo said, "it's quite possible. The school gets a number of requests for consultants, and if they were to recommend anyone, Woodbury would certainly be a likely candidate."

"Then he's bright," Frank said, feeling more than a little foolish that he was going through such machinations to find this out.

Gardo chuckled. "Not bright, Mr. Lorenzo. Leon is a genius. I only hope he uses his gift wisely."

"Why wouldn't he?"

"It happens . . . with more frequency than you'd imagine. The tendency to become totally fascinated by a subject, then to focus so deeply on it, to the exclusion of everything else—that's what sets apart the great from the mediocre. But also such obsessive behavior can go out of control."

"You make it sound a little eerie."

"Well, when I had Leon as a student a while back, he was caught up in some odd things. Nothing he really chose to discuss with me, just things I observed or heard."

"Can you be more specific?"

He hesitated, as though he might be questioning the ethics of such a disclosure, but apparently deciding none was in jeopardy, he went on. "Years ago Leon had come up with some kind of bird attractor—certain computer-induced sounds that attracted birds. He worked on it intensively, ironing out imperfections, making it more sophisticated. In fact, he came up with a similar device for rodents."

"Now *that's* something that might be marketable—an electronic exterminator."

"To be sure, but he had no interest in marketing it. What he wanted was to control animal behavior, working his way to higher animal forms, of course."

"To train the animals, you mean?"

"No, I mean *control*. Total programming. The level, duration, and intensity of a sound or series of sounds would react on the animal's nervous system, producing a specific response: fear, joy, excitement, anger, passivity, aggression, whatever. And of course, those responses brought about various behaviors."

"Sounds a bit Frankensteinish to me."

"Ah-hah, that's it exactly, Mr. Lorenzo. There was no real scientific purpose to any of it. Of course

he professed otherwise, saying it was a seed, a beginning to the ultimate: communication between
animal and man.

"Did any of it work?"

"Well, I don't know how far he went with it, but
I did once see him put a pigeon into such a frenzy,
it literally spun itself in circles. And it didn't stop
until it fell over dead."

CHAPTER
Twenty-one

In his small cellar den, Woody stood in front of the bookshelves while the invisible computer eye decoded his appearance and released the wall lock. He pushed on the shelves, cracking the wall open just enough to fit through, then closed it.

The workroom was gigantic—measuring thirty-five by forty, not including storage space and bathroom. The plain unadorned cement walls along with the pounds of sand his granddad had packed between the ceiling's sheet rock and upper floor joists, made it soundproof. On the floor, off to the right, was the round steel hatch that accessed the underground passageway, which went deep under the road, ending finally in the cellar at 8 Garden Place.

Sam Egan was the mastermind, a genius in his own right, they said. Woody though had difficulty recalling the man who—along with his wife—was killed in a plane crash when Woody was three years old. But according to Woody's father, who married into the family construction business, the room was Sam's headquarters.

And the little ranch house was a good example of Sam's clever sense of mischief: the passageway known only to a few provided ready access to the house where he hosted his current whore. Quarters not so fancy as to swell a lady's head, yet comfortable enough to make her think she had a good thing. And always of course, of prime concern was convenience and discretion. Sam Egan had no desire to cause his wife or lovely, talented daughter, Eleanor, either grief or embarrassment.

Woody's father had seldom used the room. But when he died, Woody, then sixteen, took possession of it. He added furniture, appliances, the animals' quarters, and of course, his work station. And the food and other supplies, which were mostly stored in the deep recesses of the tunnel, were enough to keep him in comfort indefinitely.

Now he sat at his computer, booted it up. He punched in the entry code, which lit up the color monitors set into the wall directly in front of his work station. Monitors which together had the capability to view every inch of 8 Garden Place. Finally satisfied that everything was in order—the children safe and asleep—he zeroed in on Hollie's bedroom.

The microscopic camera—he had ever so carefully tucked one into each of the overhead light fixtures—caught her perfectly: her right leg bent, her nightgown yanked high enough to expose her thigh . . . and even a little higher. He zoomed in so close he could actually make out the short, curly blond hairs that she likely shaved only in the warmer summer months. The image was so clear that when he reached out to touch the glass monitor, he could feel himself grow hard.

Heart hammering, he pulled his hand back, aware that for now he was there to watch, to keep away those who would only use her. No one would reach her without going through him first—not Dylan, not Roger, not Charlie, surely not Jeremy. Soon his role in her life would be clear—no more having to watch her terror. But he just once wanted her to admit that she needed him.

That's all there is to it, Hollie. . . . Is that so much to ask?

Sleep was something she caught snatches of between getting up, checking and rechecking the children . . . jumping up and out of bed at the least noise, worrying if the lump in her throat was real, and if so, cancerous? And still that awful sense of being watched. Was fear becoming a way of life?

The first decision she made the next morning was to call in sick at work. She might ultimately be risking her job, and though losing her job would surely be a financial catastrophe, worrying about it today was simply too far down on her list of worries.

First, she would keep her promise to Jake and look for Jeremy. Next, if the apartment he'd told her about was still available, she would go and see it. If not, she'd get a copy of the *Courant*, which carried classifieds for Hartford and surrounding areas.

Something decent and cheap. Cheap . . . How cheap did apartments go while still qualifying as 'decent'? Not nearly low enough to fit her budget while she'd need to keep up mortgage payments on

8 Garden Place. Would she be forced to go to her parents again? Oh, Lord, she couldn't bear to even think of that now. Instead she showered, dressed, made breakfast for the children, and sent them off to school. Then she headed to Hartford. Once she got there she'd stop at a phone booth to call work.

Hollie knew about a half-dozen places in Hartford's north end that were known to host around-the-clock poker games. Jeremy's old stomping grounds.

Frank Lorenzo hadn't gotten to sleep until late— the little anecdote about the pigeon reminding him of Hollie's dog, and Paterson's strange assertion that it looked like the animal had battered its own head against the wall. Coincidence?

Frank wasn't much of an expert when it came to operating computers: it began and ended with his familiarity with the few programs Lois used on the office IBM, but that didn't mean he was wholly ignorant of the capabilities. Still, the possibilities hadn't really begun to dawn on him until now.

So after playing the conversation with Woody's MIT prof in his head a dozen times, he was suddenly struck by something more—something that he wasn't sure was possible. Could a computer-produced sound cause a window to smash?

And what about all the explained noises in the house . . . or for that matter, phone wire screw-up? *Come on, Frank, take it slower here.* First off, Dylan had admitted to the phone calls in open court, so dump that theory. Next, sure the kid was a wizard, no doubt capable, but what in the hell might his motive be? He had just met Hollie for the first time . . . what, about three months ago? What could he have against her?

That morning Frank woke earlier than usual, eager for Lois to dig out information on the Woodbury kid. He shaved, showered, and not bothering with breakfast, took a banana to eat on the way. The more he thought about it, the more he felt he might be on to something. In any event, it wouldn't hurt to have another talk with Gardo or Alan. And he would give Hollie a call, just to be sure that she and the kids stayed away from Woodbury—at least till he'd been cleared.

Woody saw Hollie leave for work ahead of schedule—probably trying to make up for the time she took off—then went upstairs to the kitchen to prepare his mother's breakfast. He wasn't all that hungry himself, not with his stomach doing flipflops. He had come to the only decision available to him: he would move Hollie and the kids in with him.

Last night he began to act, getting the four upstairs rooms aired and dusted. All private, away from mother's probing, all quickly and easily fitted with the same audiovisual equipment so that he could keep his eye on them from his work station. But as fine as the accommodations were, they were too unsecured for now. First he'd take them to his workroom, where the acclimation process would begin. Woody spent the next few hours sweeping, opening up cots, cleaning, trying to make the area as pleasant and nonthreatening as possible: still, a cement interior was not exactly *House Beautiful.*

All she had to do was lie back, relax, and enjoy—put Woody Woodpecker in the driver's seat, so to speak. No more fears, no more anxieties, no more worries about being late for work or where her next nickel was coming from. Whatever she wanted, she had only to ask him. And to think that not long ago he had actually considered selling 8 Garden Place to a stranger. Fortunately there had always been something that held him back.

And now look at him . . . about to have his own instant family. Of course he had yet to determine how he'd get them over to the house, but he'd have at least a few days to consider what was involved. And certainly a call to her work and note to her girl-friend Elaine would be in order: "Off with the kids on a much needed vacation to pull myself together. Doctor's orders." At this point, not a difficult concept to buy.

Woody spooned the oatmeal into a bowl, then placing it on a tray next to a glass of OJ, he headed toward his mother's bedroom. He smiled, picturing what he must look like: disheveled, flushed, bright-eyed, and eager, running around doing a bunch of crummy little chores. Here he was with an IQ straight through the stratosphere, always an over-abundance of work waiting at his work station, and what was he doing? Fussing, fussing, fussing, and always for the same fucking woman.

He set the tray on the bedside stand, then hurried to the bathroom to make himself decent. Finally back, he sat on the bed and took a taste of the oat-meal. He set down the spoon, picked up a napkin, and delicately wiped his mouth. Then, in that usual sneering voice, he said, "It's sticky and gummy—no better than pig slop, Leon. After dining in the finest restaurants in Paris, surely you don't expect me to eat this, do you?"

Always a complaint, never a thank you. He stole a peek in her mirror over the vanity, then, sashaying his head in that same way he'd seen Mother do a hundred times, he smiled to her fans.

She had managed to push her conversation with Lenore to the back of her mind, but now it returned. So Jeremy was gambling again . . . couldn't that explain it all? But not returning to his apartment for nearly a week? *Disappeared.* Maybe it was simply Lenore's choice of words that made her so uncomfortable.

Jeremy would not be pleased when he learned she was chasing after him in his sleazy hangouts. And maybe she hadn't a right to do it, but weren't the children to be considered here too? Particularly Jake, so troubled and distracted and uncommunicative—but absolutely determined to reach his father.

The first two places she went to were locked, and though she banged on the doors, there was no answer. Was the recession having an impact on gambling? The next place someone finally came to the door: the man was thin, wore red suspenders, and his eyes were sunken so deep they were nearly lost in his face. The heavy cigarette smoke curled toward the door, and she heard voices in the background.

"Can I do something for you, ma'am?"

"I'm looking for Jeremy Ganz."

"Who're you?"

''His wife,'' she said, clutching her purse to her as she tried to pass him by.

But he moved in front of her, shaking his head. ''Sorry, ma'am, house rules—no women.''

She looked into his face, trying to decide how best to handle the situation. ''I need to see him,'' she said. ''It's important.''

He shrugged.

She started to cry. It came far easier than she had anticipated. And once it started, she couldn't stop it. ''I'm not here to make trouble, I just need to talk to him.''

After an initial annoyance, he sighed. ''Okay, wait here a minute,'' he said, shutting the door in her face. She took out tissues from her pocket, wiped her tears, but more came. She looked around, two criminal types passed through the alley, eyeing her suspiciously. *Damn you to hell, Jeremy, do I really need this too?*

Finally the man was back. ''Not here.''

''I don't believe you.''

''Your prerogative, lady. According to one of the guys, the last your old man was here was about two weeks back. So take it or leave it.'' He shut the door again. This time the lock snapped.

As soon as Frank got to the office, he put in another call to Alan Gray—he left a message on Gray's voicemail telling him to get back to him. Next, he asked Lois to get him a complete rundown on Leon Woodbury.

Finally he tried Hollie's house, but apparently he'd missed her. He followed with a call to her work, which was answered on the twelfth ring by a fellow named Harvey Boynton. According to Boynton, who sounded annoyed, Hollie had only a few minutes earlier phoned in sick. Frank called Gus Paterson and filled him in on his suspicions.

"Do me a favor, Gus. It may be just that she wanted to take a day off, but go to the house, ring the bell, force your way inside if you have to. But make sure everything is kosher."

"I'll get back to you."

He glanced at his watch. "I'm due in court in forty-five minutes. If I'm not here, leave a message with Lois."

He got off the phone and Lois came in with a sheet that she placed in front of him. "A report on Leon Woodbury. Just preliminary stuff so far. But you seemed a little anxious."

He looked at the sheet, mostly information that could be picked up off an extended credit application. One thing that hit him smack in the face, though, was the name, Hollie Ganz. From its construction in 1952 until a little more than three months ago, 8 Garden Place had been owned by S&E, Inc., based in Hartford. The multimillion dollar corporation founded by one Samuel Egan was now owned lock, stock, and barrel by his grandson, Leon Woodbury.

Okay, no major deal . . . in fact, maybe Hollie even knew that Woodbury owned her house. Frank tried Hollie's number again. He let it ring a dozen times—nothing. *Come on, Gus, move it.*

Two more men's clubs, both of which said they hadn't seen Jeremy in months. Finally she drove to his apartment complex on Farmington Avenue, found his name on the lobby index . . . 304, rang his bell. Meanwhile she looked at his mailbox: stuffed to capacity. Finally she gave up and rang the bell marked MANAGEMENT. The buzzer came on immediately, letting her inside.

They exchanged introductions, then the manager, Wally Perkins, led her past a receptionist with fancy, red-framed glasses to an inner office just large enough for a desk, filing cabinet, and two vinyl-covered chairs.

"We have two apartments available," Wally said, one hand scratching his prematurely bald head, the other reaching toward the filing cabinet. He opened the top drawer. "Both one-bedrooms, so if you have any kids I'm afraid you're out of luck."

"That's not why I'm here, Mr. Perkins. My husband, Jeremy Ganz, rents Apartment 304. I've been trying to get a hold of him for more than a week now."

He considered this a moment, then opened the middle drawer and fingered through the G files until he came to Jeremy's. He pulled it out and opened it.

"What I need you to do is—" she began.

He raised his hand. "Uh-uh, sorry, we don't get involved in domestic disputes."

She sat forward, putting her hands on his desk. "No, but this isn't—"

He threw one of his arms out. "According to this, you two are separated. That's reason enough for me to back off." He stood up, snapping a corner of the file with his fingers. "I did my good deed once, a real mistake: I let a guy's wife in his apartment while he was out—she said she wanted to surprise him. So what does she do? She leaves with a purse full of my tenant's personal papers. And I come within inches of losing my job."

"I just need to see if he's all right."

"Call him at work."

Was he really this stupid or was he just acting? "Don't you think I've done that? He hasn't been there."

He backed up a couple of steps to the file cabinet. "Look, I don't mean to be cruel, but what about a girlfriend? Did it ever occur to you he might be shacking up elsewhere? And as for his work, maybe he's just playing hooky."

"I spoke to his friend last night. She was concerned over his absence as well."

He looked down at the floor, shaking his head. "Look, I don't know what you expect me to do."

She stood up and walked toward him. "Just use your master key, let yourself into his apartment, and look around. That's all. And I'll wait right here while you do it. Let me be able to satisfy my little boy when I go home tonight. He's gotten it into his head that something bad has happened to his daddy."

He put Jeremy's file back in the cabinet and slammed the drawer closed. He uttered a loud sigh, then pulled out his key ring. "You wait here," he said.

It was five minutes tops before she heard the hurried footsteps pounding down the carpeted corridor, coming toward the management office. Wally Perkins, pale and out of breath, ran in and shouted to the receptionist.

"Oh, shit, get the police!"

Hollie swallowed, having difficulty getting over the lump that had immediately risen in her throat. She stood up, walked from the inner room to the doorway.

"What's wrong, Mr. Perkins?" the receptionist asked, lifting the receiver.

But he snatched the phone from her hands and, fumbling with the digits, pressed in some numbers.

"What?" Hollie knew she was asking, but was unable to hear her own words above the strange swishing noise in her head. She saw Wally's eyes reflect that someone had picked up the line, then heard his voice odd and far away. She strained to hear the words, but all she could assimilate were bits and pieces: *manager, Brandywine, bloodbath* . . .

He wasn't even aware of Hollie standing there, much less that the ground was suddenly reaching up to grab her. But the receptionist must have been watching, because before Hollie lost consciousness, she heard the woman shout, "Get her, she's fainting!"

CHAPTER
Twenty-two

She woke up in a car . . . an ambulance? She tried to sit up, but a large hand reached out, stopping her. "Hey, take it easy, it's okay," the attendant said.

"Stop . . . where're—"

"We're on our way to Mount Sinai Hospital. You passed out and banged your head. Not to worry, though, they'll have you patched up in no time."

Her mouth opened as the memories pumped in. Jeremy was dead . . . murdered! Who? Again she tried to sit up, but her head only rose a few inches before dizziness again forced her down. She grabbed the attendant's arm, squeezing it. "You don't understand, I need to get to my children!"

Once in the emergency room, she managed to get herself into a sitting position, but just when she'd begun to dismount from the gurney, the nurse, who had left her momentarily, was back to fight her. It finally escalated to a shouting match and a doctor came over.

"What's going on here?"

The nurse put her hands on her hips. "She insists on getting up. She wants to go."

"You have no right to stop me. Tell her!" Hollie insisted.

The doctor picked up her file, then glancing at the pre-admission sheet, nodded to the nurse. "She's right, we can't make her stay." But he gestured to Hollie's scalp, where a towel packed with ice hadn't yet managed to stop the bleeding. "It looks like you might need a few stitches there. And I'd like to order an X ray just to be sure there's no concussion."

Later . . . she didn't have time to deal with that now. First she had to get the kids safely out of Union. She pushed herself up again, and this time she stayed up. She slid down, letting her feet touch the floor, but when she tried to stand alone her weight sank her. The doctor caught her before she hit the floor, and she began to cry.

"Please, let us call someone for you," he said.

Someone had already explained the circumstances to Elaine, so Hollie didn't have to go through it, but still it took her a little time before she could stop crying.

"Oh, honey, I'm so sorry," Elaine said. "You don't have to talk. I'm coming right down there."

"No!" She didn't know how, but she knew for certain that the children were in danger. And she had to make Elaine believe it, too. "Please listen to me, don't come here. Go get the children."

"Of course, not a problem. You can all stay with me . . . through the funeral, through Christmas. As long as you need to."

"They're in danger, Elaine."

"Why, what do you mean?"

"Dylan . . . Jeremy's been murdered."

"No, Hollie, you're wrong about this. I'm sure. Dylan is a nasty kid, but not a murderer. Besides, he didn't even know Jeremy. I think there's a far more rational motive. We both know Jeremy had gone back to gambling. How hard would it be to believe he'd gotten himself in too deep again?"

And this time there was no house, no savings to bail him out of the mess. Hollie supposed it was logical, but to her mind, not wholly convincing. "Elaine, just get the children here, please."

Frank got back to the office at one. On his desk were a folder and three messages. One, an offer of settlement in a malpractice suit, he tossed aside. Another was from Paterson: he had picked the back door lock at the Ganz house and gone inside. No one home, everything in order. The third message was from Alan Gray. On his way to a seminar, he'd left a number where he could be reached at one-thirty.

Finally he opened the file and took out two additional sheets on Leon Woodbury: little out of the ordinary—except for an entry near the bottom of the second page. Leon Woodbury had been questioned extensively on the reported disappearance of one Nina Richards.

He pressed the intercom. "Lois, there's a 'Nina Richards' mentioned in this report. I'd like you to get—"

"Coming . . . just this minute picked it up." She came in, handed him the file.

"Lois, don't ever leave me, okay?"

Though she was in her forties, she was built like a teen—slim and athletic, with an energy level close to a ten. "Does that mean you're ready for another pay hit?"

"See me in three months," he said, already beginning to thumb through all the notes and interviews. Nina Richards had been brought over from Paris at age fifteen by Eleanor Egan Woodbury to be a live-in nanny for her son, Leon. The girl had resided with the Woodbury family for five years, at which time Eleanor dismissed her—for reasons unknown.

Leon, only nine but heir to his grandfather's estate and distraught over the girl's sudden dismissal, set her up at 8 Garden Place, where she continued to reside for the next thirteen years. Rent-free, and with a generous monthly allowance.

At age thirty-three, she disappeared. Her missing status was reported by a neighbor, Roger Spear, who claimed she had told him she was leaving the state. Leon Woodbury, under questioning, said Nina had phoned him, telling him of her plans to move to Colorado. A telephone call *was* found to have been made from her number to his at the time he'd claimed. Apparently she'd said her thank you's and farewells, and though he tried to dissuade her from leaving so suddenly, she insisted she needed to start a new life. Not being privy to her personal life, he could only hope she was making the right decision.

On the other hand, Roger claimed she had been

extremely apprehensive about telling Leon her intentions.

"Why would that be?" the investigating officer had asked.

Roger wasn't quite sure himself. "She said she felt a sense of obligation to Leon. After all, the boy had been good to her for a lot of years—free rent, a living allowance, and all." But to Roger's mind, it seemed like more: "The tie seemed deeper and darker," he said. "Of course, she would never admit to it, being more than eleven years his senior, but I got the feeling that she was intimidated by him."

Frank picked up the phone, tried Hollie's number . . . let it ring about twenty times. He hung up, pressed the intercom. "Lois, see if you can find me some bio on Hollie Ganz, maybe some nearby relatives, someplace she might be now."

Elaine quickly rescheduled a client and left a note for her son. Connecting up her telephone answering machine in her downstairs realty office, she got in her car and headed to Union. She still couldn't believe that Jeremy was dead. It was too horrible to believe.

And Hollie . . . Though Elaine hadn't been able to get through to her last night to learn the results of the hearing, she assumed that Dylan had been scolded and sent home. The little bastard had really done his absolute best to unstring Hollie.

And now Jeremy murdered . . . How many times—seeing the effect Dylan was having on Hollie—had Elaine wanted to advise her to pick up and move back? But always she'd pulled back from saying it, afraid the advice was motivated by her own interests—she so missed Hollie. She did believe Dylan would ultimately stop, and her best friend would get back to her old self, even begin to enjoy her new home.

But not now . . . enough was enough. If Hollie really believed Dylan was capable of murder—then true or not true, it was time she got out of there. And though the subject of moving hadn't been brought up, if Elaine interpreted correctly what Hollie was saying, her friend was more than ready to give up on Union permanently. Elaine glanced at her watch, trying to gauge how much time she had. Fortunately she had Hollie's house key. She would have plenty of time before the kids got home to pack a few boxes of clothes and necessities.

Enough for at least a couple of weeks. The rest could be dealt with later.

Woody still hadn't been able to decide what the cop had been doing there. He had entered illegally, then gone through the house—what was it he expected to find? Whatever it was, he didn't like it, and he liked it less when at one-thirty, after making himself a sandwich, he noticed more activity on the monitor.

He recognized her as she came in the front door, locking it after herself. Hollie's girlfriend: sable-brown hair, a wide, heavy lipped mouth, and good teeth—the one who had helped her paint, who had helped her move in. But what was she doing there now, while Hollie was at work? He watched her go to the phone, dial a number, then after listening a few moments, hang up. Then she went to the cellar door, opened it, and went downstairs. In the basement she picked out a half-dozen empty boxes, brought them up. Two she took to Hollie's bedroom and began to select things to put inside.

Does she think she's going to leave just like that: send a messenger to pack and not even say good-bye?

It took the doctor only a few stitches to close the wound. Then Hollie was transported to X-ray, where they took her without the usual delay. Once the doctor was assured there was no concussion, he agreed to let her go, providing she followed his orders. At her request, he had the receptionist leave a message on Elaine's answering machine, telling her to come by for Hollie once she got back. And Elaine, according to prior plan, would call in to her machine once she'd arrived at Hollie's house.

She looked at the big clock over the nurse's station: one-thirty. Elaine should be getting into Union, if she wasn't there already. In another ninety minutes they'd all be safely on the turnpike, on their way to get her. Once they'd arrive at Elaine's house, she'd phone Frank and let him know what had happened. Then came the awful part, to tell the children that their father had been murdered.

Doctor's orders were bed rest through tomorrow, and with that came three prescriptions: one for penicillin, to be taken for five days to prevent infection; another for Tylenol with codeine, to be used only as needed; and a third for Librium, to be taken four times a day for three days minimum, and thereafter as needed. She had already taken the antibiotic and tranquilizer, the latter hitting her like a Mack truck: though it didn't touch the sadness, she felt a thick barrier between it and her, allowing a strange calm to settle over her.

"No local relatives," Lois said. "No brothers or sisters. The parents live in a retirement community in Palm Beach, Florida. I do have a home and work number for the estranged husband."

"Try him. What about friends?"

"I have an Elaine Byers, she lives in Bloomfield. She's used for a 'call for emergency' number on several forms. Two numbers, one's a realty office."

"Try her as well." He looked at his watch: finally, one-thirty. Gray should be back from the seminar.

The first thing Elaine had done was to call her answering machine, and the message from the hospital was already waiting. She sighed in relief that Hollie was at least physically all right. Trying to select what Hollie would want from her closet and drawers, she stopped for a moment, thinking she might have heard something. She listened, but now hearing nothing, she went back to packing. It was only a few minutes later when something made her look toward the doorway: a boy was standing there, watching her. She gasped, her arms jerking upward.

"Dylan?" she said finally.

"Who, me?" he said, putting his hand to his chest, then smiling. "Not a nice thing to say."

"Then who are you, and what're you doing in here?"

"Easy now, I didn't mean to freak you. I'm from across the street, Leon Woodbury . . . Woody."

Elaine nodded, then smiled. "Hollie's mentioned you. My gosh, you didn't have to scare me like that. Well, it's good to meet you. I'm a friend, Elaine Byers."

"Did she really mention me? What'd she say?" Woody asked, ignoring the rest of what she'd said.

Elaine shrugged, then similarly ignored his question. "How did you get in here?"

"You locked the front door, not the back."

"What makes you think I locked the front?"

"I surmised as much. You look like a careful lady. And I'm sure you know all the trouble Hollie's been having."

"Why didn't you just knock?"

"Hollie and I have gotten pretty close, we don't stand on ceremony." He gestured to the boxes. "So what's going on here?"

She looked at him, wondering if she should tell him. But from all Hollie had told her, he was a good neighbor. So clearly he'd want to know. "Jeremy was killed," she said. "Hollie just found it out."

"Jesus, no—hasn't she been through enough?"

If he was a good actor, he wasn't bothering to put on his best performance for her. Obviously insincere. Elaine went back to packing, not commenting.

"Do they know who did it?"

She shook her head.

"Well, where's Hollie?"

"When she found out, she passed out . . . and as

luck would have it, fell and hurt her head. Nothing serious, but she needed a few stitches. Right now she's in the Mount Sinai emergency room waiting for me to pick her up. She and the kids will be staying with me for a while, at least until this is over.''

He nodded to the two cardboard boxes. ''It looks like you're packing for a month.''

She shrugged. ''Well, it's not been decided yet if she's coming back.''

''I think that would be a mistake.''

''Really? Well, I don't.''

''Why, because you'd rather she be with you?''

She felt thrown a little off-balance—if she was interpreting what he'd said right, it sounded more like something from a jealous boyfriend than a concerned neighbor. She stood up. ''I *would* like her closer; sure, I won't deny that. But I also want to see her happy. And I'm afraid she got off to a bad start here.''

''She'll be a lot happier with Jeremy out of her life. He was an albatross, in case you didn't happen to notice. Not that anyone wished harm to come to him, but life is funny. It sometimes knows the right road to pick and takes it without asking permission.''

She stared at him, then edged toward the doorway. He wasn't especially big—but nevertheless strangely threatening. ''Listen, do you mind? Could we continue this outside? I have a few things Hollie asked me to find in—''

But just as she made it through the doorway to the hall, he grabbed her from behind, one strong arm clamped across her chest and the other hand clutching a small knife at her throat.

Her voice came out a whisper. "You're really Dylan, aren't you?"

"No. Why would I lie about such a thing? I'm Hollie's best friend, what's there to hide?" He began to drag her through the house toward the kitchen, then down the basement stairs to the finished room. The wall of bookcases was turned . . . like a huge mouth, leading down a dozen steps, into some kind of dark cavern. *Woody was the one doing all those things to Hollie, not Dylan! Oh God, how can that be?*

"Oh, please, no." she begged. "Why're you doing this?"

He didn't have much time to get her bloodstained clothes off her and put them on himself. Then, holding a brown shopping bag stuffed with his own clothes high in his arms to partially hide his face, he walked to Elaine's car, got in, and drove off. He parked two streets away, took the backyard route to his own house and entered through the rear door. It was two-fifteen when he got into his kitchen and took off her snugly-fitted coat, stretch slacks, and high heels. Allison would be home any time now.

Al Gray verified Frank's thoughts on computer-generated sound, how it could break glass, even going into some of the technicalities that were not as easy to follow. He described how a computer could trigger telephone A to ring telephone B at a predetermined time, without the computer being in the proximity of either telephone.

Would Dylan have confessed to making those calls if he hadn't done it. Maybe Charlie had told him it was not worth the fight just to be double-stamped a liar, then not believed on anything else he might say. After all, there was "proof" of him making those calls.

Okay, so what did he have on this kid, Woody? He was oddly possessive of Hollie; there was a mystery surrounding Nina Richards, but no indication of wrongdoing; no signs of struggle, no blood, no body. Woody, despite his generosity to his former nanny, was never seen socializing with her, not even any neighborly visiting from one house to another. Wasn't it possible Nina had just taken off and Roger's accusations were those of a rejected suitor, trying to soothe a bruised ego?

And most important here with respect to Hollie, there was no motive. Some sick kind of love, but he hardly knew her. And this had all started what . . . within a week of her moving to Union? Maybe she had known him before. Maybe she had known Woody was the one who'd sold her the house. . . .

He picked up the phone and got Sampson Realty, the same outfit that had sold Hollie the house. He asked for the owner, Kathryn Morrison, but she wasn't expected in until later. He left a message asking that she get back to him. As soon as he put down the phone, the intercom buzzed.

"Yeah?"

"Funny things happening around here."

"Really? Tell me."

"Well, I couldn't reach the girlfriend, Elaine. Home line no answer, work number she has a message on her answering machine that she'll be back at four. At Jeremy Ganz's work, they as much as said he was no longer an employee. In any event, they haven't heard from him in over a week."

"You try his home?"

"That's the part I was getting to. It was answered by a police officer."

"Why?"

"He wouldn't say. I told him this was the state's attorney's office in Union, but he said he couldn't give out information. If we wanted some, to get in touch with headquarters."

"Okay, why don't—"

"Hold your socks, Frank—I already called Hartford headquarters. A Detective Steven Lancer is in charge of the case, but he wasn't available. I did talk to one of the office staff, though, and she filled me in. Jeremy Ganz was found in his apartment, dead. Stab wounds."

"Jesus Christ," Frank said, immediately wondering if there was a tie-in. "What about suspects?"

"They think it has to do with gambling debts."

"Yeah," he said, slightly relieved, remembering when Gus had tailed him. "I suppose that's possible. When did it happen?"

"Management discovered the body this afternoon, but according to the coroner he's been dead several days."

"What made them open the apartment, some kind of tip?"

"That's all she knew."

He looked at his watch: he had a deposition in ten minutes in Manchester. "Keep on trying Lancer, okay? If you get him, ask him to fax whatever he's got. Tell him I might have a different perspective on this, and I'll get back to him. And Hollie's friend Elaine, call her again at four. Keep trying the house, too."

"Do you think that Woodbury kid is involved in all this?"

"Thinking's not enough. And listen, if you do reach Hollie, I want you to call me at the deposition. I want to talk to her right away. There are questions I need to ask her."

Had she known Woody was the one who'd sold her the house? Had he known her before? Gus Paterson, mostly in jest, had implied there was something more than friendship between the kid and Hollie that night Jeremy had showed up half-cocked and taking swings at the kid. Could he have been right? If so, then why had she lied, told him just yesterday that it was strictly a friendship between them?

If Woody was connected to the Ganz murder, it meant the kid was way over the edge. But there was nothing at all to connect him to the murder, and he was letting his imagination run amok. Frank came up to the elevator outside his office and banged his fist against the wall. Dammit, so where was Hollie?

At two o'clock, late already for his deposition but suddenly realizing high school was about to get dismissed, Frank stopped at a phone booth on the road to call the office.

"Lois, call the chief, tell him what's going on with the Ganz case and ask him to get a car over to Garden Place, okay? The kids will be arriving home from school soon—that is, assuming Hollie hasn't already gotten them dismissed—you check that out first. Anyway, I'd feel better if there was someone keeping an eye on them. Tell the officer not to stick too close to the house—no need to alarm the kids unnecessarily. Particularly if they don't yet know about their father. But the bottom line is, under no circumstances is Woodbury to be alone with them."

"Okay, Frank."

"And tell whoever is assigned there not to leave until Hollie Ganz is home, at which time she's to contact me."

CHAPTER
Twenty-three

Things were starting to look up already, ever since her mother had told her and Jake they'd be leaving Union. Though Mom didn't say they'd be moving back to Bloomfield, Allison fully intended to try to push her mother's thinking in that direction. She knew it wasn't convenient to her mom's office, but there were other jobs in this world, weren't there?

When she noticed a police car up the street, she wondered who'd called them. But since it was parked two houses away, she didn't think any more about it.

Allison went up to her front door, took out her key. As soon as she began to turn the knob, she felt that something was wrong. But she had to stop being such a baby someday, so she pushed open the door. And of all people, there was Woody standing not a foot away, grinning like he'd really put something over on her. She sighed, closed the door, her hand pressed against her chest. "What're you doing, trying to scare me like that?" she began.

Then suddenly there was something putrid being

held over her mouth and nose, making her nauseous, dizzy. And there was Woody still grinning, as though this were a game. Why was he doing this to her?

Woody carefully transported Allison to his workroom, not wanting to hurt her. When he got back to 8 Garden Place, he unpacked the boxes, then returned them to the cellar. By the time all that was done, Jake was about due to come home . . . and Woody had forgotten the chloroform. He began to run, and had just gotten into the tunnel when he heard the door open and Jake call out, ''Allison, you home?''

Well, he didn't need a drug really, did he? The boy was only eight years old. He took a deep breath, walked back through Hollie's office, then to the bottom of the stairs. Finally he called to Jake. First no answer, then Jake opened the cellar door in the kitchen and looked down.

''What're you doing there, Woody?'' he asked.

''Just checking for mice.''

''Why?''

''Your mom's always complaining of noises down here. So I figured I'd check it out, bring a few traps over. And no sooner had I set one with some of my best strong cheddar, I picked up a victim. Want to come see?''

Jake came down a few stairs. ''Where's Allison?''

Woody shrugged. ''I guess not yet home.''

''Maybe I should go look for her.''

''Come on, she doesn't need someone checking on her. She's probably with her boyfriend.''

"She doesn't have one anymore." He shook his head, began to turn. "Besides, she's never late. I think I'd better—"

Woody took a leap toward him, and Jake ran, heading for the front door. Just as Jake's hand reached the doorknob, Woody caught up to him and grabbed him.

"Hey, Jake, you're a pretty decent runner," he said, now holding him by the back of the collar.

"Let me go!" Jake cried, fighting to get free. "I want to go and find Allison!"

"You listen to me, do what I say, and you won't get hurt."

"I'm going to tell my father on you!"

"Sorry to have to tell you this, buddy, but your dad's dead." His tone was menacing. No more fun and games.

Jake's eyes widened, then a low whimpering began to come from somewhere inside him.

"You knew, didn't you, Jake? Come on, be up front with Woody. Besides, I could tell. Why else would you have gone through all that silly business trying to call him?"

Jake swung out, his thumb poking Woody in the eye. Woody grabbed Jake and shook him so hard his glasses fell to the floor. The child's body suddenly went limp. Woody picked up the glasses, put them back on him.

"From now on think of *me* as your daddy. Okay, Jake?"

Tears started to well up in the little kid's eyes, but he grasped Woody's hand like he was supposed to and went right along with him through the secret tunnel. It wasn't until Woody had settled him on the cot alongside his sister, exited the workroom, and climbed the stairs to his mother's bedroom that he even thought about the injury to his eye. He stood in front of the vanity mirror for a few moments, examining it.

There was a cop sitting quietly in his cruiser up the street when Woody pulled his car out from the garage, backed it out of the driveway, and headed toward Hartford.

Hollie had slept some . . . or maybe just blanked out—snatches of time passing with no memories. She now looked at the clock again, playing silly mind games guessing how far Elaine and the kids were from the hospital. Assuming Elaine had left Union the moment Jake got home from school, they ought to be here any minute. She should have told Elaine to pack a few things for her and the kids. *Oh, who cares? We can borrow, buy, whatever . . .*

And the next thing she knew, she was hearing what sounded like Woody's voice. How was that? She lifted her head a bit and sure enough, she saw Woody standing at the reception desk—his usual jeans and sweatshirt and short out-of-date haircut—talking to a clerk, nodding his head, picking up some papers: Hollie's prescriptions.

Where's Elaine? she thought, and as she did it occurred to her: if not for the tranquilizer gratefully buffing her perceptions, she would by now be geared up for the worst possible scenario.

* * *

"I can sit up," she said, but he wasn't hearing any of it as he settled her down in the backseat with a pillow and down quilt. "Besides, Elaine lives only fifteen minutes away. I still don't understand why she couldn't pick me up."

"Doctor's orders: bed rest, total calm," he said, ignoring her last question. "And if you think I'm going against those orders, you're mistaken. Oh yes, I need to stop, pick up those prescriptions. It's almost that time again."

Maybe I should only take a half-dose of the Librium, she thought, but later when Woody came out of the pharmacy and gave her two pills with fruit juice to wash them down, she didn't argue. She wondered what had happened to his eye—it looked a little swollen. But lying down and with the car once again in motion, she felt too exhausted to even wonder, let alone ask.

Jeremy was dead . . . she remembered that. Oh, how she wished she could forget.

It was after four when Frank again called the office. "What's happening, Lois?"

"Parks is watching the house. He checked in with me about fifteen minutes ago. According to him, the kids came home as expected, so all is well on that front. But no sign of the mother yet. I did get through to Elaine Byers' house. A boy about twelve answered, said she wasn't home—he too expected her back about four. But so far, nada."

"Damn it."

"I could call the kids. . . . "

A pause as he thought about it. "I don't want

them frightened or suspicious while they're all alone.''

''Leave it to me, I'll be low-key. One positive thing is, Leon Woodbury's not home to bother anyone. Parks saw him drive off before three.''

Frank got back to the office about an hour later.

''Talk to Allison?''

''Line's been busy since I spoke to you. I would have had the operator cut in, but I didn't want to alarm the kids.''

''You did right,'' he said starting into his office.

''Wait,'' she said, standing. ''Before you go in there. Something came through about fifteen minutes ago. I figured you to be on your way back, so I didn't even bother trying to catch you. Besides, I thought maybe it was me seeing something not really there. I mean, I only saw Hollie Ganz once.''

''What're you talking about?''

''Come,'' she said, leading him into his office. She went to his desk, picked up a picture. ''Look at this.''

''Hollie.''

''No, that's just it. You would think that at first glance, wouldn't you? But that's actually a photograph of Nina Richards. Roger Spear gave it to the police when he reported her disappearance.''

Frank took the picture from Lois and studied it. She was right: once you looked more closely, you could see the differences. But with the coloring, the hair, even the shape of face, well, the resemblance was remarkable.

So was it a coincidence the house had been empty,

according to Frank's calculation, about two years, before Woodbury had finally decided to sell it to Hollie Ganz? A woman who looked like his childhood nanny, the same woman he now didn't want to see leave?

She would have stayed in that semiconscious state if Woody had not begun to talk off the wall. Did he know she was listening, or was he just hoping she was?

"I want her to rethink her position, is all," he said at first. And Hollie came close to saying *Who?* when she heard the reply come back in an old woman's voice: "Stop lying! Don't put on your act with me, young man! I can see right through you."

Was she going crazy, or was that his mother's voice? Hollie forced her eyes open to see if maybe, in her state, she hadn't noticed someone sitting up in the passenger seat. But, no, only Woody.

"I need her, Mommy." The little-boy voice whined, "Please, oh, please, don't make her go."

"Little boys mustn't argue with their mommies."

"You gave her to me, she's mine! And I won't let you take her away!"

Hollie swallowed hard. She closed her eyes— better not to see. Where was he taking her? To Elaine's? No, not likely there. She could feel hot tears sliding from beneath her eyelids into her hair.

Oh, God, the children—where are they?

CHAPTER
Twenty-four

"Jake?"

He sat on the cot beside her, staring into space.

Now Allison fully opened her eyes, and looked around. Where were they? She reached her arm out. "Jake?"

Still silence.

It was Woody who had put that smelly stuff over her mouth, taken her here . . . and, she guessed, taken Jake too. But it didn't make sense. Why? She sat up and put her hand on her brother's arm. He didn't even try to push her away.

"Did he hurt you?" she asked.

Finally he looked up at her as though he had just realized she was there. "He killed Daddy," he said.

Her hand pressed down hard against his arm. "Jake! Don't say that."

He just stared at her, not a trace of emotion on his face. "But he did."

"I said, stop!"

Big tears began to fill his eyes, then spill over, sliding down his cheeks.

"I want you to take it back." He shook his head, and she pleaded, "Please. Oh, please, Jake."

Now he began to sob, strange, terrible wails of pain that frightened her. She put her arms around him, and he clung to her as a heaviness settled in her chest. She could taste the salt of his tears, hers too. *Daddy is dead.* . . . Her mind kept on saying those words over and over and over. And Woody had killed him.

Frank was just walking out the door, heading to Hollie's house, when the phone rang again. Lois answered it, then covered the mouthpiece, gesturing him to stop.

"You put in a call earlier to a Kathryn Morrison from Sampson Realty?"

He came back and took the receiver. "Thanks for calling back, Miss Morrison. Listen, I have a few questions I need answered. Related to the property at 8 Garden Place."

"Oh really, what a coincidence. That property is just about to be put on the market again."

Surprised, he sank down onto the corner of Lois's desk. "Oh?"

"Yes, the owner called late yesterday afternoon."

He lifted his arm, cupped his hand across the back of his neck. "Hollie Ganz."

"That's right. She left a message with the receptionist to that effect, though I haven't been able to reach her yet to find out the particulars. In any event, what can I do for you?"

"I want to know if Hollie Ganz knew who S&E, Inc. was when she purchased the property."

"I don't know what you mean by that."

"Did she know it was Leon Woodbury who actually sold her the property?" he could tell she was weighing her answer—thinking how she might best cover her ass, he supposed.

"Well, no, not unless he told her. But I didn't do anything illegal. After all, Leon simply wanted his privacy. There's no law saying the seller can't remain behind the scenes."

"Why such a need for privacy?"

"I really don't know. And to be honest, I didn't think it was my place to ask."

"Did he meet Mrs. Ganz first?"

"Oh no, nothing like that."

It didn't make sense—too coincidental. In fact, Frank would have been willing to bet his paycheck that Woodbury had a hand in this Nina lookalike buying the house. "Were there other prospects?" he asked.

"Well, sure. It was a bad market, but the price he was asking was not unreasonable. I'd say in the two years we had the exclusive on it, we had quite a number of parties interested."

"And none offered to buy?"

"Actually, several met his price. But it was always one thing or another they couldn't agree upon. Twice Leon changed his mind and refused to sell, for apparently no reason. After that I was so ticked off, I not only cut off advertising, I tried to discourage people from looking at the property. If I could interest them in something else, I did."

"So how did Mrs. Ganz learn of it?"

"Word of mouth, which is usually the best advertisement. In her case, I think she said her boss had heard about it and, knowing she was looking, told her."

"Miss Morrison, it's important to think about this: could Leon have seen Mrs. Ganz before the passing of papers, perhaps informally when you were showing her around the outside?"

A pause; then: "Well, I suppose it's possible, but . . . No, Leon wasn't outdoors that first day. I even remember looking over at his well-manicured lawn and wondering why he hadn't had his gardener do a little work on number 8."

"You say that *first* day. Was there another?"

"A couple of days later she came back to show her girlfriend the inside, but it was at night and we parked in the driveway. No way Leon could have seen her. But what if he did, what's this about?"

"Bear with me a little," he said. "So you say you personally took her both times."

"Right."

"And she liked the house right off?"

"I think what she liked most was the location, but still there was hesitation—after all, the property needed work. Actually what made the sale was S&E dropping the price a ridiculous thirty thousand. Bringing it down to eighty-five."

Frank's antenna went up: somehow, some way, Woodbury had to have seen Hollie. "Quite an unusual bargain for that neighborhood, wouldn't you say?"

"Oh, no doubt about it. It was an absolute steal, and she was aware of it."

"So why do you suppose Woodbury suddenly dropped the price like that?"

"I assume he wanted to sell it."

"But in the past he was ambivalent."

"Well, people do make up their minds eventually, don't they?"

"Yeah, sure, but from what you say, he'd had other offers meeting his original price. Besides don't you think it peculiar that the person he dropped the price for was a lady who resembled the former tenant?"

A pause; then: "I don't know, I didn't really think about it."

"Then you did know Nina Richards?"

"I'd seen her a number of times, if that's what you mean. She never really impressed me."

"Oh, why's that?"

"My father and aunt live on the street—Margaret and Roger Spear. Well, my father used to have a crush on her, as did a number of the other men in the neighborhood. She was one of those sweet, helpless types. Pretending shyness—that is, until she'd sunbathe on the front lawn in a string bikini. One of those females that other women might not want for a neighbor."

"Did you notice the physical resemblance between Hollie Ganz and her?"

"Yes, actually, I did. I didn't say anything, though. I mean, it wasn't exactly relevant to our business. And then with the negative association to the house . . . well, what was the point?"

"What happened to Nina Richards?"

"Well, I don't know. Leon says she moved to Colorado. But my father insists there was foul play."

The cruiser was still parked in the same place when Woody came up Garden Place at four-thirty. He pulled into the driveway, pressed the remote for the garage door, and drove in. Once the car had cleared the door, it closed automatically. Hollie was so weak from the double medication he'd given her, combined with the trauma she'd gone through, that it was not surprising he had to carry her in.

"Welcome," he said, putting his face very close to hers. His features looked loose and large, like they were being reflected to her from a trick mirror. "This is going to be your home, Hollie, a place where none of the other men will bother you. How does it feel? Finally, you don't have to be afraid."

Reality still seemed to be at a distance. Though she was aware of what was happening to her, she seemed to be seeing and hearing it secondhand. What she wanted to ask—that is, if she could get her voice to operate—was, *Where are the children and Elaine?*

He took her into a wide hallway, opened a door, and began to take her downstairs. Then, as though he'd somehow read her mind, he said, "The kids are fine, waiting patiently for their mommy. And best to forget Elaine—she's not family."

No, he's right—Elaine isn't family, she thought fuzzily.

"Oh, by the way, I told Jake about Jeremy to give

him a head start in the recovery process. I imagine by now he's told Allison, which will make your job with them all that much easier. And if you can't yet see it for yourself, Hollie, let me give you a well-thought-out and objective view: Jeremy was a leech, the kind that refuses to unhook from your skin until he manages to suck you bloodless and drag you under with him. I'm serious about this, Hollie. Think about what I'm saying when you talk to the kids, okay?''

Yes, I'll think about it when my mind lets me.

He stopped in a small den downstairs and laid her on a sofa. ''Before I settle you in with the kids, I want to explain some things. For starters, there's nothing to be afraid of. All I want to do, all I've ever wanted to do, is love and take care of you. That's it—not so bad, huh?'' He gave her his crooked, boyish grin.

She didn't answer or even gesture.

''Now, where you and the kids are staying temporarily is my workroom. I just about live there myself.'' He raised his hand. ''It's underground.''

Uh-uh, don't like it. Tell him so. Open your mouth and make him hear you. What's the matter with you?

''But not to let it spook you,'' he went on, apparently having known it would. ''Of course, once things are better understood between us, the rooms upstairs will be much more to your liking. You'll see what I mean. But first off, we need to get you and the kids healed.''

The rooms upstairs? But what about his mother, didn't he once tell her that she didn't like guests? No, that wasn't quite it. There was something else

Hollie knew about Woody's mother, something so terrible and ugly that she absolutely refused to think about it now.

He reached out and with his fingers wiped away tears that must have been trailing down her face. His wet fingers went into her hair, playing little roads and channels through it, then moving back again to touch her skin—rough, bitten fingertips scratching along her face. He smiled down at her, and she shut her eyes tightly. *Go away, whoever you are. Scat, scat, go away!*

Finally, with a deep sigh, he lifted his hands off her, stood up, and went to the wall of bookcases. He pushed it . . . and it moved. Just like the bookshelves that night at her house. He came back, lifted her, then through the space created by the moving wall, carried her inside. As he set her down again, she could make out the faces of Allison and Jake in the background.

She wanted to run to them, hug them, explain to them that this was only a nightmare and soon they would all wake. But she still couldn't make her voice or body work. . . .

When Frank turned the corner onto Garden Place it was already dark—the lights in the living room at number 8 were on, but there was no car in the driveway, so Hollie hadn't yet arrived. He looked at his watch: five-thirty. If she had gone to work, she'd likely be home by now. He pulled up beside the cruiser. Parks put down a comic book and rolled down his window.

"Nothing exciting here, Frank. The kids are fine, haven't left the house once."

"Which house is Woodbury's?"

Parks pointed to the stone house across the way. "Not a problem there. He drove off before three, came home just before dark, about a quarter to five. Nothing at all unusual."

"Okay, I'm going to the house to wait with the kids. I don't suppose there's any need for you to stick around. Do me a favor, tell the chief I might need surveillance here tonight."

Frank pulled into the driveway, went to the door. He rang the bell, waited a minute, then rang again. He tried to look in through the front window, but the drapes were pulled. He went around back, climbed the back steps, banged on the door. Nothing. No one.

Finally he went to one of the bedroom windows, and wrapping his handkerchief around his hand, broke the glass. He unlocked the window and climbed in, calling out again as he began to run from one empty room to the next. Okay, what was going on here—where the hell were the kids?

He rushed to the phone, called the precinct dispatcher, and asked to be connected through to Parks.

"Christ, can't a guy go home?" he said, picking up Frank's call from his cruiser.

"The kids aren't here."

Frank waited a moment for Parks to digest it. "That's impossible, Frank," he said finally. "No way they could have gotten by me."

''Well, it seems they did. When I drove up you were reading a comic book. . . . ''

''Hey, hold it there a minute! I just picked the stupid thing off the floor not five minutes earlier. So if you're insinuating that I—''

''Okay, forget it. What about the back door?'' Frank glanced out toward the backyard: there was a small wooded area that covered the distance to the next street. ''Any way they might have gotten out through there?''

He thought about it a moment. ''Well, I suppose anything is possible . . . but damn it, I would have seen if they went through the yard to the woods. Or alternatively, if someone came in through that route. At least I would have before it got dark.''

''Did you see the lights go on in the Ganz living room?''

Again he thought about it. ''I didn't really notice when they came on,'' he said.

''And you're sure about the Woodbury kid getting home before dark?''

''Absolutely. I saw him, the same kid who left about ninety minutes earlier.''

''Alone?''

''Yes, alone.''

''Describe him.''

''I don't know, plain features, wide jaw. Crew cut.''

''Okay.'' None of it made sense. The kids were here after school. Why would they suddenly disappear? His logic told him Leon had to be involved, but here was Parks giving him a clean bill of health. And where the hell was Hollie?

"Frank, you there?"

"Yeah . . . do me a favor, put me on with the chief."

CHAPTER
Twenty-five

Woody had prepared tomato soup and tuna sandwiches for dinner—something light and nutritious. He was trying his best to be as considerate as possible, leaving them to themselves as much as possible. And so far it looked like the right way to handle things: when he had brought their dinner, he noticed Hollie trying to fight through the drugs so she could communicate with the kids.

He was putting away the clean dishes when the doorbell interrupted him. He tucked the dish towel into the waist of his jeans and headed for the front door.

The first thing Frank noticed was his bloodshot eye . . . and a light bruise beneath. He was wiping his hands on the dish towel, looking slightly flustered. "Mr. Lorenzo, hello."

"Hi there, Leon. Mind if I come in?"

The door opened, letting him in. "Leon, I know you're pretty close to Hollie and the kids. I was wondering if you had an idea where they might be," he said, hoping the direct approach would catch Woody off-guard.

He shook his head. ''I didn't realize they were out.''

''Have you seen them at all today?''

''No. Yesterday Hollie was pretty despondent after that hearing, so I stayed with her a while. But then I had things to do so I left. Why, what's going on?''

Frank looked past the entry into the living room: everything neat and in place. ''There's been some trouble. Tell me, Leon, were you out of the house today?''

''Yeah, I had some computer problems. I took the computer to the college to work on it. . . . I could do it here, but they've got all the diagnostic equipment.''

There was a stairway that led to a second floor. ''About what time would you say that was?''

Woody tilted his head, then attempting to make light of what was going down, said, ''This is beginning to sound like an interrogation, Mr. Lorenzo.''

''It's real important I find Hollie and the kids.''

''Maybe if you could tell me what the trouble is, I could help.''

''I suppose I could. Jeremy Ganz was found murdered in his apartment this afternoon.''

''Whoa . . .'' Woody stepped back, shook his head.

The reaction sounded okay, but there was something in the kid's eyes that implied otherwise. ''The thing is, we're concerned that the rest of the family might be in danger.''

"Why would that be?"

"It's assumed to be gambling-related." Did he notice a glimmer of relief in Woodbury's eyes, or was he just seeing what he wanted to see? "It seems Jeremy didn't always hang out with the best people. So one never knows how far a person might go to make a collection."

Woody nodded his head a few times. "Yeah, Hollie mentioned the gambling." A pause; then: "Look, I want to help all I can. As far as me going out, it must have been about three. And I got home at about four-thirty, maybe after. You'd probably get a more accurate time from that cop who was sitting up the street."

"Look, Leon, you're a pretty bright guy, so let me be candid here. Though the Hartford police are handling the murder investigation, we're concerned here about protecting Hollie and the kids. Now, suddenly it turns out we don't know where they are. This doesn't make me or the police department happy. And considering the trouble the Ganzes have had since moving to this neighborhood, it would be sloppy of us to limit our investigation to the Bradleys."

"Sure, I understand."

"You do? Good. Then perhaps you wouldn't mind showing me around the house. We're asking cooperation of all the neighbors, so don't take it personally. Of course you may refuse if you wish, I don't have a warrant."

Woody stepped back, his hands gesturing Frank inside. "No problem," he said. "Come on, follow me."

He took Frank through the house, room by room. According to Woodbury, the rooms upstairs that were now unused had been his during his teens. ''The only way the folks could get me to stay on,'' he said. ''I was always threatening to move out on my own to get privacy.''

''I imagine you'd require it in your work. Where do you keep the computer?''

''In my bedroom normally. But as I mentioned, it's now in the lab at school.''

''And your bedroom is here,'' Frank said, walking in and looking around the first-floor bedroom.

''Right.''

''And what's this?'' Frank asked, as he came out and opened an adjacent door in the hallway.

''Oh, just the cellar. Not a big deal.''

Seeing that Frank was still curious, Woody led him downstairs. It was just a small den with built-in bookshelves, connected to a larger cellar area with the usuals: washer, dryer, gas burner and hot-water heater.

As Frank was leaving, he asked about the bruised eye. Woodbury averted his eyes some, as though he felt foolish needing to relate the details. ''That, Mr. Lorenzo, is thanks to a football. There I was walking across the parking lot minding my business, and this ball heads right for me.'' He shrugged and grinned. ''I never was much of a receiver.''

Odd: the one red silk dress hanging on the back of the kid's bedroom door, the items of makeup and flashy jewelry lying on the dressing table. Maybe a girlfriend, or better yet, maybe a cross-dresser. The bottom line was he not only cooperated, let Frank go over every inch of space, but there was no one but Woodbury in that house. So where were Hollie and the kids?

Outside, he saw Paterson's cruiser. As arranged, he and Hanks were canvassing the neighborhood, asking questions. An officer on foot was standing, watching the back of Woodbury's house. Another cruiser was manned and waiting out front. Everyone alert to ensure that the kid went nowhere without a shadow.

Frank had opted to talk to the Bradleys, and it was Charlie who answered the door. Dylan—who Frank spotted in the background—walked in closer when he heard his father say, "What's-a-matter, Lorenzo? They finally demote you to cop?"

"I want to talk to Dylan."

"I thought this shit was all over."

"Jeremy Ganz was found murdered in his apartment today."

Charlie perked up, interested. "The lady's husband, I take it?"

"Right."

Then realizing they were now talking murder, his interest turned to his son. "What do you want with Dylan?"

"We want to question him. Hollie Ganz, the girl, the boy, are all missing."

"Since when?"

"Hollie hasn't been seen all day. She called in sick to work this morning. And the kids were last seen going into their house after school. We had a cruiser out here watching all afternoon. Yet at five-thirty when I went in to search the house, it was empty.''

''Either sloppy surveillance, or Hollie Ganz and her kids are a coven of witches.'' He shook his head, eyes bright, and Frank felt like smashing him in the mouth.

''You really think this is funny?''

''No, I really think you have a problem. But you're not going to get my son involved in it. So unless you have some kind of charge here, I'm going to be saying good night.''

''Wait,'' Frank said, putting his hand on the door. ''What do you know about Leon Woodbury?''

''Why?''

''He's been friendly with the Ganz family. I think he's involved in all this.''

Charlie shook his head, chuckled. ''A little late in coming, wouldn't you say, prosecutor?'' He hesitated a moment before he said, ''Look, all I know about the kid is, he's weird.''

''Give me an example.''

He thought a minute. ''Okay, an example. Years ago—he must have been about nine, ten—he used to have a bird pavilion off his upstairs bedroom window, whatever. A big board about five by five where he'd put feed to attract them, I'd see him take some birds inside the house with him now and then. I figured he played with them, tried to train them. What else would you figure?

A rhetorical question that Frank didn't bother answering, so Charlie went on. ''One morning I was jogging past the house when I saw him put out there a cat and a bird with a busted wing. One pecked, the other scratched, and both of them squealed and danced—each other trying to do in the other without going off the edge."

"What finally happened?"

"I don't know, I left. It was a little too sick for my blood."

Lois was still in the office when Frank called her at seven-thirty.

"Anything?"

"Only that I reached Mike Byers, Elaine's husband. According to him, it's not like her to be late and not call in. He's contacted friends, neighbors. He's really concerned."

"Did you get a make on her car?"

"No."

"Get one . . . for Hollie's car too. Ask whoever's covering the radios to put a line on both. Were you able to reach Detective Lancer?"

"Still trying to get more information. It's a madhouse over there—apparently a fire broke out in the state house. People trapped in elevators, traffic tie-ups, you name it."

He got off the phone, walked around the house, again looking through the rooms. Then, getting a flashlight from one of the kitchen drawers, he went out the back door, down a few steps to the yard. He stopped, turned: from where Parks was sitting earlier, he would have easily seen the kids if they'd left through the yard. Or if Woody or anyone else had tried to get inside. He looked to the right-side yard: if they had hung close to the back of the house, cut over to the next yard or the one after, then crossed to the next street . . .

As he was determining how Parks might possibly have missed seeing them, he heard footsteps come up behind. Not the men—they would have immediately identified themselves. Frank turned quickly, surprising and grabbing the arm of his possible assailant.

"Hey, wait, it's me!" the voice said, trying to pull away. Frank focused on the face of Dylan Bradley.

"What're you doing here?"

He was wearing a blue-and-white parka and jeans. "Just thought maybe I could help."

"Are you saying you know where they are?"

He took a stick of gum from his pocket, tossed the wrapper, then put the gum in his mouth. "Uh-uh, I'm not saying that."

"Then what?"

"Just that I know things maybe no one else does. About Nina Richards, about Woodbury."

None of it had gone the way he'd planned: Hollie's girlfriend coming to take the kids away, him needing to pick Hollie up at the hospital in Hartford. All unplanned and therefore risky. And now Frank Lorenzo was on his tail. What was he going to do now? He looked out the living room window across the street: a car was parked in Hollie's driveway. Likely it was Frank's car.

He didn't have much choice, now. He needed to see what Frank Lorenzo was thinking.

He headed downstairs to his control center.

* * *

"Okay, I'm listening," Frank said, unzipping his coat and sitting across from Dylan at the kitchen table.

"I think you're right about it being Woody."

"Yeah, why?" It was hard to take this kid seriously after all that had gone down. But so far—at least, from what Frank could tell by his face—Dylan seemed to be leveling at last.

"I figure it has to be. You see, there's a lady named Nina Richards. She's—"

Frank waved his arm impatiently. "I know who she is."

"Okay. Well, Hollie Ganz looks a lot like Nina. Allison does too, but a younger version."

"Okay, so they look alike. What does it mean?"

"Just that there was a thing between those two."

Finally he was getting into new territory. "Clarify," Frank said.

"I mean Woody and Nina were getting it on together." Dylan passed him one of those macho looks as he added, "Big-time."

"Is that right? Funny, I was told they didn't have much to do with each other. For instance, they were never seen going out together, or even visiting back and forth between houses."

"Well, I don't know about when Woody got older, but when he was a kid."

Frank's eyebrows drew together, and he moved in closer. "How do you know that?"

"When I was about six, seven—Woody must have been about twelve—Nina used to take care of me a few afternoons a week. Once school was out, Woody would be right over.''

''So far it only sounds like some kind of after-school babysitting arrangement between Nina and Woody's mother.''

''Uh-uh, no way it was that. Sometimes they'd go into her bedroom alone. Whenever they did that, no one was supposed to bother them. Well, once it was taking so long, I went and cracked open the door.'' He shook his head, smiled. ''She was taking care of him, all right, but not likely the way his mother would have had in mind.''

A pause; then: ''Twelve years old?''

Dylan nodded. ''It was weird; I remember thinking it then, too. . . . I mean, Woody was smart, he could do anything on a computer. But still he was the kind of kid none of the other kids could stomach—they made fun of him. In fact, I don't think he ever had one friend his own age. But Nina treated him real special. He could pretty much tell her when to piss and fart, and she'd do it.''

''You're saying she was scared of him?''

''Maybe . . . I never looked at it that way. I mean, she was an adult and he wasn't big enough to really hurt her physically. But who knows? Sometimes I thought he had powers.''

''You want to run that by me again?''

''Okay, laugh if you want, but I'm not putting you on. Like he could do things that couldn't be explained.''

''What kind of things?''

''Like for instance, Nina and me and maybe some other kid would be in the kitchen making candy apples or fudge. We used to do those kind of corny things. And suddenly there'd be Leon, standing right next to us. And not one of us had seen or heard him come in.''

CHAPTER
Twenty-six

Though Hollie had spoken to the children some, she kept falling in and out of sleep. This time when Woody entered the room, she woke with a start. He rushed to the computer, keyed in some letters, and the monitors brightened instantly: two faces . . . familiar faces, came up on the screen. Frank and Dylan? But how could that be?

It took her minutes into their conversation before she was hit with the full impact: it wasn't just the eavesdropping or hearing those awful things about Woody's past. But it was the setting, which at first she hadn't even noticed. It was *her* house. Dylan and Frank were sitting at *her* kitchen table, obviously unaware that they were being seen or heard. Did that mean that the whole time she and the children had been living in that house, Woody had been listening to and watching them?

She drew in her breath, her head reeling with one humiliating scene after another. She felt fury, shock, invaded.

Gus Paterson walked in then, about to talk but stopping when he saw Dylan.

"It's okay. What?" Frank said.

"The lady across the street, Margaret Spear?"

"The window-watcher."

Gus nodded. "According to her and her brother, about one o'clock this afternoon a car pulled into this driveway. A woman got out, went in the house, came out about a half-hour later. Alone, and carrying a brown paper bag."

"What make car?"

"They didn't know. But it was silver . . . compact. And another thing—" The phone rang. Frank raised a hand, stopping him. With the other hand he lifted the receiver.

"Frank Lorenzo here."

"Frank, it's Lois."

"Hi, what do you have?"

"A lot. I didn't speak to Detective Lancer, but I did get to one of the officers who was at the Brandywine Village apartments today. One who wasn't as hesitant to talk."

"I'm listening."

"It was actually Hollie Ganz who asked the manager to open up her husband's apartment. Apparently she hadn't heard from him in some time and was worried."

"Okay, so where is she now?"

"I'm getting to that. When she heard what happened, she passed out, fell and hit her head. She was taken by ambulance to Mount Sinai Hospital."

"How badly—" he began, apparently not sounding good himself the way Lois picked right up.

"Frank, shut up and listen. Not a concussion, but a couple of stitches to close the wound. The Hartford police eventually tracked her to the emergency room to question her, but she left before they arrived. So I called the hospital, and from what I could get from the admittance clerk, Hollie Ganz was picked up at about three forty-five by a young man. About five-ten, a hundred and seventy pounds, average-looking, with a crew cut. Does that ring any bells?"

"Leon Woodbury."

"I figured it must be."

Frank ran his hand through his hair, then sat there with his eyes shut, not talking. Trying to fit pieces together that didn't seem to go to the same puzzle.

"Frank, you still there?"

"I'm here. Listen, did you get a make on Elaine Byers' car?"

"Yeah, the chief put out an APB. It's a Honda Civic, four-door, silver exterior, 1991."

So Elaine Byers had been the one here earlier. She had left, though—at least, according to the neighbors.

So Woodbury was lying—he had picked Hollie up from the hospital, likely the last one to see her. And somehow he had got a hold of both kids. But how? And where were they now?

In addition, according to Gus Paterson, it had come up in questioning the Spears that Eleanor Woods, Leon's mother, was to their knowledge alive and living with Woodbury. Which could account for the dress and women's jewelry in the bedroom. Still, where had she been when Frank went through the house earlier?

"I don't know," Paterson said, "but I say we bring him in for questioning."

They headed over there together, Dylan tagging along, trying not to miss the excitement. When there was no answer at the door, they forced their way in through a window. But despite the three armed officers outside watching, the front and back of the house, Leon Woodbury had managed to disappear.

"See that?" Dylan said, after Frank and the others had searched every last room and Frank hammered his fist against the wall. "What'd I say about his powers?"

An APB went out on Leon Woodbury, and Paterson and Parks went off to search the neighborhood. Frank headed back to the Ganz house, with Dylan on his heels.

He walked around the kitchen, trying to dismiss Dylan's hocus-pocus explanation so that he could concentrate on the facts. He picked up the telephone—maybe he could catch Lois before she left, tell her to check to see if there was a death certificate for Woody's mother. But he put down the phone—that could wait. Meanwhile, the list of people who had disappeared was steadily mounting: Nina Richards, Eleanor Woods, Hollie, Elaine, the kids.

As he stood at the telephone, he suddenly noticed the light fixture in the living room. He turned, eyed it more carefully. It was the same as the one in the kitchen; in fact, the same as the ones in the upstairs rooms in Woody's house. He walked up closer to

the one in the living room and examined the little
brass contraption with the hole attached to the un-
derside.

"What's wrong?" Dylan asked.

"Get me a knife."

He gestured to his pockets. "I don't carry—"

"A kitchen knife from the drawer, Dylan."

Dylan got it, brought it over, and handed it to
him. "What's wrong?"

"Watch."

Frank unscrewed the brass contraption, then examined the little square box with wires and anten-
nae sticking out of it.

"Shit, is that a camera?" Dylan asked.

Frank tossed the fixture cover aside, then went
around to the other rooms. Taking Dylan by the elbow, he led him out the back door. Once outside,
Frank asked, "How long have those fixtures been
there?"

"I don't remember them from when I was a kid.
But then again, I don't remember what was there. I
was right what I said though, huh? It was a camera?"

It gave Frank the creeps to even say it—the idea
that Hollie and the kids had been sitting under this
kid's microscope this entire time. "I'm no expert,
but I'd be willing to bet that it wasn't just a camera,
but a microphone as well."

"You mean all the while they've been living
here, weird Woody's been watching . . . listening to
them?"

Frank's mind had already moved on to the next
question—where was the receiving monitor? He

hadn't seen one when he went through Woodbury's house. In fact, he hadn't see any work equipment, not even a file cabinet with data. Wasn't that odd, considering the kid pretty much spent his life conducting experiments? Surely he hadn't taken *everything* to be fixed?

Which could only mean one thing: somewhere in that house was another room.

Now knowing that some of the cameras had been found, Woody—in near panic—paced the room back and forth like a frenzied animal. Still feeling disoriented, Hollie managed to sit up. The children huddled together on the bunk beside her, stunned and terrified as they watched Woody pace.

He was caught, wasn't he? They knew about the cameras. But still the question was, would Frank and the police be able to find them sealed away like this? She tried to make better order of her thoughts, but couldn't.

"I want you to let us out of here, Woody," she said, finally daring to make a demand.

"I knew it wouldn't work," another voiced piped out of Woody.

And as it did she shuddered, remembering the voice she had heard in the car. This must be the mother who would never leave him alone. The kids—now more terrified than ever—rushed over to her, and she put her arms around them, trying to comfort and protect them. She heard Jake humming softly to himself.

"You're finally getting what you deserve, young man. How many times did I warn you to stay away from her? But would you listen? Grown women don't do things like that to little boys, and nice little boys would never let them."

Woody now took a deep breath, and his expression turned calmer as he stood up and directed his attention at Hollie. "I wanted it to turn out so differently. I didn't want any of the others involved. Can you forgive me for botching it?"

She nodded, hoping against hope that this meant . . .

But her hopes were short-lived. "We'll have to go without the kids," he said. "Just us."

She thought about leaving the children behind, and though she hated the idea, it was clearly for the best. Frank knew about the cameras: he wouldn't stop until he had found the source and with it, the children. But the rescue would come too late for her. Though Woody's perception was that he loved Hollie, he more likely hated her. Like his mother, like Nina. He was taking her away to kill her. "Where?" she asked, barely able to hear her own question.

But he heard it and answered. "To our place."

Frank got in touch with Justin Todd, the building inspector, at his home, and within forty-five minutes he was meeting with Frank at City Hall, using his pass key to get inside.

"The problem is the date," Todd said. "Not that we won't have it. Just that any building plans more than thirty years old are kept in the storage room in the basement. It's one of those cases where we're always promising ourselves to get things in better order."

So it was an hour more before Todd had pulled Sam Egan's plans out of one of twenty-four cardboard boxes.

"Here, Frank, looks like we've got it," he said, bringing the thick roll of papers to a long table. With Frank close at his elbow, he spread out the first sheet.

"Yep, this appears to be the game plan. Interesting how Egan seemed to carve it right into the landscape. . . . Really was an artist, not many of those around. Real good-looking, solidly built houses, too. Okay, let's see now, you're interested in numbers . . ." His thick finger began to move sideways on the plans.

"Numbers eight and eleven."

He started with eleven, which was the seventh sheet. He looked at it, marveling at the size of the rooms and the quality of design. Finally he looked at the lower level.

"Okay, what part were you in?" Todd asked.

"There was a small den and a cellar containing the boiler, hot-water heater, that kind of thing."

"Think about it. Doesn't it seem odd that area being so small—I mean, considering the size of the first floor?" Todd ran his hand over a larger area in the basement, about two-thirds of the two-thousand-square-foot foundation.

Frank bumped the heel of his palm to his forehead. "Of course, I should have realized immediately. And with a room that size, how could I have missed it?"

"People are trained to seek out doors."

"Are you saying it doesn't—"

"If it does, not so it shows on these plans."

"How could it have passed inspection?"

"Hey, don't look at me to take the blame. I was in kindergarten the year it was built."

"Okay, comedian . . . So you tell me, how do we go about finding an entrance?"

"Up to me, I'd say, don't bother. Take the easier route, and create your own."

CHAPTER
Twenty-seven

Woody stuffed a wad of cloth into Hollie's mouth and she immediately began to gag. Jake ran over, kicked Woody in the legs, and Woody slammed his fist into his face. Jake fell back, and Hollie, finally able to control her gag response, tried to get up, but Woody pushed her back. Allison grabbed Jake while he was fixing his glasses, lifting him under the arms and pulling him away.

"You're going to be sorry once they find us," Allison threatened, her voice shaking.

Woody looked to the monitor, which showed only the empty, darkened rooms in the house across the street, then turned to Hollie and placed three strips of adhesive over her mouth. She felt certain she would vomit and choke to death.

"I'm sorry I have to do it this way," he said gently.

He used a key combination on the computer and then, taking a woolen scarf from a drawer, wrapped it around her lower face, hiding the adhesive. Finally taking one of his own sweatshirts, he slipped it over her head and forced her arms through the sleeves. Over that went the winter jacket.

"Where're you taking her?" Allison cried.

Woody put Hollie's prescriptions, two heavy sweaters, a blanket, matches, a flashlight, and a butcher knife into a knapsack, put on his jacket, followed by the knapsack over his shoulders, then directed her toward a round sewer-like hole.

Suddenly Allison jumped onto Woody's back, her arms circling his neck, her hands trying to choke him. But he twisted her fingers loose, jerked her hands away, and swung her to the floor. Just as he raised his hand to smack her, Hollie grabbed his arm. . . .

He paused, looked at her, then rubbing where Allison had hurt his neck, said, "You saw what she did. I didn't deserve that. Now either see that they behave, or I'll punish them."

Hollie nodded, looked at her children, pleading with her eyes. They both backed up against the wall, causing no further disturbance as Woody lifted the cover to the sewer.

When she saw the steep curvature of stairs, she froze. She wouldn't go in there, she couldn't. *Oh, please, no, no, don't make me!* But as terror wiped out all other thoughts, she was being manipulated closer and closer until suddenly she was standing on the top step. He pushed her down a step, and he climbed in after her. Now he stretched his foot down and kicked her arm, and she took another step, then another, each one taking her deeper and farther away. Like the stairs to hell . . . Would she ever see her children again?

She reached level ground before Woody, and her first thought was to run. But the moment she saw her surroundings, the thought quickly left her: everything was dirt and cement, top, bottom, sides—similar to the room above, only now they were in a narrow channel.

With nowhere to run.

Allison rushed to the hatch. Grabbing the handle, she tried to pull it up again, but it wouldn't budge.

"Don't bother," Jake said.

She turned to him. He was now standing in front of Woody's computer. "The lock is controlled by this."

"If that's so, then can't you . . . ?"

"I don't know, it's not that easy. I'd have to find what program controls the lock." He stopped, sat down in Woody's chair, tried to swallow down whatever that thing was lodged in his throat, then took himself into the system.

He must have been concentrating hard, because he hadn't even seen Allison standing at the door with the little round peephole—not until she gasped.

"What?" he asked.

"Animals," she said in a funny voice. She backed away from the door and he dragged his chair over, climbed on it, and looked inside: there were dozens of animal cages filled with birds, rodents, even cats. The animals were racing and jumping and flying, banging into cage walls and each other as though they were drunk or blind . . . or maybe sick. Some just lay there, battered and bruised. Probably dead.

Jake thought of Popeye . . . and Chester.

What has Woody done?

Todd had arranged for two masons to meet him and Frank at the Woodbury house. According to him, they would use fourteen-inch stone-blade saws to cut through the cement block.

"Overtime for these fellows, my friend, and no small bucks either. I assume you're taking any heat that may result."

Frank nodded. "How long do you expect this to take?"

"Basement walls are usually eight, ten inches thick. With luck we ought to have an opening large enough for a man to fit through in half an hour."

A lot could happen in thirty minutes, particularly with someone out of control like this kid. "Will they hear us coming?"

"Not at the start, but certainly once we get in closer."

Damn, he didn't like the idea of not having some element of surprise. What would the kid do once he knew they were moving in on him? Todd, apparently following his thoughts, said, "I can only suggest when we get in close enough, you start doing some fast talking. The kind of stuff you lawyers are supposed to be good at."

"You confuse me with a shrink. This one scares me." Frank had taken along the house plans for both number 8 and number 11 Garden Place. Now he rolled out number 8 on Woody's kitchen table and examined it. "Out of curiosity, Todd, what do you think of this?"

Todd looked, then shrugged. "A basic ranch; simple, not worth a third of what the neighbors' houses are worth. And like you, I don't have a clue as to why Sam Egan would build it here."

Hollie felt claustrophobic. Where were they going? It had only been a few minutes in the tunnel, but it was hot and close, and sweat was dripping down her face. The stone path was bumpy and uneven, and with the combination of low heeled pumps and her limbs being so weak and shaky, she occasionally lost her footing and tripped.

Several times they passed trails cut off to the sides, like road intersections. It was one of those times that she heard sounds. She stopped and listened—it sounded like moaning. But Woody was right there, with his hand pushing on her back. She began to turn, to push him, when he swung his hand out, smacking her in the face with the back of it. Stunned, as though shot, she fell to the ground, the skin on her knees and palms scraping and tearing against the stone. He lifted her roughly to her feet, then forced her ahead.

But it was Elaine she had heard. She was sure it was Elaine.

Though they couldn't be positive from hitting against it, the masons decided the wall of bookshelves was likely the original entrance, so they began there. All of them stood back: Todd, Frank, Paterson, Parks, Foster and Dylan, who Frank shooed out repeatedly, only to return while they weren't paying attention. Though Dylan had said nothing since the whole process started, he watched in silent fascination.

Todd looked into the cellar area, then summoned Frank inside. He pointed out the wires, pipes, leading down and likely in the direction of the room.

"Heat, electricity, water, he's got everything in there."

"Maybe old Sam was building a bomb shelter," Frank said. "A lot of those were built in the fifties. Or maybe just one of those eccentrics, enamored of weird, secret things."

"What about his grandson?"

Frank looked into the other room, at the saw gnawing away at the cement, spewing out dust. "He thinks Hollie's his nanny, who played sex games with him when he was a kid."

"So he wants her back? Wants to reinvent her?"

Frank leaned his arms against the wall, for a moment shutting his eyes. He could never remember feeling so scared.

There must have been a thousand items and documents to choose from, and only one of them had access to the code of Woody's locking system. Jake was now lost in the search, his fingers flying over the keyboard, opening icons, looking inside . . .

Allison was watching, her arms folded at her chest, when suddenly she turned and looked around. "What's that noise?" she asked.

Jake's fingers didn't leave the keyboard, his eyes riveted to the screen.

"Jake, I hear something."

"Allison, I think I have it."

She ran to the wall and screamed, "Here! We're in here!"

Her basement. They'd climbed stairs first, then Woody had released a bar and pushed . . . and there they were, in *her* basement! The wall, the bookcase, Woody. It had been him in her house all along, making noises to scare her, doing all those awful things, even killing the dog!

The house was dark as he pushed her along—stopping at the kitchen drawer and taking out a length of thin strong clothesline. With one of her knives he cut off a long piece, then looped it around her neck in such a way that the two long end pieces pulled together and wrapped around his hand. When yanked, they would tighten the noose on her neck. Together they went out the back door into the darkness.

He used no flashlight, just led her through the backyard, the wooded area, then out onto the next street. They went through yards and fields, and though she wasn't sure where they were headed, it seemed they had circled back.

Though exhausted and beginning to get cold, barely able to stand on her feet, he wouldn't let her stop once—not until they came to a car she recognized immediately: Elaine's. He unlocked the door, pushed her into the passenger seat, and tied the leash of her collar to the headrest behind the seat.

"I know none of this is comfortable," he said, once he'd gotten in and started the car. "I wanted to take you along slowly, but you wrecked all that. Now it's a problem with time. People are pressing in on us, trying to take control of our lives. You're just going to have to take what's known as a crash course—learn to follow my directions. Once you have it down pat, you'll be able to give up your gag and leash. Now you tell me, is Woody Woodpecker not one hell of a reasonable guy?" He reached out, lowered her scarf, then ran his scratchy fingertips along her face, down her neck, stopping when he reached her cleavage.

"It would never work out, I told you that to begin with," the old woman's voice came in. "You're a dirty pig to ever touch a young boy! To make him want you!"

Hollie jerked back at the words, forcing the cord tighter around her neck. Tears were coming again . . . and here she'd thought that by now they were all gone.

"We're going to get you out of there! Give us five more minutes!" Frank shouted. "Who's with you, Allison?"

"Just me and Jake. Woody took Mommy down under."

"I got it!" Jake cried as he jumped off the chair and ran for the hatch. He pulled it open. "Look, Allison!"

She whirled around. "Good, Jake. Don't go down

there alone though, wait for Frank and the police.''
She turned back to the wall, to the roar of the saw,
as if by watching it would go faster.

"It's not even a room down there," he said as he
descended a few steps, the trip getting there earlier
now coming back to him. "Come see, Allison, it's a
tunnel.''

It was less than five minutes later when one of the
masons shouted, "You kids stand back, away from
the wall!''

And it was then that Allison turned and saw that
Jake had disappeared. *Oh, God, no.* "Jake!''

"Okay, coming through!" one of the men
shouted.

Jake kept going forward until he heard a noise—
was it his mother crying? He stopped, backed up,
and went down a side path, barely able to see.
"Mommy!" he called out. "Is that you?''

He heard another moan. He climbed onto a rock,
walked along to another rock, then looked down into
a small cavern. And that's when he saw her lying
there. But it wasn't Mommy at all—it was Aunt
Elaine . . . and she had blood all over her!

He started to yell as loud as he could.

Allison heard Jake's call, and she was at the top
step when everyone burst through. Frank came
rushing to her, but she could barely get the words
out of her mouth. "Jake's down there too!" she cried
finally.

"I'll stay with her . . . if you want," Dylan said
hesitantly.

She felt confused—what was *he* doing there? But
Frank handed him one of the walkie-talkies and said,
"Okay, Allison?"

She nodded, trembling. "Just find them please."

Now with the rest of them downstairs, she was
shaking so hard she had to lean against one of the
walls to stay up. Dylan came over, stood in front of
her, opened his mouth to say something, then shut
it. He looked at her, at the ground, then again at
her.

And she began to cry, this time really bawling.
So when he put his hand on her shoulder, she
turned toward him. Then he put his other hand on
her other shoulder, and as she sank in against his
chest, his arms came around her. Grateful for any
arms, the tears came even harder, drenching his
shirt front.

They all knew Woody was crazy. He had already
killed her father, and now her mother and brother
were with him. She wasn't used to praying. If there
was a God, would he even bother to listen? But still
she began to think of tradeoffs. Anything, she'd do
anything at all, just please don't let him kill them
too. . . .

"Remember the first time, the very first time?"

"Our place, let's go to our place."

"Not if I catch you first, you bitch!"

"It won't work, those kind of things never work!
Listen to your mommy!"

"Do you like when I touch you, Leon?"

"I just want us to be together—me, you, and the
kids. So what's so bad?"

"She's got to go, she's a tramp!"

A jumble of voices, none of them touching, all of them touching. Hollie had kept her eyes closed, as if that would help to quash the voices. Now that she had opened her eyes, she could see that they were driving through a darkly wooded area. No cars, no people, no place to run.

Was this how she was to die?

Elaine had lost a lot of blood from stab wounds to her chest and abdomen, but she was still conscious. Paterson quickly covered her with his jacket while Hanks lifted her out of the cavern and Jake led Todd and Frank, who was carrying Gus's gun, to the end of the tunnel. They climbed the stairs, pushed the wall, and it turned. "See, I told you, it's my house!" Jake said, wanting to rush inside and look for his mother.

Frank put his hand out, stopping Jake. "Wait, Jake, let me go first."

Todd stood there, shaking his head, marveling over what he was seeing.

"Tell the guys to bring the victim in this way," Frank said to Todd. "It'll save time. And alert the kids to what's happening." With his last words he was up the stairs.

Frank took a quick look through the rooms, then picked up the telephone in Hollie's bedroom and had an ambulance dispatched. By the time he was off the phone, Jake was standing there.

"She's not here!" he cried.

Frank went to him, crouched down. "I know. Maybe you can help us find her."

He shook his head, tears welling . . . but he fought to hold them in place. "I don't know where she is," he said.

"What did Woody say when he took her?"

"Nothing."

"Are you certain?"

His expression rose, then fell. "He did say something. I just can't remember what."

"Come on, let's get Allison."

They had gone a couple of miles when Woody pulled off to the right, then down and around into a heavily wooded area. He stopped, got out of the car and, after taking a flashlight from his knapsack, climbed around through the thick bush to open the passenger-side door.

Holding the leash, he walked her down a steep hill to a pond. "Remember?" he asked, smiling, as though Hollie ought to remember. He pulled off the strips of adhesive, dug the cloth out of her mouth.

She coughed, took some deep breaths, then nearly laughed as she realized the sheer lunacy of what had just passed through her: relief . . . wonderful relief, as though with the luxury to breathe freely, it was suddenly all fixed. She forgot for an instant that she was freezing and in the middle of the woods with a madman.

"It's all relative, isn't it?" he said, knowing instantly what she was feeling. She didn't respond.

"First lesson well taken—you're good at this. You see, that's how we relieve our burdens, our bogeymen, so to speak. First go the limit, then once you pull back, it's easy as pie.''

Except the ease was short-lived. She could feel her body beginning to tremble as he forced her to sit on the ground in front of him.

He opened the knapsack, took out the prescription vials, then uncapping them, shook a penicillin and a Librium into her hand. ''This will help for the time being.''

She looked at the tranquilizer hungrily. ''Maybe I'll wait a little before I—'' she began.

''Did I ask you?'' he said brusquely, cutting her off.

''I can't swallow them without water.''

He shined the flashlight at the pond, then handed her a cup from the knapsack. He got onto his knees and removed the collar from her neck. ''Now, doesn't that feel better?''

He waited for her response. Finally she nodded.

''Remember how *much* better when you go to the water . . . Because if you try to run, do anything other than what I assign you to do, I won't be so quick to take it off again.''

She took a shuddering breath, stared at him.

''Go ahead, get up. I'll beam the light on the pond so you can see.''

She stood up.

''Get water, take your pills, then come back. And oh yes, wash your face. It's bleeding around your nose where I hit you.''

She walked to the edge of the water, knelt down, and filled the cup. The large pill, the antibiotic, she swallowed with the water. But it was the tranquilizer every nerve in her body screamed for that she still had cupped in her hand.

She had to do it. If she had any chance of getting away, she couldn't be slowed by drugs. But as she let the tablet slip through her fingers into the water, she couldn't remember ever doing anything as hard. And to top it off, she would have to feign calm. She cupped water in her hands, washed the blood off her face, and as instructed, headed back to Woody.

When she had returned he wiped her face, then began to put the collar on her neck.

"But I did what you said!" she protested, pulling away.

"You did, and I'm proud of you. But it takes more time than that. Tomorrow you'll get more free time, and if you use it wisely, I'll increase it. Soon you'll be a totally free lady. You'll see how it works. Leave it to Woody Woodpecker."

She wanted to scream, but what good would that do? She wanted to kill him—a desire both frightening and overwhelming, one she had never experienced before. But all she could do was come closer and let him put the collar back on. He tied the two ends around the tree she was leaning against, forcing her to sit upright.

Then, taking off his knapsack and tossing it aside with the lantern, he sprawled out on the ground, putting his face in her lap. "Please tickle the back of my neck, Nina," he said.

"No, Woody, don't you see? I'm not Nina."

"Of course you are. Know why?"

He was smiling up at her like a little kid on a picnic. She didn't answer him.

"Go ahead, it's all part of the bigger picture. You might as well ask."

"Why?"

"Because I said so."

CHAPTER
Twenty-eight

Dylan and Allison had climbed through the opening. By the time they got outside, the ambulance was coming down the street and Jake was coming toward them.

Allison looked at him, stunned. "How did you—"

"There must be a passageway between the houses," Dylan said, dismayed. But she ignored the explanation, too much for her to take in at once. She got down, hugged Jake to her. "Mommy's hurt?" she asked, watching as the ambulance stopped in front of the house.

"No, Aunt Elaine."

"Elaine . . . how? Then where's Mommy?"

He shook his head. The ambulance attendants were coming out of the house when Allison reached them. She looked at Elaine who was covered with a blanket, then Frank. "Will she be okay?"

"I think so."

Then, knowing her mother hadn't been found,

panic began to spread once more across her face. "And Mommy, what about my mother?"

He took her face gently between his hands. "Allison, I want you to take it easy for a minute and think. Jake says when Woody took your mother, he said something about where he was taking her."

Her eyes grew large. "I remember. He said to 'our place.' At first I thought he meant to my house. But then he took her down into that dungeon—I mean, that path to our house. Oh God, I just can't believe . . . But it *was* to my house, so maybe that's what he did mean."

Dylan was standing in back of her, listening. Frank looked at him. "Maybe you know."

His shoulders rose and fell. "How would I know?"

"Now remember, we're likely not even talking about Hollie, we're talking about Nina. Where would 'our place' have meant to the little boy Woody?"

"I don't know. I'm telling you, I don't know."

Frank tried to think of a better approach. Dylan was the only one who'd been around Nina and Woody—he was his only hope. Somewhere there was a tie-in, and Frank had to get to it.

"Look, when you took Allison in the car that afternoon, you ended up at a place called Dugan Square. The peculiar part was, when Woody learned Allison was missing, that you had taken her, he found her immediately. It's like he knew instinctively where you might have taken her. Why was that?"

Suddenly Dylan began nodding his head. "Okay,

yeah, you're right. Nina used to take us on outings. In the nice weather. Sometimes they were small ones. We'd walk, and only go as far as the ice cream place on Hopper or Franklin Square or Fieldstone Plaza. But on other outings we'd take along a picnic lunch, spend the whole day there. Those times she drove us.''

''Where?''

''Let me see. . . . There was, I think, about four places. Dugan Square Park was one. Magic Mountain in Codders Creek another.'' He paused a moment. ''Bowers' Animal Farm in Ranger City and . . . wait a second, right, that's it!'' He swung a mock punch. ''The place Woody liked most was the state forest, the duck pond.''

She was cold, so cold. But she didn't dare break Woody's mood.

''I love you, Nina,'' the little boy's voice said over and over. ''I wish you'd be my mommy.'' This time he reached his hand in her blouse, letting his fingers slide inside her bra. She bit down hard on her lip—anything not to scream.

Suddenly his body jerked, and his hand pulled away. ''You dirty bitch! What are you doing with my little boy?''

''It's okay, Woody,'' Hollie whispered. ''It's all okay.'' She could feel the tension begin to ease out of him. ''I want you to close your eyes now and go to sleep.''

''And what?''

''When you wake, Nina will take you to our favorite place.''

"And what will you do?"

"Whatever you want."

She only had a small amount of light from the lantern lying on the ground. Hollie couldn't see if his eyes were really closed, but soon she could hear his deep breathing. If she could only get to the knapsack, to the knife, maybe even the car keys. But she couldn't reach out that far, not with the cord around her neck. She kicked off her shoes, began to feel around the area with her stockinged feet, stretching her long legs, her toes. . . .

Until finally her right foot touched the nylon knapsack.

Todd took Allison and Jake to the hospital to stay with Elaine. The hospital would call Elaine's husband, let him know what had happened. Meanwhile, three more cruisers were being dispatched to join Paterson, Hanks, Frank, and Dylan.

From the start Dylan fought with Frank to let him go, arguing that if anyone knew the state forest, particularly where Nina used to take them, it was him. Besides which, they used to walk through all those trails at one time or another. And of course, Dylan was right on every point. On the other hand he was only seventeen, a kid. He really had no business being with them.

They were going into the woods at night to hunt down a killer who might be at a particular pond, or alternatively, anywhere within a twenty-mile radius. A psychotic who had murdered more than once, so chances were he would think little of killing again.

Finally Frank gave in, after he'd extracted a solemn promise from Dylan that he would remain in the car with the doors locked, and that any help he gave them would come strictly through his radio.

It took Hollie several agonizingly long minutes to inch the knapsack toward her without disturbing Woody's head on her lap. But finally it was close enough for her to reach out and grab. Now that it was in her hands, she froze. *Suppose he wakes while* . . . No, she mustn't even think like that. Just do it.

She took a couple of deep breaths, then slowly unzipped the knapsack. She removed the knife, then sliding it inside the cord around her neck, began to saw through it. It took only a few quick motions before it snapped and fell away.

Should she bring the knife down—stab him? Could she? And if she could, how much force should be behind the plunge? Did she have the guts to force it in deep, and the strength?

If she only wounded him superficially, he would surely retaliate by killing her. She . . . Nina . . . being disloyal, not returning his love. And with the way she was sitting, the awkwardness of his head in her lap, would she have an opportunity to run from him?

She took another deep breath. She couldn't sit all night analyzing it, she had to act. Finally she decided to try to lift his head off, move it onto the grass while she carefully slid from beneath him. If he woke during that time, she would have no other choice but to use the knife.

And hope that she could use it well.

* * *

By radio, the four cops plus Frank split up the territory they would cover initially—Frank, Paterson, and Hanks took the pond within a three-square-mile area, each mile assigned a number. Dylan, who was sitting in the car with a map of the entire conservation area and the positions of the officers, would be available on his radio to answer questions relating to trails or other particulars. If Woodbury was spotted, the spotting officer would call the others for backup.

Though neither Allison nor Jake had seen Woodbury take a gun, they couldn't rule out that he had one. They did know, however, that he was carrying a knife. And if his victim was near him, their guns would be useless, unless they could get a clear shot, which was next to impossible in the dark.

They pulled into the conservation area. Frank stopped to let Hanks out, then a little farther down, Gus. Each had a lantern and radio clipped to his belt.

Areas one and two covered. Area three was the main entrance to the pond.

It worked. Hollie slipped out, laid Woody's head carefully on a pile of leaves. She picked up the knapsack, went through it trying to find Elaine's car keys, but they weren't there. Dare she try to put her hand in his pocket? No, best to run, get away as fast as she could.

The drive here hadn't been that long. How deep in the woods could they be? She went to lift the lantern, which was on and lying beside Woody, when she heard him move.

She gripped her hand tighter around the knife, swallowed down the ball in her throat, waited. . . . Nothing. She reached down again, and this time he made a guttural sound. *Forget about the damn light, Hollie.* She turned, began to step away: one step, two, then three. She had just reached the hilltop when she was aware of a beam of light shining directly on her.

Run, Hollie, run. . . .

Frank had parked a couple of hundred feet from the entrance to the pond area, not wanting to leave Dylan sitting too close. He had already gone down to the water, shined the light around the shoreline—it was about a three-quarter-of-a-mile circumference. But except for little animals roaming about, there were no signs of life.

He traveled farther up the hill and began to circle the area. Ten minutes into the search he came upon a car practically buried beneath the brush. He flashed the light on it, trying to make out the color—it was difficult to distinguish. Maybe silver, but he couldn't be certain. He went around the car until he came to the make: it was a Honda Civic.

He quickly took his radio from his pocket, held it up to his mouth, and spoke.

"Okay, fellows, station three. Come on in, we've got the car."

She had been running at top speed for several minutes, but her lungs, about ready to burst, made it seem like an hour. Thinking she might have lost him, she crawled into a nearby bush and sank down. Her feet were burning, her throat was burning. If only she could rest just a little longer. But she didn't dare.

She started to crawl out on all fours when she heard movement in back of her, then a sweet little-boy voice whispered. "Nina, it's me. Come out, come out, wherever you are." Then, sinking into a deeper, huskier tone, one she hadn't heard him use before: "It's time to die."

Dylan thought he had seen something earlier, but when he threw on the headlights, all he saw was a squirrel chasing another squirrel up a tree. But this time he heard noise, he was sure of it. He opened the window and listened: footsteps, running. Maybe he ought to call out. But no, that probably wasn't such a hot idea.

He looked around—what the hell was he supposed to do now? He could call the cops on his radio, but was there time? Screw this. Without further deliberation, he slid into the driver's seat, turned the ignition, and with the headlights purposely kept off, backed up, turned, and followed in the direction of the footsteps.

When he had reached the top of the hill he put on the headlights, high-beam . . . and began down the bumpy slope.

She had been running in and out of bushes, around trees, but he was gaining ground. Now hearing him only steps behind her, she stopped, turned, and raised the knife.

He was just reaching for her when she swung out. The knife slashed across his chest, and he shrieked in pain. Horrified by what she had done, her hands flew up and the knife sailed into the darkness. Suddenly she felt powerful fingers wrap around her throat.

She kicked out, kneed him, got away, only to trip and have him lift her off the ground. Then by twisting her arms back, he dragged her down the hill. She bit his arms, hands, tried to turn to fight him off, but nothing would stop him. And she was wearing down.

Until she felt the icy water in her shoes. Oh, God, the pond . . . He was going to drown her!

Again she began to fight, this time with even more maniacal fury. ''Help! Someone help!'' she screamed. But only an echo came back to taunt her.

The police had already begun spreading over the area, but it was slow going in the darkness. It wasn't until Frank heard what sounded like a woman's scream that he stopped. It seemed to have come from across the pond. He shined his light over. . . .

He pulled out his radio and called into it. ''It sounds like a struggle going on. At the shoreline, about a half-mile east of the pond entrance.''

Then he began to run.

No matter how hard she fought, she was no match for his strength or stamina. He pressed her head under the freezing water, and just as she thought she couldn't bear another moment, she miraculously pried his hand off her head. She came up for air, but no sooner had she refilled her lungs than she was plunged under again. And finally, after it all, she felt herself let go. She could feel the water, now seeming warm as it began to seep into her lungs. Quiet, peaceful . . . almost comforting . . .

Suddenly, she heard a loud slap in her ears, then someone yanking her hair, pulling her to the surface and forcing her to break through it! Then the hand let go, leaving her on her own. She stumbled, gagged, choked, spit up water. Then as her senses slowly began to return, she became aware of the fight. And the bright light, where was it coming from?

She looked at the fighters. Somewhere as if in a dream, she recognized Dylan and Woody. She watched in a stupor as they slammed and punched. It wasn't until she realized Woody was holding Dylan's head underwater that her mind broke through the fog and began to function.

She rushed to Woody, tearing at his hair, slapping at his face, trying anything and everything to stop him, but nothing would. She ran to the shore, lifted a rock, ran back, then holding it high over her head, she drew in her breath. *Do it, Hollie, this time do it!*

Down, down, down . . . she heard the crack!

He let go.

Epilogue

As Hollie sat on the mall bench, resting her aching feet, Allison was off trying on just one more swimsuit, and Jake was looking through the computer software store. Only a few months since it had all happened, yet much of the horror seemed so far away.

She had arranged for Jeremy's funeral, saw the kids through it, then as soon as she was assured Elaine was okay, proceeded to fall apart. She started off by renting a three-room apartment over a grocery store—reminiscent of that first horrible place with Jeremy. Frank Lorenzo called her several times, wanting to help, but each time she cut him off.

"What is this about, to punish yourself?" her mother said, when she arrived in town and took a look at the utterly awful apartment. Allison—it turned out—had called Hollie's folks in Palm Beach, asking them to please come.

"If I had listened to Jeremy, he wouldn't be dead."

"Agh," her mother said, dismissing the statement with a wave of her hand. "What does that nonsense mean? So, if I had listened to your father, you would never have been born."

"Dad didn't want me?"

"Sure, he wanted you, I wanted you, but we weren't so young by then, nor were we familiar with the country. So your father was frightened about starting a family." She smiled. "And as it turned out, with ample reason. You weren't such an easy one."

Hollie laughed. "Still not, I'm afraid."

Her mother got down next to her, put her arm around her. "What is it, what is it really?"

It took her a long time to say it, but she did finally. "I killed a twenty-two-year-old boy, Ma. I can still hear the crack of his skull when the rock came down on it. It's not at all like the movies, where you kill someone, then go on to the next scene. I can't get past that moment."

"You had no choice. He would have murdered you and put your ashes in a vat beside his fireplace, and that boy Dylan as well. Just like he did to his mother and nanny. Would you rather have given him that opportunity?"

"Of course not, but—"

"No buts. Cut-and-dried, those were your options. Sometimes you don't *get* options. So thank God you did, and I'll thank God you chose right."

Hollie hugged her then, thinking she had never loved her mother as much as she did at that moment.

* * *

Hollie quit her job at Stern-Adler. Actually Harvey Boynton was quite understanding, or perhaps quite relieved to finally be rid of her. Several weeks later she found a job in an advertising agency in Hartford—only a couple of steps up from a peon, but with definite potential. Next she rented a comfortable five-room, second-floor apartment in West Hartford. The kids were thrilled—fifteen minutes from Bloomfield and no toll charge to their friends.

And the mortgage payments on the little ranch? Well, the folks took them over, with Hollie's stipulation that once the house had sold, they'd deduct the payments from the proceeds. Though sometimes she was doubtful that it would ever sell. Edna Bradley, whose deceased husband had been close friends with Sam Egan, was apparently the only one still alive besides Woody who'd known about the passageway . . . and the original purpose of the house. And when the story came out, she filled in the pieces. Of course, the passageway had now been sealed.

The children, of course, missed their father. They had been seeing a counselor since January, and seemed to like her. It had been particularly hard on Jake, who had been the first to catch on to Woody's madness, the reason he was so desperate to reach Jeremy.

A few weeks ago, after talking to Elaine about the children's progress, actually about all of their progress, she'd had an urge to call Frank Lorenzo. Months had gone by, so he had naturally given up on her. But after a little deliberation, she did call.

And they met one night in Hartford: she had known all along there was something special about Frank, and she felt it again the moment she saw him. Not only the physical attraction, which there was clearly no denying, but something so real and honest about him. They talked about lots of things, even Dylan, who ironically was the one who had pulled her head from the water and saved her life. Though Hollie and Allison had run into him later in the hospital and thanked him for his part in the rescue, they hadn't really had much more to say to each other. Frank mentioned that Dylan would be starting Boston College in September.

Since that first meeting with Frank there had been others, as well as more long-into-the-night telephone conversations than she cared to admit to. But admit it or not, when it came to chatting on the phone, Allison could not be bamboozled. Just this morning, wearing a stern look to cover a smile, she had said, ''Better tell Frank to go easy on those long-distance charges. Besides which, don't you guys have anything better to do?''

Exciting SIGNET Fiction For Your Library